OLD HOPE ROAD

by Matthew James Carvalho

Honneur!

Papa Legba

Soley Levey!

This book is dedicated to my wife Norma

Peace and Prosperity...

This work is dedicated to my wife Norma, without whom this work would not have been written.

For his work on the front cover art, I owe Jeremy Willett a huge debt of gratitude. Likewise, I am forever grateful to Elias Hernandez for allowing me to quote him in the very last sentence of the epilogue. Finally, Damien Martin of Kingston Jamaica was kind enough to provide me with the photographs used for the book's interior photography.

Betsy, Carole, Cheryl and Gretchen of the Woodside Writers Group - my ever-patient readers and critics.

For time spent reading the early manuscripts, opinions and feedback, I am forever grateful to Michael Hall, Tom Mendall, Linda Peters and Ana Marie Wilson.

I am also grateful to the good people of Jamaica for the two years I lived there. The Geoghagen clan of Montego Bay and Lucille Smith of Kingston are particularly special to me.

For errors and misattributes regarding the people, places, and traditions of Jamaica and Haiti, I have only myself to blame. For this story, I am closely indebted to Nora Zeale Hurston, Milo Rigaud, Joseph Campbell, Peter J. Carroll and Edwidge Danticat for any aspect of my translation that rings true.

Since we are also what we read; JRR Tolkien, Christopher Hitchens, Frank Herbert, Nassim Nicolas Taleb, Iaian /M/ Banks, Sam Harris, Greg Bear, Daniel Dennett, Neal Stephenson and China Mieville is one shortlist.

SOUNDTRACK (to the book)

1. St. Mark's Philharmonic Orchestra – Finale
2. Bob Marley & The Wailers – So Much Trouble In The World
3. Joseph Nechvatal - Ego Masher
4. Omar Sosa – Raya
5. Lady Saw – Cyaan Get Me
6. Metallica – Wherever I May Roam
7. Vodou – Negue Nago
8. The Ettes – Teeth
9. Bann Madigra St. Jacques – Se Ayizan Mwen Mande; St. Jacques Bann Vodou Song
10. Nick Cave & The Bad Seeds – Brother, My Cup is Empty
11. Finley Quaye – The Emperor
12. Eek-A-Mouse – Born Traveller
13. The Academy of St. Martin in the Fields – Saint-Saëns: Danse macabre, Op.40
14. Tapping The Vein – Complicate It
15. Pearl Jam – Who You Are

PROLOGUE

This is a work of pure, unadulterated fiction (a declaration to which the author refers any inquiries about the autobiographical nature of the story). The narrative occurs at an undefined time in the future, decades hence, rather than centuries. The technology is advanced three to five generations beyond what exists today, save the uses to which it is put. The place is a fictional island in the Caribbean, loosely modeled after Jamaica (but not Jamaica) and references the Haitian tradition of *Vodou* (in concept, rather than practice or experience). Both a foreigner's attempt at written Jamaican Patois (courtesy of two years the author lived in Jamaica) and Haitian Creole (courtesy of an unnamed web-based translator) are employed. The narrative suggests economic, strategic, technological, and social drivers of change; yet, the variety of human experience is no less profuse, random or varied. Neither is it more efficient or just.

Although population trends were projected to stabilize by the end of 2020, even with falling fertility rates in the developed world, the much anticipated and in some circles, necessary and required, population stabilization did not continue past 2025. The global population reached 8 billion human beings by 2042. While some blamed advances in medicine addressing the worst human plagues and sickness, others found a dark irony in the milestone, as it occurred in tandem with an unprecedented influenza pandemic in 2041 and again in 2106. Strange and rare bugs continued to garner the lion's share of peer-reviewed papers and research funding. However, an irrational but persistent objection to vaccines among large swathes of the developed world proved only one factor in the reprise of the simple influenza virus that wreaked havoc again on a global scale, though mostly in southern tier states. Fatalities in the 2041 pandemic were estimated to be 100 million and up to 320 million for the 2106 pandemic.

New discoveries of vast energy deposits in North America, the Gulf of Mexico and the Arctic, combined with developments in extraction and production techniques, allowed for continued reliance on fossil fuels. These discoveries marginalized most renewable energy sources for development and production on a mass scale. By 2030, the majority of world governments nationalized their oil-producing sectors in a public/private partnership. Public shareholders received approximately $1.10 on the dollar over a period of 20 years. While this led to short-term inefficiencies, the majority of voting publics determined that public ownership of public resources, the use of profit for further research, technology advancement and community benefit to be acceptable trade offs. Since energy continued to be sold on the open market at market prices, the sector generated huge profits for their constituent governments. Because of this public benefit, most northern tier countries passed legislation limiting the workweek to four days.

Though advances in geo-engineering and manipulation of the so-called Criegee bi-radical, alleviated water and temperature stresses in some microclimates, access to potable water continued to place stresses on the same areas of the globe where it has always been problematic – Africa, the Middle East and northern China. Advances in agricultural and food production techniques such as genetically modified seed stocks, hybrid products and the increased utilization of food irradiation, allowed for the meeting overall global needs. Last-mile distribution continues to be a problem in some southern-tier states, chronic conflict areas and for some enclaves, which have boycotted the controversial techniques.

On the military or strategic front, open combat, involving not heavy armor and guns, but stealth code, darknets and anarchist hacktivism prevailed, presupposing the acknowledged decline in the utility of traditional uses of force. The advent of the Stuxnet virus in 2011 (reaching the twelfth generation by 2017) and the thousands of variants it spawned marked the start of the ongoing and some termed 'permanent' state of cyber war, which emerged into full light between 2019 and 2022. The lack of fatalities, body bags and costs of traditional military logistics made cyber war a 'natural' choice, not only between political entities such as states, but also between corporations, institutions, and individuals.

A second generation United Nations Charter and Treaty (UN2), developed over twenty years and entered into force in 2055, completely gutted the United Nations Charter and Treaty of 1945. It was recognized by all but two (Iran and the United States) of the two hundred eighteen state entities in existence at the time and contained both major donor and non-aligned country reforms. While the General Assembly remained largely unchanged, the UN Security Council expanded to include 10 members with rotating membership and no permanent members. UN2 Security Council membership and voting rights were tied to the state's status at the International Court of Justice (ICJ). A member-state could have no investigations or indictments pending for any current or former member of its government. Additionally, having served on the Security Council as a sitting, voting member, that country could not again serve on the Council for a period of two years.

One of the first and more interesting, least-worst solutions to emerge out of UN2 was the creation of "New Sumer" encompassing the former states of Israel, Palestine, and Lebanon. Based on the partition of Berlin in the San Francisco treaty of 1951, New Sumer provided three partitions of that geography each with its own access to the Mediterranean Sea. The temple in Jerusalem, destroyed in a Christian Eschatologist terrorist attack in 2023, was rebuilt on the same ground – crossing the Israel/Palestine partition exactly in half. On the Israeli side a synagogue; on the Palestinian side a mosque.

CHAPTER I

THE PRESIDENTIAL PALACE - CAPITAL – TODAY

<<Finale – Saint Saens: Carnival of the Animals>>

Near the city-center, a ten-axle, 26-wheel truck made its way slowly down a road it had not traveled before -- the road to the Presidential Palace. The fully loaded vehicle contained garbage from all over the world – exactly the type of thing the President promised would never happen. The truck would make the President eat his words.

As it approached the Presidential Palace it picked up speed – a highly discouraged behavior on this particular road. The guards in the first guardhouse watched, nervously adjusting binoculars to slow the truck down. Still, it picked up speed. Near the guard station on the outer perimeter fence, it veered left toward the guard station. The sound of the decades-old dirty diesel engine drowned out the yelling of the guards. They dove simultaneously in different directions -- away from the guardhouse and their OIC weaponry with which they could have shot around corners or at targets a half-mile away.

Other than a heavily guarded front entrance, the intruder truck used a private entrance, not found on any map and lacking signage, intentionally obscured by a front of overgrown trees and a false dead end. The Presidential Palace sat well protected inside three concentric circles of electrified fencing. The truck had only to reach the second ring of fencing to complete its mission, and having breached the first line of defense, it ploughed through the electrified fencing along the road to its target. Within the inner circle of fencing, the residence stood three stories in a facade of arches, columns, a high gabled roof and windows with wooden shutters – classic Paramaribo architecture. The white gleaming monstrosity sat on 3000 acres of pristine real estate, lush greenery, elaborate water features, palm trees, well-kept roads, a small designer golf course, an Olympic sized swimming pool, a running track and of course, electrified fences. The front portico looked out over a circular driveway featuring a large fountain with a statue of a lion. The state flag flew on a flagpole three times as high as the highest roof gable. ISEC, the island's not so secret but opaque Internal Security organization maintained the bulk of its Presidential and national security apparatus on the first floor of the Residence, fronted by a large lobby and ornate receiving and conference rooms. The President and his family took up the entire second floor. ISECs technical wing filled the third floor with large computing and data storage arrays. However, the residence was not the target. The breach at the outer perimeter fence triggered emergency measures in secret data rooms and messaging devices of serious men in expensive suits, whose coat jackets hid more expensive weaponry. Though the residence happened to be empty, the intrusion proved no less of an insult.

Standard ISEC response protocol followed an iterative and autonomous cycle of RECON/INTEL, ANALYZE, ACT, and MEASURE. The RECON/INTEL step deployed ten thousand micro-miniature, bio-mimetic flybots with 2-micrometer oxide-wafer wings and ultra-high sensitivity video sensors. They swarmed into the air like the insects they were modeled after. Each individual flybot sending its data to distributed control centers around the city, complete with GPS/GIS coordinates. Ten thousand individual perspectives merged into one integrated image much as a compound eye might produce. Armed ARV's -- multi-function robotic units -- with both lethal and non-lethal, silent, DREAD weapon technology consumed the data ravenously. Although the DREAD technology produced no recoil, no heat signature, with a variable rate of fire up to 150,000 rounds per minute, in this instance, information over body count seemed the better part of valor and the ARV's deployed with 1000 kilograms of Locator Dust, sub-micrometer RFID tags, indistinguishable in size and texture from the average dust mite.

While the ARVs coated the entire scene with Locator Dust, the flybots gave the guards in the second guardhouse a bird's eye view to the newest security travesty. Large computing arrays provided integrated analyses to the first responders, updating it eight times per second. They took no chances, because the same technology, which bequeathed them a sense of superior confidence in times of peace, precluded simple human errors that proliferated in times of crisis and adrenalin -- eliminating the need to take chances. Also equipped with OIC weaponry, the guards in the second guardhouse commenced a standard offensive cycle, their projectiles aided by the precision-guidance systems in the ISEC control center on the third floor of the Presidential Palace. Few trifled with their marksmanship skills. Initially, their projectiles wandered and strayed instead of running true, indicating countermeasures had thwarted electronically enhanced marksmanship. They had no time to analyze those countermeasures so the ARV's adjusted for the new development in conjunction with the flybot data streaming into their data feeds. Because budgets precluded the treatment of the high-cost ammunition now in use as consumables, most governments adopted the use of evidence-based firing, and a single lethal projectile found its mark, entering the truck driver's left eye. It exited the back of the driver's head, shattered the rear window of the cab and came to ignoble rest in a steel panel on the outer wall of the first trailer. The guards in the second guardhouse could not have been happier – their marksmanship had found its mark. The breach of the second guardhouse spawned more emergency measures in and around the residence. Large blocks, four feet by four feet, rose out of the ground to surround the residence with a cement skirt. While inside the residence, people made for underground emergency bunkers.

ISEC deployed its YAL-9b Airborne Laser – a directive energy platform on an old jumbo jet chassis accompanied by two unmanned Avenger/PredatorG combat drones equipped with advanced low observable, embedded reconnaissance and a solid-state laser weapon – capabilities just outside limits of the Missile Technology Control Regime. The now driverless truck would not reach the cement cordon but they took no chances. A scant 250 meters separated the middle and inner fences and a large truck could coast that distance on inertia alone. They worried in vain for inertia was not the point.

The impact of the bullet triggered a small device on the other side of the panel inside the trailer. A massive nanotech deuterium-tritium explosion shook the ground and sent six tons of international garbage flying thousands of feet into the air. Some of it landed three kilometers away but most fell where intended, on or about the Presidential Palace, including a large radiator from an American car, which found its way inside the Presidential Palace through the roof. Except for the driver of the truck, no one else died and the YAL 9B returned to base having served no purpose. The blast radius was later measured at over seven hundred meters. The incident transpired too quickly for technology to respond to a multi-layered agenda.

The incident triggered the Civil Defense clause of the constitution and martial law. For 72 hours, penalties for all crimes doubled, group gatherings of more than four people in public spaces prohibited and the use of social media for criminal purposes carried a mandatory prison sentence. Though some were sympathetic and many speculated, even dreamed, no claims of responsibility followed. Military checkpoints arose at every major thoroughfare – the huge white bridges hastily constructed across streets and sidewalks. Made of ultra-light plastic, the bridges served as a 15-meter funnel through which all traffic, both vehicle and pedestrian were required to pass. Inside the tunnel, RFID readers identified anyone connected or who had come into contact with anything remotely to do with the incident in question. The dust had proven extremely effective identifying those involved in flash mobs and other types of large hacktivist or anarchist protests. In this incident, the RFID dust did not produce the kind of results ISEC had grown accustomed to.

Though all claimed innocence or ignorance, government shock troops arrested many, tortured many, and killed some, releasing the maimed bodies to relatives since the government did not kill and bury its enemies at the same time. The President and his family slept in a secret government location (the executive suite of an undisclosed, foreign-owned hotel) just outside Capital, as they tended to have better security. The people of Capital snickered under their breaths and tried to beat the heat.

THE CONSPIRACY -- TWO DAYS EARLIER

<<Bob Marley & The Wailers – So Much Trouble In The World>>

Roads in most cities tended towards a boring sameness, life on either side sequestered in structures of varying reputation and appearance, haphazardly thrown together refuse and debris -- some of it breathing, walking and talking. A road could smell of a singular or mixed gambit, reminding the nostalgic of person, unpleasant encounter, emergency or family feud. It might wind and meander between tall rocks and old trees. But whatever the smell and however pocked the sun along the road, roads everywhere arrived at places of refuge, conspiracy, power, and other places where kings refused to be castled.

One road in particular cut through a sleepy town with hand painted signs, squat dingy buildings, a few open drains and an un-intimidating police station. Time construed a crowded vibrant town square with professional signage advertising local department stores and fast food restaurants. The town seemed clean and built up, perhaps benefiting from a coat of paint. Narrow roads that might have held two cars side by side held four abreast and sometimes a fifth. Drivers yelled and cursed each other. Horns honked and cars swerved to avoid the mass of people walking on the road – in between cars, beside the cars, stepping out in front of cars and cursing the driver who came too close. The sidewalks, where visible, became impassable for all the uncaring, hurried, unfocused faces, stricken with isolation. If careless, an elbow hanging outside the window of the car might catch on the side mirror of the car next to it. Sometimes the drivers knew each other, horns honked, drivers smiled and the two cars squeezed by without challenge or conflict. If not…it made one shrink in the uncomfortable car seat.

Well out of the city, the road meandered and wound between sugar cane fields and piles of garbage. Narrow and often traveled by children and stray cattle, one could see only the sky because of the height of the sugar cane. The *cachaca* would be good this year. Driving for the space of an hour, the road climbed a small hill towards an un-menacing gate, fronted by overgrown bird-of-paradise plants, grapefruit trees and a water pipe. Looking to the left as the car approached, a grubby child with a very large gun emerged from a small lean-to constructed of corrugated tin and burnt wood. Shirtless and shoeless, he suffered from an uncorrected cleft palate. Brown eyes, because all eyes were in that locale, they reflected blankness, as if his eyes did not belong to him, as if the world was not to be seen with them. His blank eyes were good; the only reason life itself, such as it was, smiled upon him. The car stopped because the boy shot to kill.

The boy yelled something unintelligible and the driver handed food in a plastic bag from inside the car to waiting hands. They took great pains to ignore his thick barrel-like trunk; skeletal brittle legs covered with infected sores, shaved head and bifurcated earlobes hanging like necklaces to his shoulders. The rear window closest to the boy opened and a face peered out. Recognized, the gate opened, past which the car meandered upward past a series of corrugated tin houses. Out of each, as the car passed, a grubby child emerged holding a clean but very large gun -- all veterans of small and petty wars as numerous as their days. In a flat open space at the end of the road, the visitor left the car and traversed the rest of the narrow walkway on foot. To reach this point meant one or two things out of all possible things: blood on the hands of the visitor or blood money to change hands. Either way, to be alive at this height on the hill, this close to the old sugar plantation house, created a life marker for the visitor.

Though Ashton, with hair the color of wood-ash and sand that grew straight up like corn or sunflowers made this journey many times. Sweat created huge dark spots on his linen clothing, like elephant eyes during *mustt*. He raised his arm to block the sun, to see if he could see those who watched his approach. Another child appeared from behind a tree holding a modified made M-16. For the first time, the gun did not seem bigger than the boy. He did not look ravaged by violence, hunger, or marred from birth. Free of visible scars, he wore new khaki green, pleated pants, shiny, white tennis shoes, rope for a belt, no shirt, no hat. Not afraid of his visitor, he seemed terrified all the same. Having confirmed the identity of the visitor, he gave a lazy wave of his arm towards the house and disappeared again behind the tree. Outside the gate, the boys along the road had been nameless but his one had a name and Ashton wondered what they called him.

Some roads exacted a price before arriving at the destination. The road that lead to the front verandah of the old plantation house carried a heavy price; one that Ashton paid over and over again and would soon find out how he would pay again. Two more children stood guard on the front verandah. These two carried no weapons and spoke clearly as if they went to school. The boy watched while the girl opened the gate and ushered Ashton into the house. Too old to qualify his judgment, he found them beautiful even if they did not smile. They eyed him as if he carried the last known contagious disease, pressing them selves against the wall so that his linen clothes would not touch them as he passed. Inside the house, the business for which Ashton made his journey began with shared ice-cold *cachaca* and silence. Between the *cachaca* and the sudden change in temperature, he shivered in the dark room, hoping no one noticed his weakness. If they did, they ignored it. More *cachaca* to drink and silence to share, three people and two chairs -- Ashton stood. He had never seen these two before -- a meaningless detail. They sat inside the house waiting for him to agree to do as they bid -- whatever and however terrible.

The campaign of which we spoke will begin: Prepare and redeem yourself.

He tried not to blink and raised his glass to his lips to take another sip of *cachaca*. It made his head hurt.

RINCON DU NORD -TWENTY-FOUR YEARS AGO

Landing her small apartment in the building proved to be a step up for the young dance-hall star baby-mama. The twelve-story building sat on the landscape like a swollen finger, out of place and out of sorts. Originally constructed as a place of business, the contracting buyer walked away, leaving the building half complete. Abhorring a vacuum, the empty building filled quickly with hordes of ungrateful squatters who turned it into a tenement worthy of the worst reputations. Civil protection forces refused to enter the building. It had no connection to municipal water, sewer, or power. Multiple attempts to evict the occupants failed in embarrassing ways for the successive governments that made the attempt. All the glass had been broken out of the windows and garbage piled two stories high all around the bottom of the building. The smell of garbage made the first four floors uninhabitable.

This was one of the better neighborhoods she had lived in. Still, she read the sounds of violence outside like a book she did not have to open to read. She felt forced by a perverse sense of curiosity to steal glances through the threadbare cloth that covered the barred window. She considered herself lucky to have those bars – they meant the difference between one more day of life or death. However, she did not have glass windows and bars alone could not obliterate the sound of spilled blood outside the window. She heard something sharp against something soft – like the sound of a machete against a soft mango. She heard screaming followed by a spattering sound, then nothing. She used one hand to pull the cloth across the space in the wall. She heard laughter. The laughter made her skin cold and her face burn with fear. She covered the ears of her little one.

She imagined blood because she knew how blood behaved. She let her child suckle from her breast though it pained her to do it. The rest followed like an after birth: the body taken somewhere, the ground raked clean with a tree branch as if nothing happened, as if she imagined it. Those who laughed hid themselves in the shadows, faces obscured, only their bodies in full light. Their jewelry and nonchalance about the death they made gave them away in her mind. She hated their laughter above all things. She peered through the cloth at an angle so those gathered could not see the white of her eye and call on her. She had money to give them, but she wanted to buy a new dress. She tried not to think their name for fear she would say it out loud and invite their insidious attention. Her little one bit her. She winced but did not cry out. The little one bit her again and she returned her injured breast to the cover of her slip. The little one seemed not to care, either way, and moments later fell asleep on its own. She smiled for this meant that she would have time to play with her hair in front of a small mirror. She lived for that: imagining the luxury of another hand making her hair beautiful. So powerful was this longing that she preferred this imagining to the longing for a man to come to her. They came whether she longed for them or not.

It never failed that she began to cry while she played with her hair, as if the brushing drew water from her eyes the way water is pulled from a well. The little one could be awake or asleep, a man could be there or have just left or have come not at all for a week. Her money drawer and breasts could be full or empty. She cried all the same. She did not ask why or discern the reasons for her tears and neither did she did call it sadness or grief. She had no name for it. It simply happened and she accepted such things in good faith. She asked only that it end as abruptly as it started and usually it did, though water once poured from her eyes for three days. She did not like to recall that time but she found it difficult to forget and difficult not to wonder if this night's tears would again last three days. She did nothing differently except hide her face in her skirt hoping to muffle the sound, in case the death-mongers still lingered. After a few moments, she received her composure and smiled with gratefulness.

She spread a threadbare sheet over the little one against mosquitoes and danced away not wanting to wake the child. Though she had not much room for dancing, she felt graceful and young. A cool breeze made its way through the small space and she stopped for a moment to revel in it. She lived her life as a series of tragedies and small pleasures to be had. If only she lived long enough to feel a cool breeze, watch the little one sleep, or have her hair combed out. She kept her bedtime ritual because she could, the only thing she could afford to be particular about. She washed her hands in tepid water she saved in a small white porcelain bowl – one of her valued possessions. She hummed quietly to herself a made-up tune. This went on for some time, longer than one might imagine it to take. The water on her skin felt soft and sensual and she loathed finishing washing her hands. Next to the porcelain bowl a small gray towel received some of the tepid water from the porcelain bowl. With this she carefully took the sweat and dust from the parts of her body she could reach with her hands. With the remaining water she washed her hands again. Then and only then, she removed the slip she wore and donned a clean slip, sighing as the fabric fell around her, covering her body and ending her vulnerability. She washed her hands again though she had used most of the water. She did not fret. She paused to pray but gave up before any prayer came to mind, all part of going to sleep. Thoughts came unbidden, like men expecting her to worship them.

She got the child from a man who expected her to worship him and the power he collected around him. He found her after a concert she played in Capital and bribed his way into her dressing room. She thought she recognized him – a politician of some sort, one of the hungry who thought he could change the world with his passion. He gave her flowers and wanted to take her to dinner. She was bored so she let him show her how much of the world he had at his beck and call: a shiny new car and driver, a government house in the hills, money to spend, money to burn, a soft voice, shopping trips, a perfumed bed, white flowers, red roses, chocolate and wine, tables at the best restaurants. How could she not fall in love? He disappeared long before she told him she loved him; that she had made a baby. She heard he went back to his place of birth. She would not keep the child. That was her revenge. Guede Baron Semedi would take the *mingi* child with a star shaped birthmark on his hip to the Sisters of Mercy orphanage and she would be rid of it.

DIPLOMATIC SECTION - CAPITAL – YESTERDAY

The Diplomatic Section of Capital consisted of a twelve-square mile section of the city that remained squarely under central government control. Foreign countries kept their embassies there and the government maintained offices for the most prestigious of its agencies. The University relocated to the area, bringing with it those who could ill-afford the new cost structures the influx of national and international funds produced. Clean, well-kept, and secure, *avante garde* art galleries and restaurants sprang up like weeds, mingling with skyscrapers, official looking buildings, the flags of many different countries, motorcades with sirens and flashing blue lights, and blight in small but hidden places. Prohibitively expensive, the number of actual citizens living in the Diplomatic Section numbered very few and were most likely government employees living in a government-owned condominium or residence.

One such employee, the young, indomitable, Dominic Mercy, Defense Attaché to the Office of the President, kept his usual evening routine after leaving the ISEC building where he spent his days. He picked up jerk pork and festival from a street vendor on the way to the running track at the university (or a couple hours of sparring at the dojo). A cold green coconut from another street vendor kept him hydrated while the endorphins hummed and he headed home to clean up and take a nap. People told him he had the habits of an old man but he liked the safety of routine. He lived alone in a small two-bedroom, sixth floor, government apartment, within walking distance of his office. Unfurnished when he received the keys three years ago, he had since procured a new bed for the bedroom, a huge bean bag from which he lost himself in a seventy-two inch, 110 degree, cylindrical, mosaic projection display on a 3.02 Ghz pipe for media and gaming. He paired a Bang and Olufsen 3-channel receiver he won in a virtual bidding war with an even older VIFA

Denmark AS 3-channel speaker triplet in the front room. Instead of making rent payments, he would be paying for his media system for the next ten years. He and his on and off again girlfriend Hanna talked about a fifty-five gallon saltwater fish tank for Japanese Snapping Shrimp and Ghost Eels as the next addition to the apartment. The kitchen and bathroom cabinets remained empty except for extra toilet paper and a bar of soap. He preferred open windows to the air conditioner and sometimes fell asleep on his back patio – a small eight by 10 meter affair – on a rickety chaise lounge the former resident left when they departed.

Five Armani suits, purchased on a government account, met the dress code mandated by the nature of his office. Otherwise, he filled his small closet with pegged jeans, t-shirts, imitation Italian sport coats in black, blue or grey, and sneakers of as many colors and styles as he could afford. Except for a thick, pewter "Lion of Judah" ring on his left index finger, he wore no jewelry. He liked to people-watch and spent most evenings walking on the promenade or sitting at a sidewalk bar or small club. Hanna would not be in town for a couple of weeks, so after the sun went down and the day cooled, he donned something club-worthy and walked to the Bone Room; after all it was Tuesday. Monday nights he spent at the dojo. On Wednesdays he met up with friends from his former Special Forces unit, at an expat bar or an embassy party. On Thursdays he found a restaurant for dinner and ate until he thought he would burst. Friday's found him back at the Bone Room. Though he spent a fair amount of time around heavy drinkers and alcohol, he himself did not drink.

<<Joseph Nechvatal - Ego Masher>>

Not many people knew about the small club just a short walk from his apartment, which meant it seldom felt crowded. Not a dance club, Dominic went to hide and pass the evenings when he happened to be alone. People left him to nurse his mineral water. Though sometimes, a frazzled bald bureaucrat in a short sleeve button down shirt, damp-stained armpits and a clip-on necktie; or an overweight woman in a short skirt, one size too small, wearing too much makeup, would sit at "his" table. But they rarely talked. Hanna said they were scared of him. He laughed at her but found him self using that knowledge to his advantage, sometimes. The Bone Room played a narrow range of musical genres from lo-fidelity old-school dancehall to *Japonoise* to vintage chip noise. Haphazardly framed street art and antique mirrors punctuated the club's red walls. Black leather furniture created a dark cave like atmosphere. Billie Holiday posters, original artwork by up and coming Cuban artists coming out of commercial and artistic exile, and a few framed media pieces by the club's patron saint, Joseph Nechvatal, peppered the walls. The sparsely placed tabletops held pieces of colored glassware, broken over the years at the club. Dominic liked the place because they played the music loud enough to feel the baseline in his chest. He knew the owners and most of the staff at the bar by both face and name. They knew him because he always ordered mineral water and had established a reputation for being a decent tipper. As well as a place to hide and pass time, he discovered it a decent place to meet women. Though not outgoing by nature, he met and courted not a few women, a few of which ended up either in his apartment or her hotel room. Even in this a pattern emerged: all the women, local or expat, were in transit.

She was put on earth to be noticed, to be seen, to turn heads.

She took possession of the room, standing on the long legs of a tango dancer or a ballerina. Dominic's eyes surrendered all willpower. About an inch shorter than his 5'11, she wore a charcoal-gray business suit, cut on the runways of Milan, like a weapon. Black stiletto heels over a clenched fist tattoo on her left ankle, she wore long jet-black hair tied neatly back, framing her strong, proud and patrician face. He guessed her family as South American, maybe Cuban or Argentinian, though her clothes and makeup screamed American. Her blouse framed her neck and chest, mesmerizing him like nothing else could. Blood red lipstick and lime green manicured fingernails and toes made him smile. He thought it auspicious he had also chosen to wear lime green sneakers. He assumed her date would arrive shortly -- older, with an expensive watch and shoes, drinking expensive liquor. In which case, he was content to stare. As if to prove him wrong, she walked to his table, sat down across from him, lit a cigarette, took a few moments to take him in, then leaned forward and asked, "What the fuck kind of music is this?"

He did not answer immediately. Mesmerized by the neckline of her blouse and the v-shaped shadow it formed against her skin, words took a back seat to the eyes. He managed only to lift his drink, shrug his shoulders and smile. No words availed themselves to interrupt the momentary feast of the eyes.

She did not falter. "Are you drinking water? I was going to ask you to buy me a drink!"

Dominic signaled a young girl in a very short red leather skirt who had been serving him. All the young female wait staff at the Bone Room wore short red leather skirts. It was a signature, of sorts. The bartender, with whom Dominic occasionally went clubbing, was a nice-enough kid from the university. Though he did not wear a skirt.

She ordered a Johnny Walker Blue, lit another cigarette and said she was from Miami. He told her he was from down the street. When her drink arrived, she mouthed the words 'thank you,' and returned to smoking her cigarette, watching the few people dancing with a critical eye. After a few minutes she turned to him again and asked, "How the fuck do you dance to this shit?"

Definitely American. They swore up a storm when world markets were up and their favorite team won the championship. "Dunno," Dominic said using his North Carolina accent. "I don't dance."

"American?"

Dominic shook his head and pointed to the ground. *"Mi bahn yaso."*

"Oh no you didn't," she said, waving her drink in the air between them, "chat patois to me!"

He wondered what she would do if he touched her lips when she spoke. He moved his chair closer so he could speak without yelling, "I said I was born here."

She nodded and finished the last of her drink. "You an alcoholic?"

"No."

She laughed, "You don't even look old enough to get in here."

Dominic ignored her. Though this time it was not an old man in a musty suit, reeking of cheap liquor and an even cheaper cigar.

"Sorry. That was dumb," she said, getting the attention of the bargirl again. "So how do you pay your bills?"

Dominic shifted his chair close enough to smell the haute couture perfume she wore. It was all he could do to string two sentences together. "I use Bitcoin. Doesn't everybody?"

"Nobody likes a smartass you know…"

"I work up the street," which meant any number of high-level government agencies, foreign embassies or international organizations headquartered in the Diplomatic Section of Capital. He did not go into detail.

She laughed. "Doesn't everybody?"

She sat across from him, born to be the apple of many eyes. When not smiling, her face mirrored the fierceness and confidence of her voice – strong, directed, persistent, unwavering, and not at all fragile. She smiled and the same features which gave her strength and persistence, made him feel like a child. When his eyes and body surrendered the good sense to start a conversation, he found her easy to talk to and drawn into conversation.

Born in Argentina, schooled in Cuba, she gained American citizenship in the first wave of highly educated Cuban expatriates after the lifting of the American Embargo. He guessed correctly. Seven years older than him, she took her Masters in Political Science at a university in Havana. So mesmerized was he by her voice, it did not register that she asked him about himself. She waved her drink in front of him with a smile and repeated her question.

"Sorry. I work for the national government."

"I thought maybe you were the young scion of an international banker or something?"

"No, no international bankers in my family…"

"Not so much? Damn!" she said, laughing, lightly touching his shoulder with her hand. He wished she would do that again and as reading his mind, she did when she pulled a pack of cigarettes from a Louis Vuitton bag and handed him her lighter to light her cigarette with. "I chain smoke when I'm nervous," she told him, "and I drink."

"Why are you nervous?"

"Dunno, I'm in a bar with you, should I be nervous?" Her smile disappeared quickly and she glared expectantly.

"Maybe…"

"Ha! You are a mess! Did you grow up in the city?"

Dominic shook his head. Conversation related to his childhood, growing up and family simply did not occur.

Ever. "I came here three years ago from a Special Forces base leeward side."

"Uh oh. Sniper, Hacker, or Interrogator?"

"If I told you, I'd have to kill you…"

She rolled her eyes and laughed. "Funny, I'm not that nervous any more."

"How did you end up here?"

"My job requires me to do things I hate – travel to foreign places and spend long periods of time away from home."

"Where's home?"

"Miami. You?"

"Down the street."

"Aren't you lucky!"

"How come you don't like your job?" Dominic asked, since it never occurred to him that one had a choice.

"Oh, let's not talk shop ok?"

Dominic shrugged his shoulders in agreement. She could tell him to commit *seppuku* and he would be agreeable.

"Is it safe to go outside around here?"

"I wouldn't if I were you," Dominic said, with a fair amount of honesty. Though inside the city limits, the club lay just outside the outer boundaries of the Civil Offense Technology Regime. Any intervention, should one become necessary, would be a human intervention, rather than ubiquitous, unavoidable and failsafe identity technology.

"But I'm ok if I'm with you, right?"

Dominic laughed at the innuendo. "How am I doing so far?"

"Let's get some fresh air. It's too damn smoky in here," though she had been the only smoker. They did not discuss it and he did not ask, but he headed in the direction of his apartment. His destination didn't cross his mind until she complained about her heels and all the cracks in the pavement.

"Step on a crack, break your mommas' back," he quipped, wondering where the jingle came from, and as usual, uncomfortable with the use of the word 'momma'.

<<Omar Sosa - Raya>>

At the threshold to his apartment, she walked in as if she owned the place, stopped and sniffed. "I don't smell anything bad. Point for you!" she said, gingerly going deeper into the apartment, two paces into the kitchen and half way down the short hallway, sampling the air as she went. She saw the chaise lounge on the small patio, and smiled, "Let's sit outside." Not about to argue, Dominic sat with her on the chaise lounge and together, they watched the lights of the city flicker from a distance. Not all of it electric, they spotted pit fires and the more persistent garbage fires that pocked the mountainside. Closer to the city center, brightly lit cranes stood out from the skyline like huge metallic monsters, while the lights of the office buildings glowed warmly.

"Who do you work for again? This is kinda' swanky for government work," she said, her body achingly near his, but not too close.

"I guess I'm lucky," and with that, unable to resist any longer and seeing no reason why he should, he touched her lips with the back of his finger, which she kissed, leaving a lipstick mark on his hand.

"Why don't you go get me a drink?" she asked, looking at him with petulant eyes.

He poured a generous amount of the rare rum he kept in the kitchen. By the time he returned, she shed her shoes and suit jacket, had lit another cigarette, which she held out to him. He handed her the drink and took the cigarette, savoring the sweet clove tobacco. She sipped her drink and rubbed her ankle with the tattoo on it. If he had been a photographer there would have been no shutter setting fast enough to capture her in any light. When he sat down, she moved closer to him and began removing his shoes, then the fake Italian sport coat. She let him kiss her and she fumbled clumsily to remove his t-shirt. She put her hands on his chest and said, "Tell me I can take you."

"Take me?" Dominic asked, conversation not high on his list of things to do at that point. He felt her body against his like a surging angry sea in all the places they touched, and still she wanted to talk. "Where?"

"*Ay dios mio*," she said, dispensing finally with the spoken word.

Later, as they lay on the bed, which really had not been used up to that point, exhaustion precluded him from speaking. He lay on his back, one arm behind his head and the other cupping her breast, she rested her head on his chest, her hand fingering the line of his mouth, shoulder and belly. She had not covered herself and her body shone in the half-darkness that was the city at night through partially open windows. If Dominic knew how to paint he would have painted her just that way. She asked what he would do after the elections and he told her he would follow her and watch her smoke cigarettes every night. She laughed, called him a mess and turned over onto her belly, her arm across his chest. He didn't remember falling asleep, as such, but when he woke up in the early morning, she had already left. She never told him her name.

INTERCONTINENTAL HOTEL – DIPLOMATIC SECTION, CAPITAL - TODAY

The top-floor conference room loomed large and intimidating when Dominic first opened the double doors. With its high vaulted ceilings, minimalist furniture, impressionist art, the ambient temperature felt more appropriate for Arctic seals. He looked for the thermostat, hoping the adjustment would take effect before the circus began. He counted chairs against his list of invited participants. He made a mental note to ask for two additional chairs for the President's security detail, who now insisted they remain with the President at all times. He checked the ISEC ANTI-INFIL certification again, since one could never be too sure. Although they swept the entire floor, Dominic walked around the room closing blinds and drapes so the only light came from room lighting. They would not use nametags or a seating arrangement and protocol would be relaxed. Already, Dominic could not wait for the meeting to be over. After three years, he did not understand how the President tolerated these endless meetings, briefings and reports for never a useful thing had he heard in any of the meetings.

The pre-meeting began in the foyer with hushed, urgent conversations between ministers, aides, ministers and the usual gaggle of ISEC and military advisers. Some gathered around the coffee pot, wearing serious faces and checking messaging devices. The more urgent the conversation and serious the face, the more the participants checked their messages. Dominic emerged into the foyer about a minute after the main group of attendees arrived and politely pushed his way through the crowd. He needed to be closer to the foyer entrance in case the President arrived ahead of schedule. He had a report he knew the President wanted to see before the meeting got underway and Dominic wanted to get it to him before people took their seats. He knew most of them by name, if not by face or title, but he kept his distance. Across the room, he noticed Richard Jackson, the Minister of Education, standing with his usual group of flunkies, mostly male and mostly young. Dominic caught the man's eye and smiled with a satisfying sense of irony.

Two years ago, Dominic, just shy of twenty-one, still raw and hardened by his time with Special Forces, had not his commission with the Office of the President for more than six months when Richard Jackson stopped him in the hallway of the Parliament Building and asked to speak with him privately. Dominic agreed, flattered his position attracted the attention of those with power and influence. Though young and inexperienced, he calculated he might learn something useful from it. Richard stepped into a side room and made his first mistake by standing a little too close to Dominic and putting his hand on Dominic's shoulder, before even one word had been said. Dominic shrugged the unwelcome hand from his shoulder and stepped back, still not wanting to be rude. He kept his fight or flight response under the skin and waited for something more substantive to transpire. Richard realized his *faux paux* and it seemed to spook him. He offered Dominic two thousand Bitcoin (slightly less than half a month's salary for Dominic) for dinner, a few hours at an Embassy party and after that perhaps more time at his house in the hills. It took just a moment longer than it should have for Dominic to make the necessary connection in order to respond and thinking Dominic hard of hearing or slow to comprehend, Richard repeated himself -- not exactly the conversation Dominic envisioned when he entered the room. Dominic didn't smile, but replied in as gentle a voice as he could muster, "That's not my style, Minister."

To which Richard Jackson replied, "I could go as high as three thousand…"

Dominic took a half step closer to Richard. "Yuh nuh ovastan?" Dominic said, ratcheting the force in his voice up one level, squaring his eyes with the older man, in open opposition.

Richard stepped back, almost tripping over himself. The change in Dominic's presence spooked him even more. He closed the door to the hallway.

"No need to raise your voice. No harm, no foul, right?" Richard opened the door, nodded at Dominic, and strode out of the room, returning to his group of flunkies waiting nervously in the hall for him.

<<*Lady Saw – Cyaan Get Me*>>

There the matter might have faded from memory and come to naught, save one more effort on Richard's part to recover a wounded sense of pride. It occurred a few days later in the Pool Room showers, which Dominic used during inclement weather. Having worn himself out with his usual two hundred fifty laps in the Olympic size pool, he felt neither social nor in the mood to wrestle. As he emerged from the shower and into the locker room area in no more than the clothes nature gave him, he found none other than Richard Jackson, sitting directly in front of his locker. Richard looked up as Dominic entered the locker room, quite pleased with himself. Not anticipating a long or complex philosophical conversation, but neither wishing to stand in front of the Minister of Education in the state he was in, he improvised and grabbed a towel (since he had not brought one with him) from the used towel laundry bin and held it in front of him, all without losing ground.

"Go home. No harm, no foul, that's what you said?" Dominic said, ending his sentence in a conciliatory question but taking a step forward.

"You think you're special, eh? "

"Mi nuh know a'whadoyuh mon!" Dominic said, ignoring Richard's venomous look.

"You are a little punk," Richard spat when he spoke.

Dominic squared his eyes directly with Richard's and said, *"Mi nuh mek free wit'yuh, yuhknow!"*

Richard stood up finally to face Dominic. "I know about you!"

"Wh'yuh com' yaso?"

"To teach you a lesson."

"Yuh a ras-teacher nuh, eh Richard?"

"Who gave you permission to use my first name? You lack all respect!"

Jackson took three steps towards Dominic, the way a person might if they were going to hug a close friend, intentions belied by the seething anger on the man's face and the long string of obscenities issuing from his mouth as he closed the distance between himself and Dominic. In a heightened state of awareness from the endorphins coursing through his system, Dominic stood still, feet flat on the ground, waiting. The world faded and Dominic saw Richard's advance through binoculars worn backwards, hands outstretched in front of him instead of held close, his head slightly lowered as he advanced. He saw the weakness he needed.

But Richard carried more power in his affront than Dominic expected, catching him off guard. Realizing his fault, Dominic stepped back, absorbing some of Richard's power. He allowed himself to be pushed up against a flight of lockers, Richard's fat forearm under Dominic's chin and the other grabbing hand seeking territory on Dominic's body where he was least willing to tolerate it. Forgetting the towel as a last bastion of decency, Dominic took hold of the arm at his neck and simultaneously swept one leg across Richard's unbalanced stance. Richard's copious weight carried his body towards the ground. Dominic retained his hold at the wrist. As Richard fell, he forced the man's hand forward with all the rage he could muster until he felt the bones in the wrist break. Richard screamed in pain and as he fell, hit his face on the edge of the bench and broke his jaw.

The man lay on the shower room floor, screaming and bleeding. Dominic stepped over Richard to reach the sinks to wash his hands. He stepped over Richard a second time to get himself a clean towel since the one he had been holding was now bloodied. Taking longer than he usually did, he dried off, opened his locker, and dressed in his street clothes. Richard begged Dominic to call for help. Dominic walked over to the wall near the ISEC emergency switch and looked back at Richard, procrastinating a few moments longer. Dominic had one more thing to say to Richard before he hit the ISEC Emergency toggle. *"Man nuh dead nuh call 'im duppy,"* he said, and sat down on the bench nearest Richard's writhing body and waited.

The incident caused no end of interest, gossip and whispering in the halls of government that night. ISEC Custodial authorities placed a call to the President's Office, notifying him his young attaché had been arrested for assaulting a government minister and would not be returning to work. While the Minister was rushed to hospital with great haste, Dominic suffered the usual ministrations of ISEC Custodial. Doused with four buckets of ice-cold water, they shoved him into a room with an ambient temperature just above freezing, his hands cuffed behind his back. The controlled breathing apparatus they strapped to his face gave him a bloody nose. The laceration at the top of the forehead came from a vicious baton strike. Dominic steeled himself for worse, knowing something of their methods. But just as he expected them to start again, the rough treatment ceased suddenly and the controlled breathing device shut down by remote switch. One of the custodial staff pressed a lit cigarette into Dominic's temple before he and his colleagues disappeared. Dominic noted the temperature in the room started to warm.

Within minutes, Ashton, first among equals of the President's men, entered the room in the company of an ISEC officer. Things happened quickly. Ashton yelled for an ISEC medic. A Custodial staff member removed the handcuffs and the breathing machine. He ordered the ISEC medic to do a full 'recovery' (treated for the injuries resulting from the interrogation, in ISEC parlance). First came an ampoule of pain and sedation pharma. Ashton waited until the medic completed the recovery, barking into his COMLINK for the list of Custodial staff on duty at the time. The medic showed Ashton to a side room where Dominic sat on a gurney, under a heat lamp, wrapped in towels, oxygen feed under his nose. Ashton offered a second round of pharma but Dominic refused. Few withheld their surprise when the President himself entered the 'Recovery Room'. At first, the President stared at his damaged staff member, his anger visible and palpable. He reached out to make a simple physical connection but Dominic's hyper-withdrawal reaction, despite the pharma, said all that needed to be said.

Ordering everyone out, save Ashton, the two older men expended no small effort at dragging the story out of an embarrassed and reluctant Dominic, unaccustomed to talking about the things what happened to him. As he moved through the narrative, they laughed and whistled at the amount of Bitcoin involved, asking Dominic what his magic number was. The story turned the older men into frat brothers. They made rude gestures and pulled their chins, leaving Dominic puzzled by the long bouts of laughter his story invoked. The part about Dominic not having a towel to protect basic decency set them to belly aching laughter. It was quite some time before either of them gained control, amidst many guffawing apologies to Dominic. Partly an act, they succeeded in getting Dominic to crack a smile. They stopped laughing when Dominic told them how the bones in the man's wrist cracked in his hand; and how he finished changing before toggling the emergency switch. The President noted a new, flat-line quality in Dominic's voice, his normally warm and animated eyes looking too much like darkened glass. Uncomfortable with the sudden shift in a young man he knew as usually friendly and affable, the President advised Dominic to be wary of all politicians. He said they were all wolves in sheep's wool, catching Ashton's eye with an imperceptible nod.

Ashton took pictures of the worst of the damage done during the interrogation and harangued the Custodial staff for going too far. He slipped Dominic more pain and sedation pharma and drove him back to his apartment. On the President's orders, the incident was stricken from the record, just as the previous four incidents involving the same minister had been. Ashton visited the Minister of Education in hospital to inform him that no action would be taken and that each was expected to maintain decorum appropriate to their position. The President himself suggested that Dominic greet Richard warmly and publicly, at every opportunity. Thus, Dominic took great pleasure in greeting Richard with a smile.

As he made his way to the double doors of the foyer entrance, lime green fingernails clutching a dossier caught his eye and stopped him. Dominic straightened his suit, looked around furtively and walked over to her.

"Good afternoon, I don't think we've met."

She did not look up from the folder she had been studying but replied, "The name's Castaneda, I'm with SELAND. I should be on your list."

Dominic checked the list and found the name, agency and title -- at least he had a name to go with the face.

"Could we speak privately, Ms. Castaneda?"

She hesitated before looking up from the folder but did not hide her surprise at the face looking back at her. She looked around the room, at him and followed his cue. He ushered her towards the conference room next door and followed her into the room, making sure the door had fully closed. Her stone cold stare disappeared and she chuckled to herself.

"Really?" he said drawing the word out as long as he could.

She held up her hands in mock surrender. "Dominic! What a surprise."

"SELAND? What do you do for them?"

"Global Ops…Political. You?"

"Defense Attaché with the Office of the President."

"So you're Joseph's houseboy, eh? You were modest at the Bone Room. If I knew I never would have gone home with you."

"Really?"

"This means we can never see each other again," she said, closely investigating one of her manicured fingernails.

"*Wha'mek?*"

"I'm not supposed to fuck the natives!"

If they had been anywhere else a melee and repeat performance of the night before might have ensued but he held his ground and laughed. "Too late…Thursday night, dinner?"

"Where on Thursday?"

"The Cuban place, two doors down from the Bone Room."

"When?"

"Nine."

She nodded.

He opened the conference room door ushered her out into the foyer. He continued into the main conference room where President Joseph Santo sat at the table alone, with his head in his hands.

"Mr. President?"

The older man hesitated before removing his hands from his face, looked up and smiled. "Dominic, you are here. No problems getting here?"

"No problems, sir. I have the report you asked for," he said holding out the sheaf of papers he had been carrying around. When the President did not take the report, Dominic placed it next to him on the table.

"Have you met everyone?" the President asked.

"Not everyone but they are all here."

"Why don't you let the dogs in; I'm ready to meet my maker." He began every meeting with this verbal ritual and though Dominic heard it countless times, it still made him smile. Today was no exception. After three years in the office, Dominic still had not figured out whether the President did not like the people or that he despised the meetings themselves.

Born into privilege of a mixed South African family, he came to the island at the age of twelve. He told his parents he would be a preacher or a politician – either one was fine. His parents laughed for that was how offered encouragement. They moved back to South Africa by the time he took office as President. They laughed again when he gave them the news. The person of the President arrived by anonymous helicopter -- the kind that brought Japanese businessmen to the hotel for golf. His ISEC escort arrived in a flurry of official government vehicles, parked in front of the hotel. His security contingent waited for him at the rooftop door as the President ducked to run from the helicopter. Even the suite at the Intercontinental called in a favor. Hotel management preferred not to decline a request by a majority shareholder. They went to great pains to keep his presence a secret.

He had not seen his wife and children since the incident. He had not slept since his wife left with their young children for safer ground. He rubbed his eyes, recalling the conversation, which occurred less than thirty-six hours ago. Five minutes after she stormed out of the bedroom, a rusty radiator crashed through the ceiling, ruining the white carpet she had spent a year acquiring. The papers, folders, dossiers and manuals followed in short order - all of it as useful as six tons of garbage strewn about the Presidential Palace. He could relax now that his wife and children were confirmed off the island and en route to a closely held destination.

President Joseph Santo's paranoia led him to favor a weak image over a strongman persona, though he knew he had a reputation for ruthlessness. When those around him expected action, he remained still. Vacuum drew them in and complacency ruled the day. When they expected delay or indifference, he enacted surgical and merciless end games on those who compromised his purpose, regardless of collateral damage. But any meteoric rise to power came with a price and he had no doubts his political opponents staged the garbage incident to embarrass him. He needed evidence. He often felt alone in life, but today he did not feel it -- he knew it as fact. The power of his office consumed him. Though his to do with as he pleased only until the tectonic plates of power politics shifted, he knew death or exile would come with that shift. Not if, but when.

So it happened that far from Old Hope Road and the millions and their children, a group of distressed technocrats sat at a conference table long and wide, made from a single piece of aged mahogany which stole much of the room's real estate. High-backed chairs covered in a velvet brocade sheltered angry men and one woman, chewing on expensive pens. Around the table, papers, folders, dossiers, manuals and other tools of the trade did not preclude blank stares through bulletproof, curtained windows. Crystal goblets dotted the table, holding ice in various stages of melting and soda water flavored with slices of lime. At the top of the table, flanked by two bodyguards, the President fumed over the events of recent days. After two hours of grandstanding, posing, arguing, blaming and pointless conversation, the President could stand it no longer, "Does anybody know anything?" The question shot into the center of the room like a bull out of the gate in a rodeo. It surprised him as much as the others in the room.

Excuses began in milliseconds.

"It is too early to tell, sir," this from his chief of internal security.

"We are tracking more than five thousand groups sir. They are discreet or we would not be here," bordering on insubordination from his sister's son, he fixed the man with a stare but no more.

"Anon-Lulz has denied any activity on your NETCERT. Preliminary findings confirm this, but of course, the usual disclaimers apply, but I assure you, we will find these common criminals sir and they will pay." The only woman in the room spoke without making eye contact. She kept her eyes and her hands with lime-green manicured fingernails on the dossier. Her presence in the room a matter of deep contention, she swore allegiance to a flag of fewer colors than the one on the wall behind the President. One day he would ask why the national flag always had to be hung behind his chair at whichever table he chose to sit. Most likely he imagined they would not be able to give him a specific reason.

"I hear a confidence I would not hear in the voice of someone born here. Besides, Anon-Lulz are your people, are they not?" A fat man with hair the color of wood-ash and sand that grew straight up like corn or sunflowers fixed her silhouette with fire in his eyes – a dangerous thing to say since she had the President's confidence. No one argued but no one threw his or her lot in with him either.

"Your government requested my presence sir." She delivered her riposte sharp and true. Her eyes did not waver from the dossier she hid behind, a shield she did not need. "I don't need to brief you on the particulars of Anon-Lulz, surely."

"Ashton, that is not helpful," the President said gently to his long time senior political advisor. There had always been chemistry between them, though never discussed or questioned. Neither thought of the other as a friend – the politics of the room belied any such human artifact. None of them recognized permanent alliances.

Ms. Casteñada was smart to muddy the waters with Anon-Lulz – the archetypal 'robin hood' and metaphorical conscience of the digital sunshine era. Her statement was the ultimate oxymoron, but no one in the room called her on it. Confirming the absence of Anon-Lulz activity was much like confirming the absence of angels. From humble beginnings in the first decade of 2000, Anon-Lulz cut their teeth on the razor's edge, exposing governmental secrecy through misinformation activism, as well as exposing military misadventure, dictator's bloopers, government graft, all lumped together with a generous amount of pranksterism. For its thirtieth birthday celebration, Anon-Lulz replaced the UN2 SELAND tag with a diversion tag, taking the inquirer to a list of Anon-Lulz actions, going back to its beginning in the early 2000s. In one month, they collapsed three international child pornography rings by packaging darknet user identities and the evidence that would damn those users in SELAND evidentiary fashion, leaving the evidence at INTERPOL's ANTI-INFIL doorstep. In the same month, Anon-Lulz released the SELAND hashtags of numerous, high level, undercover intelligence agents spying in allied capitals; as well as releasing the closely guarded route of a much hated Middle East dictator through the streets of New York, from his country's embassy to a world renowned hospital for cancer treatment.

Everyone in the room heard exhaustion in his voice and recognized it as a sign of weakness in an ongoing series -- the first being the sequestering of he and his team in the penthouse suite of this hotel. "None of you have answered my question!" He cast his voice in a tone he knew made them nervous. "Dominic, I need coffee." Without a word the young man in an Armani suit behind the President rose with the grace of a mountain lion and left the room.

"To be honest I expected more. I expected to see evidence, I expected progress and as usual you come to me empty handed. You disgust me, all of you. You have seventy-two hours to bring me answers, to bring me something. If you have nothing, do not come back. Leave me." As they gathered their papers, folders, dossiers and other tools of their trade in nervous silence, he changed his mind. "Ms. Casteñada, kindly keep your seat." Still she did not look up from her dossier. She had not even moved. Dominic returned to the conference room with silver coffee service and a single demitasse, set it in front of the President, poured the thick brown liquid and returned to his chair. The President noted she did not feel the need to begin talking. She did however raise her eyes from the dossier and meet his gaze. "Do you have anything for me, Ms. Casteñada?"

She spoke carefully. "All indications so far point to a home-grown vector, most likely political rather than anarchist."

"Have you seen this year's increase in our SELAND allocation, Ms. Castaneda? It borders on criminal."

"I do not determine national allocations."

"I am aware of that, Ms. Casteñada. I just wondered if you were privy to the numbers."

"Yes, Mr. President, I have seen the numbers."

"You have seen the numbers and yet you speak to me in generalities?"

"If you are not satisfied with my performance, Mr. President, I can go home with the diplomatic pouch."

President Joseph Santo laughed. "Come now, Ms. Casteñada, it has not come to that between you and I, surely? We are colleagues, no? We need to work together."

"I am here in an advisory capacity only, sir."

"Are you being coy, Ms. Casteñada?"

"No, Mr. President. I am trying to determine whether SELAND should begin looking for my replacement."

"You don't like it here, do you?"

"I prefer to be home."

"Understood. You were reading Ashton's dossier."

"I didn't have time to read them all on the shuttle over here. Yours was next. You sent them away before I could get to it."

"Since you would rather be home, I will only extend your visa for another seventy-two hours." As she gathered her belongings, he changed his mind again. His wife would accuse him of being fickle. "I would take it as a favor if you sat at table with me for dinner. We'll make it a working dinner."

She continued to put papers into her briefcase. Anticipating the President's imminent departure, the two security men moved like synchronized swimmers to open the heavy double doors that opened into the suite's foyer. When she gathered her belongings and briefly quizzed her surroundings for anything she might have missed, she flashed a brief smile. Had he not been so tired, he might have noticed her smile directed in Dominic's direction. "I am not high enough on the food chain to accept gifts from foreign governments."

He smiled and watched her leave. Dominic did not miss her exit either. If he noticed nothing else, Dominic noticed Ms. Castañeda. He watched Dominic watching Ms. Castañeda and felt old.

Dominic gathered the coffee service with one hand and the President's brief case in the other.

"Please leave this in my suite," he said indicating the brief case with his chin. "Will you remain here if I need to find you?" A rhetorical question no doubt, and yet the young man, yet a boy even, had a remarkable ability to communicate sullenness and charm in the same expression, as if playing the flute for a room full of *Naja Ashei* spitting cobras.

"Don't worry. Get some sleep. We all need it." The young man moved as if carried by a wind, the weight of the coffee service balanced by the political weight of the briefcase he carried. "You were hoping she was going to stay for dinner, weren't you?" He tried to introduce a hint of camaraderie and smiled an approving smile, but Dominic did not answer or return the smile. Protocol did not require it and Dominic knew his protocol to the letter, at times in seeming violation of its spirit. Over the three years Dominic was at the post, Joseph Santo grew to appreciate his young aide. So far, their professional relationship fit both their personalities without requiring a lot of work or energy. The young man seemed to know intuitively what was needed. Ashton had not let him down with the referral.

As Dominic disappeared into the foyer, the President wondered at the way the conversation wound and meandered, never finding its mark. No one voiced his or her true thoughts, choosing every word for its lack of substance. Even Dominic followed the hallowed rule: *Do not speak truth to power*. Of course Dominic had hoped Ms.

Casteñada would accept. What island boy wouldn't? The thought brought a smile as he remembered life at Dominic's age, but current events impinged and he wondered again about the dossier on Ashton Ms. Casteñada had been focused on. If she had been trying to communicate some salient fact with her choice, she had chosen a blunt and overstated medium – not her style. He detached any meaning from the entire exchange and restored Ashton to his usual and favored place: a close and loyal ally of many years. He wondered again at the improbable dynamic between Dominic and Ms. Casteñada but decided he had imagined it. He had other things to worry about.

WIKIPEDIA ENTRY FOR FLASH MOB:

A group of people who assemble suddenly in a public place to perform an unusual or pointless act for a short time and then disperse, often for the purposes of entertainment, artistic expression, satire, political activism/anarchism and sometimes violence. Flash mobs came of age with the advent of social media and cheap messaging technology, which assisted large groups of people to coordinate mass actions. The first flash mob of record occurred in 2003 and by 2009, some municipalities had taken legal steps to mitigate their impact if not ban them completely.

The Promenade remained Capital's most treasured feature. Built only four years prior and billed as the foundation of a new era of civility and public-private partnership, city planners, architects, visionaries and residents argued and fought over every inch. Modeled after local architecture and the design of the Presidential Palace, it covered ten acres with lawn and garden plots, water features, open seating and shade trees. Initial planning even called for potable water fountains. The buildings that formed the outer boundary of the Promenade fast became the city's up and coming places to see and be seen, to sell and shop. Restaurants emerged, flared and disappeared. Small basement clubs, bookstores and coffee shops served both the night owl and the bookworm. A special police force rose up to protect the Promenade. However, the gentrified police force, comprised mostly of uniformed, retired civil servants, armed only with a secure COMLINK proved no match for what came to be called the "NO MORE" flash mob.

Between 11.37 am and 11.42 am, four thousand people arrived at the Promenade, dressed in black, holding little white signs reading "NO MORE". Between 11.43 am and 11.49 am another four thousand people arrived also dressed in black and holding white signs which read "NO MORE".

Between 11.50 am and 12.00 noon another three thousand people of the same provenance descended into the square. At 12.02 pm, on order of the President, ISEC deployed the first contingent of flybots. Prior to 12.02 pm the ten thousand people on the Promenade milled about like confused cattle, bumping into each other, not saying a word, signs held in front of them. As the flybots deployed, the movement became more apparent – they began to jog in a circle. If someone tripped or stumbled people around them paused to help them up.

At the edges of the crowd the Promenade began to suffer as a decidedly anarchist element took over. At 12.07 pm the first surveillance drones went airborne to supplement the flybots. At 12.10 pm ISEC deployed twelve Civil Offense drones to encircle the flash mob like the numbers on a clock. Equipped with water canon, sticky-polymer net, loud speakers, RFID dust and the latest in non-lethal crowd dispersing technology, the participants in the flash mob were ordered to disperse by order of the President. The Civil Offense drones dropped their payload of RFID dust at 12.13 pm. By this time, the crowd had stopped milling and simply stared at the flybot swarm at 1000 feet, the much larger observation and surveillance drones circling at 2500 feet and the even larger Civil Offense drones hanging in regular intervals at 5000 feet. None of this technology stopped an anarchist element from setting off tear gas, smoke bombs, and using low-power stun guns to shoot people in the crowd. Small but vicious circles of panic evolved. It did not take many to turn a milling crowd into a stampede of deadly proportions. In less than a second, the flybots located the twenty-two people with stun guns and tear gas smoke bombs. Those coordinates went to the Civil Offense drones on an encrypted satellite link, which drenched the general area with more persistent RFID dust and sticky polymer net. But even such an impressive execution of non-lethal strategy did not stop people from running and tripping. Neither was it sufficient to prevent the deaths of eight hundred and eleven people who died underfoot that day. Three people caught in sticky polymer net died of heart attacks. No one died from tear gas or stun guns.

The NO MORE flash mob triggered 72 hours of martial law and the most stringent penalties for domestic terrorism and involuntary manslaughter handed down by a Civil Defense tribunal with no option for parole or appeal: life in prison for twenty-one people caught with stun-guns in their possession, thirty days in jail for those who generated original messaging about the flash mob before it went viral, and a monetary fine for all who tested positive for the RFID in the subsequent RFID sweep. Flash mobs had not been criminalized but the monetary fine generated revenue to recoup some of the cost of the response. Either a misnomer or a non sequitur, ISEC never figured out what the "NO MORE" slogan referred to.

CHAPTER II

INTERCONTINENTAL HOTEL – DIPLOMATIC SECTION, CAPITAL, TODAY

A large truck ban led to food riots because grocery stores were empty, though the truck in the garbage incident passed nowhere near the city center. Banks closed because of the riots. Looters stepped into the void and were shot on site by civil offense drones. Garbage trucks became especially unacceptable within the confines of Capital's streets, so garbage piled up in neighborhoods everywhere. Rodents did very well. At least the government had not sat idly by; at least it had taken strong and immediate action.

The volley of trucks carrying slightly less than six tons of international garbage from the grounds of the Presidential Palace (no one thought to go into the residence to retrieve the radiator) crawled from their rallying point, flanked by armored police vehicles and more military vehicles. The men in the cars smiled smugly at the security. Absolutely nothing would go wrong because absolutely nothing could go wrong. Their lives depended on absolutely nothing going wrong. They wrote backup plans five layers deep and back up plans for each of those layers. They smiled and peered through dark sunglasses at island-clad girls standing on the side of the road to witness the spectacle, laughing at the cruise ships put off outside harbor waters, waiting for clearance to unload unhappy passengers. The planned route led them through the city center to the harbor where a ship waited to receive the garbage and take it back where it belonged – out of sight and out of mind. They designed a simple straightforward route, which required a house be demolished so the route did not have to make a turn. They had the home's residents trussed up and driven three hours into the countryside, then un-trussed and left on the side of the road. The squatters would not make it back to town in time to protest and they would miss the parade. Out of sight out of mind.

According to plan, each truck backed up to the receiving end of the largest conveyor belt contraption the island ever saw and slowly dumped its payload. It took hours and days. The crowds had long gone and the only spectators left were those paid to watch and protect. Finally the last truck offered up its load and the last piece of plastic disappeared over the top of the conveyor belt into the gaping maw of the cargo ship's hold. The security men laughed, high-fived each other, lit cigarettes and ambled over to the gathered news crews to harass them and leave greasy fingerprints on television camera lenses. For afterwards, there was only beer and dinner to look forward to. A pair of small coast guard cutters escorted the cargo ship to the edge of the harbor. A small dinghy wove in between the three ships like a mosquito – each with four black clad figures, holding massive electro-optical machine guns at ready, pointed menacingly at the choppy water. Manned and unmanned helos circled above as the cargo ship began to move ever so slowly, then more quickly, gaining on the escort, toward the narrow exit and the shallowest part of the harbor.

Ashton started sweating the moment he reached the safety of his hotel suite. He took large swigs from an open bottle of *cachaca,* overcome by claustrophobia. He struggled to open the window of the forty-eighth floor room before realizing it could not be opened. He whipped the drapes to the sides of the bulletproof window and turned the air conditioner fan as high as it would go. Standing directly in front of the wall unit spewing air a good thirty degrees cooler than the air outside, he continued to sweat as the room shrank. He forced himself to take deep breaths. He had long passed any failsafe point. He would be lumped in as a conspirator, more to blame because of his closeness to the President and their well known, decades old political association. The President could easily choose him as any of the others. The President would have many reasons to be angry with him, but was too soon and neither would benefit.

He knew the President would make good on his threat to place blame on his ministers, his own nephew even. Ashton had been in another room, in another time, after a different incident when no common citizen-criminal appeared to take the blame. The Public Health and Security Minister stood accused of treason within days. ISEC *discovered* a large amount of illegal narcotics in his government apartment and painted him into the international criminal cartel mosaic. The evidence was compiled and handed, neatly packaged, to the American ambassador, resulting in the public servant's extradition. However, during the unmanned-helo flight carrying the disgraced minister to Miami, an unfortunate accident occurred over the crater of Mont Gran Pere. The helo blew up.

The man with hair the color of wood-ash and sand that grew straight up like corn or sunflowers took more swigs from the bottle of *cachaca*. He might have been drinking water. He tried to lie down, close his eyes and stop the whirling dervish in his mind for just one minute. He watched national news feeds showing prison gangs dragging their chains over palatial lawns, picking up garbage of ill repute and mostly foreign origin. They could have used robotics to do the job but chain gangs had a stronger impact. They cut to scenes of special operations police "intercepting known criminals" in their places of habitation, bulldozing tin houses at four in the morning, creating orphans and the next generation of criminals.

MOOMA JACOBS HOUSE - FOURTEEN YEARS AGO

The Verandah kept tall vines trees cacti away from the place where milk-coffee-colored-skin creole woman drank hot tea as afternoon sun made her sweat and mop her forehead with hand-washed sun-dried handkerchief. Iron bars encircled the verandah like a cage dividing the world into parts to keep little posse boys begging money-food-water outside. Milk-coffee-skin-creole-woman did not trust them despite their youth. She knew the story down the road: two dark bad boys begged then took money-food-sex-life from generous old-broke-hip-christian-woman. Milk-coffee-colored-skin creole woman sipped tea and nodded off with mosquitos, roaches, moths, wasps, and barking lizards for company.

Outside the iron bars of the verandah, coal-colored-washer-woman drank tea from cracked cup and saucer. She peered through bars and jungle green with tired wispy eyes, longing for more energetic days. She had a strong face, indifferent as rain to prayer. The heat produced a thick pungent sweat that stained her clothes in the usual places as she hung dripping clothes on a sagging line. She did not allow a single thread to touch the ground. Her black and swollen hands broke the backs of dirty clothes with bleach, her universal solvent. She stood in the bright merciless sun with an old *burra-burra* song on her lips. She knew the song without knowing how she knew.

During the hottest portion of the day when even sleep could not be had, ten-year old Dominic sprawled on the floor where conventional wisdom placed the cooler air. He had only bad words for conventional wisdom, it having done nothing for him. He squirmed-rolled-muttered but did not, could not sleep. He called the smallest room that shared a door to the kitchen his own space. He felt safe behind his barricade from bug-bird-song that filled the air like smoke

46

carrying odors of spice, wood fires, decaying fruit, shit, and rancid cooking oil. Behind this barricade he could not be found or heard and mumbled to Wink (that sad and shifty friend of the very small) and a barking lizard that lived behind a crack in the far wall.

^yuh is hype
^yuh fruit aint rype
^yuh aint got nuh coal
^yuh ain't got nuh soal

The gray-black-white cat stalked him endlessly and stopped to lap cold sugar water tea on the flimsy card table where he ate with coffee-skin-creole-woman. Dominic peered with ginger colored eyes through cracks in the tin of his barricade, which let the shade out and the heat in. His clean but ragged clothes stuck to his skin because of his ever-present sweat which smelled like pepper sugar and coconut, gathering like blood on his chin, falling, staining the cement floor. He felt rich with his cement floor. His gut growled and boiled with hunger all day like soup in the big pots that sat on the fire from sunrise to deep night. His eyes fell on a single bright red-and-green-like-flag-big-like-mooma woman mango. It sat on the card table across from sleeping milk-coffee-colored-skin creole woman and her cold tea. A parade of thieved mangos from various tables and trees made him thick. No better feeling in the world than hunger assuaged. It drove him to a little thievery and to speak sharply to his friend, Wink.

^mi nuh tell yuh?!! 'top mek mi belly pain mi!!

Belly full, his eyes sparkled like gold in a slow river or a god in a box. He took sweat from his face and neck with both hands and dried them on his belly-skin underneath his shirt strings. His arm lashed out against the tin wall of his little space. Loud noise, breaking up, tearing down, made him smile. Milk-coffee-colored-skin-creole-woman would soon wake and find her tea cold. She would go back to sleep or call coal-colored-washerwoman with her bell to make tea again. If she waited too long big coal colored washerwoman would go home slapping her hip and singing '*hallelujah lahwd a muhcy lahwd a muhcy*'

THE CONSPIRACY – UPCOUNTRY - YESTERDAY

Inside the Plantation House at the top of the hill, four men sat in a large room with four doors. Where a chandelier might have hung or a *peristil* might have stood, a loose frame hung from the ceiling. The frame held an opaque linen covering, permitting light and shadow but not features or detail, and that suited their purposes just fine. The linen separated the room into four sections in which a man sat. Summoned by text message, each man came in through a separate door, forty minutes apart, named for the main directions on the compass – East, South, West and North. The titles gave them no hierarchy or captaincy, no subtle clues at dominance or majority.

None had been to the Plantation House before and none alone had information to make them dangerous. Each brought a battery operated electronic voice distorter and the chair they would sit on. As they took their seats, a wall-panel covering an inset hutch behind each chair opened, revealing a human-form spatter collimator attached to a projectile rifle. Each rifle held a single round in each electronically networked chamber. The guns would fire simultaneously or not at all. Though strangers, they took their seats, bound compatriots in purpose and obedience. A door slammed and from the quadrant each man knew to be east, the last man to arrive spoke through his voice distorter. "I have been given no items of concern to address."

On the heels of the man sitting in the East quadrant and from the quadrant each knew to be north, another man spoke, "I have been asked to inform you that three people were killed."

From the quadrant each knew to be west: "I have been given an item of concern to address."

From the quadrant each knew to be south: "I have been asked to inform you now is the time for patience."

Each left the Plantation House as they arrived, through a separate door with their chair and voice distorter, in forty-minute increments. As the last man left the room, the panels covering the weapons closed, returning the wall to its previous unthreatening state. An hour later, another door slammed and a diminutive woman in a plain white frock, white slippers and *gele* entered the room. She used a hook on a long pole to disconnect the linen from the frame. She then folded the linen into a square she put under her arm. The frame held a few more complications. It needed to be disassembled and its parts stored in various parts of the house. That chore could wait for another.

She had been paid only to do certain things and the simple thing she set about doing next. From another room she dragged a small collapsible card table and placed it carefully in the middle of the room. From another room, she found three folding chairs, which she placed around the table. From the same room, she found a plastic red and white plaid tablecloth, which she used to cover the table. From a kitchen cupboard, she took plastic cups and plates and an empty pitcher, placing them on the table in a setting for three. The house held no food but she did not need to worry about food – perhaps for the first time in her life. She felt as if she had missed something, as if she had forgotten to wrap her hair or left the house without shoes. Don't worry, her brother told her in the modified sign language they used. She knew her birth-star was a worrisome one. She worried those who would sit at the table might get hungry, that the tablecloth and chairs were stained and that she had been paid so much to do so little. She kept her eyes down and her worries to herself, however. Between her brother's useless eyes and her useless ears they were the perfect caretakers for the Plantation House. Being blind her brother had developed a sense of hearing rivaling some dogs. Being deaf and unable to speak she had honed her sense of smell to where she recognized an individual by their smell. She kept that secret to herself. She knew she had to leave before the other men arrived.

While she sipped lukewarm ginger tea from her own verandah a mile and a half away, three men arrived in one car and took seats at the table she had set up. A small pen like electronic instrument sat on the table along with a sweating bottle of *cachaca* and three small thimble-sized glasses. A red light on the electronic instrument flashed as the earlier conversation played back into the otherwise empty room. The three men at the table stared indiscriminately in separate directions while the recorded conversation played and ended without conclusion.

"Patience?" one man sneered, his hair the color of coal wood-ash and sand that stood straight out like corn and sunflowers

"It is not an unreasonable request," the man to the left answered, avoiding eye contact, his body language stating in no uncertain terms that if cornered he would not back down.

"Our times are beyond reason," the third ended the argument by judiciously folding his arms on the tabletop and ritually pouring three glasses from the sweating jar of *cachaca*. "It is a matter of time before the government answers. We must be ready."

"They are paralyzed."

"Escalate or stand still. That is the question on the table," said the man who had poured the drink.

They each downed their drink and gently replaced the empty glasses on the tabletop.

"Escalate," said the man with hair the color of coal wood-ash and sand that stood straight up like corn and sunflowers.

"Stand."

"Escalate."

The one who voted to stand rose, nodded dutifully at the other two, and left the table, the room, the house, and the plantation. The others sent the required text message. The plan would move forward. They did not value patience.

After a second trip to the Plantation House to do less than the first, the woman in white sat alone on her verandah and carefully removed three glasses from her pocket, placing them on the table next to her. She held each glass up to the sun to see the liquid at the bottom. With a certain ceremony, she put each glass to her lips and drained it – her own private ritual. She remembered that someone had taken the bottle but that it left its own tattoo on the plastic tablecloth – a round of moisture where the bottle sat. She took the liberty of sitting at the table for a short while, staring out the small window, but the shadow of the garrison city blocked her view. She wondered when her brother would get home from begging on the town streets and how his luck had gone.

"*Si bon ki ra,*" she thought, as she drained the three glasses again. *Good is rare.*

CAPITAL – TODAY

Joseph Santo's government, like governments across the planet before it, harbored no qualms about the use of technology to penetrate the society it governed. Governing had become impossible without it. It was both a national religion and addiction. Though powerless without data the technology provided, operational and policy bullets proved only marginally effective, reducing governance to a series of carrots and sticks. Yet the garbage incident exceeded their stunning, unprecedented capabilities in existentially disturbing ways. It took brutal advantage of a weakness they were at pains to identify. As often happens when hindsight yields less than perfect vision, they poured resources into data arrays and the latest Anti-Infiltration (ANTI-INFIL) developments.

Thus, the RQ-7C caused no great consternation when it appeared over the harbor, descending out of the clouds like a large black insect. Known to most as the 'Global Hawk', it hovered noiselessly at 25,000 feet, bathing the harbor with synthetic aperture and infrared radar. If necessary, it could maintain its position for over sixty hours. Not autonomous, it took instructions from a young SELAND combat gamer sitting in a single story innocuous, anonymous building in Miami who controlled the drone in fifteen-minute shifts. It carried no weapons and required a smaller, unmanned, armed, autonomous UAV drone, carrying 200,000 DREAD rounds. The lack of recoil and heat signature made this weaponry perfect for use on the lightweight offensive drone, its sole mission being the protection of the Global Hawk. International treaty governing its existence and use precluded the use of either drone against humans or human-based infrastructure.

Like the SELAND combat gamer in Miami, comfortably ensconced in large comfortable chairs, purveyors of brightly lit screens flashing data points, grids, tables, charts, graphs, flashing status lights, machine messaging, firmware capacity utilization alerts and memory cache warnings, the ISEC operations team running the recovery operation felt secure and untouchable in air conditioned rooms and working uniforms. They saw the world through GIS software, dispensing with copious video feeds available from the RQ. Just one of hundreds, the infrared discrepancy warning did not immediately inflame or arouse. A junior ISEC officer flagged the warning and pushed it up the electronic chain of command, where it was noted and logged. The warning sat in this innocuous state for eight seconds before being forwarded via a standard operational COMLINK to SELAND Operations in Miami. Four seconds later, the RQ's onboard control boards acknowledged a demand to explain a sudden increase in ambient temperature in the engine room.

The few that remained to watch the garbage recovery project described a sonic boom, muffled by the water. The massive cargo ship paused momentarily in the water. All eyes turned towards the sound and the stalled ship. It crossed the mind of not a single person that their well-laid plans had been foiled again. A moment later, the ship's bridge exploded like a firecracker. Garbage from the fully loaded ship sank to the harbor floor a mere one hundred meters below. Minutes later, the presence of additional government helos and a much larger coast guard assault-ship impressed on the minds of the most paranoid among them that plans had gone awry. When the huge ship began to list, one did not need paranoia to suspect the worst. When the cruise ships began to turn around outside the harbor, everyone knew the impossible had happened. They would later discover that two explosion had been effected. The first explosion dumped the garbage through the bottom of the ships hull. The second explosion seemed to have been for good measure, besmirching the name and the life of the ship's pilot, whom everyone assumed was complicit.

Once more, the man with hair the color of coal wood-ash and sand which stood straight out like corn and sunflowers growing into the sun, watched developments in the harbor from his locked hotel room. The new high definition flat screen televisions the hotel installed did not make him feel better. He turned it off in anger but silence threatened more than high definition havoc, so he turned it back on, eyes riveted on the scene playing out. The outside world so seldom affected him this way: his brain unable to process information, his gut in wrenching turmoil, his breathing quick and shallow. He had up to now always been able to maintain a clinical distance. He did not deny he would rather not have seen the name on the dossier in Ms. Casteñada's hands during the meeting. He wondered if it was an internally prepared dossier or one provided by ISEC or maybe SELAND. He consoled himself that she had a stack of them, though he doubted she had one on the President himself. If she did, he wondered what treasures it might hold.

He cursed the conspiracy's blatant lack of patience; leaving no time to recover, clean up, find fault, blame, point fingers…at least until he had left the city. They knew the reason he turned his back on his government and used it against him. He could never return to naiveté, they said. He could not argue with the grainy videotape of that sorry pandering episode from so many years ago…

…exploit unbidden - state of undress in a rigged contest - generally proscribed – the man advancing, pawing, struggling for control — the boy resisting -- power in jeopardy -- trying for some small integrity - covering a constellation shaped birthmark on his hip – fighting as best he knew -- withdrawing – surrendering to the…unpleasantness…

Ashton came out of the memory with fists clenched, manicured nails biting into his palms. He considered it nobody's business what he did in his own house, and he told them so. They laughed and asked whether he wanted to see whether the President agreed with him. He bruised his hand punching the wall; so angry was he the debauchery had been caught on the oldest of digital media – tape. In his anger, he said something he later regretted. He said he should have left the *mingi* child in the streets. In unguarded moments, he blamed Stork, his now dead wife for suggesting the child come to live with them. This only fed his anger, since her death occurred not long after, for which he also blamed himself. His anger peaked and threatened to boil over with recent events. He realized his treachery would only be fodder for the trough his country would be buried in -- a trough, despite his best efforts, not full of garbage, but of blood.

MOOMA JACOBS HOUSE - FOURTEEN YEARS AGO

When night fell and Posse boys built sound systems higher than the house around him, shaking the world with *reverse blue dub ragga ragga nyabingi* beat, Dominic could not sit still or stay inside where he could not feel the drum inside. Speakers as big as houses stood hulking and massive to one side of a large dirt clearing. Where moonlight failed, someone strung wires with bare light bulbs held up by rickety poles. The wires, bare in places, all fed into a rigged electrical box into which the loudspeaker equipment, microphones, speaker and turntable equipment were also plugged. Some of the women and girls wore wigs made out of colored strips of tin foil and small strips of cloth wrapped around their bodies for clothing. The men and boys wore huge plastic medallions sprayed with gold colored paint. They wore rings as big as a baby's fist, also made out of plastic sprayed with gold or silver metal paint. They smiled not out of happiness but to show stainless steel-capped teeth. Shirtless, they paraded like soldiers, upper bodies shining and hilts of handguns jammed into the waistlines of their *jeanspants*. Tonight one or two people might be electrocuted, another stabbed, two others shot, one struck with machetes. Only the music mattered and the clothes and the hair and the jewelry and the ever plentiful bare skin. The music throbbed in its peculiar way and the people bounced. A DJ yelled into the microphone every few moments using a badly rigged effects box to complement the music and the beat. Whenever the DJ spoke the people bounced harder and made more noise, punching the air with clenched fists (the men), or extending their arms straight out and waving them up and down in time with the beat (the women), while all moved their bodies in mysterious ways.

The crowd boiled with frenetic energy, driven by the drum and bass that reverberated and punched each sternum, middle ear and verandah for a mile around. Oblivious to the passage of time and the course of the moon across a cloudless sky, the music throbbed and the DJ babbled into the night. With no distinction between portions of "song", a moment occurred when movement ceased to be a conscious effort and the dancers achieved a trance state possessed by a new *loa*, the DJ. In this trance state, the bodily contortions became unbelievable. As others noticed this slight shift, the excitement doubled, the crowd ceased yelling at the DJ and in gratitude the DJ ceased his senseless backtalk and the music throbbed alone. After a time, only movement and beat survived -- increasingly unbelievable movement and increasingly, unbelievably faster beat. No melody, just drum and bass.

Old Wukless Rum asked him to bury something at the bottom of a tree. Rum showed Dominic a handful of coin that was his for the taking. Rum had long past the age to run with the posse, but he looked mean enough. Dominic called him "Rum" because the man always had half-filled bottle of rum in his hand. Rum didn't know it, but he made good sport for Dominic and his knee-slapping pranks. Once, Dominic put a bucket over Rum's head, as he lay passed out on the side of the road. A hard rain beating down on the bucket a few minutes later woke the old man up with quite a start. Dominic almost fell out of the tree laughing as the man ran in circles. Another time, Dominic dumped the rum out of the ever-present bottle while the man slept. He waited for him to wake up and take that first swig. Dominic did fall out of the tree for that one. Another time, Dominic took the piece of corrugated tin that served as Rum's roof, right before the afternoon rains. Needless to say, the rain woke the old man. One of his pranks almost landed him in trouble with the constabulary, but he handily outran the constable.

Wrapped in a cloth to hide its nature, Dominic knew what lay beneath - an old machete. Since he already knew, he did not ask. Likewise, he suffered no questions with his machete inside an empty watering can. He hoped no one looked inside. Getting caught with the machete would be unpleasant. Dominic broke up the clay-ridden dirt and broke a sweat hiding what needed to be hidden, then tamped the dirt back down again. No one troubled him. No one spoke to him until after he filled the can with water. One of the electrical riggers asked him for some.

Dominic returned after completing his chore later that night. After bathing in the bucket outside, he stopped to take in cricket song and bird whistle like a choir in thick leafy trees. A rat crept along the cactus between his yard and the next. Dogs barked with lolling tongues. Milk-coffee-colored-skin-creole-woman sat wide-awake and wide-eyed, worrying and fretting in her empty house. Her shoulders sagged ever so slightly when she heard the boy's shadow coming through the gate on the verandah. She heard it all -- slender feet in flapping dried vine sandals, copious folds of soft white pants made from old bed sheets. The night brought cooling and life to old and young eyes and she beckoned until she could touch him and sniffed her hand. She frowned because she did not know where he had been and because if she asked, he would pretend not to understand. Grateful to have him at night, she kept her worries to herself.

Dominic went into the kitchen where he found tepid peppermint tea, hard bread and a watermelon slice for his supper. It was coal-colored-washerwoman's singular mercy. He grated ginger and built fire for milk-coffee-colored-creole-woman's tea, singing his rhyme while he worked. She tapped her cane on the floor to tell him she did not approve. He let her tap for a while, changing the rhyme to fit the rhythm of her cane and then switched to an old spiritual he knew she liked. When she began to hum the same song, he smiled. The water boiled and he withdrew a few pieces of money from his pocket. Dominic clucked his tongue. She held her hand out and he placed the hot ginger tea in her hand. He waited while he counted the stars he could see from the kitchen window and she drank her tea.

He clucked his tongue again and she found his shoulder with her hand. He led to her bed where she spent another night with him curled up on a hard mat on the floor beneath. They slept to the sound of his *funde* song…

^ha' mercy faddah
^gi' mi strength muddah
^gi' mi hope sistah
^protec' me bruddah

She could not see him but his voice told her he was near. The sound of it, she said, would lead her to Guinée. He did not believe her. He knew many roads. None of them led to Guinée.

INTERCONTINENTAL HOTEL – CAPITAL – TODAY

The city spread out like a sore. Smoke fires dotted the smoggy horizon along with scraggly trees, corrugated metal, skyscrapers, official buildings and flags in the diplomatic section of Capital. The Intercontinental held pride of place, sandwiched between the UN2 Mission and the sprawling cement encampment of the US Embassy. It rose like an ancient and revered obelisk out of the surrounding mediocre 1970s architecture. On each corner, at the first and top floors, a Lion of Judah in copper and brass perched on steel balustrades. The tower of steel and glass reflected the brilliant morning sun back over the city. In the glass, one saw the city for what it was, a low-ceilinged quilt of hillside garbage fires, robot air shuttles on final approach, wide swathes of sugarcane, and SELAND NOC sites with their bright-red spherical rooftop beacons stabbing the air like massive lollipops. From the Presidential suite, the ground appeared petty and small. From the ground, the top floor touched the clouds. Dominic reveled in the privacy of his hotel room, its opulence still foreign and strange. The hotel was a long way from Old Hope Road even if he still remembered getting into fights over dominoes and chasing girls at the standpipe.

He missed being outside, smelling the smoke from wood fires, running his hand along iron fences protecting empty lots and vacant storefronts. He missed the graffiti. He used to stand in front of the worst of it, trying to separate different tags, wondering if they carried deeper meaning. He missed the sun's oppression in the afternoon, when the heat demanded he sit on the verandah and wait for the evening breeze. He missed drinking tea with Miss Missy, the street vendor who sold him cold green coconuts. He missed the catcalls, shout-outs, honking cars, sirens and girls on the street who smiled when he passed. His eyes went for the usual places – the top of the tube top where a necklace

61

pendant sometimes sat, or the hemline of a short skirt. Sometimes he found himself looking at ankles. He liked tattoos in particular places – on the calf or the lower back, he especially liked ankle tattoos. Just two days ago, one of the security men told him when a woman sported a tattoo on her lower back they called it a 'tramp patch.' He wanted to know whether Ms. Casteñada had a 'tramp patch'. She did not, but he said he did not know.

He pulled his body into the familiar and comforting *virabhadrasana* pose – finding satisfaction in knowing enough to include what some in his *dojo* considered beneath them – *yoga*. Switching sides, he repeated the same pose, considering breakfast on the coffee table - fresh fruit, omelet, and orange juice. He was not quite ready to be food-stoned. The Cabinet meeting had not gone long into the night, which netted him a few extra hours of sleep. The note with breakfast told him he had the morning to himself, that the Cabinet meeting would start at 2 pm. It would be good to see Ms. Casteñada again. He inspected his chin at close range, looking for a more substantial beard but found nothing different from the day before. He checked the birthmark on his hip to see whether it had faded or gotten darker, but it looked the same. Somehow, he knew it looked like a star called 'Orion'. He paced through a series of increasingly difficult stretches, feeling the muscle burn in his legs and shoulders, then the subsequent relief as he came out of the stretch. He moved through *tae kwon do* kicks, followed by weighted punches and hooks. Flushed and warm, the prelude to the light sweat of exertion he sought, he noted his elevated pulse and stood still, feet shoulder width apart clenching and unclenching his fists. He made short work of the food on the platter and like clockwork, felt sleepy again.

He skipped his usual morning diet of media feeds to avoid unwanted attention from ISEC tracers and sniffers. His schedule had not provided enough free time to correctly configure his triple-secret proxies. Dominic had not yet achieved the requisite level to have a SELAND deck assigned to his person but he already knew the unlicensed SELAND deck Ashton passed him would register as obsolete. Though pre-loaded with SELAND firmware, until Dominic was able to prove it was not a hack-job, he used the deck cautiously. ISEC took the art of paranoia to new and dizzying heights -- - thus the need for triple-secret proxies. His path to sleep wound through flashes of past memories. Not always chronological, one memory linked to another in mysterious ways, threading forwards and backwards.

<<Metallica – Wherever I May Roam>>

Mooma Jacob's death was the hardest thing life had thrown at him by the age of twelve. After making himself king in the household of a blind woman, Mooma Jacobs went to *Guinée*. In the naiveté of eleven years, he vowed to find her. He cried for hours when Ashton told him a year later what "going to *Guinée*" meant. Losing Mooma Jacobs to *Guinée* taught him to steel himself against grief and loss. He learned to fight back with his body and glass eyes, hardening what muscles he could find to keep himself strong. He knew about losing people and Mooma Jacobs had been the hardest in his short life to lose, but if she had not gone to *Guinée*, he would never have learned to lay sandbags around himself.

After Mooma Jacob's *ninenight*, he lived for three years with Ashton, his wife Stork, and their three almost grown children, where he was nothing if not the runt. He learned to run at Ashton's and it proved to be a useful tool. When he could not run, Ashton's wife, Stork fast became his ally and he learned to hide behind her, sometimes literally. He ran from bizarre hazing rituals perpetrated by the Ashton's two older children, tickle tortures that made him laugh until he couldn't breathe and then cry because they would not stop. The middle child chased him with a machete and the older one tried to dump him in a dry well. He ran away at least once a month, but someone always found him and brought him back. He went to school, causing him no end of tears. He had a lot of catching up to do. He drank his first white rum and stole and smoked his first cigarette with Ashton's youngest son, Straightedge, a few years older than Dominic. They smoked it hurriedly, hiding behind an old, dry water tank. It still amazed him they thought any one cared. He remembered how the rum and the cigarette made his head spin. There was the unpleasantness with Ashton, not every night, but most nights for two years. Ashton was not a cruel or mean man, but Dominic found it unpleasant just the same.

After Ashton's house, he spent three idyllic years up country in the middle of hectares of sugarcane, at the home of Pierre, who was blind, and his sister, Mercilia who was deaf. They taught him the strange hand-language Pierre's sister used and the creole language Pierre spoke. They taught him to sing their songs and to walk with his head up, not downcast, eyes floor-bound. They took him to ceremonies where everyone wore white. He watched them dance to the rhythm of huge drums. He learned the *Rado* and *Pethro*, about ancestors and how to dance in the *peristil*. People regarded him strangely the first time, his skin being so much lighter than those who stared. That particular strangeness passed when he began to dance. The *loa* were close to him, they said. In the silence and peace of upcountry, he fell in love with Pierre, the way a boy falls in love with a grandfather or uncle. They walked for hours in between the rows of sugarcane, Pierre's hand on Dominic's shoulder, talking about the sun and the fire that turned the cane into sugar. Twice, Dominic caught a glimpse of a large plantation style house at the top of a hill and asked Pierre about it. Pierre shook his head and said that evil lived there. After his short lifetime of being yelled at, Pierre spoke softly and Dominic fell for it. Pierre could have asked him for anything, and Dominic would have gladly complied. Pierre's sister Mercilia was more of a mystery and except when he was sick with 'Breakbone Fever' — he had cloudy memories of her sitting by his time the whole time he was sick — she mostly ignored him

The idyllium would not last, however. Wrenched away from Pierre and Mercilia, he and his life were boxed up and sent up north, to attend a military prep school in North Carolina. They called it a student exchange and he had been assigned to live with the Paxton family. The Paxton's gave him money - an allowance - to spend on anything he wanted and he spent it on coffee, energy drinks and video games. He stared in amazement at wide the roads they traveled on and the clean, un-crowded sidewalks they walked on. The Paxtons had a son just a year older than him but friendship proved difficult. They ignored each other at first, but soon found themselves talking for hours from separate bunks until the early morning hours. Many nights, he passed Kevin's father passed out on the family room couch, an empty liquor bottle on the floor. He heard Kevin's mom crying in the master bedroom as he passed it on the way to the bedroom he shared with Kevin.

Dominic taught Kevin to play Dominoes and Kevin taught Dominic to play Poker. Some weeks, they gambled their allowances away in weekend marathons of card and video games. Dominic excelled on the schools soccer team, while Kevin played second team in basketball. A source of bitter rivalry at first, Kevin's father, in an unlikely moment of lucidity, arbitrated an uneasy truce, saving them bruised knuckles and egos. He ran away once from the Paxton's in the early days, hitchhiking to the airport, hoping to get back to Pierre's house. A police officer picked him up and returned him to the Paxton's house. No one was home at the time and he let himself in and cried himself to sleep. Kevin's dark moods and the nightmarish pencil sketches he hung above his bunk infiltrated the bedroom like a contagion. They spent entire nights on their separate bunks, arguing about the capabilities of this game character or another; about the end of civilization, which was always near; about girls at school and the girls on posters that peppered the bedroom walls. For three years, they were inseparable. When their friendship twisted and turned from the unfamiliar emotional to the physical, Dominic felt neither repelled, nor did he turn Kevin away.

Again, not of his choosing, interrupting plans to attend university with Kevin, he cut his teeth with the island's Defense General Forces, as was traditional for island youth his age, and then the Defense Special Forces. He excelled in ways he never imagined at boot camp and beyond. They tried to break him and failed. Awards and promotions followed him to Special Forces unit where they tried to break him again. He woke up waiting for the next test, the next challenge and beat them all. Awards and promotions continued until he hardly knew what to do with them. He mastered weaponry others dreamed about, interrogation techniques some called torture and dissected encrypted code for traces of known vectors, sometimes for forty-eight hours at a stretch, popping little pink "WAKE" pharma capsules every four hours. He mastered SELAND sources and methods and the SELAND Evidentiary process. He wondered how a kid from Old Hope Road, who fought over dominoes at the standpipe, ended up a trusted team member in the Office of the President.

Though he found it easy to present himself as a blank slate or a chameleon, he knew he was neither. Accustomed to being ignored, he kept himself hidden behind a calm demeanor. He felt the world with his body. There was just one loose end that sometimes sent him into a tailspin, embodied in his relationship with Ashton. In real terms Ashton risked much for a shallow, one-sided friendship and it gave him pause. However, in his mind, the die was cast. Ashton had made his bed years ago and one day he would lie in it. For now, Dominic accepted without bitterness or anguish that Ashton was the President's 'right hand', untouchable in the present configuration. Things could change and Dominic had a plan, contingent only on the opportunity to execute it.

CHAPTER III

MOOMA JACOBS HOUSE - FOURTEEN YEARS AGO

Just after sunrise, morning came like quick-quiet-bright-revenge but did not silence barking dogs. Those who lived so close to the ground could not remain asleep after first light. The new day required their attention like a blameless crying demanding child. Smoke from wood fires curled around pots of soupy porridge. Children stretched yawned suckled the morning into a bright hot steamy day. The sounds of changeling voices rose as children carried water jugs from the far away standpipe. They called laughed walked ran up the hill, past the *I-tal* man with beer and rum to sell.

Dominic lay with eyes open, staring at the underside of milk-coffee-colored skin creole woman's bed, woken by the sounds of life and a tight feeling under his belly where he made water, the mat beneath him, damp from the long night, stuck to his back. He laid dead still, eyes open but not seeing. He claimed this time as private property: a few minutes stolen from the day. He played the same game every morning, careful not to make a sound. Only silence brought him the luxury of lying in. He rolled slowly out from under milk-coffee-colored-skin-creole-woman's bed and shuffled on his back, a sideways walking crab, across the cement floor to the door-less doorway. He found his clothes exactly where he left them. Coal colored washerwoman told him a *duppy* might recognize him with his clothes on at night. He dressed as if he had something on his body he wanted to hide.

His two friends caught him unaware while he peed on the cactus wall outside, something he could do only while milk coffee colored skin creole woman slept, and coal colored washerwoman stayed busy inside. Peering through the cactus, the boy called Worm bit the fingernails of one hand, his other fist full of used matchsticks found the night before. Next to Worm, stood the boy Scorn, a didgeridoo in one hand and three dice (he lost the fourth dice years ago) in the other. Neither Worm nor Scorn could keep a secret of any sort and as Dominic fixed himself, he put a finger to his mouth, begging silence. He did not want to wake milk-coffee-colored-skin-creole woman. Worm covered his mouth with his hand and chuckled, big red-afro hair shaking as his slight body convulsed in laughter until he got hiccups. Worm seldom spoke, but Dominic and Scorn knew he wanted most to find someone to talk to, and though long a lost cause, they helped him look anyway. They looked inside rum bars and churchyards, in yards behind brothel houses and inside preacher's houses. So far unsuccessful, they remained relentless. A year or two older, Scorn liked to think he knew how the world around him worked, and to prove his point he gave Dominic a rude gesture with two hands. He wore his long jet-black black hair in a topknot, standing head and shoulders above Worm. Scorn's rude gesture proved his knowledge of the world complete, replacing the more conventional greeting of *mahnin'!*, or *yes yes I*. Scorn began the morning with a second insult and Dominic kept pace, insult for insult.

^*how yuh so oogly and dark?*
^*yuh tink yuh bright? yuh'nuh'no who yuh a'deel wit...*
^*batty bwoy*

Dominic clenched his fists, feet tense, shifting to fighting stance, ready to damage maim hurt break crush tear cut stab -- though not the only solution, an immediate one. He exploded like a bomb left in the market place where children sat under a tree taunting the village fool. The fight that ensued stirred up dirt dust cockroach carcasses leaves dead grass twigs, until Worm could not distinguish between

68

bleeding and yelling friend. Jumping up and down, laughing like a loon, only he knew milk-coffee-colored-skin-creole-woman called with her bell from her bed. The fight broke the skin on both boys -- near Scorn's left eye and where Dominic's pants ripped at the knee. Dust settled and conflict forgot, adrenaline waned, and blood and sweat became profuse. Only water did the trick, which required a trip down the hill to the standpipe, a wash, and a game of street war to make the girls scream and watch their bodies move as they ran. The six-handed tribe headed down hill from the verandah, a plastic water container in each hand.

They followed one of the ten thousand paths from the house on the hill, down into the morass where the million and their children lived and spent their parent's futures. They thought nothing of the walk to the standpipe, or that on the way back the water jugs would be full and the path up hill. They had long arms by birth and strong shoulders from many such trips. Besides, fun could be had at the standpipe with no milk-coffee-colored-skin-creole-woman to ring her bell and make them stop what the moment found them doing. No uncles with big hands and fat straps to chase them; no mooma-woman to *"lawd ah massie"* them and scold the ripe and colorful language. No one told them not to waste the water. Dominic, Worm and Scorn reached the standpipe and joined the yelling cussing threatening troop of the million's children. Insults, laughter, and tears waxed abundant from the million's untried pinnacles of hope and neglect. They filled their water jugs according to unwritten order. Though most children remembered when no water flowed from the standpipe, none remembered a time when no standpipe stood at the bottom of the hill. None recalled that where they played, fought and washed, a river once ran.

Coal-colored-washerwoman kissed her teeth (that universal sound of disgust and despair) as the children returned with five-gallon water containers only three-quarters full, balanced on their heads. They turned on her with a fierce and well-practiced, curled-lip sneer.

^lahwd jeezus yuh nuh see mi cross
^yuh wukkless gyaal

She picked up the thick arm of a fallen tree and swung wide and low across the spaces where the tribe had stood just seconds ago. She spun around, pivoting with her bare feet, hoping to catch one of them with her rod of justice. Six legs and eyes moved darted taunted with hands on skinny hips, mouths panting in the hard heat. Her thick swollen soapy bleached hands caught a handful of soft red sponge hair and clamped down like a leech on virgin vein.

Worm yelled:

^rhatid!! mur-dah!

Coal-colored-washerwoman could not keep a straight face. Laughter seeped out of her and she released Worm in favor of a knee-slapping good laugh, the spaces between rotting teeth and blood red gums exposed. She leaned on Scorn, slapping her knee the whole time. She laughed until she could not breathe. When she recovered, her face softened and she talked to the children the way a teacher or mother might do.

^yuh mout' dutty lyke whot bwoy

Three bowls of porridge waited for them inside. Worm and Scorn left coal-colored-washerwoman to tend to the water jugs and ran into the house to find their breakfast. Dominic entered the old woman's bedroom with sloppy clean fresh water for milk-coffee-colored-skin-creole-woman, clicking his tongue, wiping sweat from forearms and chin with the back of his free hand. He stopped mid-step: bell on floor, milk-coffee-colored-skin-creole-woman's arm hanging like a leaf dying from lack of water, water spilled on the hand-made night table, sheet askew across the bed. He clicked his tongue again, thinking she had fallen asleep waiting for him. He still thought she saw through her blind eyes. He wondered how she knew his whereabouts before he gave the telltale sound: that soft clicking of the tongue he discovered by accident. She said she found it peaceful and he used it ever since. It always made her take notice and turn in his direction -- until now.

^*Auntie*!

He used the familial to call coal-colored-washerwoman who entered the house like a spooked warhorse. She stood by his side with as much surprise on her face as on his. A wail rose from Auntie's mouth; a loud, long, angry, sound, collecting power like a sand storm gathering strength across a thousand miles of dune. The sound took form in the air around the little house on the hill like a spirit of the newly dead; like a *duppy*. Auntie's face twisted in grief — a face Dominic knew he would not like to see again. Still confused, he wondered what made coal-colored-washerwoman so mad. He looked up again, but she would not be comforted. He stood there feeling useless. At least milk-coffee-colored-skin-creole-woman depended on him. About to turn on coal colored washerwoman for behaving badly, it occurred to him what had happened: *science come tek soal an' mek she ded.*

He did not have much time with this conclusion before coal-colored-washerwoman took him in both swollen strong soapy black hands and shook him like a rug. Her mouth moved and every part of his body moved shook hurt. Since nothing in the world made more noise than coal-colored-washerwoman, she did not hear his long string of bad words, cries of pain, more bad words and more cries of pain. After a long minute, she dropped him, not out of compassion, but because she needed her two arthritic hands to make right the sheet and cover milk-coffee-colored-skin-creole woman right up past her eyebrows. Only a thin wisp of gray hair peeked out from the edge of the sheet.

At the end of a very long day, Dominic crept walked sprinted to the beach to dig his toes in the wet sand. Hungry but without mangoes, the ocean reminded him of milk-coffee colored-skin-creole-woman's voice at night, treble for the song they sang together. He sat on the sand, his wet short-pants clinging to his body -- eyes watery and itchy. Most people called it crying.

CAPITAL - THREE YEARS AGO

President Joseph Santo assumed leadership under less than ideal circumstances -- with voter turnout at 38% — he won on the narrowest of mandates, less than 2%. Four days after the election, Santo deployed two divisions of Island Defense General Forces to quell three different flash mobs in the diplomatic quarter. Even with the kill switch to the biggest social media portals thrown, flash mobs continued and people died in the streets. Violent, anarchist flash mobs and unregistered system decks in offensive mode wreaked havoc with the new SELAND cyber structure days after the installation of the Santo government. Santo begged in soaring rhetoric for people to stay home and ordered the military to use weapons only in self-defense. People moving away from flash mob sites would not be arrested. Still, people died. His best efforts got him nowhere and in a fit of frustration and anger, Santo ordered his General Forces to clear the streets. They did so at astronomical cost in death and injury. A general forbade medical response teams to treat those injured in flash mob violence and those who died in the violence were not returned to their families for a suitable burial.

The island's neighbors to the north approached him with a proposal to fortify and extend SELAND's reach and throughput via a network of platforms in the open ocean. These platforms would serve two functions: provide additional network relays and extenders and provide participating states with a secure and offshore location to store refuse – a charged topic in rich countries. They proposed locating one of the platforms within the island's territorial waters. Anticipating a violent reaction, they included generous fees to accrue to his government in foreign currencies. The fees would make the next round of economic austerity measures, slated to take effect the next month, unnecessary. Santo accepted the proposal as the right thing to do. He promised the garbage would never touch the island and that the platforms would not be visible to the unaided eye from the island's coastline.

It made his eyes smart to sign the final agreement, for it proved in no uncertain terms that rich countries acted with impunity and poor countries waited for international institution scraps. Poor countries demanded fair play and rich countries accused them of asking for handouts. Rich countries made money by flaunting the rules with fair skin, while poor countries chafed and suffered under those same rules with darker skin and lopsided trade agreements. Of course, it was not so simple as the 'grey area' was vast and easily exploited. But it made good copy. Technology carried its own costs, a culture unto itself, forcing small countries to borrow increasingly more just to run in place. But if technology equalized some, it disenfranchised more. Despite what many saw as a rigged contest, people still had a responsibility to make sacrifices for the common good, Santo claimed in the noblest tones he could muster. Politicians could not sustain their myopic focus on small, insignificant, non-binding resolutions, spending public resources on the next re-election campaign. The real purpose of government was to help people. Nobody listened. Good government was insufficient. Unable or unwilling to enact effective policy on any front, governments all over the world wallowed in complex parliamentary maneuvers and long-winded speeches to empty chambers, like wildebeests in a mud bog. Those who could afford to exclude political advertising from their media-recording queue did so. Those who could not afford the new media portals and their accompanying subscription fees did not see Santo's impassioned speeches anyway.

Six months into his term, he had become irrelevant. Time and effort invested in finding the "right" path to governance would languish and people would curse him in every town. Though he ordered the Island Defense General Forces back to their barracks, the island pulsed with unease and restlessness, waiting for a spark to fuel the fire of undirected rage. He took personal responsibility. It was his island to lose – with nothing to win and no upside. It weighed on him in his office and in their private suites. It caused problems with his wife...but ever since the election, everything caused a problem with his wife. He wished she would take the kids up north again. He did not mind being miserable but he preferred to be miserable alone. Three months into his second term, he told Ashton to create a position within the Office of the President for a political/defense attaché. After recovering from surprise that Santo did not want a young woman (his wife would never permit it, the President said), Ashton suggested his nephew, currently serving with the Island Defense Special Forces.

The summons arrived at the leeward Level 3 NOC site at 5 am, just one hour before the end of his fourteen-hour shift. They called his name on the loudspeaker, which required he withdraw from Operations on the Theater Floor and make his way to the commanding officer's office on the Executive Floor. He hoped the summons was not another award or commendation. Since dress code for the Theater Floor was generally relaxed, he answered the summons in the tan carpenter pants and black t-shirt he wore. He swallowed his eighth WAKE dose in twenty-four hours dry, unable to remember when last he slept. The commanding officer admitted him into the office, handed him a traditional summons package and returned to his desk chair while Dominic opened and read the summons. It was a summons to meet the President, at the Presidential Palace. It took a few moments for the gravity of the situation to sink in. Dominic, being Dominic, first thought it was some kind of prank. He looked at the commanding officer's face as a checksum and decided it was not a joke. In fact, this was the first time Dominic had even seen the commanding officer face to face, much less in the confines of his own office.

"Do you need me to read it to you?" the commanding officer asked with his usual level of impatience.

"No sir."

"Then what's the problem?"

"No problem, sir. It's just a little irregular."

"Are you kidding Sargent? This is your ticket out of the humdrum."

"It's not final, sir."

"Sergeant, if you end up back here after a summons like this, I WILL kill you myself. You understand me, son?"

"Yes sir."

"You go get cleaned up and take a 45 minute nap. Report to the helipad at 6 a.m. in Dress Tactical. We have a landing slot at 6.30."

"Yes sir."

"One more thing, Sergeant. Congratulations."

"Thank you, sir."

"Get the hell out of my office."

The short helicopter ride across the island was his first and he kept his motion sickness to himself. It also gave him an additional fifteen minutes of shut-eye. He downed a protein shake that passed for rations at the NOC site, moments before they landed. Ashton met him at the heli-pad and he knew then who to either thank or curse. Ashton said nothing in the car ride to the Presidential Palace but handed him a thermos of ice-cold orange juice – a detail from childhood only Ashton would know. They entered the Palace through a side entrance and Dominic shivered involuntarily as they paced down the long hallway, elaborate rooms to either side of him. In front of the third door from the end of the hallway, Dominic saw two of his uniformed comrades standing at attention outside. This was the door Ashton opened without knocking and without even a blink in response from the security detail. Dominic shivered again. The room was empty, save a desk and two chairs. Ashton pointed to a spot just inside the room, close to the entrance. Dominic took up post there, at full attention. There was no room for error. It happened so quickly Dominic almost missed it. As if he had materialized in front of him, without coming through any doorway, the President stood in front of him, hand outstretched. For a moment, Dominic was conflicted: should he break post or shake the man's hand. He decided on the latter.

The President smiled and offered Dominic one of two chairs in the room. Then turning to Ashton, said, "Give us a few minutes, please sir."

Ashton nodded and left the room, making sure to close the door so that they knew the door had shut completely behind him.

"I hate it when they linger. Makes it hard to talk," the President said, conspiratorially. The smile on his face gave the impression he meant what he said.

"Yes sir."

"I have not yet opened your file. I wanted to talk to you first. Where are you from, Sergeant?"

"Old Hope Road." Dominic had trouble sitting without squirming a little bit. He heard blood racing in his ears.

"What is your first memory from there?"

"Running from the Uncles at the standpipe."

The President smiled. "You have family on the island?"

"No sir."

"Are they off shore?"

"No sir."

"You come highly recommended by your superior officers."

"Thank you sir."

"You also come highly recommended by your Uncle, Ashton."

"We are not kin, sir. He calls me his nephew."

"I see. I was wondering if we'd get past 'yes sir', 'no sir', 'thank you sir'."

"I'm sorry, sir."

"If you work for me, what is the one thing I should know about you?"

"I don't like to talk about my family."

"I'll remember that. What else, one more thing?"

"Nothing else, sir." Pent up nervousness peaked and he turned his gaze to the room: heavy drapery covering huge windows, richly framed artwork on the walls. Never before had he seen such a room. Not even in a dream.

"What do you do for fun?"

"Tae Kwon Do."

"A young man's martial art. Do you know why you are here?"

"You summoned me."

The President laughed out loud. "Yes, I did. Do you know why I summoned you?"

"No sir."

"No one told you?"

"No sir. My CO told me not to come back."

"Lawhdamassy! I need an aide. It would be a commission with the Office of the President. You would be working with my office, and working closely with me on the defense and security side."

"Yes sir."

"What does that mean? Are you interested?"

Dominic nodded, but kept silent. The man in front of him was disarming. Warm and informal, Dominic had a hard time figuring out the right answer to the man's endless questions. His commanding officers never asked him what he thought. In fact, this man was probably the first to ask the question and Dominic had no idea how to answer it.

"Look, son, I need you to talk to me like a normal human being, not one of your commanding officers. Loosen up. No one's listening. No one's recording."

"Yes sir. Sorry sir. I'm interested."

"There will be some school. OK, there'll be a lot of school. The commission will need to be approved by a Member of Parliament, but I think Ashton already has that in the bag. We'll give you some money to get some new clothes. Your bills will be taken care of, and your salary will triple. How are we doing so far?"

"We?"

"What do you think so far?"

"I'm interested."

"Now for the down side. Your life will not be your own and you may be put into dangerous situations. You will forever be associated with this government and myself, as the President."

"I understand."

"You don't want to think about it?"

"No."

"We'll be spending a lot of time together, so I would like us to be friends, if that is possible."

"Yes sir."

"How old are you?

"Twenty."

"Are you close to Ashton?"

"Close enough, I guess."

"When was the last time you slept all night?"

"I don't remember sir."

"Ashton will have new orders for you. You're not going back to the NOC. You have two days to get some rest. No work. No Wake. I think Ashton put you up at the Hilton in the Diplomatic Section until we get housing set up for you. I expect to see you here in this room in 72 hours. Ashton will make sure you get here."

"Yes sir."

"Anything else I should know?"

"Do you have kids?"

"I have two boys. Seven and five."

Dominic stood up, came to attention and gave the President a full dress salute. The President sighed and dismissed him. Out of Dominic's earshot, the President later needled Ashton about whether he could not have found someone who at least had started shaving. He also noted Dominic did not ask what might happen after the next election.

For months, the island experienced a period of domestic civility with no reaction to the SELAND agreement. The President thought it a dead issue. So dead, that when his chief of internal security came to him with a report involving said treaty, the President had to be reminded on the particulars. The report disturbed the entire executive team on multiple levels. Critical and protected information had been passed to unknown, unauthorized recipients via means they were unable to identify. While this alone was cause for concern at the highest levels, the content of the information gave them heartburn. While it was unclear exactly how much information had been passed, the nature of the content related to the physical structure and dimensions of the SELAND ocean-based towers. It happened right under their noses, despite multiple layers of safeguards developed to prevent such occurrences. Worse, the incident did not even provide them plausible deniability, since the data transfer left residual metadata pointing to the unauthorized transfer. ISEC notified the President. The President notified SELAND. SELAND seemed to ignore the warning, although it did update its firmware world wide, and revise the documentation. That is what passed for a SELAND surgical strike. "Don't Let the Perfect Be the Enemy of the Good" was their motto.

Santo fired the security minister and replaced him another Ashton recommendation, a personal and political enemy of both the President and Ashton. Santo liked the idea of keeping his enemies close and extended the appointment. Within days, he had a new internal security minister who loathed him, but suggested a complex plan to prioritize the investigation at the highest levels. Dominic, fresh from his first protocol and decorum training stood at attention behind the President as the new security minister met with his new boss, and his bosses 'right hand', Ashton. They followed decorum at the beginning, but not for long. The President wasted no time pointing to the elephant in the room. He played media footage of his new security minister criticizing the current administration for all kind of mishap and misstep. The new minister stood by his words, refusing to recant or explain. His appointment had been vetted and approved by both houses of Parliament. Santo's only recourse would be to fire him.

"Mr. President, I fail to see the point of replaying the past. We know where we stand."

"I am trying to figure out why Ashton would recommend you. You seem like 'opposition material'."

"Do not malign me, Mr. President, nor misunderstand me. We have our disagreements, but I am now a public servant."

"You are in NO position to instruct me!" Santo yelled, standing to full height to make his point. Dominic stepped out of position, moving closer to the President. In private settings, his charge included protection of the President. Noting the change in status, the President waved Dominic aside.

The new minister, one Mr. Wilson Toole, also noted Dominic's change in status. "I do not instruct, I only advise."

"You would do well to remember that!" the President said.

"And you would do well to remember that questioning my loyalty will not stand…not while your administration has more leaks than a rusty sieve," Toole said, not backing down, stirring the fire.

It was Ashton's turn to explode. "How dare you, sir!"

Toole stood up, as if he was finished with the conversation, in that way of old men that said in no uncertain terms, 'good day, sir'. "The 'truth' is not a 'dare'. Two completely different things." As he spoke, Toole looked directly at Ashton, as if the President had left the room.

President Santo stood up to match Toole in tone and stature. "Be careful, Toole!"

"You should do the same, Mr. President. You are an island and the sea is rising."

Ashton jumped out his chair and swung at Toole, who was saved only by Dominic's intervention. Yelling obscenities, Ashton forced Dominic to use every skill he had to keep the two from blows.

Standing between them, Dominic kept his eyes on Ashton whom he had forced back into his chair. The man was seething; the veins in his forehead standing up like tall trees.

Dominic had never seen him in such a state. Ashton had always been the epitome of control. Dominic stood, facing Ashton. "It's not worth it, sir," he said softly. Ashton looked up at him briefly, kissed his teeth and then looked away, out the window. When he glanced at the President, he swore the man had the tail end of a smile on his face.

"I like a man who comes out of his corner swinging. I think we can work together, Toole. You may go," the President said.

MOOMA JACOBS HOUSE - FOURTEEN YEARS AGO

<<Vodou – Negue Nago>>

The sun painted the sky a deep shade of red as it sank below the horizon line. The lurking dusk brought its usual orange red yellow purple haze -- the effect of light filtered through fine dust, carried by trade winds from distant continents. There was much to be done: make coffee-tea, buy rum and oil for flambeaux to mark the way. A series of naked flames would light Mooma Jacob's path to *Guinée*. Between this night and the ninth, Mooma Jacobs would begin her journey, carried by uncles, nephews and brothers. In deep caves, far from the *dedyard*, a motley collection of old, graybeard, black-tooth *nabobs* gathered to sing, drum, smoke all night for wisdom, knowledge, reason. With their songs and rheumy eyes, they promised to divine the identity of science-woman who *tek soal an' mek she ded*.

The sound of so many voices took Dominic by surprise. He had never been in a *dedyard* before, but the singing drew him in and made him catch his breath, as if about to cry. He panned his eyes across a church of brown-eyed faces, visible in flambeaux flame. In the moon-less night, the singing voices carried old *karamante* songs in a keening, shifting harmony -- simple and graceful, sleepy, and beautiful.

^blue yerry, ai
^blue yerry
^blue yerry, gallo
^blue yerry

More voices, layered like a fancy frock, joined the song as a second choir…

^bah day, bah day, oh man jah ee!
^bah day, bah day, oh man jah ee!
^bah day, bah day, oh man jah ee!

Barefoot children, thick men and beautiful women filled the *dedyard*. Men with huge gold rings on fat fingers came from town in shiny cars, carrying fat clean pretty children and women with hair the color of sunsets smelling like flowers and heavy musk, eager to see and be seen. Others came down from the hills, dressed in ill-fitting, off-white suits. Others came from shanties around the standpipe. They had no river-washed suits and dressed as if rum coursed in their veins. Sulky women wearing children for clothes stood next to them – dark, strong, mean, and gentle as coal-colored-washerwoman; talking, eating, laughing, eating, crying and eating. So much food, so little time.

Coal-colored-washerwoman taunted him while he bathed, hours before the people began to arrive. Born with a bitter seed in her mouth, she sung a *gégé nago* song and threatened to sell him to Guede Baron Semedi. He ignored her with the nonchalance and absence of his age and took a fifth mango from the tree. At least milk coffee colored skin creole woman went to Guinée during mango season, though the sweet but stringy mango did not fill his bitter belly.

^hush now, yuh hear? a' Guinée she a goh...

A big man with hair the color of coal wood-ash and sand which stood straight out like corn and sunflowers growing into the sun, put his hand on Dominic's shoulder and then on his face, brushing away the water Dominic made on his cheek and said 'hush'. The man pretended not to notice as Dominic stared up at him. He kept his hand heavily on his shoulder and shortly a new changeling voice joined the flambeaux path choir:

^bah day, bah day, oh man jah ee!
^bah day, bah day, oh man jah ee!
^bah day, bah day, oh man jah ee!

Moomma Jacobs would go to *Guinée* and not come back. They washed the body with nutmeg and lime. Ashton said these things out loud because Dominic had not heard the old stories and he believed the old stories might save him. A curtain of women in clean white dresses hid the activity around the body. On the adjacent table sat a bowl of limes and a smaller bowl of fresh nutmeg. Dominic squirmed, a skittish racehorse in the starting box. Ashton knew about curiosity and his hand stayed Dominic from sneaking underneath the curtain of women to see what should not be seen. All those Moomas would cuff him until he could not hear – no place for boy-children, Ashton said. Knowing Dominic would rather see or do, Ashton led Dominic to a group of men constructing a pine coffin. The men stopped working when Ashton's generous shadow fell over them and smiled large gap-toothed smiles. They did not return to work while Ashton stood over them. Ashton spoke in a full-hearted, generous, gregarious voice.

^*watch ya, uno mek mi likkle friend drive nail*

Dominic drove eleven nails, in the shape of nothing, about as big as his own hand in the plank covering the box. The men with large toothy gapped smiles patted Dominic gently about the head and shoulders. Ashton smiled and took him in tow again. The flambeaux shone brighter as the sun descended behind the waterline and Ashton gave Dominic coffee-tea to drink from a small glass (a glass!) and a piece of bread with codfish. The choir did not sing so strongly as before but their voices mixed with a dozen stories now being told around the yard, as small knots of people gathered around, depending on the shade of their skin, how much paper money they carried in their pockets or how much rum flowed in their veins.

^*if yuh evah see 'ar, when she likkle, she face pretty...*
^*mi 'ear one story 'bout 'ar, yuh 'no... mi cyaan believe it...*
^*a wuh do yuh mahn! How yuh speak evil 'bout 'ar, when she well ded?*

^mi seh! mi 'ear one story 'bout 'ar. mi cyaan speak evil 'bout 'ar. a good christian woman 'dat

Ashton led Dominic around the yard, his hand resting gently on the boy's shoulder until they reached the place in the yard where the broad-backed men dug a long hole. Behind them, the crowd gathered to keen cry moan wail. They swayed together as one. Left, then right, and left again. They placed a pillow filled with parched peas, corn and coffee beans sewn inside for milk coffee colored skin creole woman's head into the grave. Together, they told milk-coffee-colored-skin-creole-woman she should not linger; that she find her road to Guinée and begin her journey. She could not look back. She should not come back.

We have all changed our clothes. We have moved our beds.

A sound arose from the midst of the people. Dominic found his voice though he wished from somewhere inside she did not have to go to Guinée. The speaker threw compellance powder into the box, followed by handfuls of parched corn and peas. Four gap-tooth smiling men helped lower Mooma Jacob's coffin into the grave and somebody Dominic did not know poured a bottle of rum over the coffin. As the gap-tooth smiling men covered the coffin with soil, Dominic helped spread coffee grounds and salt around the grave so *duppy nuh com'*. Between third night and the ninth, Moomma Jacobs would travel from grave to room where she breathed last -- thus the reason for the *nine-night*. They recreated her room to appear as she left it, so she could take what she wished on the long road to Guinée. She had to be happy and reconciled for there could be no reason to linger, to seek recompense from the million and their children. They had so little to lose. People who knew her intimately and those who only heard her name in evening verandah gossip came to eat her food, sing and show their faces to Moomma Jacobs one last time. Moomma Jacobs fed them, they sang and showed her the road to *Guinée* with flambeaux. They smiled, danced and caroused as if celebrating a birth or marriage and people came and went every day; but on the ninth night, Moomma Jacobs would go.

On a long table covered with a white tablecloth and banana leaves, Dominic never saw so much food in one place at the same time: fried fish and bammy, yams, chicken, rice and beans, bottles of rum in various stages of fullness and emptiness, harddo bread, coffee, wet sugar and condensed milk. Inside the house, in Mooma Jacob's bedroom, lay another feast: white rum, white rice without salt, and white fowl without salt. A small white porcelain glass held water. Next to the table, a wooden bath bowl also full of water sat next to Mooma Jacobs' well-made white bed. More and more people filled the yard and partook of the feast that sat outside, but the food without salt in the bedroom lay unmolested. Around the walls of the room, older Moomas and nabobs sat smoking clay pipes, rheumy-eyed and rotten in the tooth. A creole Mooma pointed with enthusiasm, her clay pipe falling into her more than generous lap.

Dominic had never seen this creole mooma before the *nine-night*, but she told all the others what to do. All around the outside of the room, moomas and nabobs pointed, smiled and cooed. From doorway to feast table, bath bowl to bed, their silent gestures told the story of Mooma Jacobs' entry and approval of the *dedroom*, and of her sitting down with the other Moomas in her special place. The creole woman rose (with great effort because she was so fat) and spoke to Mooma Jacobs. Calling her by her intimate title of "Auntie", the fat creole Mooma told Mooma Jacobs that all of them were glad she had come -- two and three and four times glad. All in the room reinforced what the creole mooma said in their own ways: nodding their heads, slapping their knees, knocking clay pipes against the wall (only if the tobacco had been burned and needed to be knocked out anyway), exclaiming *tchroo sah!* or *ee-hee*. Then the singing began, led by Ashton. The songs did not vary greatly but carried emotion not shown at any other time. It went on for hours and hours, changed only by the injection of some new variation of the melody or something new untried unheard.

Some time before the sun set on the next day during the night, Hanna arrived with her parents. She came to him like a sister to protect him, like a mother to give birth, like a woman come to…he did not know. He picked out Hanna's singsong dub voice out of the ruckus and together, they ran down to the beach, helping each other wash the sadness of the day from their bodies, dissolving it in saltwater and ocean brine. When they finished, they sat on the sand near the water. They fell asleep on the beach and woke just outside the reach of the incoming tide, turning their attention to the half loaf of *harddo* bread and a few pieces of salted herring Hannah brought with her. A green coconut, broken open with a machete Hannah carried with her, quenched their thirst. At the fumbling tide's edge, he bent to splash water on his face and shoulders. As the water sloshed past his knees, he muttered to Wink, that sad and shifty friend of the very small…

^yuh cyaan gi'mi one likkle bebop song fi sing, wink?

Dirty gray sand and murky green water spread as far as their eyes took them. With whitecaps low and weak without a breakwater, no fishermen fished off these waters. No boats sat at anchor off the bay. No seabirds or land crabs called this beach home. The solitary palm tree lived only in its death agony. Yet they sat underneath it and stared at the black horizon while moonrise ignored them.

^a mahket mi a'goh, fah mi haffi find sittin fi sell
^find someone fi help yuh
^mi nuh tell yuh, mi nah mek free wit d'ras people-dem!

When they returned to coffee colored skin creole woman's house, they saw Hanna's parents deep in conversation with the big man with hair that stood up like sunflowers the color of wood-ash, and a police woman. Though Hanna and her parents had come to fetch Dominic to their home up country, the man with hair the color of wood-ash that stood up like corn or sunflowers promised to take him home and treat him as one of his own.

MARKET, NEAR MOOMA JACOBS HOUSE - FOURTEEN YEARS AGO

The millions and their children had one place where they seemed most equal. The place, they called Market. Above all a woman's place, they gathered and mingled there without malice or grudge. This place lay in the center of town and took a wide swathe of land for itself, flat and without trees or growing things. The place remained empty and barren most of the time, except on Saturdays and Sundays, when it came alive with the commerce of the millions and their children, laid out on brilliant white bed sheets, on sale to she who bartered longest and hardest. Before the sun woke the millions and their children with heavy heat and hazy light, the market women sipped peppermint tea. They wore dresses full and free like the banter that flowed between them, made from bright swaths of yellow, red, green and black hand-woven cotton. The *gele*, an intricately wrapped swath of cloth contrasted with the colors of their dress and the color of their skin, for they had much *soal*. With faces most radiant in the morning, before the day got underway, their men still asleep, they relished and indulged in the joy of sisterhood.

All of them had the same things to sell: food sown and harvested from the ground with their own hands, or useful tools and wares — made, found, or acquired. Nothing unique or novel in anything they offered except each face, each voice, offering a work of art, sadness, fierce pride and quirky superstition – grandmothers, daughters, grand daughters, mothers, sisters, all. They laughed and cried easily, quick to anger and quicker to love. They sat in their places praying, cursing and smoking fat hand-rolled cigars. To make them smile one had only to comment on her beauty and offer her a little rum mixed with cold water. Market filled with women lined up in neat lines to make efficient use of space. In two days they sold their goods and made their money for the week to avoid the treacherous trip

91

back with unsold goods, braving darkness and other no good doers. This amounted to much yelling shouting and heckling in between the neat rows of market women, keeping competition fierce and curses flying all day. None who needed to buy waited until the last few hours of Market. The millions and their children rushed to Market before the Market women finished laying their goods on the bed sheets; to be the first to touch the biggest pear, the ripest paw-paw, to go home with the best piece of salt-fish. A good haggler could get the best piece of salt fish for less than one might acquire it in the last minutes of Market. By sunrise, a visitor would find Market well underway with much buying, selling, gossip, laughter, crying, and carousing filling the day.

The crowd pressed Dominic forward -- relentless, loud, unforgiving and impatient. The entrance to Market narrowed to make collecting the entry fee easier and Dominic attached himself to anyone who could pay. Large families worked best since no one noticed one more child, but with lighter skin than most, he had to be picky. His clothes were ragged so the family had to look the same and most families dressed their children in Sunday best. Dominic had no Sunday best, only drawstring pants made out of old drapery, torn at the knee and dirty and frayed at the hem – not even one pair of *jeanspants* – and a sweat stained and grimy shirt. Getting into Market without paying would be some trick indeed. He did it. He hid behind a very fat woman, her fat man and their troop of nine children, sneaking past the women who took the Market fees.

He heard the big market woman before he saw her.

^Weh yuh deh when creole woman 'ave she dedyard?
^Mi deh a'mi yard.
^A-oh! yuh wukkless! yuh rood lyke wot!
^Mi well wan' one mango.
^See it deh? di bockabocka mango. tekki!

He took the mango with a toothy smile for thanks but the market woman's face retained its angry scowl. He continued to smile as he devoured the mango, already planning how to get a second. He watched with sad ginger eyes as people passed with either money or food in hand. Dust invaded every part of his body. He found it later in nostrils, ears, covering his feet like socks. He walked barefoot while all around him shod in heavy leather shoes. He spied a familiar face -- the big man called Ashton from the *dedyard*, with hair that stood up like sunflowers the color of wood-ash and the sand. While market woman and Ashton talked, Dominic slipped another mango from her pile and darted away. He noticed Ashton following him with his eyes. He hid long enough to almost finish his second mango when Ashton blocked the sun with his hair and his very large belly. Ashton smiled. Bigger now than at the *dedyard*, he loomed over Dominic, his shiny white teeth showing between fat bulbous lips, sleepy eyes, a double chin, and no neck. When the big man began to chuckle, Dominic laughed with Ashton trying to make the mango disappear before Ashton asked him where he got it. Ashton spoke first, his voice deep, rolling and as kind as Dominic remembered it. Ashton handed Dominic a few coins, the most money Dominic had ever held in his hands.

"*Mi nuh lyke fi see likkle pickney beg a'street*," the big man said.

DIPLOMATIC SECTION – CAPITAL - TODAY

He stayed up all night Wednesday through the early hours of Thursday morning, drinking club soda, while the rest drank bourbon, talking about the end of the world. It was an after party in a private dining room rented by the Embassy of Barbados, and Dominic stayed far longer than he intended to. The ambassador-level staff had all taken their leave at a civilized, polite hour. Those who remained were the invisibles, young and untitled, low-level consular folk and military types. Incredibly, a young woman with the US Marine Corps had been invited and stayed for the after party. She sat two seats down from Dominic, sandwiched between two men in suits from one of the international aid organizations. Dominic listened to the conversation laughing occasionally, waiting for the two suits to leave. She looked like she might need 'rescuing', he told himself. Another American, from the Consulate, Dominic thought, dominated the conversation with wild stories about poison spewing from commercial jet engines, aliens, and mysterious but powerful secret societies, which controlled the planet, if not the universe. The table laughed good-naturedly as his stories became more and more complex and intertwined, managing to explain almost absolutely everything in a narrative that was as clear to Dominic as a ball of wax.

The world was coming to an end, he said, and everyone was sleeping. Either the bourbon was very good, very bad, or this bloke truly believed himself. Even Bigfoot was involved. As crazy as the stories were, people around the table argued about the details – about the chemical make up of the poison being spread by commercial jets, about the poisoning of the population through the use of fluoride in schools, about whether the Americans would come clean about the existence of an alien species from which the fount of their success unquestionably flowed. That the world would end was incontrovertible, he claimed. The question was, what would come afterwards: who would survive, how would they survive, what would replace what had just ended.

"Toilet bowls and cockroaches. That's all that'll be left," the American Marine said, as if she had been waiting for her chance to throw the conversation. She used her comment to extricate herself, nodded to the table and made her exit.

A relative silence followed her exit. Dominic thought about following her and casting for a conversation, but something about the way she carried herself gave him the underwhelming impression she would not be interested. He poured himself another glass of club soda and leaned back in his chair as the group continued to argue, this time about the pineal gland and how it was becoming encrusted with mineral deposits (from drinking water, no doubt), making the whole world blind to reality, keeping the people of the world in a stupor, content with bad media and mediocre shopping. When someone at the table realized morning was upon them, the room cleared quickly. The military folks would be expected to be at post in less than an hour. Dominic had a little bit more time. He had time to drink tea with Miss Missy at sunrise and take a forty-five minute power nap before his office opened.

He chose a solid black theme paired with red sneakers for his date on Thursday with Olivia. She ditched the business suit for cocoon shaped, tan, linen bloomers and a Tibetan embroidered vest. She ordered Johnny Walker Blue and he stuck to his mineral water. She seemed more pensive this time, distracted, as if something weighed upon her. The evening required less conversation, which was fine with Dominic. He could not get enough of her. She asked between cigarettes if he thought anyone picked up on their dynamic. He was sure he did not know. She waved him off with the hand that held the cigarette.

"I could get fired, you know," Olivia said, in a slight scold.

"I'll put in a good word for you," Dominic said, trying to make a joke of it. He could not take his eyes from the seam of her embroidered vest at the shoulder and the light on the bare skin of her shoulder.

"I hate this place," she said, after her fifth drink.

He understood she meant the island in general rather than the restaurant specifically. "You told me." He took the cigarette out of her hand to put the ash in the ashtray and handed it back to her.

"Does that bug you?"

"It's not your place. I get that," though he wished she did not talk so much.

"That's why I drink."

"You don't have to explain yourself..." Dominic replied, reaching out to touch her shoulder, to confirm with his hands what his eyes hinted at.

Olivia followed his hand with her eyes. She glanced over at the lone bureaucrat at the next table. "He could be my boss."

Dominic knew better. He knew the man — a flunky at the UN2 mission. "He's not your boss."

Olivia laughed. "How would you know?"

"Your boss doesn't even know this place exists. They don't come this far south."

Olivia laughed again and lit another cigarette. "You're probably right. God! I hate it when you're right."

"Why don't you put in for a transfer, I mean, if you hate it here so much?"

"SELAND discourages that sort of thing, especially on short term assignments. It messes with their logistics, so they make sure those who do put in for transfers always end up someplace worse than where they came from."

"There's nothing worse than an ISEC leeward NOC site," Dominic said, speaking from experience.

"Is that the rock Santo found you under?" Olivia asked, putting her hand on top of his on the table, her way of telling him she was making a joke. She knew sometimes he did not quite get her sense of humor.

"Twenty-hour shifts and vitamin D deficiency screws with your head..." Dominic said, not bothering to tell her how WAKE pharma distorted his sleep patterns.

"I hear they're pretty liberal with 'WAKE' here."

Dominic nodded and shrugged. His body screamed and raged at him and it had nothing to do with food, the conversation, or pharma. He picked at his food, content to watch her eat. "How many countries have you been in?"

"Eighty-seven countries in three years."

"That's a lot of defense attaches..." Dominic said without thinking about the innuendo, then regretting his words.

Olivia took a drag from her cigarette and blew the smoke from her exhale in his face. "Buy me another drink, asshole."

They took a taxi to her hotel and sat on the kitchen counter drinking coffee. The windows in her room opened into the night. Dominic noticed she traveled light -- one small bag and a SELAND deck that looked smaller than his. It never occurred to him that SELAND had other form factors – he had only ever seen one. She had not unpacked. An open bottle of wine sat on the counter along with the remains from breakfast. It was a nondescript hotel room, telling him nothing more about her than he already knew. He stood in the front room of the two-room suite, staring out the open windows.

"What are you thinking?" Olivia asked, from the suite's kitchenette.

"My place has a better view."

"You don't think you're biased?"

"You don't have a chaise lounge."

"That would be a good thing."

"What does that mean?" Dominic asked, turning to face her.

"It means that what happened at your place won't happen again."

"*Wha'mek?*"

"It's like you said, eighty-seven countries is a lot of defense attaches."

He knew he would pay for his nonchalance at some point. "I didn't mean it like that."

"And that's not why I'm ending it."

"B' it nuh start yet..."

She laughed, if somewhat ruefully. "Dominic! I'm serious."

She hoisted herself off the counter and stood in front of him, but instead of a kiss, she put her hands on his waist and her mouth to his ear and told him what she knew. She said SELAND had opened an Evidentiary file on one of the President's advisors – the guy with the Don King haircut, the one the President called 'Ashton'.

***

Unsure of how he felt about his 'date' with Olivia, or unwilling to draw any particular conclusion, he went back to the Bone Room until the bartender's shift was over. He and Bryan often wandered the Red Light district after 2 am, dropping WAKE, waiting for sunrise in dark peep shows, burlesque lounges and live sex clubs. He put down good money to sip champagne with tiny Japanese Goth girls with intricate spider web face make up, layered, black lace, brocade gowns, and hushed conversation about sex toys and the strange situations the girls had gotten themselves into. They walked brashly into whorehouses where women grabbed their crotches and beckoned in a menacing way; unable to hide the fact life had used them up. They peered into live sex clubs where the cover ran to two months salary, the prize views blocked by bouncers twice their size. More than once, they got brutally manhandled for reaching out to touch the dancer, who danced amazingly and painfully close. They did not question the outrageous covers for such feasts for the eyes. They dropped large amounts of cash to sit with tall skinny African girls who spoke no English, drinking drinks with African names, smoking cigarettes laced with dried scorpion poison (most likely fake or detoxified); or blonde Ukrainian girls who spoke London English with a Russian accent and insisted on drinking only

Speyside Glenfiddich 40, but who would, after all, settle for Suntory Yamazaki 18. The girls laughed when they found out Dominic didn't drink, but it made him memorable and he liked being remembered.

Leaving Bryan with the Russian girls on their third round of Suntory Yamazaki, he picked and threaded his way towards the coastline, and Melia, a young woman of eighteen, who maintained a small room in a large house for such rendezvous'. Like him, life orphaned her at a young age. She bore invisible scars and refused to talk about them. If she wanted to see him, she put a candle in the window. If she couldn't see him, she closed the curtains. Melia was a dark wind in his life, a reminder of all that could go wrong and often did. Sometimes she took the money he left on the table, other times she told him to keep it. If his efforts to take care of her struck her as too overt, she refused to see him, sometimes for weeks at a time. She had no idea what he did during the day, and had she known, she would likely disappear and he would never see her again. He guessed her to be Nigerian, with only the slightest touch of the European. Sad, large brown eyes surveyed her melancholy world and she kissed him with full, pouty lips that seldom smiled. She had the sparse, slender beauty of her age and she used it against him. He did not mind. Unlike Hanna, she provided no refuge or sympathy. Unlike Olivia, she swung indifference like a broadsword. Seeing the lonely candle in the window, he knocked on her door. She opened the door, said, "Oh, it's you," turned around and retreated back into the room, leaving him to follow her.

Leaving Melia just after sunrise, he stopped at Miss Missy's roadside shack to dink tea and listen to her complain. Even if he had just been at her shack the day before, she greeted him as if she had not seen him in years and years and peppered him with complaints that he never came to visit. She poured them their usual two cups of tea and cleared a spot inside her cluttered shack for him to sit. Dark and fat, her eyes sparkled in the morning light and her smile never left. Dominic had no idea where she went at night, but in three years, he never managed to get to her shack before she did. Pushing sixty, she never married and had no children. She claimed him as her child though and was not shy about telling people about it. Somehow, she managed to extract most of the stories of his life and after three years, Dominic remained unsure as to exactly how she had done so. Sometimes, he fell asleep in her shack and she let him sleep. Sometimes she wanted to talk; sometimes she remained quiet. They drank tea and talked about the depths of despair into which life on the island had descended. She gave him advice he might have used if he had born one hundred years ago. She scolded him for not sleeping and for wasting his money in the red light district, but she liked hearing about the dresses the Japanese Goth girls wore and swore at the amount of money he paid for a single shot of whiskey. Once, half asleep, he called her "Mooma Jacobs," which seemed to please her. After all, they were cut of the same cloth…big-hearted women who only knew how to give and not take…and he knew already he would be beholden to both.

By Friday evening, he could think of nothing but sleep. Exhausted, he hired a taxi to take him the four blocks to his apartment. He collapsed in his beanbag and slept for eighteen hours. He woke up to eat early Sunday morning and then slept again for another five hours. When he woke up mid-morning, he was 'sleep-stoned'. There was no other word   for   it.

RINCON DU NORD - TWENTY-FIVE YEARS AGO

Jemma...

^ fa she nah 'ave skin lyke gahd give 'ar

The million's uncrowned market queen and former dance hall star arrayed around her on bleached white bed sheets (upon which two of her three children were conceived and born) artful piles of such stuff as made up her life: green peppers, scallion, mangoes, paw-paw, jack fruit, coconut, scotch bonnet pepper, grapefruit and pear. Her wares she did not name, for the millions knew those like they knew their own. But her children were less known, though infamous in their own right, and they took their rightful places on her body. Riverrun lived until the age of twelve. Though quite dumb, he grew big and strapping. He dropped out of school to carry wood. He died by a machete. Apollonia died of dehydration before she learned to talk.

Ink and scarring the only memory of her children she permitted herself, she believed that children (especially hers) had no *duppies* when they died and did not travel to *Guinée*. Instead, they wandered the earth in unknown and undiscovered forms. Thus she carved or scarred their names onto her skin, so that if they happened upon her, they would see their name on her skin and come to know the outside of her womb, her gorged breasts and the rest of her body -- especially her arms, thick and wide as a jackfruit when picked and taken to market. She kept to herself in her own way and were one of the millions to ask, she might not tell them about her three children, born a year apart, the first having been born twenty-seven years ago. The boy she named for his father, the girl after her own fantasy. Her brand of naiveté waxed strong: childlike in her stubbornness and not easily disabused of her notions of how the world around her worked.

Jemma, with feet dusky and dark, swayed with imaginary winds on a sea of haggling voices and wafting odors of goat shit, pepper sauce, jerk chicken and human sweat. As market goers passed her by in favor of another's, Jemma rubbed her wide belly with one hand, twirled her Nubian knots with the other and kissed her teeth. Those who paused in front of her she ignored until she saw money. If they bought and the correct amount of money changed hands she sent the buyers on their way with Selassie's blessings. If they returned her wares to the pile and moved on without buying, she cursed them with a loud and fierce voice, quickly devouring the offending piece. Sometimes she threw fruit or vegetable at their backs, along with handfuls of dirt. The girl children gave her wide berth and she berated them for the skin they showed. The boys she called after, hoping they would linger, allowing her to put her hands on their hips or something of that nature that would be a comfort to her. When she became pregnant with her third child she did not cease to tell anyone who might listen that someone cursed her birth canal. Her breasts filled with tears not milk. She said this last child would follow the path of its siblings. She would not wait for it nor stand idly by. Her belly continued to grow and she spent the day rubbing it and crooning. At the end of each Market day, Jemma wrapped her wares in the white sheets in which she carried them and prepared for the journey home, wondering as she did at odd moments what became of her third child — a *mingi* boy — born alive and healthy. Although she nursed it for a while, she retained neither hope nor grief for the child, her child.

In those days, Ashton's hair still stood up on his head like sunflowers, not gray like wood ash or beach sand, but black as his skin. He had a reputation for being a strong but fair and fat young man with a dubious reputation. It did not occur to him at that age, that he would one day curse time for its devastating consequences. When the sun seemed highest in the sky, when those who wore watches looked at them and thought about lunch, Ashton could not. In fact, a single thought consumed him and how this thought came to him consumed him further still -- lust. He wandered aimlessly for as long as he could without drawing undue attention to himself. In the end, he could not avoid friends, acquaintances, and accomplices who wanted to share a glass of rum or smoke with him. Though he tried, he could not pinpoint when this all-consuming thought began its work. As the day progressed, the narrow spaces between sellers seemed less crowded and most good people, having completed their buying, now turned to something to eat, drink or shade. About two hours after noon, the crowd at Market changed as those with no familial commitments or stricture woke from their beds and ventured out. The talk became crude, rancorous and confrontational, decidedly younger and by nature of their youth, more pleasing to Ashton's eye.

He smiled at seeing his children Slip, Magnum and Straightedge and his long time companion, Stork. They talked for a little while and shared green coconuts between them. He smiled at seeing Stork. She kept her hair short and curled close to her head. She dressed in loud reds yellows and greens and loved to drink great amounts of rum. Her eyes and face turned soft and radiant, and when she smiled, Ashton felt like going to sleep, his head resting on her chest as he used to do when they were young. She cursed and prayed with the best of them and kept Magnum, Slip and Straightedge under her arthritic thumb. She did not leave their yard much and he counted it as one life's few blessings that Stork had come to Market today. It would take his mind off the single thought that possessed him all day. Not a complex man he found himself often beset by complex problems and temptations. For Ashton, lust remained his greatest most complex temptation. Without that singular event, he was certain he could lead the life of a jesus or other saint.

CHAPTER IV

CAPITAL – TODAY

Instead of lobsters and crabs, two species that had long collapsed in the wild, they dredged for garbage.

From three hundred fifty yards, scoping the harbor operation remained challenging. Dredging for bodies might have been a familiar operation for some, but dredging for six tons of international garbage promised to be surlier. The earphones did a decent job of cancelling out rotor noise. With his feet resting on the glass bubble of the cockpit floor, Dominic's discomfort in the helicopter persisted in a slight case of nausea he would never admit to. Dominic had offered his seat to Ms. Casteñada, but she demurred, citing a fear of heights and smiling conspiratorially that he would have more fun. Just the four of them – Ashton, the President, the pilot and Dominic -- in the close quarters of the cockpit, they used first names though it still felt strange. Dominic called Ashton and the President, "Baba", an honorific meaning something like 'uncle'. An operation of this scope however would have been impossible a mere twenty-five years ago. The headphones made conversation difficult but the operation engendered enough awe in the cockpit for emphatic pointing at one display or another. Dominic had little time to ponder what sequence of events conspired to put him in this particular helicopter at this particular time.

Using humans for underwater work remained inefficient and with known currents inside the harbor, still far too dangerous. Submarine robotic units on the harbor floor did most of the work with the help of advanced imaging devices and the latest GIS/GPS positioning software. Using a pair of GPS-enabled binoculars on a COMLINK to the UAV above, the displays in the helicopter and what he saw with the unaided eye, Dominic made an attempt at scoping the operation in his head. For three nights prior, a pair of small, submarines scanned the harbor floor with laser range gated imaging. Underwater imagery, combined with a Spacial Data Infrastructure application on loan from SELAND, generated a geo-tagged map of the harbor floor. The underwater robotic units had a straightforward task: move the identified objects from present location to a massive wire bucket. Once the bucket filled to hastily compiled stress metrics, the crane, mounted on the floating platform, stabilized by eight tugboats each as big as two eighteen-wheel trucks side by side, winched the bucket up and onto the modified SELAND platform – the same type of platform from which the garbage came.

The executive helo shared the airspace above the operation with two other helos: the President's security helo and another all white helo with no visible windows, seconded from Ms. Casteñada's agency. No one was quite sure what it was exactly and whether it carried human cargo. It stayed quiet on the COMLINK, hovering and banking in the shifting air currents, its rotor noise muffled by strange baffles. Dominic would have given a limb to get some sort of glimpse into the capabilities of that bird, but SELAND capabilities were invisible to him. His clearance made him privy to many things, but SELAND was as inaccessible to him as the Horsehead Nebula was to a robot air shuttle. Shifting his view from the harbor operation to the shore, the military vacated a swathe of land two miles inland. Zoned industrial/commercial, the displacement proved to be not a particularly painful operation on a Saturday. Although they ran the risk of running into the regular business week, the President had a plan. If necessary, they would declare an extraordinary national holiday. The small island nation could ill afford further losses in their tourist sector.

After two hours in the air, the President began to relax, smiling as he pointed out various aspects of the operation. Dominic knew the operation impressed him, with his formal education in structural engineering. Back on land, they ate a hastily prepared white tablecloth meal inside the hangar, away from the cacophony of the operation and out of sight of whoever might have been trying to get a glimpse of them. While Dominic scarfed down the food set in front of him, he listened while the two men talked about the near future.

"I don't want a statement Ashton, or a plan. I need a way through this mess," anger once more returning to the President's voice.

"With no claims of responsibility and no demands, it is difficult to find a way forward. In principle we could assume these actions are being taken in opposition to the Garbage Treaty. I wonder if the best approach is mitigation rather than offensive obliteration."

The President stopped chewing, looked at Ashton, and then Dominic, put his fork down, finished chewing and then looked back at Ashton. "You can't be serious…"

"What are the alternatives? Give everyone free gas on Tuesdays? Require the children to wear dunce caps to school on Fridays? Perhaps you can inform Ms. Casteñada you have unilaterally vacated the SELAND treaty."

"Dominic do you have your deck with you? I want you to look something up for me. What the hell does SELAND mean anyway."

"I lost it in the security sweep."

The President stopped chewing and glared at Ashton yet again. "I authorized no such sweep."

"Something I did on my own. We can't be too careful. Besides the *pickney* had malware on it," Ashton winked conspiratorially at Dominic and chuckled as he met the President's eyes.

The President put his silverware on his plate, taking great care to line the knife and fork up with the edge of the plate. After a moment of staring at his plate he looked up first at

Dominic and then at Ashton. "Next time you decide to do something on your own Ashton, don't."

"Yes, Mr. President," Ashton said in a wise return to protocol, even if temporarily.

"Dominic you answer to me and me only. Is that clear?"

"Yes Sir."

"Wait for me in the car."

The car sat half a football field away and Dominic would have given a limb to hear what the two men were saying. In different circumstances he might read lips, but Ashton would not be saying much. He would have to imagine the conversation. He had little interest in their problems or their politics as he considered himself separate and apart. Something Ashton said gave him heartburn. Ashton told the President he found malware on Dominic's deck, implying that Dominic had put it there. Except that the entire deck consisted of malware; it had no GOVNET certificate or image, the SELAND registration a complete ruse. Ashton told him that much when he gave Dominic the system. In the short time the deck had been in his possession, he spent most of his free time meticulously compiling the mystery trace-tag he inadvertently discovered. Although the picture remained incomplete, an uncomfortable shadow took shape. As it became clearer, Dominic realized that all who smiled at him were not friends and wrote the evidence to a private SELAND Sequester, allocated to the President's office. He did not trust Ashton, but he that was his own secret. They had so far been able to maintain a mirage of trust, but with Ashton making his surprise move, he felt vulnerable to possibilities he preferred not to think about. His heart racing and his face and neck flushed, a sudden urge to bolt from the car washed over him in waves.

In its wake, he longed for the quiet he remembered at Pierre's house. Dominic had to think a little bit about the woman's name and after a moment, it came to him --

Mercilia. Thinking about the simple years he spent with Pierre made him smile, countering the impulse to run. Pierre never yelled or pried. He met Dominic's hyperactive frenetic days with the same keening voice as on slower sleepier days. When Dominic woke up angry and gloomy, Pierre suggested they walk. Walking with Pierre's hand on his shoulder to guide him, reminded him of Mooma Jacobs, which always made things better. He remembered the way Pierre put his hands on Dominic's face, to see "inside". Those big swollen gnarled hands could now do little but beg, but when Pierre pulled them away from his face, Dominic felt different – lighter, cooler, as if someone had washed his face. Pierre touched his face only three times: once when he arrived at the house, once when he left for his first day of school and once before leaving for South Carolina. But Capital, the city of lies, as Pierre called it, had long been emptied of men like him. He feigned a yawn and a stuffy nose as an excuse to hide the water in his eyes while the President settled into the backseat. The President gave instructions to the driver to take them back to the InterContinental and raised the sound proof barrier. Dominic steeled himself for whatever might come next as the motorcade careened out of the hanger.

"Dominic, listen to me. Are you listening?"

Caught off guard by the sincerity of the voice and sudden urgency, Dominic took a deep breath and nodded.

"You have been with me for three years. We are not kin and you may not consider me a friend but there are things going on that you do not understand, I do not even understand yet." The President put his hand heavily on Dominic's shoulder and gave it a gentle shake. "Do you hear?"

Dominic nodded again. Santo had never touched him or taken this tone before and it made him uncomfortable.

"I am worried about you."

"Me?"

"You may have to choose sides."

"Choose sides?"

"There is no such thing as neutral. Standing on the sidelines puts you in danger."

"What about your side?"

"It may be a losing side…"

"*Wh'yuh a-say, captain?*"

"I have grown fond of you…"

Dominic pulled back and away in the seat opposite the President.

"Dominic, please! I am telling you this so you can make your own decision for once in your life!"

Dominic relaxed again in the seat, staring blankly at the man across from him. "I could go back to the Fifth…" but he knew before he finished his sentence about the impossibility of that option.

"That is not possible."

"What about Ashton?"

"I can not answer for Ashton."

"But if Ashton was on your side you would say so, *nuh'tchroo?*"

The President said nothing

"What about Ms. Casteñada?"

"The American woman? You ask me what side she is on?" The President laughed bitterly.

"I don't know her and you did not introduce us…"

"I figured you would side with Ashton…" The President let the silence drag for a few moments more and nodded slowly.

Before the President could speak again Dominic spoke his peace. "Do you think I'll see Pierre again?"

"It is not safe in the country."

"Maybe I should have stayed up north? They had a son and we were friends. We were going to university."

"University would be good for you…it would be a more normal life."

"But that's not now…"

"No, you are right that is not now."

Dominic came to a conclusion he could not have predicted. He squared his eyes with Santo and said quietly but firmly "Now, I choose your side." Dominic surprised even himself. He had not planned to choose sides; he hadn't spent sleepless nights wondering which side to choose. He had not come to a conclusion waiting for the right time to say it.

The President exhaled as if he had been holding his breath. He did not smile but in an odd way, seemed relieved and pleased. "Say nothing to anyone! You hear me?" The President reinforced his statement by putting his hand on Dominic's hand and squeezing to the pain point. For the first time since starting with the President's office, Dominic did not recoil involuntarily, though he very much wanted to.

"Yes Sir," he said, feeling relieved and puzzled that he did not care he had no reason -- he liked the feeling -- like a reverse 'game over'. Dominic said nothing but pointed to Santo's own deck and with the President's permission, opened a draft message and keyed in the hash tag for the SELAND Sequester where he wrote the code compiled from his now missing deck.

INTERCONTINENTAL HOTEL – DIPLOMATIC SECTION – CAPITAL – TODAY

<<*The Ettes – Teeth*>>

Ashton had finished picking through his lunch when Dominic knocked on the door. They rarely saw each other, even if Dominic considered him a 'friendly' in the Cabinet. In such close quarters, confined to the secured floors, Dominic found it easy to sneak past security and steal time without the watchers. Whenever Ashton saw Dominic, he marveled at what had become of the skinny, bright-eyed, but stubborn child who lived in his home leeward side. Dominic entered diminutively (an odd characteristic retained from childhood). He dropped his bag near the door and sat down. Hoping Dominic brought his deck with him, Ashton noticed the telltale blue light inside the bag and relaxed, flashing a welcome smile. "You have lunch?" Ashton queried. The kid could still eat like an elephant.

"Yessuh."

"Are you required at Cabinet today?"

"Yessuh."

"Don't you get tired of sitting there?"

"Yessuh."

"Do you have anything else to say besides 'yessuh'?"

"*Yessuh. Yuh tink Miss Castaneda mek mi chat to 'er?.*"

"*Lawhd!NobodyKnowTheTroubleMeSeen! A'wuh do yuh, bredda?*" Ashton fired back.

"*Mek mi tell yuh sump'n, mon!*"

"*Yuh too bright! D'woman deh nuh mek free wit' pickney dem, yuh know!*"

112

Dominic laughed out loud. "*Ras!*"

Ashton shook his head. Somewhere along the line, the boy had disappeared and he had not even noticed. Somehow, he missed the transition, the flowering. The young man who sat in front of him no longer needed him, his body language screaming an indifference that pained Ashton in ways he would not have predicted. Knowing what he was about to do would either be forgotten or buried by happenstance, still he felt compelled to lay the groundwork for the personal disaster he was courting. "Listen to me now!"

"*Wha'mek?*"

"What do you think about those idiots with stun guns at the Promenade flashmob? Life sentences…"

Dominic stopped smiling. These kinds of unrelated, hanging questions from Ashton tended to carry weight only time revealed. "Going soft, Minister? You can always commute the sentence."

"I asked you what you thought."

"I haven't."

"You've never thought about what might happen if you went to prison for life? No appeal. No parole."

"*Wh'yuh a chat 'bout, bredda?*"

"Stray dog get more mercy, y'know!"

"You've been talking to stray dogs?"

"I've been thinking…"

"You know bad things happen when you do that."

"If something bad happens…"

Dominic stood up, red flags flying high, eyes fixed on Ashton. "Now you're fekkin scaring me. You know something I don't?"

"This is what I'm telling you. This is what I know. I'm a stray dog. Ovastan?"

The alarm startled them both and Dominic jumped from the couch, swept his deck from the bag on the floor and landed back on the couch, staring at it unbelievingly. "They turn socials on again, yuhknow!" 'Socials' was the new generic for the descendants of the foundational, but now legacy social networks from the chaotic early decades of the twenty-first century.

Ashton nodded, convinced the kid had sprung another of his pranks. Early in his assignment with the Office of the President, between protocol and decorum classes, Dominic decided in his youthful wisdom to amuse himself. Using his formidable coding skills provided to him by the government he served, he foisted an illusion that the SELAND decks used by both Ashton and the President had been wiped clean. The prank was executed so perfectly that three levels of ISEC Technical were unable to resolve or explain the never before seen phenomenon. The two men were apoplectic, inconsolable, angry, not amused. While the President sat on hold with SELAND Executive Escalation, Dominic killed the prank. The President and Ashton stared at their decks, as the customary interface magically reappeared. Ashton would have struck him had the President not interfered. He lost a quarter of his salary for six months and the President seconded him to ISEC ANTI-INFIL, saying he could put his skills to better use there.

"Yuh cyaan' fool me!"

"Mi cyaan' lie, Star! Socials tun on!"

Ashton grabbed the napkin on his lap and snapped it against Dominic's knee and used a voice he knew Dominic would take seriously. They had long ago agreed to avoid street names. Dominic paused and let a few moments of silence pass in apology and Ashton did not drag these things out, as boys just stopped hearing. Ashton picked up a media display and traced into the news-feeds. The restoration of

114

the social media feeds could be big news if true, since restriction of such feeds remained a key element of the recent imposition of martial law. Surprised he had not heard about the decision earlier, he read the feeds, nursing a wounded ego that he had not been consulted. Though he soon realized why -- the reconnection had not occurred through any action by the government. In fact, the government had just begun its scramble to figure out how it happened at all.

Media feeds flooded with reports of crowds gathering in city centers, flashmobs at government facilities, rioting and looting. The GOVNET page came through again, this time at a higher level of emergency. As they stared at unfolding events on screen, they heard the President's security men shouting at the front door of the suite. Dominic grabbed his suit and ran for the bathroom. Ashton shut down the media portal and readied himself for his President, *ex parte*.

The President's face exuded anger hatred and bitterness. He scanned the room and stared Ashton down until Ashton could no longer stand up to the withering eyes. "Why did you shut it down? Something frighten you Minister? So this is where Dominic is hiding. I have been looking for him. Have you seen what is going on?

"Yes, Mr. President."

"If I remember correctly, you suggested Toole for the job..."

"Yes, I did make the suggestion."

"Do you regret the suggestion?"

"No, but Winston might."

Both men laughed at Ashton's last remark as Dominic emerged from the bathroom, dressed in the same rumpled Armani suit.

In a rare moment of lightheartedness the President looked at Dominic and slowly shook his head. *"Yuh muddah neva tell yuh, yuh fi tek yuh clothes off b'fore you liedun' pon'bed?"*

Dominic's face and posture switched from relaxed and friendly, to glassy-eyed, cold, stiff, angrier than Ashton had seen in years. *"Nossuh, she neva' tell me 'dat, suh."*

The President paused and realizing his muddying of the waters, said "I'm sorry, Dominic. I meant no harm."

Dominic's shoulders relaxed slightly and he nodded, but did not look up as he often did when ready for a fight. "You will be late for the meeting, sir," Dominic said, not quite looking at the President.

Somehow, the folders dossiers pens and half-filled glasses of ice water accumulated on the table. A heavy, dark mood saturated the room and Ashton noticed that Toole, the new Minister for Internal Security, had begun to sweat. The mood would only get worse with the usual players gathered around the table, like centurions at a Roman Circus, to witness a foregone bloodbath. This time, Dominic sat angled towards the corner of the room where Ms. Castenada sat. "The most recent activity is the result of some fairly sophisticated anti-censorship software," Ms. Casteñada volunteered. This kind of information would have taken Santo's government days if not weeks to determine.

Toole countered when he should not have. "How is it that you know so quickly?"

"Our A-INFIL folks have been reviewing the logs. They report trace-tag inconsistent with our firmware," her voice soft, syrupy, polite to a fault.

"I'm listening Ms. Casteñada," the President said, putting Toole in his place.

"We have been following the development of anti-censorship tools for some time. This affords us an opportunity to learn…"

"I will not have my island be a classroom for your combat gamers! This is YOUR problem."

"We have solved the kill switch issue. The island is now invisible to your dreaded social networks."

"Thank you Ms. Casteñada. In the future, please do not patronize me."

Now the circus began with a silent crucifying gaze from the President in the direction of the Internal Security Minister. "So, Toole…what do you have to say about all this?"

Toole cleared his throat hesitantly.

He should not have done that, Ashton thought.

"The attack trumped our capabilities sir. We had no way to foresee this strategy."

Brave but foolish, Toole all but said his country's tools were inferior to the task.

Now the President broke out in sweat. "I am surrounded by idiots! Dominic, please join us at the table."

Dominic approached the group at the table. He remained standing behind the President. "Yes Mr. President?"

"Tell me what I should do, Dominic."

Ashton and Ms. Casteñada stood up, horrified looks on their faces. "This is highly irregular, sir," Ms. Casteñada said.

Ashton nodded. "He has no experience!"

"Sit down! Both of you! Do not tell me what to do in my own Cabinet!" the President thundered, staring at Ashton until he fell back into his chair. Ms. Casteñada remained standing a moment longer and then she too sat down. "You are right. It is irregular, but I mean to prove a point. Speak freely, Dominic answer the question. You have nothing to fear from me or anyone in the room."

Dominic straightened to full formal attention, filling out the wrinkled suit. "Follow the INFIL trace-tag, see where it leads."

"That is all?" the President queried.

"Yes, Mr. President."

"You do not wish to fire someone, one of these fools?"

"No Mr. President, I would not do that."

"Thank you Dominic. You are excused with my gratitude." He watched Dominic exit the room and when the door shut behind him he turned to the group, "Such simple advice, eh?" Facing Toole, the President continued "I have decided, on Dominic's advice, not to ask for your resignation," his voice dripping with irony, "But for god's sake, don't ask him for a date!" He chuckled at his own joke and his staff laughed with him, except for the Health Minister.

Wild ideas and wilder strategizing consumed the rest of the meeting. Ms. Casteñada continued in her cooperative vein, but solutions would have to be local. A-INFIL technology had grown by leaps and bounds but it remained an art. All recognized the battle would not be won with technology alone. Something continued amiss and amok, and so far they pursued only a dangerous strategy of abiding. Protected in their secure cocoon, they could afford to think philosophically. One person in the room however, knew the tendency to think strategically rather than operationally would be their undoing. He also needed to get Dominic's deck away from him and out of the hotel. He needed to do this within minutes if not seconds.

Ashton excused himself and left the conference room. He walked towards the restrooms at the other end of the hall, subtly inviting a security man to walk with him. On the premises of a private investigation, Ashton gave his instructions. The security man nodded and broke off in another direction as Ashton entered the restroom. Sure the clothes he wore had soaked through with nervous sweat, he checked himself in the mirror. He noted his nervousness had not yet shown. He laughed in a physical release of tension and recalled the jingle about paranoia. He could not be accused of being paranoid when people really were following him. The A-INFIL trace-tag would yield nothing. Still, the President danced ever closer to abyss -- coincidence or something else? He retraced his steps, his reconnaissance, his framing, agreements, promises, what habits and personality revealed and found no weak spot. He had not negotiated nor capitulated.

INTERNCONTINENTAL HOTEL – CAPITAL – TODAY

SELAND: Selective Electronic Link Array Network Delivery:

SELAND was the foundation of the ubiquitous network, the successor of the World Wide Web of decades ago. In prior architectures the network required physical structures – plastic or metallic boxes, cables, wires, power supplies, modems and routers. One 'connected' to a network -- to tune in, to gather information, to do the things one's life required. That connection became commercialized and capitalized to pay for the expansion of a necessarily limited network. With SELAND, the network became "aerosolized" as one pundit put it. The data still required physical structures but the network existed 'everywhere'. The individual, once tagged, became the universal resource locator, tracing their way through the desired data banks. Thus trace-tag evolved as the new forensic treasure trove in an architecture where anonymity was anomaly. Everyone called it and the ocean-based structures that supported it, SELAND. From any single point on the open ocean, the unaided eye did not see single SELAND tower. From the air, they appeared as massive black and yellow tower-buoys. Permanently paired to a geosynchronous communications satellite, they formed a grid around the globe powering governments, commerce, communication, conspiracies and small, quiet but lethal revolutions.

Though SELAND quickly proved itself different, better and new, old problems remained stubbornly intransigent. Commerce under the SELAND platform filled state coffers and people had both money and time. Still, when the franchise produced no consensus, negotiation and quid pro quo broke down, failing to produce a path through policy obstacles, even if budget and funding were not fundamental issues. Paralyzed by ideological extremism and institutional name-calling, governments burrowed deeper into society, parasitic and selfish. People opposed it with waves of nonsensical violence. As revolutions large and small foundered for the want of a coherent list of demands, chaos and violence cowed the people without beating or co-opting them. Riots replaced the old Roman Circus and the shock troops of law and order found ever more creative ways to inflict pain without death, to do damage without fists clubs and feet. SELAND helped. Civil Offense drones did the rest.

Each SELAND platform measured approximately forty-five meters across. From the tip of the tower to the bottom of the platform measured one hundred thirty-five meters, however only forty meters of platform could be seen above the waterline. Shaped like a circular dinghy, the visible platform consisted of three concentric layers of re-cycled tire rubber. A carbon-fiber mesh and a new bullet/explosion-proof material covered the outer layer, each layer inflated to varying pressures to maintain buoyancy. The tower consisted of a single anodized aluminum cone twenty meters wide at the base, tapering to just over six millimeters at the tip. Below the visible platform, the structure descended underwater to a depth of twenty-five meters. The underwater portion took on the shape of a massive propeller providing critical stability for the platform in open-ocean. A small nuclear reactor provided power to both the platform itself and its contingent of six unmanned Offense Drones.

Beneath the platform, torpedo-drilled into the ocean floor, a SELAND beacon kept the platform squarely in place above it via a GIS/GPS application. The geosynchronous paired satellite provided visual infrared and laser-guided imaging of the platform at all times – both above and below the waterline. The Caribbean tower had long been thought the most vulnerable because the ocean floor underneath that particular SELAND beacon could be easily accessed by deep-water submarine craft. Were the beacon to be destroyed or made inoperable, the platform would exceed its GIS/GPS coordinates, breaking the satellite link. The inoperability of one platform did not a disaster make but it would de-certify all of the operating NETCERTS for that tower's geographical jurisdiction. Havoc, confusion, violence, and chaos would quickly ensue. Commerce would halt because COMNET could not validate commercial identities. Communications would slow to a trickle as packet sniffers and identity daemons worked over time to route data packets either into A-INFIL quarantine or around what amounted to a SELAND arterial bleed. Offense Drones would deploy with weapons armed and a cadre of manned attack helos would arrive at the marine site within fifteen minutes. Up to this point it had all been contingency planning. SELAND had been operational for six years and with the exception of the usual startup and growth pains, its early life had been secure, stable and uneventful.

On Tuesday, mid morning, the Caribbean SELAND tower went AWOL and SELAND Corporation, along with its constituent governments, learned how well the Strategic Continuity consultants had done their job. Everything occurred just as they predicted. Very important people became upset and acted threateningly towards any one around them less important. Very important people released statements and held press conferences. The event triggered a rolling 24-hour period of martial law, resulting in a quadrupling of the civil offense drone population. SELAND had twenty-four hours to resolve the problem and restore the network to steady state. It was well known in the most elite of government circles, which included almost all the very important people and some of the not so important people, that the attacks would not bring commerce to a halt or overly frustrate an indifferent people with the arbitrary imposition of martial law on an irregular basis. It would not cause riots on any mass scale (although riots did occur); it would not on its own cause mayhem, confusion and violence among the population on any wide scale (although mayhem, confusion and violence did occur). Once dislodged, notwithstanding it returned to tether a mere eight hours later, the episode incurred unplanned costs of \$187 billion; payable by the treaty signatories via a pre-determined but mandatory formula. The point was well made.

On mornings like this he thought he could lie as he was forever. Hanna preferred to see him at his apartment but he convinced the right people on the President's security team to have her vetted and allowed into the hotel. It had been her birthday the day before but as usual with Hanna, he felt he had received a gift. He enjoyed watching her, especially when she slept. The abandonment of sleep intrigued him. Her hair streaked her face and the pillow beneath her. He heard her slow breathing just on the verge of a snore. He cupped her form with his body and she smiled with her eyes closed. He had always been the nomad, and she, his amber, curly-haired oasis. When they were young, she had been taller and darker in skin color, but she reminded him of an angel in a long skirt and a brightly colored *gele*. Seeing her after a time apart calmed the butterflies in his stomach and gave him a feeling of being home. People tended to underestimate her soft amber eyes and button nose on a girl's face. Of course, growing up had the usual effects and she became the woman she was almost over night, in Dominic's mind, since he saw her less often as they got older. If Olivia was a dancer, Hanna was a deep pool. Not effusive, she neither laughed nor loved quickly or easily, but what began as a childhood alliance blossomed with their bodies.

He tried to get off the bed without disturbing her but failed. She opened her eyes smiled and reached her hand out to him and they dove back underneath the sheet to savor the morning and each other one more time, interrupted by Nierika, Hanna's two-year old Belgian Malinois, when she put her nose under the sheets and found Hanna's toes.

Hanna squealed in surprise and Dominic threw a pillow at the dog. So the morning began, but being a Tuesday morning, did not end on the same note. For one thing, Ashton discovered his keycard no longer opened Dominic's suite entrance. Dominic forced himself to ignore the GOVNET emergency page for just a minute. They heard someone trying to use a key card in the suite entrance and Ashton yelling as if his hair had caught on fire. Dominic jumped off the bed, nearly tumbling onto an excited Nierika, wrapped himself in the sheet and paused at the door to give Hanna time to escape into the bathroom.

Ashton said nothing as he strode to the media portal and waited for the displays to resolve. All four screens showed SELAND shock troops hovering in black helos over the Caribbean tower, faces covered by mirrored helmets, bristling with weaponry and A-INFIL gear. They remained an impressive sight from a safe distance. Ticker tapes at the bottom of the displays announced another 24 hours of martial law, although break/fix estimates quickly fell below deadline. Ashton stood in the middle of the room staring at the media feeds, mouth agape. Dominic watched and shook his head in disbelief at this new escalation. Even if they figured out how such a stunt had been accomplished, it implied an unacceptable vulnerability that would elicit a desperate and over-stated response.

"Where's my deck?" Dominic asked after a few minutes.

"You're getting a new one, a real one. 'His' orders."

"Why'd you take mine?" Dominic shuffled and shifted to dress under the sheet that covered him.

"It was problematic, unstable." Ashton continued to stare at the displays but he shifted his weight as if uncomfortable.

"Really."

Ashton ignored him.

"Baba lost his cool in the car coming back from the harbor." Fully dressed, Dominic dropped the sheet on the bed and sat down on the couch, watching Ashton as closely as he dared.

"Did not I tell you? Did you say what I told you to say?" Ashton shot back, without taking his eyes off the display.

Dominic's body froze in place, like a seizure. He knew of it but not what it was; he did not have a name for it. Spawned during the time he lived in Ashton's house, he learned to feed and water it, growing it to unimaginable size, infinitely curled in and around itself; bounded only by his physical body. If he let it, it raged just below the skin, filling his body until he thought he might be overrun with it. Content to remain quiet when he was very young, it reared its medusa's head more frequently, provoked by less each time. Like an electric shock, it subsumed his entire being without remedy, without resolution. He learned to control 'the monster', but only barely. Ashton had no idea, but it was he who woke 'the monster' - a word, a tone, a phrase, a facial expression, and sometimes even his absence. Dominic knew the remedy, but it would require patience. Until then, he would have to mitigate rather than satiate. He would have to sit instead of stand.

"Yes," Dominic replied to Ashton's question. Except he did not say what Ashton told him to say. Ashton told him not to take sides, to give the President reason to wonder. Dominic had done the opposite and only now, in Ashton's presence, began to worry about it. Nierika sat outside the bathroom door whining. Ashton stared glumly at the displays and Dominic wondered what would become of them and whether they would survive themselves.

RINCON DU NORD – UPCOUNTRY - THIRTEEN YEARS AGO

On Old Hope Road, the wide, wide road to bedlam where the price of life ran to the lowest common denominator, the Blue Sect wrote the rules. In practice, the northern half of the island belonged to the Blue Sect or more properly to the one man who fancied himself after the old barons of baroque period but who refused colonial titles. He called himself 'Semedi' but the island called him 'Guede Baron Semedi', for the Blue Sect and Guede Baron Semedi could not be separated – one had become the other. Guede Baron Semedi owned all the cemeteries as well the land beneath Market. Market participants gladly surrendered half their profits to him for the privilege of selling at Market. The wealthiest man on Old Hope Road by far, some said he also held the record as the fattest man in the whole place. Some said he could shape-shift but Old Hope Road swam in superstitious mythology. Without question the best-dressed pariah of Old Hope Road, he traveled freely and frequently, leaving Old Hope Road for Capital and sometimes all the way to a place known to Old Hope Road only as North -- where they made money of a single color. Guede Baron Semedi dressed always in garb of the deepest blue, and while perhaps at one time the color retained some symbolism or meaning, just as the million and their children forgot that where the standpipe stood, a river used to run, so The Blue Sect forgot the reason for the color of their garments.

Women flocked to him like planets to a star. No one dared put flesh on such rumors as such things took on a life of their own and Old Hope Road gladly saturated itself with unspoken, widely held but un-proven knowledge. Parents used this knowledge to threaten their children into doing domestic things like carrying water or going to sleep — things children hated to do most. Children formed not a small part of his entourage. They made the most cacophony of all though completely without meaning. They had no bells or horns but just their mouths tongues and lungs, made strong by childhood beatings. They were not angry or troublesome, but even Guede Baron Semedi could not change the inherent nature of children. A band of angry looking men, all gone to fat in the same fashion as Guede Baron Semedi formed the main part of his entourage. On men who needed another man to follow he bestowed tools, paper money in sparing amounts, rum in overly generous amounts, cheaply made sets of dice, women, girls and sometimes boys. On women he bestowed gifts of gaudy jewelry, paper money, rum and a space in the market at half the rent. On children he bestowed gifts of an ironic kind of protection – if they did as he bid and went where he told them to go, he kept them from catastrophic harm.

Known to travel mainly at night and having come across him on one of the ten thousand paths, common wisdom had it that one should fall to the ground covering one's head (and especially the eyes) until he passed. One was not to inquire into Guede Baron Semedi's business. He attracted dramatists, voyeurs and fanatics and women of a certain kind of rough-hewn beauty. Some rumored Jemma to have been his greatest trophy and tragedy. Few spoke directly to him and of those who had, none dared hint at the nature of his relationship with Jemma, though they said she took unfathomable liberties with him and that there had been a child between them. There the whispering stopped and the humming of some old spiritual for which everyone had forgotten the words began.

Every morning the million's children made their bodies shiny with cake soap in the full light of morning. They bent their bodies in the necessary ways to reach the stream of water that flowed from the single standpipe. Small, shiny hands passed over black brown dark light bleached skin. Water and soap carried dirt tears sweat into the rocky topsoil that washed into the sea with the rains. In this way, the sea (said the millions when they thought their children were asleep) filled with other people's sins and troublesome deeds. As the morning wore on, the ground itself gathered heat and disappearing shadows devoured what little shade could be found the way a snake swallowed a boar. A few days ago, a fight broke out at the standpipe between three tall thick angry tattooed well-muscled thick-shirted canine-tooth-capped posse-boys, overturning water containers and precious dominoes. It all flew into the roiling dust. The fight went on for some time and grudges kept and bloodshed, long after the dust near the standpipe returned to its place…knife-in-stomach, machete-to-back-of-neck rum bokkle bomb thrown without care. Down the road a mother woke to find that someone had slit her son's throat. One of the thick-shirted canine-tooth-capped well-muscled posse-boys who rumbled at the standpipe did not survive the darkness. The dirt floor to their clapboard house had much clay so the blood sat on top and did not dissipate. She knew her son had not grown up to be a good boy, yet still she wanted to help or to find, but also to be helped and to be found. So she remained motionless in her clapboard house, neither helped nor helpful, not found, nor the finder of grief, alone with the hot blood of her son edging around her bare dusty feet.

Guede Baron Semedi found her in her clapboard house. Leaving his motorcade at the edge of the garrison community, he picked his way through the rubble, garbage, excrement, mangy dogs, pigs and goats, past rough looking men who refused to look at him, past worn women in worn doorways and children who wore distended bellies like medals of war. People made a point of looking away as he passed. No one pressed a gun barrel against his rib cage or a machete to his Adams apple, despite his clean pressed clothes, a gold watch and ring. He found the grieving mother on his own and brought with him two local men to help clean the dirt floor. He held her hand in silence, staring out the door less doorway through mirrored aviator sunglasses. He offered the mother white rum from a silver flask, which she refused. He offered her a cigarette from a silver cigarette case, which she accepted. Such visits had become a ritual. He put small pile of money on the table, for which she smiled and nodded, but did not touch or take. She rummaged around for a while and found a new, white candle and a clean white plate. Tears streaming down her face, she lit the candle, holding the match to the bottom of it in order to secure the candle to the plate. She placed the lit candle just inside the door, behind the door, had one still been hanging. He cursed a world that spent children so carelessly.

He remembered the *mingi* child Jemma had given to him and how much it pained him to surrender it to the nuns at the Sisters of Mercy orphanage. Because he refused to tell them the name he had given the child, the nuns in their infinite wisdom named him, in part after the founder of their Dominican order, and in part after the name of their own order. He watched from a distance. He donated infant formula, money for a teacher's salary and food and clothes for the children. Baskets of ripe mangoes, heavy bags of frozen *chickenback* and dumpling flour arrived anonymously at the doorstep of the orphanage. At year-end he sent jugs of sweet *sorrell* (without the rum) and goat head so the nuns could make soup. The boy grew like an avocado tree - a good-looking but hardscrabble kid whose only piece of good luck in the mad world he had been born into would most likely be his light complexion.

INTERCONTINENTAL HOTEL – CAPITAL – TODAY

Dominic saw and felt fear in the room and though the air conditioner worked double time as usual, Dominic saw only one dry forehead. The pressure on the department heads became more unbearable with each passing minute. Dominic saw no relief in sight. Ms. Casteñada alone sat in a perfectly untroubled state. No one took different seats or ruffled the assumed order of the table. Dominic made a point of catching Ms. Casteñada's eye and nodding. He had not expected it but she returned the greeting. The papers and dossiers and folders and expensive pens had all been left behind. The government could ill afford to continue its political maneuvering and posturing, but found itself unable to do otherwise. Few in the room knew how to do anything else. He wondered and hoped the President knew a little bit more.

President Joseph Santo strode into the room on the heels of his announcement and took his place at the head of the table but did not sit down. Dominic followed the President's lead and remained standing. The President looked coolly around the room, meeting the gaze of each person, not settling on any of them before he spoke. When he did speak everyone in the room understood just how little their maneuvering and posturing paid off.

"I am dissolving this Cabinet. You will keep your departments, offices, residences and salary but I refuse to waste any more time than I already have." He worked up to such a crescendo and volume by his last word that Ms. Casteñada winced.

A stunned silence followed, though the Finance Minister made a valorous attempt to argue: "Excellency, but this is unconstitutional!"

"Thank you for your resignation. Good bye, sir!"

Ashton shifted his weight as if preparing to speak, but seeing the President ready for fisticuffs, only shifted his weight.

Dominic sneezed, making everybody jump.

"You are all dismissed, save Ashton and Ms. Casteñada. You may go home to your families, I'm sure they have missed you. I…I will not miss you."

It took every shred of self-control Dominic possessed to conceal his amusement as the line of disgraced ministers filed out of the room, faces aghast. The door slammed on the last one and a brief moment of silence passed before both the President and Ashton burst into unrestrained laughter. Ms. Casteñada observed them with her usual bemused expression and Dominic had a hard time keeping a straight face. Their eyes met but she held one finger to pursed lips, counseling restraint. It took minutes before the laughter came under control and either could speak.

"You surprised me," Ms. Casteñada said.

"I ran out of options."

"How will you proceed?" Ms. Casteñada queried.

"As you suggested…" the President said, the rest of his sentence cut off by another bout of laughter.

Ms. Casteñada stood up. "How will you respond to recent events?"

Ashton exhaled loudly. "Let me say, the President and I disagree on the approach. I suggested mitigation but the President found that in wanting."

"It feels weak Ashton. You may be right but it feels weak. That was my objection but we should talk about it. Tell me how would 'mitigation' work?"

"Mitigation until we understand what is at risk and what we can give up; until we better understand those who oppose us. Mitigation buys us time…to recover, to repair, to stop reacting."

"That is a dangerous strategy Ashton," Ms. Casteñada added. "It is equivalent to appeasement."

"The truth, if I may be so foolish, is that we have no choice. There is no ideal answer thus I see no option but to wait until our understanding increases."

"Maybe it's an organic, spontaneous, conflagration that must run its course," President Santo countered.

"Then mitigation is still the wisest course, otherwise we risk burdening the people."

Dominic regretted it as soon as he said it, but he could restrain himself no longer. *"Peeple do dem 'ting, y'kno!"* He bowed his head in embarrassment for the outburst but not shame for his Patois in the hallowed halls of government. He lifted his head again and made a point to lock eyes with Ashton then with the President. Ms. Casteñada remained aloof.

Ashton nodded. "But which people? All of them?"

The President nodded as well. "But we know those who have opposed us before. Why not call on them? Why not ask them?"

"You wish to let them into your inner circle? To show weakness, to truck with common criminals?"

"The man in blue, what's his name?"

"Science keep us! Baron Semedi? You aren't serious?"

"Why not? More than half our people believe what he says?"

"Will he talk to you?" Ms. Casteñada asked looking up from her reports for the first time.

"We have spoken before through back channels." The President's answer surprised everyone.

"That is NOT what I had in mind," Ashton said, standing to make his point.

The President stared icily at Ashton and said "I have made up my mind. I need time to think. You are dismissed."

In the now empty room, the President turned to Dominic and motioned him to sit at the conference table. "You have spoken with this man before, do you remember?" he said when Dominic sat down.

Dominic nodded.

"I don't know why but he will talk to you. That is the card in our hand. Can you play it?"

Dominic nodded. This would get him out of the hotel, in the fresh air and hot sun. He could wear street clothes, eat street

133

food and walk with normal people, free from the usual entourage.

"Try your best again." The President put his hand on Dominic's shoulder. "Don't get cocky and don't say anything more than you need to."

Dominic nodded again and kept still even though the man's hand on his shoulder made him want to pull away.

"Meet me at 9 pm at the bar on the top floor. We'll find somewhere private to talk and I will give you my question for the Man in Blue."

No one knew how the bar on the top floor of the Intercontinental Hotel got its name. In either a fit sarcasm or irony, the sign on the wall read 'The View'. Surrounded by walls of glass on three sides, very little pleased the eye outside. To the north lay the windblown airport, 'international' in name only. To the east lay the low foothills pocked by squatter settlements, burned out buildings and garrison communities. To the south lay only endless fields of sugarcane that turned into a sea of pitch black at night. Besides, no one sat near the window any more – too dangerous. A safe distance away from the windows, the hotel set up a plush but uncomfortable array of couches, loveseats, tables and chairs. The bar had a minimum drink limit and they did not take cash – very few legitimate vendors did.

Dominic arrived early and ordered orange juice. They left him to think about the conversation that would occur in a few minutes and to think back to the last time Santo asked to talk to Baron Semedi. But he couldn't start there, he needed to review more recent events: the break with Ashton, his siding with Santo and the chaos of the last two weeks. Only now it began to bother him that no good reason emerged to explain his actions. Santo turned him so easily and for so little, perhaps nothing. He thought about his deck, Ashton's private security sweep and the fact that he had been without a deck for more than twenty-four hours -- such things were unheard of. He thought about the trace-tag he uncovered and documented, grateful for the ::Q:: level SELAND Sequester the President had assigned him. The trace for his compression algorithm would be discoverable but aside from limited metadata, the file he created could not be derived. As these thoughts coursed through his mind and body, he knew what he would ask Santo for in exchange for his journey to Baron Semedi.

Santo surprised him by entering the bar without the usual heraldry, taking the seat across from Dominic before he had come out of his reverie.

"Daydreaming?" Santo asked as he settled into a high-back chair. His security team took up positions at the entrance to the bar and in a chair a discreet distance away.

"Nossuh! I didn't see you." Protocol called for Dominic to stand when the President entered a room.

"At ease. Tonight we are two men in a bar, yes?"

Dominic had seen this relaxed cheerful side of Santo only once or twice in three years. Dominic nodded but did not smile. He thought he had missed something crucial.

"You don't mind doing this thing for me, captain?" Santo called him "captain" in informal moments and although his actual rank in the defense force, Santo rarely used it in that fashion.

"I need something from you, though." As soon as the words were loose he knew he should have found better ways to say it.

"So you say," Santo mused, settling back in his chair as if to brace him self to receive unsettling news.

"I need my deck back."

Santo pursed his lips and inhaled deeply. "That could be difficult. Ashton has been so…how should I say it…bitchy … lately."

Dominic said nothing.

"And you won't settle for a new one? It has to be that specific deck?"

Dominic nodded, knowing this would be the tipping point.

"Why? What's so special about that deck?"

"That's what I was trying to get to when Ashton took it."

"How is it every time we talk, you worry me?" The President asked only somewhat rhetorically, staring him down.

"I'm sorry sir."

"What are you saying to me?" Santo hissed in a whisper.

"Mi seh! Sump'n special 'bout dat ting y'kno!"

"Uno see mi cross!"

"I won't know for sure unless I get it back."

"If it's not in your room when you get back, there was a problem."

Dominic nodded and shrugged his shoulders at the same time. He could not have hoped for more under the circumstances. "What do I tell Baron Semedi?"

Turning to the crisis at hand Santo resettled himself in his seat, took the first drink from his glass and took a deep breath. "You ask him this, captain. I want to know who I have forgotten. Say it just like that, you hear? 'Baba Santo wants to know who he has forgotten'."

About to make a counterpoint, Dominic thought better of it. "When?"

"In the morning, after 10. I'll make sure Ashton is busy." Before he finished his sentence, Santo stood up, nodded to his security escort, placed his clenched fist softly on Dominic's shoulder for a brief second, and then disappeared into the entrance hall, his security people following behind him.

PERISTIL OF GUEDE BARON SEMEDI – TEN YEARS AGO

A single massive stone, rising to the height of a man's chest, on a rectangular platform, is the focal point for the gathering. It is called pạ. *Around it are many an odd thing: rattles, flags, jewelry, a worn djembe drum, a bell, an assortment of coins, candles of white, red, black wax, and glasses full to overflowing with fresh, clean water. Around the pạ are large porcelain jars painted with various designs and hand-drawn images. In the middle of the* pạ *stone itself is a hollow interior, large enough to harbor a snake. On this night, though the* pạ *was vacant, it was no less important for being so.*

The pós mitain *defined the absolute center of the room and the pạ stone sat at a height of 33 degrees relative to the intersection of the* pós mitain *and the ground into which it was driven. From the cross beams that comprise the* om'fa *ceiling hung a small plastic ship, the significance of the ship forgotten but nevertheless it remained.*

The pạ *stone lived in the* om'fa, *a covered, circular place, circumnavigating a tall central post, the* pós mitain. *The top of the* pós mitain *defined the center of the sky, and the bottom of it the center of hell. From the ground where the* pós mitain *originated, to the top of the* om'fa *where the* pós mitain *terminated, two figures intertwined -- either humans or snakes. A rendering of* Pwezidan *and a flag of solid blue hung in repose above the* pạ *stone.*

This place was known as peristil.

<<Bann Madigra St. Jacques – Se Ayizan Mwen Mande; St. Jacques Bann Vodou Song>>

On the night of the little moon, Pierre told Dominic, now taller, less diminutive, still growing into the frame of his body, he would dance in the *peristil*. Dominic stood in a line of people dressed in white just as he was, waiting to enter the *peristil*. He began the line of others his age that would dance with him. The girl in front would enter first, spinning in one direction and then the other, before placing a candle on the ground and lighting it. An older woman followed, repeating the motion, carrying a clay jar and creating a *veve* on the ground with cornmeal. She offered water to the cardinal points of the compass, to the *pos mitain*, each of the drums and the entrance through which the dancers would enter. He followed the line of initiates into the temple and around the *pos mitain* counter-clockwise, following the woman's actions. Each dancer made water offerings to the cardinal points, the drums, the entrance to the *peristil* and finally the *pos mitain*. When they had done this, they performed the *bo te*, prostrating themselves to kiss the ground of the *peristil*. A man he did not know stood up and recited a short verse in a language he had never heard before but which sounded beautiful all the same.

Ahi, manman, hen!
Tambour moin rele
Jou-m allonge....Ahi!
Ahi! Manman

The *peristil* filled with flags, tables with white tablecloths piled with rice, salt, pitchers of water, white candles, ornate flags, model ships and old black and white pictures of people he had never seen before. All the treasures of the *peristil* sat on tables surrounding the *pos mitain* – bowls of rice, pitchers of water, baskets of fruit, bottles of liquor and perfumes in various stages of fullness. Those who came to watch stood in the outer circle, fanning their faces furiously in the heat. Another entered, carrying a large fighting saber and the most beautiful flag he had ever seen. He wanted to be that man carrying the saber, touching the flags with its tip, prostrating himself before the big woman with the *asson* and bell in her hands and presenting her with the saber.

He could hardly contain himself as the drums began their relentless, driving song. He felt each beat inside his body, like a sea of clocks striking the hours at different times; first, the drum of the thunderbolt, hot and dangerous, followed by the drum of *Guinea*, receiving the lightning bolt. The sound of the drums assaulted him and he fell in love with the different syncopations, woven into a singular overwhelming rhythm. The woman's voice rose over all and the drums carried it out into the air and to the stars. Not soon enough, the time to dance arrived, bodies and minds turned inward, attracting something that could not be seen. The drums continued speaking into the night through arms, eyes, faces and feet of the dancers, rhythm and counter rhythm rhyming. Dancers poured water and spirits on the ground; they lit candles and drew *veve's* with cornmeal on the ground. Women waved their arms, eyes wide open, tears streaming down their faces, smiling. Men carrying flags, bottles of liquor and baskets of fruit passed him, touching his forehead with their hands. He felt the rhythm in his chest and something welling up inside: something different, foreign and unknown, a creeping power welling up from his belly, radiating outwards. He felt a fire inside and it did not burn.

All these things he would forget by morning, the memories driven into the dirt floor of the *peristil* by his dancing feet.

CHAPTER V

THE PERISTIL OF GUEDE BARON SEMEDI – UP COUNTRY - TODAY

Not the *peristil* -- though Dominic did not expect to be received in the *peristil* -- on appearances, this appeared to be a receiving room, like a library lounge. Dusty bookshelves paired with clean carpets and wood floors; old books with fresh flowers in the many vases spread around the room. The room smelled smoky like incense, but he saw no incense burning. Cracked windows opened to the sun, framing a ceiling fan, turning lazily as if it preferred to remain still. Inside the room, Dominic felt a pleasant breeze, yet he heard no telltale hum of an electric air conditioner. He saw no paraphernalia, nothing that would overtly call out this place for anything other than an average sitting room. Although he could not pinpoint a reason, the thought of entering a real *peristil* made him uncomfortable, as if about to break out in a cold sweat.

Baron Semedi strode into the room wearing dark slacks and a white button down shirt, hanging loosely over his generous frame. He did not wear shoes but he wore thick eyeglasses and had begun to go bald. No more than three people could brag of seeing him in such a state. Dominic stood quickly in respect but Baron Semedi shook his head and proffered the open seat to Dominic. He himself sat on a stool across from Dominic on the other side of the room. He did not smile but his face and manner seemed welcoming all the same. "You are less conspicuous this time."

Dominic nodded. The last time he had worn his uniform and Baron Semedi told him that if he showed himself again in that uniform that he would not live out the day.

"But you do not come for your self."

Dominic made a point to avoid eye contact when he spoke and keep his head bowed. "I do not."

"Pity…"

"I come on errand for someone else. I think you know him, Baba Santo."

"You come on a fool's errand!" Baron Semedi snapped his fingers as he spat out his words and stomped his foot on the floor.

"As you say…" Dominic knew not to argue.

"These happenings that puzzle your superiors have naught to do with me. Or perhaps I should say, I have naught to do with them. However, I agree to one question." Baron Semedi smiled as if the thought he could name terms amused him.

"I am ready."

"Speak, child!"

"Baba Santo want to know who he has forgot."

Blue Semedi put the palms of his hands together beneath his chin and gave Dominic a long look. "He has forgotten how things used to be done…when what needed to be done could not be done in plain sight, when what was important was hidden and what was in plain sight could be disregarded."

Dominic repeated Baron Semedi's words verbatim in order to commit them to memory.

"You have been here twice for others. Do not come back unless you come for yourself." With that cryptic sentence Baron Semedi left the room.

The trip back to Capital happened much the same as the journey out. Two men entered the room on Baron Semedi's heels and escorted Dominic through the house and out into a back alley where a car waited. They hooded their guest with a black hood and let him hit his head on the car door as they shoved him into the back seat. Dominic had not settled in the seat when the car jumped into the road like a jackrabbit and they were off to the bus station. This time, the two men did not sit next to him in the back seat. Dominic heard them chatting in a language or dialect he did not understand. He smelled bus exhaust before as they approached the bus station. One man removed the hood and pointed at the rear door as the car slowed. Dominic opened the door, thinking the car would stop, but the man in the passenger seat reached back, grabbed Dominic's shirt and yanked him out through the open car door. As soon as Dominic's feet hit the ground, the car jumped forward again, screaming away from the bus station. No one paid him a second glance.

Out in the open air, Dominic felt alive, vital, anonymous and ready for anything the world might throw at him. He had no good reason for feeling this way but he did not care. People ignored or pushed past as they rushed to their next destination. He felt the heat and the crush of people, swarming and pushing. He had no escort or entourage. For the first time in weeks, he felt the sun on his body. The hotel was so sterile, quiet and devoid of color and smell, as if the building itself muted language and emotion, changing the meaning of everything. He passed two Island Defense sergeants on patrol, locked eyes with them as they passed and gave a slight nod. They returned the greeting and kept walking. They would not believe him if he told them he had come from the waiting room of Baron Semedi. No one would.

Baron Semedi's last and closing words stuck in his brain, repeating over and over as if Dominic had some reason to call again. It made no sense and he chalked it up to the man's strangeness. Cash in hand, he bought a cold green coconut for its water, a meat patty, and a bus ticket back to Capital. He would ride back on the crowded public bus, five people to a bench meant to seat three. It would be a hot and uncomfortable five-hour ride. If it rained, they would close all the windows, turning the bus into a steam room. Dominic preferred this to the quiet government cars with their car phones, ceiling lights and wet bar. He would get yelled at when he got back to Capital for taking unnecessary risks, but he would pay that small price with ease. He asked the man next to him for a cigarette and savored the simple act of smoking while waiting for the bus to depart. So much he missed on a daily basis and yet the commission with the President gave him a certain pride he could not remember feeling previously.

It was not pride that led him and his two childhood friends, Worm and Scorn, to set off on their epic journey, stealing mangoes and cups of fish soup, sleeping on the beach after Mooma Jacobs died. It was fear. Not more than twelve, maybe younger, closer to ten, they thought they had embarked on the journey of a life time, but only three days had passed. An observant constable saw them running from a roadside shack — warm, unpaid for meat patties in grubby hands. Neither of his friend's parents was happy about the escapade. They placed the blame squarely on Dominic; and no, they would not take the *mingi* child, even for a single night. Dominic remembered sitting in a large empty room with the bright lights at the police station. He turned his back on his friend's parents when they began yelling at him. A police constable told them to stop but they ignored the advice. The same police constable used his heft to push the angry parents out of the police station and still they kept yelling. Another constable brought him blankets, food and more food. He spent his first night in jail after Mooma Jacobs died, alone in a cell built for twenty, the on duty constable visible from the locked cell. When they turned the lights off at the end of a long day, he asked them to turn them back on again.

Ashton's wife Stork died and Ashton's family imploded only three short years after Mooma Jacobs went to Guinée Dominic swore he would not spend another night in a police station. He waited for just the right moment to run. He did not stay for the christian funeral, although Stork always treated him gently. He hid behind crumbling sections of the beach retaining wall, and being older, knew how to put hunger behind him. He stayed out of city centers. He jogged in between walls of sugar cane and scraggly acacia trees. He ran all the way to Hanna's house in the country, collapsing on their verandah at 3.30 in the morning, feeling safer at the mercy of the black night than he had ever felt at Ashton's house. The sun woke him before it woke Hanna and her parents and he hid under the porch, unsure of how to present himself to the unsuspecting family sharing coffee-tea inside. The dust made him sneeze which led to his denouement. Hanna's mother kissed her teeth and insisted he take a bath. Hanna's father shook his head and laid out a hefty breakfast. Dominic ate for three hours. Only later would he realize the awkward position he put the family in. Neither he nor Hanna were children anymore. Hanna's parents could not conscience an unrelated male living in the same house. Of course, they did not tell him this while they watched him eat their food. Dominic saw it in their faces though.

He drank his first *cachaca* while Pierre was asleep. Mercilia, Pierre's sister, saw him opening the cabinet and cuffed him on the ear. She taught him their sign language but ignored him for the most part. He went to school, which made him feel dumb, until one day he discovered he could read the same silly books the little ones read. He waited until all the other kids left to read another book. He read lots of silly books about cats and pots and dogs and logs. He read them two and three times. He stopped feeling dumb. All the kids in his class were smarter than him, until they were not. When he answered a question no one else could, the teacher accused him of cheating. The teacher made him sit inside while the other kids played outside. He could not stop smiling, even while he watched the kids outside playing, infuriating the teacher. He had to stay after school by himself again. When Pierre came to find out why he had not come home, the teacher gave Pierre a full report. Pierre asked Dominic a question — not the same question but similar. Dominic answered. The teacher did not have time to apologize. Pierre let loose a barrage of more curse words than Dominic had heard in his life. No one accused of him of cheating again and Pierre made a friend, for life. Like a small child, Dominic attached himself to Pierre. He was in love.

His love for Pierre made the trip to North Carolina a wall he feared he could not climb. Sixteen by then, he made it through the long shuttle flight and the awkward, stilting introductions. He cried the first few nights when he would have killed to sit on the verandah with Pierre and watch the moon rise. He ironed his uniform every night. He went grocery shopping on Monday evenings. He went to church on Sundays. The Paxtons seemed nice enough but everything about them and their place felt strange. Their streets were clean and quiet. They drove on orderly streets in an orderly fashion, windows rolled up. They came and went from their houses, talking to their neighbors at most twice a year. Kevin, the Paxton's son proved a hard nut to crack. The friendships Dominic remembered had always been easy, almost assumed. Kevin kept his distance, although they became friends after a few months. Kevin's father liked to drink, his mother cried a lot and Kevin drew dark, foreboding sketches in pencil. He learned many things while he lived with the Paxtons. The most important were video games, texting and pornography.

INTERCONTINENTAL HOTEL – DIPLOMATIC SECTION – CAPITAL – TODAY

From the public bus station, two of Santo's men swooped in on him as he sauntered off the bus and walked him furtively to their car. They said nothing on the ride back to the hotel though Dominic knew no one at the hotel would be happy about his choice to cross the island on the island's unlucky public bus system. He would get yelled at, but he did not care. People had been yelling at him for most of his life and he easily ignored them. The people who talked softly threw him for a loop – like Pierre and Santo. The car moved quickly through the city by reason of its siren and flashing blue light. Dominic noticed an escort car keeping pace. Both Santo and Ashton waited for him at the entrance to the government suite.

Santo's face looked grim and Ashton shook his head in disbelief.

"You want to get yourself killed?" Ashton began the tirade.

"That was a foolish thing to do Dominic," the President spoke more softly than Ashton.

"I'm back now." He did not take this tone with Santo or Ashton often but he grew tired of their bitchiness.

"Promise me you won't do that again," Santo said, his voice scolding but soft. Like Pierre, Santo used his voice to get inside Dominic's head.

"I didn't go for myself," Dominic said, oddly reprising something Semedi said.

"OK. Let's finish this in the conference room," Ashton said and walked towards the rear of the suite. He followed

148

Ashton and the President followed him. For whatever reason Dominic noticed a smile on the President's face. Behind the closed doors of the conference room, Dominic told Santo and Ashton what Blue Semedi said. He told them about the waiting room – how it felt cool without an air conditioner.

He has forgotten how things used to be done...when what needed to be done could not be done in plain sight when what was important was hidden and what was in plain sight could be disregarded.

"What the hell does that mean?" Ashton blurted out, striking the table with the palm of his hand.

"I know what it means," Santo said quietly.

Both Dominic and Ashton turned towards the President, waiting for him to reveal what he knew.

An odor made them wrinkle their noses. Unmistakable and familiar: dog shit. The two men looked at Dominic who dutifully checked his shoes. They were clean. The stink crept into their nasal passages forcing them to cover their noses with their hands. Another putrid layer made itself known, the nauseating odor of rotting meat assaulting them and making them retch. Knowing more than most about the latest in stink bomb tech, running was the only rational solution. They jogged from the conference room into the reception area, only to find the rest of the national government milling around, holding their noses like lemmings trying to decide which way to stampede. Another wave of nauseating odor assaulted them, so thick it felt like the odor causing material had settled on their skin. This new wave smelled like old stale urine. The disgusting odors continued coming in waves, each stronger than the wave before it. Retching proved contagious and at least a dozen people vomited on the hotel carpet. Oddly, this was the breaking point. Finally, the group made for the stairwell, but they carried some of the odor with them on their bodies and the lack of air conditioning only exacerbated the odor. Both Santo and Ashton would have sworn violent revenge on the perpetrators of this malodorous disturbance, but they dared not remove their hands from their noses, thus the threat remained unspoken. Only time would tell whether they would remember this sad event the next time they ordered the use of stink bombs for the simple purpose of crowd control.

The common citizen on the street must have found it amusing to see what amounted to the entire national government stampeding through the front doors of the hotel, as if running for their lives. Common citizens pointed, gawked and laughed. Within minutes, military and police squadrons arrived with a contingent of crowd control drones. Together, they formed a blockade on one side of the street and began parsing individuals from the uncontrolled group on one side of the blockade to the other. They isolated regular hotel customers who were none too pleased from the contingent of government employees requiring their protection. Ms. Casteñada could not seem to convince the police lieutenant her badge was authentic, releasing her into the care of President Santo only on a direct order from Ashton. Still the junior member of the President's staff, it fell to Dominic to don a breathing apparatus and join a military squad who entered the building to retrieve sensitive items left behind in the stampede. He barely extracted himself out of the apparatus when he, Ashton, Santo and Ms. Casteñada were hurried into a waiting military vehicle and escorted away from the hotel. Santo made the decision in the car to return the government to its rightful place – the Presidential Palace. The upper echelons of both the defense force and ISEC objected, to no avail. Santo listened patiently to their well thought out objections. He extracted a promise from his winging ISEC people: he wanted to keep the radiator from a 1974 Ford Maverick as a collector's item.

Dominic could not have been happier. He could go back to moving about the city without an escort or asking permission. He could open the apartment window; see the sun unfiltered through bulletproof glass -- call, text, maybe see Hanna. Against the advice of their security people, they opened the car windows to flush their noses of the horrific smell. Dominic could not wait to get out of his clothes, as the smell seemed permanently lodged on his clothes, skin and nostrils. Much sniffing and snuffling in the car provided no relief.

"Our enemy is a secret society…a capable one at that," Santo said, as they screamed through town. "Most of them aren't dangerous so we turn a blind eye. This one is different. They think they are sending messages so we must find a way to let them know we are listening. We must do it carefully but we must do it quickly," Santo said nodding as he spoke.

Dominic stared in disbelief. *"Ras peeple dem do all dis an' yuh wan fi chat?"* Ms. Casteñada caught his eye and motioned for him to back off. She held her index finger in front of her lips in a friendly caution. He had to keep himself from reaching over and touching her. That would really give the old men something to bitch about!

THE CONSPIRACY – UP COUNTRY - TWO DAYS LATER

At the Plantation House, three men sat at the card table with small glasses of *cachaca* sweating in their hands. The windows had been covered with old drapes that kept the room dark but also kept the heat inside. Outside, the heat loomed even more oppressive. They were not worried, stressed or tense. In fact, they seemed to be waiting. As if on cue, a text message arrived and the man who received the message drained his glass and cleared his throat.

"They are looking for religious groups."

"We are invisible."

"We have our man on the top floor…"

"He may be compromised…"

"When will we know?"

"When he is dead."

"How should we proceed?"

"We wait for their response."

"What if it does not come?"

"It will come. They will act."

When the house emptied once more, the woman in white emerged from a small shack behind the house to do what she had been paid to do. Humming tunelessly, she went about her business with a confident efficiency, allowing nothing that deserved it to escape her attention. There could be no hint that people had been in the house – she would make sure of that. She adjusted her white *gele* and went on with her chores. As usual, she drained the glasses of the last drops of *cachaca* before dropping the glasses gently in the pocket of her frock. She used a square of special material to wipe the last of the moisture from the table, as well as the chairs and all surfaces she could see. She put her face close to the chairs to glean some smell of the men who sat in them. She smiled to herself as she looked around the house, checking for anything she might have forgotten. It was so little to go on, the old smells, the empty glasses and the creaking house but it was all she knew of them and why they paid so much for so little. Sometimes she thought she should give the money back but quickly thought better of it. Why give the money back? She herself had done no wrong. She could dance in the *peristil* with a clean heart.

After the meeting at the Plantation House, Ashton went home and opened a bottle of *cachaca* just after sunset. He owed more than he would be able to repay and had sunk too far to be recovered. Every day he took another step out over an abyss with no ledge to break his fall. Against a firing wall, he provoked the executioners. He made promises he knew he would never keep. Dominic would likely escape unharmed but it was by no means guaranteed. Santo called it 'glass eyes', but Ashton knew better. He sensed something dark behind Dominic's tranquil personality but he claimed no responsibility; no direct, and certainly no singular cause and effect relationship. All the same, it frightened him. His own children fared far worse than Dominic. There also, he saw no direct or singular cause and effect, even if he was the last remaining common factor. Children were born with their own devils; they seldom needed adults to bring those devils into full light.

He emptied his house of his last two bottles of *cahaca* before he passed out. Four hours later, he regained a sort of consciousness with a hangover he ranked as the fiercest he had ever experienced. He chalked it up to getting old. He just could not drink the way he used to. Though he should have slept straight through, he came to in the middle of the night, unable to get back to sleep. His head felt like it might split open with every heartbeat. He sat up in bed and put his head in his hands, hoping he could find the will to sleep again. The nervousness grew more powerful. Despite the fact his brain would not permit him to sleep, exhaustion plagued every muscle in his body. It hurt his back to standup. It hurt his head to sit up. When he lay down his skin crawled. Now the system deck that might send him to his grave had been taken from the storeroom, probably handed back to the one person he could least afford to have it. He cursed himself and his birthday with ripe, angry curses as well as the fact that he would simply have to retrieve the deck, at considerable cost. Doing so would force him to reveal his game so his hands would have to remain clean. Ashton knew how to go about such things and considered himself lucky that Dominic had not yet learned the art of paranoia.

Cursing again and needing to bring his brain to a full stop, he reached into the drawer of the nightstand and extracted a pill from an unmarked bottle -- a new, non-narcotic, invisible to known tox-screens, intrusive or remote. They were also illegal. He swallowed it with some effort and within minutes felt its effects – as if various switches in his body had been thrown. His brain and heartbeat slowed, the crawling sensations of his skin eased, blood withdrew from the surface, racing to the core, making him feel cool; his brain downshifted again and his limbs gained weight as if waterlogged. The headache drifted slowly away and in his final voluntary act, he closed his eyes to the blessed blackness of pharmaceutical sleep.

CAPITAL - GOVERNMENT HOSPITAL – SEVENTY-TWO HOURS LATER

<<Nick Cave & The Bad Seeds – Brother, My Cup is Empty>>

He felt as if he would fall forever into a cave or off a cliff. Aside from the sickening sensation of falling, he couldn't move. His muscles froze. As much as he thought his life depended on it, he could not open his eyes. Free fall continued. His brain streamed panic. Adrenaline pulsed through his body, but neither fight nor flight seemed possible. Approaching some sort of fail-safe if he could not break his fall, he knew armageddon waited for his physical self below. A blinding light pierced eyes that would not open no matter how much he willed it. He wanted to yell. He wanted to reach out and break his fall. He wanted to open his eyes. He could do none of these things. Then, in a terrifying moment of lucidity he never wanted to experience again, he woke up, yelling at the top of his lungs.

They stood in a semi-circle around him looking like they had seen a ghost. One of them had a pen light in her hand, pulling away from him with a startled look on her face. The room had white walls and the bed had two rows of metal bars around it. He tried to lash out but something stopped his arm with a loud noise. He tried to jump out of the bed but again something stopped him with an even louder noise. No longer yelling, fear turned to anger. Exhaustion consumed him. He felt submerged against his will in a deep pool. Not until he fell back onto the bed did he realize who the people in the room were: Santo, Ashton, a doctor, two nurses and someone in an ISEC uniform. Seeing familiar faces made things a little better and he closed his eyes to reset, to get control of the moment.

A nurse went around the bed releasing the straps that had a moment ago saved them from his flying arms and legs. He rubbed his wrists and stared at them, confused and flabbergasted, realizing he had been tied to a hospital bed. His hands and legs free, he straightened the bed sheets to regain some small dignity, though it was not nearly enough. He recognized one other person in the room: blind Pierre stood off to the side, staring in the wrong direction with a worried look on his face. A nurse led the blind man to the side of the bed. Pierre put both hands on Dominic's face for the fourth time, reading him in ways that no one else could. Dominic melted into the hospital bed as the blind man maintained his contact. After a minute or so, Dominic took Pierre's hands in his, guided them away from his face, touched them to his chest and kissed the man's forehead.

A moment later, Dominic could speak again. *"Yuh see mi duppy?"*

Ashton winced and pushed his way past Joseph to look Dominic over, to reassure himself that no permanent damage had occurred. "We almost did."

Then Santo spoke. "There was a security breach at your complex. We think you were the target. You had an allergic reaction to the pharma they used - we're not sure what it was. The restraints were in case you had a seizure. You've been semi-comatose for three days."

"You're not sure?" Dominic said incredulously. Drug screens had advanced by leaps and bounds over the last few years. Comprehensive drug screens could be run remotely and return results over distances as great as 40 feet. No substance the human body metabolized escaped the most advanced screens. Claustrophobia and nausea joined him in the room and on the bed. He methodically removed all of the IVs and medical monitors from the various places on his body and pushed and yanked the bars until they retreated.

He saw the light in the water closet and jumped off the bed, slamming the door to the water closet behind him. In the small confined space, with the light off, he avoided hyperventilation. He did not avoid the hot tears that came involuntarily to his eyes and stayed there without cresting or streaming down his face -- they were always so close. He heard the doctor scold the visitors and ask them to leave.

"I should not have allowed this. You must leave now. The old man may stay but just for a few minutes."

Dominic heard shuffling footsteps, found the light switch with his hand but then thought better of it. In darkness, he regained a burgeoning but fragile sense of control. When he woke next, he found himself back in bed but without the straps that secured him earlier and though he felt weak, he noticed that Pierre had not left. The old man sat next to the bed, hands folded in his lap, lips moving without sound. When Dominic shifted his weight, hoping Pierre would notice, Pierre turned to the noise, held out his hand and let Dominique put his arm beneath it. That simple contact with the swollen gnarled hand resting on his made things much better than they had been since he woke up yelling. He muttered under his breath, knowing Pierre would hear. *"Mwen ta dwe te rete kanpe la avè ou, Pierre."* (I should have stayed with you, Pierre.) He could easily leave all this behind. It would not be difficult.

In the peculiar way of people blind since birth, Pierre's eyes either wandered away from a single point of focus or pointed inward, as if the eyes knew they had become unnecessary. Pierre had never been an emotional man but today he wore a worried look. He placed Dominic's arm on the bed, palm up, and put his closed fist in Dominic's palm. Staring off in a different direction, Dominic focused on the slow movement of Pierre's fist in his hand. Dominic recognized the sign language Pierre had taught him long ago and it took a few moments for the syntax to come back to him. Though Pierre's blindness did not extend to his voice, he thought it necessary to conceal his communication in syntax only the two of them and Mercilia understood. Not a sentence, but a series of symbols: Dominic...safe...no...uncle...snake. These four symbols repeated themselves over and over again in Dominic's palm until Dominic closed his hand around Pierre's and the symbols stopped. Abruptly, Pierre stood up and rapped on the wall behind him. A nurse appeared and Dominic watched the old man shuffle out of the room, Pierre's hand resting on the nurse's shoulder. In no uncertain terms, Dominic wished it was his own.

Two days later, two ISEC officers arrived for his release from hospital. He felt a thousand times better. For the first time in days, he felt solid on his feet as he walked, albeit slowly, down the hall to the waiting motorcade. Santo had taken no chances, sending a full government escort to bring him back. He rarely saw ISEC people outside government buildings, as they tended to be secretive and mostly unwilling to appear in public. Although one member of his escort sported familiar insignia, the other wore no insignia. There were four cars, two primaries and two escorts with one motorcycle each. They ushered him into the back seat of the second primary and joined him in the front seat of the same vehicle. The motorcade sped off with full lights and sirens. At the exit to the hospital, the back windows of the primary vehicles darkened and the motorcade split, with the two primaries going in opposite directions. Within fifteen meters, their vehicle picked up another escort car and motorcycle and they proceeded apace to the front of the Presidential Palace. His ISEC escort took him not to his apartment, but to a wing of the Presidential Palace itself and ushered him into a private guest suite. They handed him a note, written in freehand by Santo, nodded and closed the door with Dominic inside.

I have taken the liberty of moving you inside the residence. You will be safer here. You must rest and regain your strength. My wife and children are coming to visit. You will have dinner with us tonight. I will explain later.

Exhausted, but happy to see his media system already set up, he spent too much time checking the calibration specs, speaker cube positioning, satellite positions and leveling the display. When the calibration specs in the manual became blurry and he realized he was sweating from the simple effort he had so far expended, he lay down on the floor, using the spec documents as a pillow. He slept right up until dinner, which happened much as he imagined it would. Between bites of food, children laughed, said silly things and complained about the food. Santo and his wife Carly drank wine and picked at their food. The kids drank milk and squirmed in their seats. Dominic ate as if he had not eaten in days, ignoring the conversation. Though he often felt like a fifth wheel, he had no inkling of that tonight. Friendly, outgoing and concerned, both Carly and Santo seemed happy. Engrossed in the pork chop and apple chutney, he did not hear Carly asking how he fared. Santo tapped his glass with a fork to get Dominic's attention. Carly told stories about the kids when they were away and Santo told Carly that he saved the radiator. Dominic laughed when the kids begged him to throw it away in exaggerated kid voices. If an ideal family dinner existed he thought this was it, savoring the last of the pork chop with a generous mound of apple chutney to spare. After dinner, Carly and the kids left the dining room to retire upstairs and Dominic and Santo had a few moments alone. "If you don't like it here you can thank Carly. She insisted we move you here. She threatened dire consequences if I did not agree," Santo said smiling conspiratorially.

"The two ISEC men you met at the hospital are assigned to you. They go where you go."

"You don't have to do that Baba," Dominic said, knowing his claim rang empty.

"Perhaps, but Carly and I think highly of you and it would make us happy if you stayed with us for a while. This is personal. Be a part of our family for a while…"

The words rang true, though Dominic had a hard time hearing the word 'family,' much less thinking about it. All family was short-lived, temporary and the best 'family' always the most fleeting. "I'm ok here." Dominic turned to go before he showed emotion he preferred to keep to himself.

"Remember what the doctor said. Nothing strenuous. No running, none of that judo stuff. Understood?"

"It's not judo. Its…"

Santo cut him off. "Whatever you call it, leave it alone. We'll talk when Ashton returns from the errand I sent him on."

Part Two

On My Own...

Ten thousand roads wind and meander through dwelling spaces of the millions and their children who call this place the place they live.

On ten thousand roads, the millions and their children live dusty, hopeful, violent lives.

Cornmeal dumpling, yam, salt fish, a little oil, a little flour, and sometimes blood: these are the currencies by which their lives are paid for and fed.

The roads keep the millions and their children moving from misery to misery.

Ten thousand opportunities for unmapped, unplanned births, deaths, joys, crimes.

CHAPTER I

CAPITAL - TODAY

The government response to recent events impressed and frightened no one. No secret arrest warrants were issued and minor civilian civil defense nodes were summarily deactivated. Defense forces stationed in the most restive areas returned to their barracks. Threat levels and corresponding security regimes for government personnel remained elevated -- they were none of them safe. The President appeared on national television to vacate restrictions on social networks, restoring full access via SELAND for residents and citizens of the island. Penalties for disturbing the peace and flash mobs that turned violent or destructive doubled. Offensive drones decreased by one-sixth, except in major urban areas where the most destructive and dangerous flash mobs had occurred. The new policies reduced the number of surveillance drones by one-fourth, as long as no further destructive hacktivist or anarchistic riots occurred. In the event something illegal did transpire, offensive drones would be given autonomous kill shot authority if citizens did not heed its five verbal warnings (increased from three). The incident-based automatic trigger for 24 hours of martial law was also vacated. Bitcoin transactions under certain amounts reverted to anonymous status, however SELAND and ISEC took a more active role in domestic security monitoring and control tactics. Sensitivity thresholds for residual trace-tag increased by a factor and though arbitrary, the additional metadata generated left SELAND and ISEC feeling a little less uncomfortable. Santo did not expect to be thanked or praised but he did expect that citizens recognize their civil responsibilities and act accordingly.

The government gambled that opening the gates to sources of information and social networks would come at some future cost but that the additional data gathered would increase exponentially as people reverted to the easiest methods of communication and networking, rather than the most anonymous methods, which were fast becoming nearly impossible. Sealed, hardcopy, hand-delivered communication had long been rejected for SELAND-based messaging and governments wasted no time in removing the expenses of the traditional post/mail house from tightening budgets. Parallel to the loosening of control on civilians, ISEC launched a deep probe into the role of secret societies and their impact on island life, beginning with the premise that the more the government knew, the less danger a group posed in aggregate. Once compiled, analyzed and presented, it became apparent that most groups that fashioned themselves as a secret society were in fact relatively open, public and indexed, thus making it unnecessary to go to the level of trace-tag to find them, even if membership rolls were protected and privileged. However the list of groups that did require trace-tag methods to gather data on grew far too long and ISEC expressed the very real concern that they would run out of time utilizing usual methods.

He listened to his ISEC advisors with a jaundiced ear, physically weary of governing. He knew there were no ideal answers and that those who governed would live as pariahs or come to an early grave. Governments in general had never wielded more power over the societies they governed and yet those same societies stayed home on election day, passed conflicting initiatives and passed judgment on public policy based on nothing less than what they believed to be true, never mind those beliefs had no basis in fact. For the most part they preferred to know something for sure, even if hoax, than to wade unsure into unfamiliar waters and admit the unthinkable: that they simply did not know. Although it made him uncomfortable, the President admitted that he did not know how to resolve the contradiction. The monomania of his ISEC people frightened him, events of the last few weeks unsettled him, the challenge of governance overwhelmed him, the safety of his family made him lose sleep and the politics of his government gave him a headache. Seeing Dominic on the floor, playing Legos with his two young sons the night before, was the only thing to bring him a smile in weeks, if not months.

Game theory's 'Tragedy of the Commons' scenario expressed his conundrum: common good, valued so highly by rational thought, required that the costs of common good be shared, even if bearing those costs meant greater sacrifices for some than others. For those with only two apples the surrender of half an apple for the common good represented a much greater sacrifice than for those who had ten apples or ten thousand. Yet no inexhaustible supply of common good had been uncovered and its finite shadow passed quickly, unless perpetually renewed. Command societies outlived their usefulness either in declining utility or self-immolation, while demand societies routinely found themselves on a perpetual precipice – self-absolved of anything common to all, while unquestioningly beholden to outdated assumptions. What rational human sought power under such circumstances?

Two days later, they broadcast images of the Caribbean SELAND tower as empty and clean as the day they raised it. They streamed the images across both certified and uncertified NETCERTs. People passed store windows where the media feeds could be seen from the sidewalk and while some paused to get caught up, most ignored the scenes in the window and pressed on. Local monitoring stations showed people shrugging their shoulders and laughing. The feeds did not show the results the latest ISEC algorithms produced from big data collected on various groups and splinter groups, the shape of the trace-tag or the math of their collection techniques. The feeds did not release information gleaned from Ashton's movements around the island. They also did not reveal the deployment of a high altitude, long endurance, Gladiator drone stationed over a plantation house in the middle of hectares of sugar cane. It carried 1500 pounds of kinetic energy projectiles -- armor-piercing, fin-stabilized, discarding Sabot rounds -- and could remain on station for close to sixty hours. ISEC slaved the drone to a combat satellite whose firepower and advanced capabilities it could call on autonomously. The fate of the plantation house and anyone inside the house had been ceded to a relatively small batch of ISEC code. However, according to the data the drone sent back, the house remained empty. Someone had cleaned the house of all biological evidence or they were smart enough to fool the drone's very sensitive sensors, broadcasting a complex data-mirage to cover what lay beneath.

THE CONSPIRACY – UPCOUNTRY - TODAY

Inside the Plantation House at the top of the hill, four men sat in a large room with four doors. From the center of the room where a chandelier might have hung or a *peristil* might have stood, hung the loose frame on which one might hang mosquito netting. For their purposes the frame had been hung not with opaque linen but a different material, like thick aluminum foil but not made from aluminum. It cascaded over their collection of chairs, covering them like a tent divided into four quadrants. As before, it permitted light and shadow but not features or detail. In each quadrant a man sat in a folding chair he had brought with him. Summoned by text message, each man had come in through his separate door, forty minutes apart, each named for the main directions on the compass – East, South, West and North. None of them had been to the Plantation House before and none alone had the information that would make any one of them dangerous. Each of them had a battery operated electronic voice distorter through which spoke in turn. As they took their seats, a panel covering an inset hutch in the wall behind each chair opened to reveal a kinetic energy projectile weapon with a human-form spatter-pattern collimator. The chamber in each weapon held one round and would fire simultaneously or not at all. The weapons were electronically networked so if one activated, the other three automatically emptied their chambers. Though strangers, they found themselves bound as compatriots in purpose and obedience. Somewhere in the house a door slammed. From the quadrant each man knew to be east, the first man spoke through his voice distorter. "I have been given no items of concern to address."

On the heels of the man sitting in the East quadrant, from the quadrant each man knew to be north, another man said, "I have been given no items of concern to address." From the quadrant each knew to be west: "I have been given no

167

items of concern to address." From the quadrant each knew to be south: "I have been given no items of concern to address."

Each man left the Plantation House as they had arrived, each through their separate door, with the chair they had sat on and their voice distorter, in forty-minute increments. As the last man left the room, the panels covering the weapons closed, returning the wall to its unthreatening state. Within minutes a diminutive woman in a plain white frock, white slippers and a white *gele* entered the room and used a hook on a long pole to remove the strange material from its hook in the ceiling. She carefully disconnected the material from the frame and folded it quickly into a square she could put under her arm. It crackled as she folded it and it felt metallic in her hands.

She held it up to her face to smell it and it smelled like an unpleasant mix of chemicals. From another room she dragged a small collapsible card table and placed it carefully in the middle of the room. From another room she found three folding chairs, which she placed around the table. From the same room where she found the chairs she found a plastic red and white plaid tablecloth that she used to cover the table. Also in the cupboard were plastic cups and plates and an empty pitcher. These also she placed on the table, setting a table for three. Having her brother back from his journey to Capital pleased her. She hated to be alone and she worried about him, especially when he set off alone as he did a few days ago. Knowing why he went did not make his absence easier. She did not quite understand what Pierre saw in that hulking sulking boy-man who lived with them some time ago. Perhaps Pierre fancied himself a father. She knew her own position on children very well: evil and vile. They called her names and threw things at her when she walked in town, laughed at her as she passed and whispered rude things behind her as she walked. One of the vile creatures not much older than the boy-man who lived with them, tried to rape her. Though she looked old and fragile, she surprised him with a letter opener to his throat, watching him bleed out on the road before the police arrived. They let her go after a few hours but did not give her the letter opener back. It did not matter. She had another within the hour, sharpened to a razor point – just like the one the police had taken from her. She could still dance in the *peristil*; her heart and body clean for the *loa* of her life.

For the time period during which the men were at the Plantation House, the slaved autonomous drone high above recorded no movement in or out of the house; it recorded no change in status of the surrounding area and nothing in the multifarious signals it monitored gave any indication that anything of import had occurred on the ground beneath it. Were the data to be reconstructed to recreate a visual image of the area under surveillance, one would see a house in the middle of hectares of sugarcane, silent and empty, unwelcoming and ignored.

THE PRESIDENTIAL PALACE – CAPITAL – TODAY

The hospital administrator found it difficult to hide his nervousness as he waited for an audience with the President. He clutched his sheaf of papers to his body and tried to make himself small on the large bench. A small man, he combed his thin shock of hair over his growing baldness as best he could and dressed for the occasion in clean black slacks, a loose linen shirt and leather shoes that made his feet hurt. The whole episode made him uncomfortable and he wished it over and done with. He did not like what he had been asked to do, uncomfortable with the origin of the request and even more uncomfortable with the results he held in his hand. The door to the President's office opened and the President himself emerged to greet him.

The President greeted him by name, shook his hand, offered him a seat and then a drink. "Vincent, I'm glad you could come. I know it's irregular but I needed someone who could employ the requisite level of discretion."

"Yes, Mr. President."

"There is nothing in writing, this is just between us. It is not political and no one will be hurt. Does that calm your fears?"

"I am not afraid Mr. President."

"Good! You have the results I asked for?" the President said, eagerly taking a long drink from his glass.

"Yes Mr. President."

"And do you plan to tell me or keep it a secret?"

"You asked to have two DNA samples compared, one from one of your staff and the other, a blind sample."

"Vincent, speak up man! You are not on trial!"

"Mr. President the two samples are a familial match, most likely, father and son."

The President, who had been standing, pursed his lips and sat down, as if something pushed him. His demeanor changed from gracious and gregarious to quiet and reflective. Drink still in hand, he set it gently on the desk, clasped hands under his chin and closed his eyes. "Thank you Vincent. I appreciate your discretion. I owe you. Shall I tell you the back-story?"

"No Mr. President, I do not want to know," the hospital administrator said as he stood up to go.

"You must call on me if I can help, Vincent. Do you understand?"

The hospital administrator nodded, downed his drink in one gulp and left the President's office, the sheaf of papers he brought with him still firmly under his arm. He would burn them when he returned to the hospital. He declined the back-story to be polite but had already drawn his own conclusions.

After dinner with Baba Santo and his family, Dominic allowed himself a controlled collapse on the bed and did not wake up for twenty-four hours. When he woke up again, hunger pangs shot through his gut. The clock on the bedside table told him just minutes had passed. Then his SELAND message queue caught his eye: two messages from Hanna, one from Santo, six from Ashton. He realized the reason for the hunger pangs – he had slept a full twenty-four hours. He demolished a bag of plantain chips, two bananas, a quart of orange juice, a mango, and half a box of peanut butter cookies. He thought he might go to sleep again but he decided to message Ashton first.

Never had he heard so much panic in Ashton's voice. Ashton had always been collected and calm, always knowing what to do, whom to call, how to get through the impasse. If it had not been for Ashton he could not imagine what would have happened to him after Mooma Jacobs died. He owed quite a bit to Ashton though the man had taken payment for his kindness in ways not unfamiliar, but still the most unpleasant experience of his childhood. Despite the one shortfall, Dominic could not dismiss Ashton all together, finding himself drawn to Ashton's independence, sarcasm and his ability to move through life in a relatively straight line, even when all around him crumbled and disintegrated. Ashton kept Dominic's life going in a relatively straight line, appearing at the exact moment to point Dominic in a new direction, even if Dominic never expressed appreciation for the trouble he took. Dominic did fault Ashton for yanking him out of Pierre's house and swore he would neither forgive nor forget the travesty and unnecessary upheaval. He did eventually though.

Panic and fear unlike anything encountered before overwhelmed him. Ashton had fallen victim to the Columbian Necktie: an IED on a collar with the trigger embedded in gigabytes of encrypted garbage code. The timeline: between 72 and 96 hours. The hyperventilation attack he narrowly managed to avoid at the hospital overcame him for a brief moment but he did not let it take him. The water in his eyes that merely burned but did not crest at the hospital now crested but did not run. It pooled around his eyes and made it hard to see. He managed to toggle the ISEC emergency flag on his message board, but only barely.

COLUMBIAN NECKTIE: the latest development in placing the human body under a maximum amount of stress. The IED aspect of the device was well known – a collar bomb fueled with whatever explosive material could be obtained. The trigger code was typically embedded and encrypted in gigabytes of trace-tag. The victim was given two numbers, both in terms of hours; a minimum and maximum number of hours of life the victim had left to live. Recent experience indicated the actual trigger was coded for a random interim time period between the two given numbers. Additionally, some were intentional duds.

Response to such events developed into a pre-determined protocol with responsibility shared between the defense forces and ISEC. In this case, elements of the President's protective services also responded. Within minutes, each deployed the agreed on mitigation strategy. None succeeded in saving the life of the collar bomb victim (when the collar had not been a dud) but they certainly reduced, if not eliminated, collateral damage. Five layers of explosive damping structures surrounded Ashton (who happened to be sitting on a curb outside the newly built and dedicated Ministry of Internal Security). The surrounding area had been evacuated to a three-mile radius. Though not always obvious to the victim, a coroner's van rather than a medical response team also responded. It took them two events to keep the coroner's van hidden from the victim.

Ashton remained within the first damping layer -- they did not give him a chair. The only task that mattered -- and they hardly needed Ashton's help – would be to un-encrypt and decode the trace-tag to isolate and countermand the trigger. So far they had been wildly unsuccessful, but still they tried. The work proceeded in shifts, like an archeological dig. Small pieces of trace tag were isolated, indexed and bounced against ISEC's considerable databases. Most trace-tag could be compared to junk DNA – gigabytes of it. But each 250 MB slice had to be analyzed separately. To date, their best time from isolation of one slice to decryption, decoding and identification of the slice as either junk or relevant, held at twelve minutes. A more relevant measure might be their worst time – five days. The longest maximum time they had encountered on any one Colombian Necktie — 96 hours — although to be fair that one had been a dud. Once copied and securely backed-up, the mitigation teams had no more use for Ashton. They gave him water, a COMLINK transponder, and left him alone to contemplate the beauty and pain of randomness.

ISEC intercepted Dominic as he arrived on the scene and shuffled him into the control station — a bus chassis converted to a roving emergency management crisis center. Although the video displays gave Dominic the full picture, a much fuller picture than he would have gotten were he standing on the street, he wanted to go outside. His ISEC escort told him they had permission to handcuff him inside if they had to. He did not believe them but decided not to push. He did not know these ISEC men and what he did not know had a tendency to hurt him. After twenty minutes, he wondered out loud why the responders were standing around, waiting. Dominic had no idea what they could possibly be waiting for.

A voice on the line made him jump -- Santo talking to Ashton. Dominic swore he heard a smile in Santo's voice. "Ashton, this is Joseph. Are you all right?"

"Why ask such stupid questions?" Ashton yelled back.

"I want to make sure you can hear me. It seems that you can. "

"Yuh mad? Tell di people-dem fi tek 'dis ras ting from mi neck! A'wha do yuh'mon?"

"You have nothing to say?"

"Science keep me! Yuh lose yuh mind?"

"No, but I thought maybe you had?" A long silence followed but the President had more to say. "I will tell you what we know. The collar is not a dud and the timeline is short. We have very little time. Do you understand?" More silence. Ashton appeared to be holding his breath. "This time we know more than usual. Are you happy about that Ashton?"

"Yuh mind gone?" Ashton whispered.

"That's good Ashton! You are listening now." The President strode into the crisis center van met by two ISEC agents and a confused Dominic. Santo side stepped Dominic and went directly to the display wall to get a better view of Ashton. He turned off his COMLINK and spoke quietly to Dominic, "This will get ugly. Are you ready for that?"

"Yessuh." Dominic could not imagine a scenario where he would leave.

The President turned his attention to Ashton. "You have been busy, Ashton, have you not?"

"We have all been busy."

"Do not misunderstand me, the necktie you wear is just like the others with one small difference. Would you like to know what it is?"

"Tell me…"

"We know who built it! Isn't that wonderful?"

"But I am still wearing it…"

"If I were you I would find that strange."

"This is your evil Joseph!"

Now Santo took his turn at yelling. "I return evil for evil!"

"Which evil, sir? Mine alone or the evil we share?"

"We share NOTHING sir!"

"So you say…"

"I have evidence you conspired against this government to bring it to ruin and commit treason."

"Why do you say such things?"

"There's a house up country in the middle of a sugarcane field where these plots are hatched. Do you know of it?"

"No sir, I do not."

"We've been looking at this house very closely and do you know what we've found?"

"No, I do not."

"Absolutely nothing."

"I don't understand…"

"You must be under considerable stress. You are usually much quicker about these things."

"You play with me…"

"Oh that's MUCH better. I like it when I don't have to explain everything. This house that you know nothing of, returns zero biologicals. Do you find that interesting?"

At this point Ashton's head bowed. He had held his head up in defiance and kept pace with Santo's taunts but the last question turned the tide. His chin sank to his chest and they heard his labored breathing. Dominic rose from his chair and stood next to Santo.

"It is possible to be too careful," Ashton said.

"We did find it interesting but I wish you had been there when we cracked the SELAND deck you procured for Dominic. Do you remember? The one you confiscated? Can you tell me what we found?"

"You should ask Dominic."

"Ashton, you waste time, the one thing you don't have! Let me tell you. We found a very sophisticated Stuxnet-variant."

"Why do you think I confiscated it?" Ashton's chin still rested on his chest but now everyone could see that he had begun to cry. "You cannot win, Joseph."

Joseph smiled and pounded the fragile table inside the crisis center with his fist. "Now you understand! You must also understand that your life is in my hands!"

Ashton repeated himself. "You cannot win."

"Tell me, when did you decide to throw your nephew to the lions?"

"He is not my nephew."

Dominic fell back into his chair nauseated.

The President glanced at Dominic and then at the ISEC agents with them. The COMLINK clicked off again. "I warned you this would get ugly. You do not need to be here."

Something unknown inside him made him want to stay. Dominic shook his head.

"Really, you should go."

"I want to know why…" Dominic replied, shaking his head in opposition.

"Then you are bound by the State Secrets Law."

"I'm staying…"

"This will make you feel small. Are you ready?"

Dominic nodded again.

The President did not like Dominic's decision but did object further. He waited a few moments for him to change his mind. When nothing happened, he turned back to the displays, re-activating his COMLINK.

Something had changed. Ashton's chin no longer rested on his chest and he no longer sat on the curb despondently. He stood up, facing the tenting as if facing the President himself. "I made my bed. I will lie in it."

"It's over, Ashton. We will wrap this up with or without you."

"There is nothing left to do. You cannot win. I never expected to."

"What about your children, Ashton?"

"Do not blackmail me, Joseph."

"Like you were blackmailed?"

"Perhaps…"

"Then we shall watch you die from a safe distance."

"So be it. Why are you waiting?"

"I wanted to hear your side of the story."

"I will not tell you."

"Then allow me."

Ashton stumbled over his own feet at the President's last sentence. "If you know the story, why ask?"

"Tell me how they turned you. You, a man who risked his life and lost all for his country! What did they have on you, Ashton?"

"I will not tell you…"

"Are you such the narcissist you had to record yourself meeting a man's needs with a twelve year old boy, in your own home?"

Ashton did not respond but his chin fell back to his chest. "I bought you time. You! Not me!"

"On that account you may be right," the President said, surprising everyone in the makeshift crisis center.

Before the President finished his sentence, ISEC shock troops appeared, cordoning off the tenting under which Ashton sat. They pushed back the first responders and onlookers and began dismantling the tenting except for the last layer. Screened from public view an ISEC Custodial van backed up to the last tenting layer, two ISEC uniforms lifted the tenting about four feet. Those in the crisis center saw Ashton shoved into the back of the van, the collar bomb still around his neck. Once the Custody vehicle put a safe distance between itself and the scene, the shock troops spent a few more minutes dealing with the tenting and then disappeared from all displays. The entire area was cleared of all responders and equipment. A medium size explosion ensued, just as everyone expected. Later that same night, the newsfeeds announced a senior government minister had been targeted by a collar bomb and had not survived. In less than a minute, ISEC coded instructions to the drone above the plantation house. Up country in a field of sugarcane, the big plantation house imploded inwards and then upwards in a plume of fire, smoke, and ash. As quietly as it had been deployed, the autonomous drone returned to its in-country base of operations.

<<Finley Quaye – The Emperor>>

No one expected him to bolt from his seat, out the rear door of the crisis center, around the primary scene, past a caggle of ISEC people, and through an unsecured alley between two separate sections of the Ministry building. If he knew nothing at all, Dominic knew how to run. Still, this kind of running remained an involuntary reaction. Neither destination nor distance entered the equation. He knew how to run when his lungs burned and his legs muscles cramped. He began at sprinting speed, which did not last long, maybe half a mile. He pared back slightly for the next mile, drawing blank or open-mouthed looks from onlookers. Though he did not remember exactly how he got back to the Presidential Palace, Melia would tell him he showed up at her place, out of breath and unable to stand. When she opened the door, he puked his greeting on the verandah of the house. She did not scold or chastise, but helped him clean up and put him in a taxi, using her own money to send him back where he belonged. Carly would tell him that a taxi had dropped him off at the public entrance to the Presidential Palace, six hours after the conclusion of the Ashton incident. He remembered none of it, time forever lost. Dominic collapsed in his usual chair in front of an open window, facing the southern sky. The room darkened with the moonless evening until the stars glowed like candles. He would have preferred to disappear like a shadow at noontime or the moon below the elliptic. Carly came by to check on him, but said nothing. She put her hand on his shoulder, left it there for a few seconds, and then left him alone.

Some time later, Dominic heard someone else. By the footfall he could tell it belonged to Santo -- the man walked with a slight limp. He had something in his hand and set it down on the arm of Dominic's chair -- a glass of something golden, a liquor of some sort. Santo sat down in the chair next to Dominic and joined him in staring at the southern sky for a good thirty minutes. The sitting and the silence harkened back Pierre's house and he was grateful for it. Though he swore he and Santo would not be friends, Dominic felt the sandbags he built around him begin to shed their sand, in the Presidential Palace of all places, with the person of the President, of all people. He felt pushed and pulled towards a connection of a kind that always ended badly. Santo had shown himself an ally when he had no reason to do so, when no expediency forced his hand. Something nibbled at Dominic from inside, a strange and foreign desire to be 'found', 'recognized', castled, and brought into the fold, any fold. He felt drawn in much like he had been drawn to Pierre, finding something he did not know he had been in search of; finding something he wanted but which frightened him.

"Are you ok?" Santo asked.

"I'm all right…"

"I'm sorry it happened this way."

"I'm all right, Baba," Dominic reiterated.

"We removed the collar."

"How did you know?"

"I've known for some time, but I had to wait until he played his hand…"

"No, I mean, when I was a kid, when you said I'd feel small…"

"I could forgive him for the coup, but not what he did to you. You're strong enough to get past it, yes?"

"I am?" Dominic had not intended to make it a question, but there it was, hanging between them and he did not correct himself.

"Ashton will pay, I will see to it."

"You did this for me?" Dominic had to ask if only to hear the expected negative.

Santo cut the question down the middle. "I did it for both of us."

"Do you think he was right, that he bought you time?"

"If this had broken earlier, it would have been the end. He delayed the inevitable."

"The inevitable?"

"This is how power changes. A coup is a message – a request for new rules."

"So what now?" Dominic asked, hoping to continue the conversation since Santo had just recently begun talking to him on these terms.

Santo sighed heavily. "We will wait…"

"For what?"

"Have you heard the expression, 'trouble comes in threes'?"

"No…trouble everywhere…"

"You don't subscribe to limits on trouble, eh?"

"Noosuh!"

"It's not as bad as that, captain. It will even out…it takes time." Santo shook his head – the conversation had come to an end. "Something to help you sleep," he said pushing the glass closer to Dominic.

Dominic pushed it gently away.

"Don't be a fool Dominic, not tonight." He pushed the glass back towards Dominic. "It's Hakushu, a Japanese single malt…a drink for a man."

That night Dominic broke years of tradition and downed the drink in one gulp.

Hanna arrived two days later, though Dominic slept for most of the first day of her visit, as he never had the chance to rest the way the doctors wanted him to. She sat on a couch across from the bed and passed the time reading. When Dominic thrashed, rocking back and forth on the bed, she called his name and he stopped. She stepped out to take a walk and he slept through it. She nibbled on food he had in the suite and he slept through it. She paged through some of the news feeds, frowning, and he slept through that as well. When a woman in an ISEC uniform rapped softly on the door, she answered it and went back to reading. He slept through that as well. When he woke up, she had fallen asleep on the couch. He did not wake her. He did not tell her he had been promoted to the rank of Major and he did not tell her about the scotch he had taken. He finished the food Hanna only nibbled on, did some light stretching and felt tired again. He gently woke Hanna and they moved to the bed where they slept through the night.

They ate breakfast the next morning in the executive kitchen, swiping pastries and cups of coffee, fresh fruit and more coffee. They went to the track and walked in the morning sun before it became too hot to be outside. They walked together in silence. Nierika, Hanna's faithful companion, would have preferred a faster pace or perhaps a rousing game of Frisbee but it did not happen. She soon settled in with the slow pace. Just looking at her made them smile, even if Dominic had not gotten over his fear of dogs. He napped. She read some more. She napped. He picked up her book and read from where she put the book down.

Reading made him sleepy and he put the book down after just four pages and slept on the couch.

A knock on the door to the suite woke them both. Dominic ignored it at first but then remembered where he was. He checked the video feed and saw a visitor he could not ignore. Santo wanted to walk so Dominic grabbed sunglasses and a 'lid' (as he called it) and followed Santo out to the running track. Nierika followed them but gave up and left them alone.

"Walk with me, Major," Santo said, motioning with his hand.

"Whapp'nssuh?" Dominic said, when he had caught up.

"You all right?"

"I've been sleeping a lot."

"Good. How is Hanna?"

"She's ok."

"Are you going to introduce us?"

"Maybe…"

Santo laughed a full, throaty laugh, something Dominic had not heard in a long time. "Good man! Good man! You keep her safe, you hear?"

"Yessuh."

"Ashton is talking, telling us everything."

"He is?"

"Yes. He wants to see you."

"What's going to happen to him?"

"He will die in prison, Dominic. There is no other way."

"He wasn't all bad…" Dominic said, squinting in the bright sun as they walked, trying to catch the expression on Santo's face.

"We are mixed breed Dominic, some good, some bad, some indifferent. Ashton got himself into trouble and couldn't see his way out of it."

"He said I owed him…"

"You owe him nothing!"

"It was only twice…"

"A man has only one life to pay for his crimes. He will spend the rest of his life in prison."

"He wants to see me?"

Santo nodded, then put his arm around Dominic's shoulders. They walked a few paces and Santo squeezed his shoulder, removed his arm and they kept walking.

"I didn't tell Hanna."

"It's not over, you know. I need you back tomorrow. We have work to do. I did not give you that new rank so you could sleep!"

They walked in silence back to Dominic's suite where Hanna waited for them. Santo smiled and nodded his head at her as he passed but did not stop to be introduced. Dominic called to him as he walked away and Santo paused mid-step. Dominic thought at first he would thank Santo but changed his mind and simply waved him off. What exactly would he have thanked him for anyway?

THE INVESTIGATION – PLANTATION HOUSE – UP COUNTRY – PRESENT DAY

The Plantation House investigation took on massive proportions and utilized technology known to only the top layers of the government. After tenting the blast site to avoid further contamination, they cordoned off an area five square miles around the house with an electrified chain link fence. Twenty-four hour, heavily armed guards took up post every 100 yards around the perimeter. ISEC recreated the area's signals intelligence for 36 hours prior to the destruction of the house, as well as 24 hours afterwards. Ultra sensitive robotic crawlers deployed into the blast area. Keyed to biological, chemical, explosive residue/wake and DNA trace, if the crawlers could not find it, it did not exist. The investigators established that prior readings of the Plantation House which showed a complete lack of biologicals, to be a sophisticated data-mirage. The evidence and the destroyed hardware supporting the data mirage proved to be technologically novel and made the ISEC folks drool. The apocalypse they fear-mongered about finally occurred in their own back yard and damned if they would not prove themselves right, if only in hindsight. Evidentiary data streams were sequestered and backed up every 3 seconds. In one 24-hour period, the investigation generated 900 petabytes of data. Sophisticated algorithms would do the brunt of the work. ISEC would write queries.

SELAND provided the throughput to convey the data to similar data farms in other capital cities. Barred by SELAND Treaty, electronic compartmentalization and redaction had long been abandoned. Since sources and methods were known and largely the same worldwide, few governments found inter-institutional secrecy efficient. In an international environment of persistent, constant, electronic signal warfare and aggressive, offensive journalism, compartmentalized data risked exposure in uncontrolled and unauthorized releases. Ironically, the compartmentalization of times past repeated itself in single copy, irreproducible, hardcopy printouts, stored in heavily fortified rooms, impervious to all but a direct nuclear blast. In some agencies, even print drivers, much less a printer itself, were cause for a termination investigation.

The technical hardware supporting the data mirage consisted of un-serialized, cannibalized components, some of which appeared to have been produced solely for the operation. The human form spatter collimator attached to the machine gun network survived the blast. ISEC found some explosive wake that did not match the explosives used to destroy the house but not in amounts significant enough to draw any conclusions. They retrieved some DNA but that would take more time than they liked to admit. Processing and matching time frames tended only to increase, as forensic scientists felt compelled to match against ever-growing worldwide databases. In addition, international standards had, in less than a decade, doubled the number of core-loci set criteria. Additionally, maximum random-match probability factors required to produce adventitious evidence rose to a level never before approached in forensic science.

They did find traces of a liquor alcohol; most probably some sort of *cachaca*, but it too appeared to be home made – the product of a back room sugar cane still. Though somewhat embarrassing, it was their strongest lead.

CHAPTER II

THE PRESIDENTIAL PALACE – CAPITAL – PRESENT DAY

Hanna stayed in Dominic's suite when ISEC announced they would bring Ashton to the front portico of the Presidential Palace. Though unnecessary, they shackled the man's hands and feet. His head and beard completely shaved, he wore the ridiculously large, baggy yellow and blue-checkered prison jumpsuit for the occasion. Dominic tried to act normal, as difficult as it was to do so. The man he knew had diminished and faded so that Dominic wondered how Ashton ever frightened him.

"Mi nuh'know why yuh wan' fi see me…" Dominic spoke first, unable to look directly at Ashton.

"You know why…" ISEC had positioned Ashton facing the bright afternoon sun, so he saw Dominic only in silhouette.

"Wha' mek yuh do dem ting deh?"

"I am a stupid man…"

"Yuh cyaan say nuttin' else?"

"I wanted to say I'm sorry, if you will have it…"

"Too much 'sorry' a'go round yaso yuhknow!"

Ashton motioned to his ISEC interlocutors, seeing no reason to prolong a painful audience. They waited for Dominic to reply and when he did not, made away with their prisoner. Santo's two young sons came bounding out of the residence, shouting and laughing, begging Dominic to play football with them, giving him the easiest decision he had made in the last month, his doctor be damned. The children bounded and bounced like fireflies, kicking a new ball during the hottest part of the day. Dominic willingly and enthusiastically jogged after them.

189

President Joseph Santo wasted little time in reconvening his former Cabinet. Shell-shocked but not entirely surprised, their sudden re-instatement made them compliant for a few minutes, each content to save their own skin. They nodded in unison as Santo recalled the recent chain of events. Ashton's spot remained empty, a black cloth draped over his chair. They each mourned in private ways, never imagining the man who had the President's ear just weeks ago, now languished in a small cell, three levels below them. Dominic wore a black armband on his upper arm, over his suit jacket. The President did not. In this new configuration, the President asked Dominic to sit at the table. Ms. Casteñada, fresh from a shopping trip to Miami, sat on his right. This made the traditional ministers uncomfortable but they kept their concerns to themselves.

"I will tell you what we know so far. What we found at the Plantation house can so far only be linked with the SELAND tower mishaps -- both of them. We have not found any evidence that this group involved itself in any of the other events. You are all familiar with our sources and methods so you know that our conclusions are at this point unimpeachable."

"But that means..."

"Multiple vectors. So far no demands or claims of responsibility have been made."

"It is impossible to govern under these circumstances! How can we negotiate with multiple vectors with no stated position?"

"We can reward good behavior," the President said quietly.

"That is tantamount to appeasement!"

"But there is no one to appease; these mishaps were perpetrated by just a few people. The rest are sympathetic perhaps, but innocent of any wrongdoing, let's be sure they are rewarded for keeping their hands clean."

"Reward them how?"

"That is what I expect my newly-re-instated Cabinet to determine!"

Each of the ministers nodded in understanding and an exaggerated sense of self-importance. Santo couldn't wait to clear the room. He realized hated aspects of each of them. At first he self-censored on the word 'hate' but changed his mind. He really did <u>hate</u> all of them. They had their uses, but together they were useless and dangerous, a combustible combination. He dreaded going to the parliamentary houses, but his was a representative market state engaged in a battle for civil tranquility – they expected no less. Overly attached to hotly held opinions based on little more than rumor and innuendo, people voted based on feelings, not evidence, their voting patterns patently irrational. He rued the day the theory of the 'rational man' had been disproven; likening it to the day the philosopher declared that god was dead. Most people preferred to be fooled, especially if it meant they could be sure about something. With every sub-group the existential enemy of every other sub-group, no room for compromise or concession emerged. Every sub-group claimed some social high ground, making every middle ground worthy of conflict. For a people on a four-day workweek and a fair amount of free time on their hands, sufficient ground remained to fight over, even if they employed anti-social methods. The usual carrots, sticks and policy bullets had been exhausted. The advent of secure Bitcoin made short work of manipulation of the money supply by national or private bankers. Interest rates were already near zero, with both credit and labor markets inconsequential bit-players. SELAND made censorship either unnecessary or technically impossible. The advent of socially acceptable and embedded drone technology made the combat/civil service draft irrelevant. People had time to pick non-fatal fights, making each fight more brutal but leaving the combatants to fight again another day. Only brute force remained but that had been declared internationally illegal and in declining utility in any case. At times, Santo understood the wisdom, utility, and tragedy of the old Roman Circuses.

*

Dominic's request for five days personal leave sailed through the system in record time. He told Santo he would stay at the villa, which seemed to calm the old man's nerves. Biding his time inside the suite until after sunset, he packed extra clothes in a non-descript backpack, securing his COMLINK in the backpack's false bottom. He did not plan on using it while he was away. Old, tattered shorts, a pepper sauce-stained t-shirt, and sneakers with holes in the toes made him feel more anonymous. He left his telltale ring in the suite. Once outside the palace grounds, he hitched a ride into town to pick up Brian. Together, they would take Brian's old, unregistered Mini Cooper out to the coast, to the beachfront villa.

The morning sun crested just as they reached the turnoff for the villa. Brian rubbed his eyes as if rubbing them would actually help and leaned his head out the window as bald tires spun and slipped on the rocky, sandy turf. Dominic dove for sunglasses in the backpack. The salt-laden ocean air filled the car and their lungs temporarily masking their acute lack of sleep. More than once, Dominic thought he might have to get out and push the car out of one of the gaping potholes in the road. They split a warm beer – a surprise from underneath the front passenger seat and the last of the WAKE. They parked behind the villa, carried the copious boxes of liquor – beer, tequila, rum and bourbon inside, where they found the food they ordered neatly arranged in boxes in the villa kitchen. Food and liquor sorted, they set to closing blinds, curtains and shutters wherever they could. Their eyes thanked them almost immediately. Dominic removed the sunglasses. Still wobbly and intoxicated from the previous evening's adventures, Dominic fell onto one of the couches while Brian had the good sense to mix two protein shakes before he collapsed on the bed in the other room. Besides a bloody nose, a nice bump on his forehead and a sprained knee, Brian was not the worse for wear. Dominic nursed what was most likely a broken hand, a shallow knife wound on the upper arm and a nasty bruise covering half his face. These things happened when they were too drunk to recognize they were wading into other people's battles. In return for the protein shake, Dominic pulled himself off the couch to share his sleep pharma with Brian. That would give them a good twelve hours of respite but they would wake up hung over and very sore. But they had a civil commendation from a downtown, policing unit. The irony was almost too much.

They had not been looking for a fight – there were plenty of fight clubs for that sort of thing. In fact, they had closed their tab with the Russian girls, finished the last drops of Suntory Yamazaki and set out to find the car, calling it a night. A few blocks down, with the car in sight at the end of a short alleyway, they had only to get around a budding disturbance between three young posse hooligans and an older, very drunk guy in a suit, who sounded terrified through slurred speech. Dominic's usual habit was to ignore that sort of thing, but the guy called him by name. As soon as he did so, the three hooligans turned their anger and rage on Dominic and Brian. The ensuing melee was neither balanced nor fair. Though the kids had a club and a knife between them, Dominic and Brian incapacitated them in short order, surrendering them to the policing constabulary when it responded. Only afterwards did Dominic realize whom he had rescued. It was none other than Richard Jackson – his nemesis and one time suitor. The man seemed sincerely grateful, going as far as to sign the commendation, leaning heavily on Brian as he signed the electronic document with a shaky hand. They refused medical attention. WAKE residual made aggression easy to come by. Sleep pharma made it easy to forget.

They passed hours without talking, nursing their wounds, building a mound of empty beer bottles. Brian left Dominic to himself to sit in the surf, allowing the water to creep up his legs as the tide followed the moon. Dominic ventured outside to lay flat on his back under a tree as the sun set on their third day at the villa. The bruise on his face had gotten darker. It hurt to talk. It hurt to laugh. They no longer needed sleep pharma to sleep. They began to feel human by the fourth day. They sat under an acacia tree before the afternoon sun became unbearable, a half-full bottle of Spanish rum in each of their hands.

"You're on the razor edge, *bredda*," Brian said, sitting up in a rare moment of lucidity, looking at his friend with a concerned eye.

"Too much sorry go around *yaso*…" Dominic said, not bothering to lift his head or look at Brian from his perch on the sand.

"*Man nuh dead, nuh call im duppy…*"

"There's a lot going on…"

"You can't drink it away, you know that…"

"OK Answer-man…"

"You want me to smother you?" Brian sat up to ask the question, with just a hint of a smile to belie his choice of words.

The absurdity of the question made them both laugh. Dominic held out his bottle for a toast. Brian drank with him. One more wake-up and they would head back to Capital with only the one conversation between them. Somehow, Dominic felt better for it.

THE INVESTIGATION – CAPITAL – PRESENT DAY

Though grateful Ashton decided to cooperate, saving them the intensity of "special techniques", Dominic did not view the interrogation. He learned through ISEC briefings, passed to him by the President, what the man revealed. Ashton revealed the existence of an old darknet on an unused portion of the SELAND NETCERT -- open, available and functioning, but invisible. He never learned the group's name in all the time he worked with them, but he knew they violently objected to SELAND – not the network itself, but the inability to remain anonymous. He had not seen or talked to the same person more than once.

Yet SELAND had been in existence for 6 years and opt-out blocks could have been utilized, Santo countered. Ashton shook his head. SELAND had been presented as *fait accompli* – and people flocked to it like a new religion. A federal vote garnered a 38% turnout, but response to the free bio-tag tattoos, required to access SELAND, came in at 99% within the first 6 months. With bio-tag, confirmed identity became wearable. People put the bio-tag tattoo in strange places, though the majority of people accepted the recommended placement, just behind the left ear. Pundits marveled at the near 100% acceptance rate of the SELAND premium – the loss of anonymity. They should have worried about the less than 1% who rejected it. People reveled in their new religion and did not notice what they did not choose to see.

Ashton knew about the machine gun network and the body-pattern collimator. He knew about homeless children as trigger wires, but only after confronted with pictures of small, blackened corpses. He volunteered nothing, waiting to be confronted by specific evidence. He admitted going to the Plantation House and drinking *cachaca*. He knew no names. He had no knowledge of whether other incidents, such as the stink bomb at the hotel, resulted from the same group. He thought not, as it diluted the impact of the group's other actions. He took great pains to stress the group's efforts to avoid death or injury. He claimed the group's actions were made possible by the malware on the SELAND deck he had given Dominic. When asked why he used Dominic, Ashton admitted he hurt those he loved and had done so all his life. He also now deeply regretted it. Ashton had almost succeeded in splitting Dominic into two – on one side a kind of friendship, and on the other, abhorrence. He had a hard time reconciling the two and did not often try

The information from Ashton came from three weeks of interrogations, four hours a day, three days a week. Ensconced in a comfortable, air-conditioned cell, they granted him access to a limited number of media feeds, all censored. His interlocutors remained soft-spoken, polite, accommodating and friendly. The *cahaca* was the key, they insisted. Ashton mentioned it in passing early on, but that was the element of commonality ISEC had been seeking. The two weeks of interrogations that followed made Ashton believe himself more important to the government than he was. At least ISEC positioned them selves that way. When pressed by the President ISEC conceded the hidden cellular network to be slightly interesting as well. Within an hour, ISEC, SELAND and other government agencies placed more trace technology on that single darknet than any network of any kind had ever sustained. For their trouble, ISEC recorded a single text message sent to two camouflaged recipients. The message read simply: <::poof::>

ISEC still insisted *cachaca* to be the key. Advances in thin-layer chromatography technology allowed investigators to work backwards from known explosive residue to trace amounts of sugars in the blast residue. They proposed to derive a chemical signature for the *cachaca* consumed in the Plantation House. The Cabinet remained skeptical down to the last man; even Ms. Casteñada raised her perfectly shaped eyebrows at the concept. Even if they could derive the signature, if homegrown, the signature would not be registered and there would be nothing to compare against. ISEC remained optimistic and no one thought to argue, since they did not often maintain such optimism.

INTERCONTINENTAL HOTEL – CAPITAL – PRESENT DAY

<<Eek-A-Mouse – Born Traveller>>

In the InterContinental front lobby, Dominic detected nothing of the stink bomb which only weeks ago had the entire government running for the doors. People went about their business as they always had -- hurried, frowning, absent-minded, juggling multiple conversations. Kevin had arrived at the shuttle-port a few minutes ago and would be driven to the InterContinental by a driver who appeared to be a normal taxi driver. In fact, he was Dominic's driver in a dumbed-down government car, made to look like a common taxi. Curiosity as to how Kevin fared won out over the discomfort he felt having Kevin in country. He retained few friends from a tumultuous childhood and with Ashton in prison and the unpleasantness of their relationship exposed and known, Dominic drifted to fixed elements, of which Kevin was perhaps one of only two still living. The fight for the limited independence Kevin's stay required was uncomfortable and took far longer than it should have. His first idea had been to go the coast, where the government maintained a beachfront villa, but ISEC would not permit it and the President chose not to override them. The Intercontinental was a default fallback location, a known quantity. For ISEC, Dominic himself was the variable.

As he waited for Kevin's arrival, his thoughts turned to Hanna, and he wished he had taken her with him. He thought about her at random moments throughout the day, more often now than before. He wondered what it meant for him, for Hanna; if it meant anything at all. Before he had the chance to thread his thoughts out, Kevin arrived. Easy to spot, Kevin screamed "foreigner," from his face to his clothes to his walk. Sporting two days of facial hair, blonde hair shaved close, Kevin lifted a pair of expensive sunglasses and peered deep into the hotel. Baggy shorts, tank top and flip-flops completed the picture – in a hotel where people dressed more formally. People regarded him coolly in the foyer, but the front desk people called to him by name. His near constant smile also gave him away. He offered his credit card, which the front desk took but did not charge. While he waited for his room key, he turned to peer again into the hotel looking for something, someone.

Dominic waited for his driver to drop Kevin's bags with the bellhop and made his way to the lobby. Seeing Kevin propelled him towards their reunion of sorts, after five short but formative years. He reached the front desk just as Kevin accepted his room key. Kevin turned slightly, as the clerk must have seen Dominic approaching, ruining the surprise. It felt good to see a friend uncompromised by other things and Kevin laughed out loud in a friendly way as they shook hands and hugged awkwardly in public.

Dominic opened with the local patois, "Wahpensuh?"

Kevin laughed again, a warm, deep rolling chuckle. "What?" Kevin reached out and took the fabric of Dominic's coat sleeve between two fingers. "Holy shit dude, you wearin' Armani?"

Dominic winced at Kevin's language. He remembered the difference between the two places; here people were more reserved, less ebullient and effusive. In North Carolina, people were more open. They laughed out loud, yelled, cursed and laughed again. "You can have it if you want it." Dominic said shrugging his shoulders. Kevin had changed very little except for the growing up that occurred between seventeen and twenty-five. A year older, Kevin acted younger, less inhibited. An awkward moment followed when neither had anything to say, nothing to move the moment forward. The driver stopped to shake Kevin's hand but when Kevin proffered a small tip the driver smiled and declined. Dominic gave Kevin his messaging hashtag and suggested Kevin get settled in his room and meet at the bar on the top floor in two hours. When Kevin disappeared into the elevator, Dominic realized he had been holding his breath. Hanna once told him he held his breath when nervous. He denied the accusation in the same way he denied her accusation that he snored.

Three hours later, they met at the "The View". Kevin ordered a local beer and Dominic ordered mineral water. Kevin apologized for being late, saying he had fallen asleep, then took his beer with him as he walked slowly around the glass-walled perimeter of the bar. Dominic followed a few paces behind, in case Kevin drifted too close to the windows. Kevin picked up on the space between the chairs and the windows. "Why don't they put the chairs next to the windows?" Kevin asked, standing in the wasted real estate. Dominic shrugged, not wanting to get into detail. Dominic did his stint as 'tour guide', pointing out the airport, garrison tenements, squatter settlements and sugar cane. Kevin returned to his seat still smiling, shaking his head and nursing his beer. "It's good to see you, dude! You look hella different! What's up with the Armani?"

"I'm with the President's office."

"No shit! You have the craziest life!" Kevin said, shaking his head and finishing his beer. Dominic motioned the bar staff for another one. "I remember the stories you told us back when. My mom probably still thinks you're a really good liar."

"How is your mom?" Dominic queried, remembering Kevin's mother for the first time in a long time.

Kevin's face darkened and he lost his smile. "She has breast cancer. You knew that, right?"

"I didn't know..." Dominic shared Kevin's palpable darkness.

"She's strong though...she still gives me a hard time about getting married and having kids..."

"I'm sorry to hear about the cancer…"

"You know they got divorced a couple years after you left…"

"No, I didn't know that either…" The conversation turned in the very direction Dominic had been so uncomfortable about earlier. "How about your dad?"

"Dad? Still an alcoholic, shacked up with some chick my age in California, calls me every week. He's cool but he pretends he's 25, pisses me off sometimes."

Kevin had not changed as Dominic remembered him -- everything revealed, nothing hidden. "What are you doing?"

"I'm supposed to be finishing school. I went with this combined Bachelors/Masters program in Artificial Intelligence. It's fukken' killin' me. I got another two years left."

"SELAND?"

"Hell no, those gray-hat bastards!"

Dominic smiled as the Kevin he remembered came back to him -- so sure of himself, an indignant expert. He remembered Kevin's dad never found it amusing. "I'm glad you flew down, Kevin," Dominic said unsure of where to take the conversation.

"Dude! I've been trying to get a hold of you for years bro'!"

"Sorry, my hashtag changed."

Kevin's incredulity showed. "How does that happen?" SELAND's foundation -- globally verifiable, universal and persistent identity services -- one's tag-hash was the key to all of it.

"It happened…" Dominic replied without going into detail.

"Dude, that is insane! You gotta' tell me!"

"I will, but not here." Dominic motioned for another beer for Kevin and because the nervousness inside had started to grow, he decided to order scotch, a 'man's drink' as Santo called it.

"You got a girlfriend yet?"

Dominic nodded. "Her name is Hanna. She's a year older than me and she's into all that AI stuff too. She's part of the DF as well. I think she wants to get into ISEC."

"DF? ISEC? You talking that patois again?"

"Sorry, 'DF' is the defense force. ISEC is like your FBI, CIA and NSA combined."

"No shit! You work with them too?"

"Not really…" Dominic hoped his white lie held water.

"I saw the newsfeeds coming into the airport. Sounds crazy…"

"Crazy's one word for it."

"Dayum! You're all growed up! I would have never guessed, dude, and you're life is STILL crazy!" Kevin shook his head in amazement and made short work of his third beer.

Right on time, his COMLINK chimed ten minutes into the conversation, just as he asked. He dutifully checked the display and apologized to Kevin. He had to take care of something, but if Kevin wanted, they could have dinner later. Always easygoing and agreeable, Dominic ordered Kevin a fifth beer, closed the tab and made his way to his room, grateful Kevin decided to make his visit short. The country had been placed on multiple watch lists because of recent unrest and having Kevin in the capital ran the usual risks. There were ministerial 'response-only' security teams in both adjacent rooms. They had no 'eyes' or 'ears', Santo's one concession – that Dominic would know trouble when it struck, even if Santo did not believe it himself. Where Dominic hoped to feel closer to Kevin for their shared past, he felt distant; where he hoped to feel something in common, he felt further apart than he imagined two people could be, with not just distance and time separating them. Despite the distance, real or imagined, something propelled him to connect, like a ship, repeatedly dropping an anchor in rough seas, hoping to catch on something solid.

By the time they sat down for dinner, Dominic felt less nervous in the familiar surrounds of the restaurant, with its clinking glass, snatches of conversation, and piano music wafting through the room. The lights seemed bright, the ambient volume high and the food, not quite hot enough. With Ashton's treachery fresh in his mind, he began to wonder whether some basic things now needed guarding, that he had put his faith in the wrong faces, and that despite the friendship he and Kevin forged, his brain screamed caution. He found it strange to feel the way he did, not having had reason to think that way before. They ate slowly, neither picking nor eating voraciously. They drank more than they ate, but Dominic went back to mineral water. They talked about high school teachers they liked and the ones they hated; about girls who rejected them outright and the ones who merely ignored them; about beach parties and bonfires with cheap beer and cheaper tequila. They talked about football practice (for Kevin) and soccer (for Dominic), about an adolescent athletic rivalry centered primarily on opposing opinions of the other's sport, or more to the point, whether each was truly a sport. The jokes were crude and rancid but they both laughed. They talked about Kevin's parents and talking about Kevin's parents. Kevin graciously honored the unspoken rule of not asking about Dominic's family, or his past. They laughed about smoking pot at the boardwalk in Atlantic City, skateboards and porno pin ups. Dominic told Kevin about Hanna and Kevin told Dominic he met a girl he wanted to spend his life with.

Deep in conversation, their waiter told them apologetically the restaurant had closed. The hands of the clock had traveled four hours since they had taken their seats. Dominic paid with a wave of his hand.

They went back to Kevin's room, taking separate couches to vivisect the past. They broke the seal on the wet bar and emptied it of the four Jack Daniels bottles in four toasts, each a little more raucous than the last. When those were done, they ordered twelve more, finishing those in short order in a mere six toasts.

"I'm not doing so good with my moms being sick, dude. You have no idea."

"I don't know what to say…except, 'I'm sorry'. *Too much 'sorry' go 'round yaso.*"

"I know. You don't have to say anything. I had to tell someone."

"You don't talk to your dad?"

"Oh, I talk to him. Most of the time, he passes out in the first five minutes. Doesn't even remember talking to me the next time I call."

"What about your girlfriend?"

"I try to be strong for her…"

Dominic nodded. His brain stalled. Even if he had wanted to say something, he would not have been able to.

"Don't you have problems you can't figure out?" Kevin asked, standing up and moving to the window.

"My problems are state secrets. If I told you, I'd have to kill you."

"What doesn't kill me makes me stronger, right?"

"That's what they say."

"You ever wonder who "they" are?"

"Nope."

"Never?"

"Nope."

"You got it all figured out, don't you."

"Nope."

"Seems like you do. Your life's all buttoned up, not like mine, with everything up in the air, always on the verge of collapse."

"Nope."

"Really? Then you're a better fukken liar than I thought! You still a runner?" That's what the cop called Dominic in North Carolina when he filed his report, 'a runner'.

Dominic lied. "Not so much."

"See?"

"Maybe it'll even out after a while…" Dominic countered, using a line he'd heard Santo use, though he did not quite believe it himself.

"Maybe," Kevin said. His wandering around the room led him to sit on the opposite end of the couch Dominic sat on.

After a night of conversation and words, a physicality found a tense then tentative, awkward, then comfortable reprise -- one light skinned and sunburned, the other darker skinned and self-conscious, eyes open, absently covering the constellation shaped birthmark on his hip. It was comfortable because familiar. Dominic passed no judgment, excusing himself around 4.30 in the morning.

INTERCONTINENTAL HOTEL – CAPITAL – PRESENT DAY

The GOVNET page came during a late brunch. Kevin wore dark sunglasses and Dominic wished he had done the same. Dominic stared at the message because he had not seen this particular urgency/priority code before. It came through as a "Z" code. He excused himself to call into the standing ISEC control center. He learned the "Z" priority superseded ALL other GOVNET priority codes and that it meant crisis in progress, or emerging. ISEC would not let him return without an escort, so he authorized them to "retrieve" him, to use ISEC parlance. He barely made it back to their table when eight ISEC agents stormed the restaurant, surrounded Dominic and hustled him out of the restaurant, the hotel, and into their waiting motorcade.

<< The Academy of St. Martin in the Fields – Saint-Saëns: Danse macabre, Op.40>>

He joined the President in the control center along with a few high ranking Cabinet members, the leaders of both houses of parliament and two flag staff generals who ignored him completely -- a prestigious gathering on an inauspicious day. The displays showed swarms of tiny, robotic, marine assaultbots attacking the SELAND tower, like a colony of ants attacking an elephant carcass. Each assaultbot was outfitted with a twelve-inch reciprocating saw, attached to the external flotation ring. It seemed they meant to sink the thing. Three hundred feet away, large black boxes floated ominously on the water, from which the swarms of assaultbots originated. They had no contingency plan for this unprecedented attack and the top tier of government watched in utter fascination as the basic unit of SELAND fell under attack. For a few minutes, they could only watch. The horror had not yet set in. Someone had enough foresight to deploy the YAL Directed Energy Platform and two Gladiator drones with DREAD weapons on board. Already on-scene, the RQ-9C hovered above the other hardware, escorted by its own contingent of two unmanned Firescout helos. No one thought to think operationally, even the ISEC bosses stood speechless. The paralysis in the room grew more and more frustrating for Dominic as he watched multiple layers of assaultbots swarming, using the layer underneath to find a clean spot with which to begin their terrible task. The Gladiator drones attempted conventional weaponry to no effect, as the damaged assaultbots simply fell into the water and sank, replaced by a dozen or more new assaultbots. The RQ-9C with all of its fearsome capabilities produced no usable imagery of the mysterious black boxes floating on the ocean surface. Something blocked the RQ's imaging capability, which meant "shock and awe" remained their only option.

For the first time since his induction into the President's office, Dominic did not ask permission. He hopped over the railing and knelt down next to the Operations Chief's console chair. After a brief conversation, Dominic keyed in the President's authorization code on the control board. Coaching the Operations Chief, he first he called the YAL, tying it to the new authorization level. Then he accessed its weapons systems, taking inventory of what it could muster. Santo noticed and put a hand of caution on Dominic's shoulder. Dominic then asked the Operations Chief to order the most detailed satellite recon and SIGINT ISEC could produce on the entire theater.

Realizing he needed better reaction time, he asked the Operations Chief to surrender his chair. Dominic nodded an apology to the surprised officer and jumped into the chair to review the recon. Despite the technology at his fingertips, what he did not see concerned him. The assaultbots appeared to be mechanical, though with some indeterminable power source. The black boxes were the bigger concern because they appeared to be masked to the most advanced SIGINT and recon methods available. Nothing in his substantial and detailed training prepared him for this – forced into acting blindly, without evidence, without context. He entered two commands, ceding both timing and execution to the routines on board the YAL. The Global Hawk released a swarm of Limited Tactical Destruction Polymer rounds ("buckyballs"), raining them on the skirt of assaultbots the SELAND tower had acquired. On contact with the metallic, mechanical assaultbots, the "buckyballs" released their polymer payloads, freezing any moving mechanical object it came into contact in less than a second. The Gladiator used a similar torpedo based polymer weapon to shut down, but not destroy, all three controlling black boxes by closing the portal from which the assaultbots had been spewing. Immediately, the assaultbots, which had so far escaped the "buckyball" swarm, began to detach and fall into the water like metal insect carcasses. Each carcass floated for a few seconds or so until it sank into the ocean depths. Eight seconds later the YAL used its directive energy laser to evaporate two of the three black boxes in an explosion of light, fire, and steam. The third would be retrieved for further investigation. The ISEC reinforcement helo, which had been ordered at the start of the crisis, before the unmanned technology had been ordered, arrived finally with its complement of human shock troops, but the immediate crisis had been resolved. There was very little for them to do.

But they would be remiss if they did not learn something from the experience and Dominic's actions had been calculated to stop the destruction without completely destroying the agents of that destruction. Before surrendering the console chair back to its rightful owner, Dominic ordered all the recon from the incident into a Presidential level SELAND Sequester for future analysis. He asked the Operations Chief to order the physical retrieval of the remaining black box and a few of the assaultbots for post-mishap inspection. When he stood up finally to survey the wall displays, Santo stood next to him. Dominic focused his next remark for Santo's ears alone, *"Mi seh, wi bredda cyaan jus forget 'bout dis ting-deh!"* Santo put his fist on Dominic's shoulder in relief, to congratulate him; then his whole hand on the shoulder, the way Pierre had done. Santo proposed Dominic be promoted but Dominic deferred, choosing to avoid the objections of the ISEC boss and the senior generals in the room. It would have been too much too soon and they would never forgive him. Dominic did ask that the Operations Chief be given a commendation, which went over well with everyone.

Just as they congratulated themselves on the success of their intervention, as the manned attack helo turned around, Santo pointed at the displays with a look of horror. Everyone realized they had succeeded only in instigating the next layer of attack. Similar suitcase type boxes floated up from the depths as if released by the destruction of their precursors. These were much bigger, their purpose not immediately obvious. They navigated closer to the tower where it met the water. After a few minutes, at a distance of a few meters, a nozzle emerged on each of the visible surfaces of the cube shaped objects. Most of the nozzles pointed at the thick rubber of the massive flotation device the tower rested on. However, the nozzle on the top surface pointed upwards towards the metallic portion of the tower. As they watched, the new larger black boxes began shooting concentrated acid under pressure. The acid mixed with seawater and rubber of the tower's flotation raft with terrible consequence. The tiny razor sharp stream of acid that came into contact with the anodized aluminum base of the tower presented a much greater danger.

ISEC could not guarantee their newest polymers would withstand the acid being used in the attack – they had not tested the polymers against acid. The drones exhausted their supply of polymer torpedoes in the first wave. Simple explosives would mix the acid inside the boxes in great quantities, with unknown but fearful effects. The drones had ample supplies of traditional explosive weapons, but the acid made them all useless. They settled on an EMF blast, realizing it would destroy the internal mechanics of both the acid boxes and the sensitive electronics contained within the tower. SELAND asked for 15 minutes to divert its traffic around the Caribbean tower. They had five, at the most. Santo told SELAND he would not call again, preferring to apologize rather than ask permission. SELAND called back in three minutes to report the Caribbean tower had been quarantined. Santo gave the order after confirming the manned helo to be safely away and the drones complied. The control center lost their video of the scene with the blast. Two minutes later the displays lit up again, courtesy of the Global Hawk, stationed high above at a high enough altitude to escape the consequences of the EMF blast. The acid baths stopped but the tower sustained mortal wounds. It would need to be replaced rather than repaired.

This time, they waited before beginning their round of congratulatory high fives and smiles. Their eyes glued to the displays, Dominic felt certain there would be one last wave, that they had survived the first two waves too easily. He waited holding his breath. They almost missed it – yet another black suitcase size cube emerged behind one of the others. They could only wait to see what sort of destruction this new wave would bring and they were not long to find out. Two sides of the cube opened to reveal a cannon. As soon as the cannon stabilized, it fired. All assumed its target would be the tower. Within milliseconds, the Global Hawk soared, putting considerable altitude between it and the canon on the surface, pushing its stress metrics to the absolute outer envelope. As it did, it fired a special kind of projectile, homing in on the heat the surface firing generated. The projectile hit the canon before the canon's mortar found the top of its parabola and fell harmlessly in to the churning water. For less than half a second, their displays went dark as the drone moved its power resources away from reconnaissance and into weapons and evasive action.

They slumped in their seats. No one smiled or high-fived each other, no congratulations were in order. Santo stormed out alone and no one followed. Two AEGIS VI cutters and DF/ISEC helos arrived to cordon the theater. SELAND measured a slight drop in network throughput, but advance warning had prevented the worst damage to network performance. The Global Hawk proved itself well worth the $650 billion prototype investment – one of two on the planet. Replacing the tower would come a little more cheaply at $75 million.

Santo declared martial law. They had the metrics: for every day of martial law the island would lose 0.0035% in annualized GDP.

ISEC CUSTODIAL FACILITY – PRESIDENTIAL PALACE – TODAY

Ashton sat at a heavy metal table, his wrists manacled to the tabletop, ankles manacled to hooks in the floor. Uncomfortably hot in the room, he began to sweat. He had been sitting in that room for the last twenty-four hours with the most horrendous music Dominic ever heard blasting from huge speakers in each corner of the room, this after three days of pitch-black solitary confinement. The temperature in the room sat at 99 degrees with 92% humidity, an ultra-controlled environment. His daily insulin injection had been withheld and instead they injected a diuretic. A glass of ice water sat on the table in front of Ashton, just out of reach, sweating in the hot room. They expected him to break within the next four hours or pass into a coma in the next twelve. Three questions written in green chalk on an old fashioned chalkboard stared back at him: 'Who?, 'Where?', and 'How?'. Ashton only needed to answer two of the three to be released. Simply watching made Dominic sweat, although his training included both sides of 'Special Techniques'. DF resistance training required he submit to Level 1 Special Techniques for twenty-four hours and Level 2 techniques for one hour. Though difficult to watch, he assumed Ashton would give in, that there would be a point to this institutionalized cruelty.

Santo hardened to a steel point and personally supervised the techniques applied to Ashton. Four hours later they commenced with Level 2. Ashton's clothes were removed except for his underwear and the room cooled down to a chilly ten degrees Celcius. When the ambient temperature in the room reached the desired temperature, they dumped a bucket of ice-cold water over him. He had not eaten or drank anything in 30 hours. They injected him with small amounts of adrenaline and the lowest dosage of insulin to avoid diabetic coma. A belt tightened around his chest made

212

breathing visibly difficult and a low voltage stun gun, fired randomly, caused pain and temporary paralysis.

Dominic never wanted to be in this position again. If he knew nothing else, he knew this to be wrong on as many levels as he could imagine. The images came back to him at inopportune moments, making him feel spun out and dirty. Though he did not expect it, Dominic broke as the President ordered Level 3. Dominic pulled Santo to the side and then out of the observation room. He asked for a chance to take a different tack. At first Santo refused, dismissing Dominic's request with a vengefulness Dominic had not witnessed before. Dominic countered that even the Americans had rejected this approach; a low blow in context, but it gave Santo pause.

"You still think you owe him, don't you," Santo said, the steel point of his vengefulness softening.

"I don't think that," Dominic answered, treading carefully and lightly.

"Then why do you want to do this?"

"So your hands are clean..." Dominic said, reprising advice Santo had given him over the course of his assignment.

Santo sighed loudly. "Altruism will get you nowhere. But since you asked me directly, I will give you one hour to the second but it is a favor. You do not owe me, but I may remind you of it. That reminder may be unpleasant."

Dominic nodded without misunderstanding. The granting and payment of favors formed the currency of the Office of the President in reverse reciprocity or *quid pro quo* relationships encompassing both sins of omission and commission. Dominic moved to pass, but the President had more to say. He put his hand on Dominic's shoulder holding him back.

"Do not think of him as the old man from Old Hope Road. I will be watching and I will pull you out if I think he is gaining ground. If that happens you cannot ask me for more time. If you do I will order you to stand down."

Dominic decided to respond in kind. He came to full military attention and gave the President a full dress salute.

Santo nodded and smiled. "Good. You understand the gravity of the situation."

On Dominic's orders, ISEC brought the room temperature up to normal temperature, gave Ashton towels and a clean prison jumpsuit. They removed the belt around his chest and the manacles from one hand and both ankles. Slowly Ashton drank room temperature water. They gave him a candy bar in small bites, a high protein shake and metered his insulin based on blood sugar readings. Dominic left him alone for two hours to 'recover,' after which he donned an ISEC-blue paper jumpsuit and entered the interrogation room, rank with the smells of shit, urine, sweat. Ashton regarded Dominic in silence, his eyes full of fear, exhaustion, defiance and hate. Dominic reached for the glass of ice water and pushed it closer to Ashton so he could reach it with his one un-manacled hand. Dominic realized he had been holding his breath and took a deep breath to compensate.

"So Joseph sends a boy to do a man's job," Ashton said, spitting blood.

Dominic ignored him and used one of the clean towels to dry a chair for him self. He reviewed Ashton's latest physiological vitals on a display only he could see, pretending to be more interested in the display than he really was. After a minute, Dominic looked up, squared his eyes with Ashton and said, "You used to scare me."

"You were easily frightened…"

"I thought you wanted it that way…"

"I know all the tricks, Dominic. You will not succeed where they have failed and you are a fool to try..."

"Straightedge was scared of you…"

"I will not talk about my children!"

"You haven't seen them in years…" Dominic countered, utilizing information Ashton did not know he had.

"You are running out of time."

"Why do you say that?"

"Those butchers can't wait to restart the protocol," Ashton said with no small amount of contempt, spitting blood again.

"You are right, I am running out of time."

"No tricks from your bag, Dominic? No script?"

"I came for myself, Baba."

"Do not call me that!"

"What shall I call you? Ashton? Star? I don't know you anymore," Dominic said, looking up from the display and locking eyes with a broken man. Dominic's refusal to engage in any one specific interrogation technique began to have effect, throwing Ashton off guard and giving him no hold against the incline facing him.

"I don't care what you call me just do not call me Baba. I don't know why you started calling me that." Ashton was bleeding profusely from the mouth, spitting blood with every sentence, every breath. The glass of ice water turned a shade of red from the one sip Ashton had taken.

Dominic signaled for a medic, who entered silently to clean up the blood and give Ashton medicated gauze for his mouth and refill the glass with fresh water. "Are you willing to barter, Ashton?" Dominic asked, getting to the heart of the matter.

"Surely they trained you better than that," Ashton scoffed, his laughter muffled by the gauze in his mouth.

"So how shall we pass the time?"

"You came in here of your own accord or they sent you in here?"

"I am here for myself."

"Why?"

"I don't know…"

Ashton removed the stained gauze from his mouth. "You want to barter? I am already dead. I have nothing to barter."

"The veins in your arms still stand up. It would be a shame if the sins of the father were visited on the children."

"You said 'barter'. Why do you threaten me?"

"Happenstance is a harsh mistress and Trouble is a pimp, I know them both well."

"What do you barter?"

"I have only assurances…"

"About my children?"

Dominic nodded.

"Why should I believe you?"

"Because you have no other choice. No one else will sit here."

"What do you know?"

"What I know would make a father cry…"

"If I give you what you want?"

"Your children will find assistance is more easily obtained."

"How is it you hid this propensity for evil from me all your years?"

"Hanna will be here soon and I am hungry…" Dominic replied, purposefully focusing his attention on a loose string on a seam of the paper jumpsuit.

Ashton shook the table with his manacled arm and spat as he yelled, "You are a devil!"

Dominic did not look up or react but continued to worry the loose string on the jumpsuit. He knew that Ashton could not take being ignored.

"Look at me when I speak to you, boy!" Ashton yelled again, his face twisted in anger and rage, his entire form shaking as if buffeted by a strong wind.

Dominic remained motionless, wrapping the thread around his finger to snap it free, purposely keeping his head down and his body language indifferent and relaxed. Without looking up he replied, "You don't scare me, old man." Dominic stood up, shut off the display and used yet another clean towel to energetically wipe his face and hands as if they needed to be cleaned. "We are finished then." He threw the towel at Ashton, turned around and made for the door. "Your butcher friends will return shortly," he said as the door slammed behind him and the lights in the interrogation room switched off.

Dominic entered the observation room and collapsed on one of the metal chairs, tearing at the paper jumpsuit as if it was on fire. He stared at the wall. Santo sank into another chair, covering his face with his hands. The ISEC officers shuffled papers and made notes, entered things into various systems, avoiding looking at the mess of a man on the other side of the glass, shown in their infrared displays in varying shades of gray.

"You made it personal," Santo said to Dominic.

"It is personal," Dominic said, exhaustion palpable in his voice and on his face.

"Are you giving up?"

"He is weighing the odds…I think he will decide in our favor."

"How can you be sure?"

"His daughter Slip is pregnant and living in the garrison tenement at Rincon du Nord. His oldest son Magnum is a heroin addict living in a tent city south of the airport. His youngest, Straightedge, is a paranoid schizophrenic. He's sitting in his own shit, tied to a chair in a local ward."

"And you are here, a trusted team member in the highest office of the land," Santo said quietly.

Now it was Dominic's turn to cover his face with his hands as he replied to Santo. "He put me there."

"Your concern is genuine…" Santo observed.

"I don't care about Slip and Magnum, but Straightedge…we were friends…"

Although there was much more to the conversation, they were interrupted, as Dominic predicted, by Ashton using his manacled hand to shake the table, making a thunderous racket via the speakers in the observation room. Dominic did not bother with the jumpsuit this time. He entered the room, triggering the lights and stood near the door. He handed Ashton a pencil and a pad of paper and waited.

Ashton took the pad and pencil and started writing. After writing three lines he stopped and looked up at Dominic. "Are they ok?"

"They are not OK."

"Are they doing better than a stray dog?" Ashton said, meeting eyes with Dominic as if his question was particularly relevant.

"Keep writing. I am not your friend."

Completely broken, Ashton returned to writing his confession. It took him less than five minutes after which Dominic took the pad back to the observation room.

*

Though it took every ounce of internal will power, Dominic cleaned up for the trip back to the InterContinental. He needed to see Kevin off the island in case the civil situation became unstable. He sent Kevin a message telling him to pack and wait for him in the lobby, that he would take Kevin to the airport for an earlier flight. Kevin did not argue. He did not take the ISEC escort this time, but a small group of men in Santo's detail he still trusted. Dominic went into the hotel alone, found Kevin trying to pay for his room at the front desk and hustled him and his bags outside and into the waiting car. A two-car police escort took them to the airport through the diplomatic entrance and into the VIP airport lounge.

Kevin extended his hand and Dominic shook it. "When are you coming to North Carolina?"

"Maybe sooner than you think!" Dominic said, wondering how much more his commission he could stand.

"You have to come up for my wedding dude! If you don't, you are dirt! Dirt!"

"I never pictured you the marrying type…" Dominic said with a goading voice.

"Dude! Shut the fuck up. I'll be married with five kids before you grow a fukken beard!"

"All right, all right! I promise. I'll come up for your wedding." They shook hands again and one of Dominic's security men hinted that Kevin should board his plane. Kevin waved as he disappeared through the boarding gate, still smiling.

In the car on his way back to the Presidential Palace, Ashton's reference to a stray dog stuck in Dominic's head as it seemed a *non sequitur*, an oxymoron, unrelated to anything that preceded it, directly or indirectly, recent and not so recent. Dominic attached importance to the words and did not know why. He assumed meaning though he was at a loss to define it. By the time he reached the Palace grounds, current events conspired to make him forget, in favor of a continued crisis, an ongoing and persistent emergency.

*

As a measure of the power even an embattled leader can muster when threatened, slaved MULE assaultbots the size of large trucks quickly and quietly surrounded ISEC's executive headquarters. MQ12 Reaper drones accompanied by Firescouts, both with anti-tank, line of site weapons systems, armed and ready, stationed themselves high overhead. Three Special Forces platoons followed behind the assault bots, followed by the President himself in a phalanx of heavily armed SELAND shock troops, past the entrance to the barracks. A 2-star general emerged from a side room, looking as if he had just woken up, saluting in his rumpled uniform. The SELAND phalanx spread out to cover the room's entrances, exits and weak points. President Joseph Santo demanded the audience of the agency's director, a former five-star general and ISEC career officer, whom many assumed would retire after a long and illustrious career.

While waiting for the Director to comply with a presidential summons, a COMLINK burst informed them that a SWORDS combat robot apprehended the Director attempting an escape through an undefined exit and was now in custody. Simultaneous to the arrest of ISEC's Director, a different cast of the President's men invaded the headquarters of the Defense Force's Third Regiment, taking its ranking general into custody and duly sealing and locking down that facility. The President issued the order freezing all ISEC facilities, as well as the barracks of the Third Regiment. No exceptions. With ISEC's technical facilities "frozen", SELAND pledged full cooperation, ensuring all traffic in and out of any ISEC facility would be mirrored and stored at the highest level of security it could muster. SELAND went into full discovery mode invading all aspects of any bit and byte of data that passed through its network – financial, official and personal communication, places people visited, where they stopped or stood, how they got there and those they traveled with. Authority for ISEC operations ceded to the President, who promoted Dominic as its nominal and functional head. Santo needed someone he could trust, he said as his excuse, and the number of people he could trust had just dwindled to one.

ISEC CUSTODIAL FACILITY – PRESIDENTIAL PALACE – TODAY

ISEC Custodial placed the former, now disgraced, DF General and ISEC Director in a room similar to the room Ashton had been in only days earlier. Their arms manacled at the wrists above their heads and over a bar, they found it difficult to keep their manacled feet on the ground. Hooded and clothes removed, ISEC Custodial started at Level 2. They started with an injection of high doses of adrenaline and a so-called 'truth serum,' which had extreme paranoia, nausea and migraines as side effects. They received large doses, not to ensure the truth, but to intensify the side effects. They hung lifeless, like exsanguinated hogs on the hooks that killed them. A young Custodial conscript peppered the two men with nonsensical questions yelled through a loudspeaker held directly in front of their ears. They had no time to answer before the next question battered their eardrums. Other Custodial staff sharpened long knives in between the questions and brought in three dogs whose viciousness on command turned the room into a cacophony of barking, growling, yelling, screaming and involuntary bodily functions. The water from the fire hose in the room made short work of any mess they made, but it left bruises on their bodies even if they could not see them. Though unpleasant, he could not muster feelings about 'wrong' or 'right'. He did not hold his breath. Dominic watched episode without feeling.

The Level 2 treatment continued for two hours, on forty minutes, off for twenty. Leaving the manacles and hoods in place, they removed the bar above them without warning so that they crumbled to the ground with a thud. They were given no food and only sparing amounts of water. At the end of two hours, they were hosed down with the fire hose one last time, released from the manacles and given a slice of bread and water. They did not leave the room and the hoods were not removed. Thus they remained for another two hours after which they were offered the opportunity to confess. One accepted; the other did not.

Removed from the room but still hooded, the confessor found himself in a different room with three uniformed police officers. Injected with a substance known to cause extreme dizziness, the police officers shoved the confessor back and forth between them, against the walls, threw him to the floor, for a good half hour. After thirty minutes, they gave him another injection of adrenalin and began the manhandling again, this time markedly rougher, beating him about the head and kidneys with bare fists. They hung him upside down and swung him back and forth until his head slammed into the walls on both sides of the room. Ten minutes later, the man had a heart attack. When they dropped him to the floor, he was dead at fifty-nine. The second man, the one who had not confessed also died, a result of repeatedly being dropped on his head from a height of about eight feet. His neck broke on the third drop.

Though Dominic had few feelings about the fate of the two men, he felt dirty afterwards. Needing to push the world away from him, he went to the track and did his usual collection of sprints. Instead of giving up when his chest burned and felt like it would explode, when his leg muscles felt like jelly, he pressed further until exhaustion made him so nauseous he could not stand. It took him a good thirty minutes until he recovered sufficiently to make it back to his suite. There he collapsed on the floor, breathing heavily, unable or unwilling to stand up, much less shower, or move to the bed. He lay on the floor staring at the ceiling. As his body recovered, he felt the familiar flush of natural endorphins coursing through his bloodstream. At its most powerful point it overwhelmed his thought processes and made him feel as if the world had been pushed away from him, not isolated or protected, just at arms length, which had been the point all along.

Too much happened too quickly for Dominic to incorporate into a coherent story line. He possessed little logic or explanation other than the fact these things occurred. He traveled with the trappings of power, though he found it useless. He learned things he never wanted to know but nothing about the one thing he thought he should know. He saw a man broken and watched men die and the broken man made him more uncomfortable. Friends turned to enemies. The one person he thought he would not befriend or become attached to, treated him like a member of his family -- Santo even talked about Dominic joining them on a family vacation. He berated himself for getting things so wrong but also recognized that somehow, against unreasonable odds, he kept landing on his feet. None of this dulled the question of history -- his mother and father, his grandparents. Without knowing why, these questions took on increasing urgency, eclipsing everything else, not an unpleasant distraction given the events of recent weeks, but perhaps a more hopeless one.

CHAPTER III

PRESIDENTIAL PALACE – CAPITAL - TODAY

The President announced the foiled coup in a dinnertime media feed. He blamed the conspirators for the garbage bomb, the ship sinking in the harbor, the SELAND tower de-linking and the attempt to destroy the SELAND tower. There had been other incidents but the government generously chalked those incidents to copycat crimes and let sleeping dogs lie. He announced the arrests of the conspirators and that if there were others, they should come forward during the leniency period. If discovered after the leniency period, the government could not guarantee their wellbeing. With martial law lifted, the President repeated his call for people to live peacefully, help their neighbors and raise their children to do the same. He apologized for the unrest and inconvenience the conspirators brought upon the island and its residents, expressing his hope life would settle into its usual rhythm.

He made this announcement with his wife and children on the portico of the President's Palace, as well as announcing elections in six months. Employing neither a triumphalist, nor a belligerent tone, if one word described his manner, it would be 'indifferent'. Dominic watched the feed and got the impression Santo had stopped caring. After the media feed concluded, Santo came inside and joined Dominic in the small sunroom Dominic adopted as his own. At sunset, Dominic could open the windows and position his chair so the evening breeze crossed his face and he had a perfect view of the evening sky. Santo poured them both a finger of *Hakushu* and sank into the chair across from Dominic.

"I'm tired, bredda…"

"Running on empty?" Dominic asked, reprising an expression he heard Kevin use years ago.

"It does feel like that," Santo tipped his hand, holding his drink toward Dominic and took another long swig.

"Maybe 'tings settle' nuh…"

"I hope so, son." Santo said.

"Me too," Dominic replied, unsure and uncomfortable with the honorific.

"You made us proud a couple days ago, Dominic. More than one person complimented you, people who don't give compliments lightly."

"Yessuh. Who told you?"

"You don't know them and even if you did I wouldn't tell you. I can tell you that there is room for you with SELAND or ISEC…when this is over."

"When this is over?" Dominic asked, immediately more uncomfortable.

"Nothing lasts forever. You know that. Some day the government will change; a different family will live here. We will move on and do other things."

"*Nuttin' fi changeup nuh, tchroo?*"

"Not now, but I don't want it to be a surprise for you. Think about it and tell me what you want to do next."

"I was thinking of looking for my family…" Dominic said quietly, unsure how to frame what he wanted.

Santo nodded knowingly. "If you find them? What then, captain?"

"Then I'll know…"

"How long has this been on your mind?"

"Not so much before, but…"

"I think I understand…"

"It's a wall I have to climb…"

"Do you…have to," Santo asked, sounding worried. Then, before Dominic could answer, "I'm sorry. That was unfair."

After a few minutes of silence Dominic asked a question. "Remember the day we met you said you wanted us to be friends?"

"Yes, I remember…"

"When you said that, I thought you were crazy. But now…it doesn't sound so crazy…to say that we're friends…" Dominic said quietly but confidently.

Santo downed his drink, smiled, stood up and put his hand on Dominic's shoulder. He made his way to the hallway and then stopped as if he thought of something he had forgotten. "Think about after you climb that wall, what you want to do…school, ISEC, SELAND. Then come talk to me, as a friend."

Dominic nodded but said nothing. It seemed the better course of action to concentrate on finishing his drink.

Hanna and Dominic walked on the palace grounds in the cool of the morning, sometimes hands clasped together, other times at their own separate paces, as if strangers. Nierika jumped and bounded between them in complete happiness, tail up and wagging slightly to the right, eyes bright and engaged, her body shivering with enthusiasm. Relieved and grateful for quiet time to share, they walked unclouded by the urgent and the unimportant. The weather chose to be less foreboding, with a high-pressure system that kept the humidity low and the sky free of intimidating thunderclouds. Dominic smiled as they walked and watched the dog move through her repertoire of tricks and antics – trying to get them to do something. Finally, she resorted to standing in their path and barking at them, raising her whole body with each bark and landing squarely on her front feet. She did this over and over and over until Dominic could stand the barking no more and picked up whatever he could find and tossed it as far as it would go. Nierika fled in the direction of the object, her head and shoulders low, her whole body propelled in the direction the twig had been thrown. She flew across the ground, her paws barely touching the ground.

Dominic laughed and called her a fool. Hanna feigned dismay and scolded him for insulting the dog. The dog gave them no time to argue, for Nierika returned to Dominic's side again, the precious twig placed directly between his feet. She did not wait this time but immediately commenced her insistent barking. Once more, Dominic threw the twig for Nierika…and again…and again…and again…and again…until foam flew from her mouth and her breathing sounded like a freight train crossing a mountain bridge at full speed. She took her twig and ran to a spot about 20 yards away and lay down, her long tongue lolling, tail wagging and the twig safely secure under one paw.

With Nierika's chase instinct temporarily satisfied, Dominic and Hanna argued testily about the difference between making love and fucking. Hanna thought of 'making love' as something done at night and 'fucking' during the day. Dominic thought it hardly mattered day or night. She feigned dismay and pushed him away from her. He asked why the time of day made any difference and she did not know. He smiled out of a sense of vindication and got a frown from her for his efforts. She claimed 'making love' as something she invited, invoked and elicited; a part of herself she gave up but did not lose. He shook his head and pulled her into a bear hug. She pretended to struggle but he held her to him and she stopped pretending to struggle. With her head near his chin he put his lips on her forehead; a favorite place of his, his other mercy seat. She told him about her plans to go to law school and he said he would deal with that when he had to. He ignored her when she asked him what he thought about going to school off shore. She asked again, on the chance he had not heard her. He ignored her again. They talked about Ashton being right, wrong or somewhere in between. Dominic talked about watching the treatment of the other two conspirators and how he was unmoved, how he did not hold his breath. He started to describe what he had seen but Hanna stopped him with her finger on his lips. Dominic defended Ashton for taking him in and making him a part of his family. Hanna did not argue but he knew she disagreed. Dominic defended Ashton for getting him the commission with the President, something about which Hanna argued passionately.

"He did not do that for you, he did it for himself!" She stopped walking and turned to face him.

He kept walking. "But I got something out of it."

"You made something out of it! You can't tell me you don't see that!"

"Sometimes, I still feel like I owe him something…"

"The way your mind works is a natural mystery! Ashton used you!"

"It wasn't like that…I don't think…"

"You don't think? What world do you live in?" She was upset, not feigned.

Since seeing her upset bothered him more than capitulating in the conversation, he took the path of least resistance though it pained him to do so. "A crazy world. I live in a crazy world." He extended his hand towards her and although it took her a moment to reciprocate, they resumed their walk in a troubled silence.

They nursed beers by the pool. Hanna sat in the sun while Dominic did belly flops and cannonball dives to see if he could get her wet. He tried to coax her into the pool and she resisted. He watched her putting suntan lotion on herself, on her arms, on her legs. If she caught him staring at her, he turned away as if there were rules against that sort of thing, as if he was not to be watching her or be entranced by her. She asked him to put lotion on her back and he pushed himself out of the pool to do as she asked. He swore the water that dripped from his chin onto her back was a mistake. She laughed and called him a liar. Nierika pranced around the edge of the pool barking frantically. Whenever Dominic went into the pool, Nierika jumped in, swam to him, placed her jaws gently on his wrist and pulled him to the side of the pool. The first time surprised and amazed them both. The second time, their amazement increased by leaps and bounds. The next time Dominic came to the pool, it would be without Nierika.

After scalping a dinner of beer, ice-cold papaya, fish soup and fried cassava cake from the executive kitchens, they reserved a movie feed for themselves in the theater room and watched a Quentin Tarantino movie (again). Dominic loved Quentin Tarantino movies more than she did, but she liked to watch movies more than once, so they saw a Tarantino flick they'd seen before. Picking movies to see together remained an art and it did not always work out so well. When the movie finished they ran back to his suite and 'fucked' on the living room floor, then 'made love' on the bed later. In the afterglow, in the shadows of natural and artificial light, she traced her favorite lines — shoulders, chest, stomach, hip with the star. He kept his hand on the small of her back, his fingers just the space where her buttocks separated, his other mercy seat – a place with no name, though he longed to give it one.

In the morning, they repeatedly told Nierika to lie down and shut up and they slept in. They slept much later than usual with no particular reason not to. It was a peaceful time and although Dominic woke frequently, he would check on Hanna, see that she was still sleeping and then feel tired again. Dominic's message board chimed around noon. It woke them both up. Not in a hurry to check the message it sat in queue for an hour.

"Visitor at the front gate. Deaf/dumb woman. Carries note. Wants to talk to you urgently."

Dominic knew who had come calling. Immediately worried, he jogged out towards the front gate. He saw her before she saw him – white clothes shining in the hot sun, the security troops regarding her as an anomaly. He stopped for a moment, gathering his thoughts, steeling him self for the message the woman brought. She did not smile but allowed herself a sigh of relief. Dominic offered the usual honorific: he took her extended hand in his and placed it on his forehead and then his chest. She then held out her other hand. Dominic enfolded her hand in his and waited. She did not hear with her ears or speak with her tongue but had her own way of communicating with her hands, her own special language, which Dominic learned when he lived with her and her brother, Pierre.

Her fingers moved and she told him:, "Pierre is very sick. Wants to see you. Will you come?"

Dominic signed back: Yes. She nodded at Dominic and turned to walk away, her business finished. Dominic called after her, but realizing the uselessness of it, ran after her, tapping her on the shoulder. Surprised, she looked at him expectantly. He extended his arm and she took his hand in both of her hands. He asked her to wait, that he would go back up country with her. She nodded again and walked back to the bench and sat down.

It took four hours to arrange the trip up country. ISEC moaned, complained and insisted he pre-plan excursions. They checked databases and maps, displays and threat matrices. They woke up logistics managers and drivers and surveyed garages and equipment. Initially, due to the recent unrest, they proposed an eight-vehicle convoy, which Dominic rejected out of hand. After an hour of argument and negotiation, Dominic succeeded in reducing the convoy to four vehicles, though Dominic found this still too big a footprint – especially to go up country where opinion of the government in Capital ran to the less favorable. He did not want to get Santo involved but pretended to be willing to do so. That got him down to three vehicles, still ridiculous for a trip up country, but it would not get better. Santo refused to vacate his promotion, adding an additional layer of complexity. Other than making some budget appropriation decisions and mediating an internal dispute between department heads, he had little to do with ISEC's day-to-day operations. They treated him as the President's houseboy. They departed finally in the second of a three-car motorcade. The woman Mercilia rode in the last car. One car would remain with Dominic in case he needed to move around. The two protective detail officers would have to bunk outside on the veranda of Pierre and Mercilia's small house. He hated traveling this way, calling so much attention to himself, having to ignore the stares of people on the road as he passed. However on this occasion it was a small price to pay to see Pierre again.

PIERRE AND MERCILIA'S HOUSE –
UPCOUNTRY – PRESENT DAY

The small house stood just as Dominic remembered. Built on stilts to protect from flash flooding endemic to the area, the house looked run down and in need of a coat of paint. Only one window had a glass pane it – the rest barred and shuttered. A basic square house with four rooms: a front room, a kitchen, a bedroom and a bathroom -- decades old, the wear and tear of time remained its most telling feature. Decrepit and creaky stairs led to the front door hanging on hinges by a single screw, a small verandah and the outwardly facing window with a glass pane. The inside of the house presented the visitor with a more welcoming feel. Despite the clapboard floors, Mercilia collected a couple of chairs, a sitting room rug and a small sofa that collapsed in the middle when you sat in it. The kitchen contained a small sink, a wood stove and a card table with no chairs. A bare hallway led to the bedroom containing two small beds one on each side of the room. The water closet had been an add-on and one had to step over a one inch gap between the floor of the house and the floor of the water-closet.

Pierre lay in his bed, small and helpless. Even with the open-air windows, the room smelled bad and Dominic noticed one leg swollen to twice the size of the other. Hanna covered her nose and mouth with her hand. Mercilia stood back in the hallway where Dominic used to sleep. The two men from Dominic's protective detail held their fingers under their noses. One of them – a trained combat medic -- approached Pierre on the bed and made eye contact. Dominic had already taken position on the other side of the bed, his hand on the old man's forehead.

"Honneur! Bonswa mesye...pou nou wè?" (Hello, may we take a look?)

The ISEC man followed his greeting by lifting the blanket on the side of the obviously swollen leg, the sight making them all nauseous: twice its normal size, the flesh mottled red, purple, pink and white, two black blisters, easily mistaken for large, shiny headless beetles. The ISEC man gently lowered the blanket, caught Dominic's eye and shook his head. "Gas gangrene. He needs a hospital now!"

Pierre spoke in a strong voice, *"Lopital pa!"*

Mercilia signed to Dominic: 'His time to die'. Dominic understood but did not translate.

The ISEC medic thought he needed to translate. "He says no hospital."

The dialect returned to Dominic, a French Creole as opposed to the English Patois more familiar to him. *"Moun ki konnen lè pou l'mouri?"*

Annoyingly, the ISEC man continued translating, "What man knows the time of his death?"

Dominic desperately wanted privacy but knew he would not get it. Raw emotion welled in his eyes from his gut, as he knew would happen. *"Nou te kapab ede…si ou kite nou…"* (We can help if you let us…). He glanced at his inconvenient translator and held his hand up before the man could speak again.

Pierre held his ground and shook his head. *"Li se sa ase w'a isit la."* (It is enough that you are here…).

"Ou pa pale pou m, tonton…" (You do not speak for me, uncle…), Dominic replied more strongly than he intended, his voice breaking mid sentence. The water in his eyes crested and Dominic let it dampen his face. Hanna put her hand on his shoulder. She needed no translator to understand. The ISEC escort excused themselves to wait on the tiny verandah.

Pierre raised both his hands with considerable effort and gently placed them on Dominic's face. For most of his life these hands had been magical, but today they were cold and dry. The smell made him sick to his stomach, but Dominic did not withdraw. As he had always done, Pierre used his hands to "see": forehead, temples, cheekbones, and chin. *"Poukisa èske ou kriye, mon timoun?"* (Why do you cry, child?)

"Paske ou gen denye moun ki pou rele m sa." (Because you are the last to call me so) Pierre kept his hands where Dominic used to find such comfort and renewal a moment longer and then let them fall to his side. The small effort caused sweat to bead on the old man's forehead and face.

"Le sa amwen pa janm ka mouri pou ou," (Then I can never be dead to you...) Pierre said, smiling for the first time. *"Chita an sanm avè m' pou yon ti an. Wè ou se yon renmed ase."* (Sit with me for a while. Seeing you, is medicine enough.)

How many times had Dominic heard that before... *'Chita an sanm avè m' pou yon ti an'*, It was Pierre's response for happiness and joy, sorrow and grief. Dominic heard it when he came home with a book to read out loud and after coming home exhausted from dancing in the *peristil*. He heard it when a gang of boys in town attached Mercilia, and after being sick for three months with 'Breakbone Fever'. He heard it when Ashton appeared and told Dominic he would be going to boarding school in a foreign country. As these memories floated through Dominic's thoughts he began to accept Pierre's decision in a way he never imagined he would, for in Pierre's world they had only a little time to sit together. So Dominic sat with his two hands over Pierre's hand while Hanna stood next to him, her hand on his shoulder.

Chita an sanm avè m' pou yon ti an.

Pierre tired himself out just with the few sentences he had spoken and fell asleep. Dominic put his other hand briefly on the old man's forehead. Fever consumed him. Hanna placed a kiss gently on Pierre's forehead and the top of

Dominic's head and excused herself. She did not often express her inner emotions so she went outside to stand by one of the cars, her back to the house, head bowed. She once told him she had absolutely no idea what she would do when her parents died; even contemplating the possibility brought on threats of a panic attack.

Mercilia entered the room as Hanna left it and sat down on her bed across the room from her brother's bed. She stared first at Pierre's face for a few minutes then turned her gaze to Dominic. Dominic signed a greeting: 'Honneur'. She nodded and returned her gaze to Pierre.

'My brother is a stubborn man…" she signed.

"Yes, Auntie," he signed back.

Mercilia continued signing. "He does not fear death like I do…"

Dominic could think of no response so he nodded. "Yes, Auntie,"

Mercilia had more to say, more to say in this one sitting than Dominic had heard in the years he lived with them. "You are much changed…"

"Yes, Auntie."

"Do you remember us well?"

"Yes, Auntie."

"What do you remember?"

"Ever since I was small, I have danced…"

"You do remember!" she signed as a smile came to her face. "Have you found your ancestors?"

Her question made Dominic catch his breath as if she had heard the conversation he and Santo shared just a few days ago. "No, Auntie…"

"You must find them so you are not afraid to die…" Mercilia had never spoken more than one or two words to him in one sitting, making her veritable lecture quite remarkable. "You must find them so you can make peace with them."

"Where do I start?"

"You must find a *houngan* who will help you…"

"They have all left Capital."

"Maybe you will find one here in the country where the air is clean and our voices clear."

"I will try, Auntie."

"We will help you. If Pierre cannot, I will." Mercilia stood up crossed the room and put her hand on Dominic's shoulder. "You sleep here tonight – I will give you a blanket. The girl will sleep on my bed. Tell the government men they must sleep on the verandah."

He did not remind her he too was a government man. She rose and came back with two thin blankets. Although threadbare, they felt soft enough and clean. Mercilia left for a few minutes and returned leading Hanna into the room by the hand. Dominic could tell she had been crying. Before she left the room Mercilia, took one last look at her brother and then disappeared into the hallway. Hanna lay down immediately, her back to Dominic and Pierre. Dominic gave her the space she wanted. Before settling in for the night he went outside to speak with his escort. The verandah being creaky and rickety they decided to sleep in their cars. At least they could keep the sensors on and have a bit more security in the black night. When Dominic returned to the room, Hanna had fallen asleep and he let her be. Alone in the familiar house, he shed his clothes to his shorts and lay down on the floor. The evening coolness seeped into the room following its usual tracks, falling from the window over his skin, cooling like no air conditioner could. He dreamed of the *cata*, *seconde* and *maman*, the three drums of the *peristil*. He dreamed of people dancing -- not ritualized or allegorical, but simple repetitive steps of resolution. Partial to the offbeat, unforgiving rhythms of *Pethro*, full of rage and delirium, he dreamed of the fire at the foot of the *poteau mitan* and how easily he found it burning inside.

He woke up to sunlight, birdsong and Pierre asking for water. Mercilia gave him one of Pierre's long hand-washed shirts to wear and harddo bread, saltfish, tea and mangoes for breakfast. They sat on the veranda waiting for the rest of the house to wake up. Mercilia resumed her silence, her only nod to the social, a smile she bestowed on Hanna when she joined them. Dominic and Hanna took turns sitting with Pierre during the day; wiping his face with a cloth soaked in cool water, offering him small mouthfuls of soup and sips of water. Pierre had begun to breathe more quickly and shallow. His heart rate had quickened. The medic shook his head, having a hard time doing nothing for a treatable condition. Pierre complained he could not feel his legs. Dominic noticed a rash that had not been there the night before. All symptoms of septic shock, the medic said, Pierre could die within hours. Dominic remained resolute he would honor Pierre's wishes. Hanna did not argue but she made her objections known. The two security men stayed on the veranda waiting. They were used to waiting.

When Pierre began mumbling incoherently, Dominic struggled to maintain resolve. Painful to watch, he began thinking about the kit the medic had with him. He wondered whether it contained something to make Pierre, if not comfortable, then oblivious. As if he had been thinking out loud, the medic entered the room and silently handed Dominic four tiny ampoules from his closed fist. Dominic took them and the medic left in silence. What seemed the easier path now loomed as a distinct possibility with the ampoules in his hand. He stared at the slight figure on the bed and could not follow through. He could not take Pierre's life even in a fit of sadness, which made him angry. If only they arrived sooner. If Mercilia had not waited, a doctor might have intervened. If Pierre had been born a less stubborn man, Dominic's choices would be less murky.

Dominic heard a car, actually more than one car, and at first thought his security detail had departed and returned. He glanced out the window and noticed the government cars had not moved. Three black SUV's joined them in the small yard and his security detail was apoplectic. Four men emerged from the first and last vehicles and held up their hands, palms facing outward. One of them opened the rear door of the middle SUV and an older man emerged and then made his way into the house. Dominic knew this man, though Baron Semedi did not have a reputation for making house calls.

The older man walked through the house, unsurprised to find Dominic in the bedroom, next to Pierre. He smiled in greeting and said, "We meet again."

"You?" The surprise on Dominic's face and in his voice must have been noticeable.

Baron Semedi smiled. "Capital belongs to you, but this part of the island belongs more to me…but you knew that…"

"As you say…" Dominic replied knowing better than to argue.

"Many things here are as I say they are, such as your safe passage."

"I am grateful…"

"I will take your word." Baron Semedi looked down at Pierre, touching the back of his hand to the sick man's forehead. "He is not well."

"I asked him to let us help him but he refused."

"You cannot help him," the older man said dismissively.

"It is too late now…"

"He has made his peace. He does not fear death."

"As you say…"

"You should spend some time up country, see how the people live, how they dance. You live in a dream in that city of lies."

"You came to Pierre's house to tell me this?"

Baron Semedi laughed. "I came here to make Mercilia strong."

"She is afraid…"

"She has no reason to fear."

"Why? You will take care of her?"

"As she and Pierre took care of you."

Dominic thought he had a handle on surprise, that nothing much caught him off guard, but the old man upended all that. He must have missed something, overlooked some crucial detail. "How do you know?" Dominic asked feeling his face flush with warmth.

"Ah! Good! You can still be surprised." Baron Semedi clenched his fist and struck an invisible tabletop as he spoke. "How can I not know the child who came with Pierre and his sister to dance in my peristil?"

"I do not remember…"

"I know you do not remember." Baron Semedi sat down carefully on the edge of Pierre's bed. "You will remember him well, yes?"

Dominic nodded. He felt like a small child again, as if he had done something wrong or was about to and gotten caught.

"What do you clutch so tightly in your hand?" Baron Semedi indicated the hand that held the ampoules. "It must be valuable for you to hold on so tightly…"

Dominic had intentions to resist the inquiry, to not give this strange man any more advantage but he lost what willpower he thought to summon. Like an automaton, he opened his fist and held it out.

"This is your help?" Baron Semedi said, taking the ampoules deftly out of Dominic's hand.

"To take away the pain…"

"He does not feel pain, *pitit mwen*…"

"I am not your child…"

"Forgive me, I spoke in general terms, not as a literal expression." Baron Semedi smiled as he spoke, as if the conversation amused him.

"I hardly know you."

The old man held up both hands, chuckling. "Peace, brother, I withdraw the expression, *ètranger*."

Frustrated Baron Semedi kept the upper hand Dominic nodded and backed out of Pierre's bedroom, leaving the two older men together.

Mercilia seemed to have disappeared and as he peered out the window, he noticed his security detail in the midst of a crisis, brows wrinkled, transponders squawking. Hanna ran towards the house, an urgent look on her face. He met her on the veranda and took her into a strong hug, more for him than for her. Two vice ministers had been kidnapped and threatened with Colombian neckties, though no one had taken credit or made demands. Hanna agreed to stay with Pierre and Mercilia while Dominic returned to Capital. In the end, the medic stayed with Hanna, keeping one of the vehicles. Dominic and the other security man took the other car. On the drive back, Dominic replayed his conversation with Baron Semedi trying to find the key to unlock meaning in the words. Something had gone awry and Dominic could not put words or feelings to it. Every time he encountered

Baron Semedi, a living, breathing puzzle made itself known; a private mystery building up in front of him.

PRESIDENTIAL PALACE – CAPITAL – PRESENT DAY

The night he returned, Santo invited Dominic to breakfast the next morning. Dominic arrived before Santo but left the table untouched; although sorely tempted by the array of fresh fruit, pastries and orange juice. He sat in the back of the room and waited. If he had learned one thing, he too had learned how to wait. A few minutes later, Santo arrived, alone. He sat at the table and motioned for Dominic to join him. They ate in silence for the first few minutes until Dominic could stand it no longer.

"The suspense is killing me…"

Santo looked at Dominic as he sipped his coffee and shook his head. "I did not intend this to be suspenseful. I wanted to talk to you before the meeting."

"About what?"

"A decision I've made…"

Dominic's body shifted to warning mode, tense, courting fight or flight. Adrenalin coursed through the bloodstream and his heart pounded inside his chest. "About what?"

"We will not stand in the next election."

The words hit like an unexploded cannonball, though he understood how Santo had led up to it, with the conversation about the future and what he wanted to do. In hindsight, it all fit together. "*D'people-dem wear you dun?*"

"You could say that."

Dominic nodded. He should have seen it. If he had, he could have fleshed it out, considered options, played out a million scenarios at the expense of a few nights of sleep. But he had not done that. He had not thought about it at all.

"Things will get messy, maybe even bloody, so we need to be prepared."

Dominic nodded.

"I can help you land on your feet but you have to tell me where you want to land."

"I thought you would keep fighting..."

"I did too..."

"I can fend for myself...no need to worry about me."

"The time you have spent here has marked you. There are those who will hold it against you."

"Who?"

"Those who lead are drummed off the island or killed."

"Where will you go?"

"I am making plans now. I need to know whether I should include you."

"Like part of your family?"

Santo nodded; relieved Dominic seemed to 'get it'. "If 'family' makes you uncomfortable, then don't think about it that way. Going with us will be the safest way. I tried to tell you earlier but I missed the mark."

"Even if I am not kin?"

"I'm offering you a way out, a way to save your skin and land on your feet. It doesn't have to mean anything. I wouldn't over think this, captain."

"I thought you were calling elections in six months."

"I may be forced to call them earlier. The situation is fluid."

Dominic emptied his glass of orange juice and looked around the ornately decorated room. The shock of the situation had worn off and the heaviness that assaulted him lightened. He took a deep breath and his mind cleared and he understood. He decided once more to cast his lot with Santo; unsure whether he was more pleased that Santo asked, than about the actual decision itself. "I will go with you…"

Santo sighed. "I couldn't be happier. Carly will be thrilled."

"Carly?"

"She likes you more than I do!"

"But what will happen?"

"Making plans will take time."

"What if I change my mind?"

"If you do you, will hurt me, but you are your own man. It would be very dangerous."

Dominic remembered what Ashton said when he still wore the Colombian Necktie, that Santo could not win. In light of what he had just heard, Dominic concluded Ashton had been right and Santo knew all along. Ashton was Santo's curtain call. He cursed himself for not seeing this earlier, for not reading the tealeaves. "Ashton was right -- he said you could not win."

"Ashton has been right more often than he has been wrong but that is his own tragedy. We have our own to consider."

"So now what?" Dominic pushed back from the table. He had consumed a whole tray of fresh fruit as well as half a tray of pastries and a pitcher of orange juice. He did not remember eating any of it.

"You must act normally and you must always be reachable. Always."

Dominic nodded.

"Things may change quickly and we may not have time to talk things out so you must be ready."

"Ready for what?"

"Anything. That is the hand we must play."

"I'm ready."

Santo smiled. "Good. We'll talk in two weeks."

Dominic rose to leave.

"I read the ISEC report on Pierre. I'm sorry."

"He's stubborn…" Dominic said, holding his true feelings back. "I want to see him before…" Dominic could not say the word.

"Of course. "

Speaking of Pierre made it difficult for Dominic to contain his emotions but he gave it a good stead.

"ISEC will take you back up country."

***

ISEC REPORT: PLANTATION HOUSE COUP
REPORT GROUP: POLITICAL
REPORT AUTH.:   ::Q::
REPORT TIME: POST EVENT
VERSION: PRINTED-REDACTED

A.   THE PLANTATION HOUSE COUP IS THE NAME GIVEN TO A SERIES OF EVENTS PERPETRATED BY _____, _____, AND _____. OTHERS WERE INVOLVED BUT THIS REPORT NAMES ONLY THESE PERPETRATORS, HEREAFTER REFERRED TO AS 'THE PERPETRATORS'.

B.   THE PERPETRATORS ARE ACCUSED OF TREASON, SEEKING THE OVERTHROW OF THE GOVERNMENT BY SUBVERSIVE MEANS, COMMITTING ACTS OF TERRORISM, FOMENTING CIVIL UNREST, AND MURDER.

C.   THE PERPETRATORS ACCOMPLISHED THIS BY INSTALLING AN AGENT IN THE INNER CIRCLE OF PRESIDENT SANTO. THIS AGENT HAS BEEN IDENTIFIED AS _____.

D.   THE PERPETRATORS TOOK THE FOLLOWING ACTIONS IN THEIR EFFORT TO VIOLENTLY OVERTHROW THE GOVERNMENT OF PRESIDENT JOSEPH SANTO:

   ☐   THE HIJACKING AND EXPLOSION OF A FULLY LOADED GARBAGE RIG ON THE GROUNDS OF THE PRESIDENTIAL PALACE.

   ☐   THE EXPLOSION, DESTRUCTION AND SINKING COMMERCIAL HARBOR.

   ☐   THE DE-COUPLING OF THE CARIBBEAN SELAND TOWER FROM ITS LOCATOR BRINGING SELAND NETWORK TRAFFIC TO A VIRTUAL STANDSTILL.

- THE ATTACK ON THE CARIBBEAN SELAND TOWER USING MARINE ASSAULTBOTS, CAUSING REPLACEMENT.

- THE KIDNAPPING AND MURDER OF _____, UTILIZING A COLLAR BOMB.

- THIS INDICTMENT IS SUPPORTED BY EVIDENCE PROVIDED BY SELANDSEC, INTERPOL, AND ISEC AND IS ACCESSIBLE AT THE ::Q:: AUTHORIZATION LEVEL; AT

E. ::SELAND:POLITICAL:PLANTATIONCOUP:EVIDE NCE:SEQUESTER~50 4C 41 4E 54 41 54 49 4F 4E 43 4F 55 50::

F. SOURCES AND METHODS: NORMAL

G. DISPOSITION: CLOSED

Although chaotic, things had been stable, even predictable since Dominic cast his lot with the President. Santo's decision threatened to change all of that. Dominic read and reread the ISEC report sitting on the floor in Pierre's bedroom. It made no mention of special techniques used on Ashton, the victim of the collar bomb, and for whose death the main perpetrators were accused; or the fact Ashton was in custody and very much alive. It also made no mention of the main perpetrators, who were dead, indicted but not convicted. He began to understand Santo's decision not to seek re-election.

Though no one knew how, Pierre continued to mumble incoherently and periodically ask for water. His leg deteriorated as expected – the colors deepening and streaking, the stench fouler, and the leg itself more bloated. Three more shiny black blisters emerged. Although he continued to take in tiny amounts of water, Mercilia said he had not urinated in more than 30 hours. He did not appear to be in pain but looked much closer to death. He no longer had a fever so his skin felt cool to the touch and he had trouble breathing. Dominic knew Pierre would die before the sun rose again. He had done some reading in the car from Capital and quizzed a couple ISEC physicians. They told him Pierre should not have waited so long, but that waiting remained a common reaction in the country. People avoided hospitals out of basic mistrust, afraid neither of pain nor death.

Dominic fell asleep as he sat against the wall, the ISEC report falling to the floor. Mercilia sat in the front room staring blankly at an empty wall. Hanna slept on Mercilia's narrow lumpy bed. Dominic woke up with a start as if a loud noise had startled him. Yet Hanna slept, as she had been, her back to him. He heard Mercilia humming tunelessly from the front room. In the still night, he heard neither owl, cicada or barking lizard. He checked his watch: 1.13 a.m. Convinced something had changed he padded through the small house to satisfy himself all was well.

Though quiet, a small discomfort kept him more highly strung than he liked and as an afterthought, he reached down to check Pierre's forehead. His arm reacted as if it touched fire. He had not touched fire though. Sometime during the night Pierre had passed from the world of the living. Pierre was dead. Dominic returned to his seat next to the bed. In the darkness he steeled himself against grief and loss. He would pass this time alone with a secret knowledge. He felt his body reacting in its usual ways and he fought back, hardening what muscles he could to stay strong. He knew about losing people and he knew how to lay sandbags against such breaches. Feeling small again as Santo described it; Dominic invoked that sad, shadowy and shifty character of the very small...

^yuh cyaan gi'mi nuttin fi keep mi, wink?

He felt bad for leaving but staying would have been an inconvenience and although it made little sense to him, he trusted Baron Semedi to take care of Mercilia. He had nothing to base this trust on, other than what the man said, but he had trusted others on less. The world had become smaller, shrinking and receding around him. If his world had visible lines, they were in flux, knotted and tangled. If the world could be made into sound, the chords would be asynchronous and the rhythm minimalist. These were dangerous times because very little kept its shape under pressure and every thing became open to debate, question and perhaps rejection, until only he remained, like a clock tower or a sundial. He and Hanna rode back to Capital in silence. He fell asleep in the car leaning against Hanna's shoulder.

She had pulled away during their stay in the country. He could not tell when, but he read the difference in the way she moved and her facial expressions in reaction to routine events, when he leaned in to kiss her or when he reached out to touch her. He wondered if perhaps she had come to some decision or conclusion; that their alliance forged in childhood and strengthened as they grew closer but further apart, had begun to fray.

Two weeks after Pierre died, Hanna arrived, unannounced at Dominic's office, in the middle of the day. She had been crying and she ignored the small gestures they shared – the ones that asked or gave freely. He followed her to an old banyan tree and they sat down underneath its branches. She took his hand and released it. She put her hand on his leg then removed it. She touched his cheek, chin, brow, then folded her hands in her lap. He wanted to gather her closer to him, to be her great coat, to envelop her like a cave, but she would object.

"I've been keeping a secret and it's killing me," she said, finally looking at him with her eyes.

"Then tell me…"

"I couldn't tell you before because of Pierre, but if I don't tell you, I will die…"

"Don't do that, Hanna…" he gambled and got a way with wrapping her hand in both of his.

"I'm going to school, Dominic…"

"Hanna! You should be happy! Why are you crying and carrying on like this! Why wouldn't you tell me?" She had wanted to go to school for some time and they spent hours talking about what she would study, where she would go.

"Dominic, the school, it's not here. It's not on the island."

There: the reason for her anguish, her tears! No doubt there would be anguish for him but it would not be now. It would come later. When he remembered the conversation later he would remember he saw it coming, that her secret had been

251

inevitable, but he played the stoic because he was good at it. "Where is the school, Hanna?

"Montreal..."

"Aren't your parents in Montreal?"

"Yes..."

"Have you decided what to study?"

"Law..."

"That's a long way from artificial intelligence..."

"Montreal is a long way from here...from you..."

"The world is a small place..."

She laughed, at least she could still laugh at him. "The world is a huge vast place, Dominic."

"No it's not..." He felt himself closing, his body blocking the world and though he knew he needed to fight it, part of him did not mind -- time to lay down sandbags.

Hanna thumped his leg with her knuckles. "Don't do that, Dominic! Don't shut me out!" She pounded his leg with her fist two more times to make her point. He said nothing but put her arms around her and they sat together without another word for the better part of half an hour.

"My dad asked if you would take me to the airport...you know how the airport can be..."

"Of course... I'll take you."

"You're not mad?"

"Mad? How could I be mad? My best friend is going to school! How could I be mad?"

"You won't miss me then?"

"Of course I'll miss you. Are you crazy?"

Working for the President had its advantages. He took a full escort to pick Hanna up from the base where she was stationed. Though not an official motorcade it still looked impressive: two black Audis, two motorcycle units and an ISEC security vehicle. Before they left the base they took pictures of themselves with the trappings of power and messaged them to Hanna's parents and themselves. They left the lights and sirens off and flew no flags but people still made way for them. When they got to the airport they followed the frontage road circling around the rear of the airport and went through the rear entrance used only by government or diplomats. Someone carried her bags, checked them, stamped her passport and paid her departure taxes, while Dominic and Hanna had the private government lounge on the top floor of the main building to themselves.

Dominic's escort gave them privacy. They agreed they would not be mushy or emotional – airports were not the place for all that. Dominic gave her a media-cube with some music he had collected to see her off with. Hanna gave him a kiss on the mouth and forehead and a piece of paper with a poem she had written on it. The loud speaker announced Hanna's flight, Dominic gave Hanna one last hug and then he watched her walk down the boarding tunnel and onto her plane.

PRESIDENTIAL PALACE – CAPITAL - PRESENT DAY

In the chair he had taken as his own, facing the southern sky, two fingers of Hakushu in the glass on the armrest, the emotion he held back at the airport threatened to overwhelm and turn into an avalanche. The stars in the southern sky blurred by reason of the water in his eyes. He had avoided this for a few hours by gaming with the Santo kids, but eventually their attention turned and they left him with his own private emptiness. He sipped his drink but it tasted salty. Returning the glass to its place on the armrest, seeing Carly sitting in the chair Santo usually sat in gave him a start. Out of surprise or instinct, he stood up. "I'm sorry, I didn't hear you sit down," he said.

Carly shook her head. "Joseph called, he said you could use some company. Sit down, please."

Dominic followed her cue and settled back in the chair. "Where'd he go?"

"A conference in Barbados."

"Do you invite every attaché to live in your house?"

"No, I can't say that we do. You are the first."

"Hanna got on a plane for Montreal today…"

"Hanna, that's the young woman you've been seeing, right?"

"We've been friends since I was ten…"

"That is a special friendship," Carly said, closely examining the bottle of Hakushu standing on the side table near her chair. "Did Joesph turn you on to this jet fuel?"

Dominic chuckled at her question. "Yeah…he poured my first shot…"

"I thought you didn't drink. I swear I remember Joseph telling me that."

"I didn't."

"Shame on him, then!" Carly said. She sounded truly disappointed. "Will you keep in touch?"

"I'n'I bahn yaso…mi nuh know wha'do'er…"

"You didn't say that to her, did you?"

Dominic shook his head.

"Maybe Joesph can find a reason to take you along the next time he goes up north."

"Yuh 'tink 'im do 'dat fi mi?"

"You won't know unless you ask."

"I don't have a passport…"

"That is a very weak excuse, Dominic," Carly said with a smile, her eyes deadly serious.

Dominic chuckled again, avoiding her serious eyes.

For a few days, Dominic distracted himself by combing historical records and datacubes for traces of people he had not thought about in years. For reasons he did not yet understand, he entertained a small obsession with the fates of his two childhood friends, whom he knew only as Worm and Scorn. When he thought he should be using what little time he had to find his own past, he focused on shadows. For on Old Hope Road, few data links existed to tie person to place, or name to face. Property deeds and lot numbers meant little to nothing to the squatter. Data links proved useless to people living on top of each other. Corrugated tin roofs held no antennas. Tenements and garrisons, by nature, escaped most civil defense regimes. He had found Ashton's children, almost too easily and he promised himself he would keep his promise to Ashton. He told himself a life could not pass completely unnoticed. Both Worm and Scorn had parents and extended families. He knew how many houses up the road from Mooma Jacobs they lived. However convinced he might have been he would find some trace of his boyhood friends, the task proved more daunting than he ever imagined. For all SELAND's bragging rights about consistent, persistent identity across an entire planet, he had stumbled across two out of all possible ghosts. After fourteen hours of data-shape immersion, datacube gymnastics and SELAND search fatigue, not even WAKE could bridge the exhaustion gap. He managed to create and task a searchbot to continue the search without him before fell asleep sitting upright, data-shapes dancing across the displays, datacube hyperlinks dancing behind SELAND search matrices.

He woke a mere four hours later with an overwhelming urge to see Olivia. He knew it was WAKE talking, but he could not ignore it. He stalled for a few hours, telling himself it would be disrespectful to Hanna. Although that particular story didn't last very long, seeing Olivia again proved more difficult he would have liked. She refused to see him at the usual places: the Intercontinental, the Bone Room, his apartment or her hotel – those were her rules. Dominic's new ISEC position only complicated things, since he now traveled with a detail. He could not contact her on a COMLINK or via SELAND messaging to avoid data linkage. Any money he spent in his quest would have to be in cash markets. If she agreed to see him, they would have to find a place to meet, perhaps a hotel in the cash market. His detail would need to spec different approaches and escape routes. He would have no advance team, no 'eyes and ears'. They would use false names and most likely not stay the night. Dominic knew people who could still navigate the cash markets, people who had taken advantage of the small number of SELAND opt-out blocks when they first became available. They would need to use cash to reserve a room. It would not be a five-star establishment but the hotel would not ask questions. He would need to convince his security detail on the bona fides of his little field trip, but they were not unwilling partners in this one small deception or even a series of small deceptions. For Dominic was not the first to require such discretion.

Olivia arrived late, causing no small worry for Dominic and a couple of trips to the clapboard bar at the end of the road to use the beacon cell phone. They settled in a small, clean room, with a window air conditioner, an old clock radio, twin beds and plastic curtains on the windows. The twin bed they had sex on was not the quietest bed had ever encountered, but it served its purpose. Hanna would have called it "fucking" - it was still light outside. Though he had not planned to, the narrative of the last couple of weeks filled the room in a flood of words. She listened in silence, knowing people found it easier to talk to someone they did not know very well as opposed to someone who knew them inside and out.

"You'll have some great stories to tell your kids, did you ever think about that?" she asked, when he finished talking. She knew he was done because he stopped to take a breath, as if speaking all that time on a single breath.

Dominic lay back on the bed and stared at the ceiling, feeling the muscles in his neck and shoulders thanking him for telling his stories. "You want kids?" he asked sitting up, looking at her quizzically.

"Hell yeah! I want a church of kids!"

"LahwdJeezuz…"

"The President's calling elections, you know that right?" Olivia asked switching from the personal to business.

"Is that 'the' SELAND assessment?"

"It is now."

"How soon?"

"Maybe two weeks, a month at the most."

"That soon?" Dominic heard surprise in his voice.

"Decent leaders are never long in office, the worst hang on forever."

"Is that a compliment?"

"Could be."

"What about after the election?

"Bad to worse." Olivia wore her cabinet meeting face; hard and cynical.

"Why do I feel like you're not telling me everything…"

"Those two ministers weren't kidnapped. They ran for their lives."

"I haven't seen this on the ISEC side, which means you're breaking SELAND SCI."

"I'm doing you a favor."

"Why not use normal channels?"

"These are not normal times."

"Sounds like a pol-game." Dominic immediately regretted saying so, but she did not blink.

"You don't read your own Estimates, do you? Fukken amazing! By every assessment I've read, you should be dead or in prison!"

Her words stung like pepper in the nose or a Scotch Bonnet seed on the face. Dominic stood up as if to leave, head spinning and stomach nauseous, but he stayed and used an expression Kevin used often, "What the fuck are you talking about?"

Olivia softened and held out her hand to him. He did not take it immediately but she persisted and finally he sat down next to her and took her hand. "If you don't have a game, they'll fuck you nine ways from Sunday."

"You're giving me a game?" Dominic asked, letting his hand stray to his favorite parts of her.

"I'm giving you information. He wants to trust you. Everybody wants to trust someone."

"You don't think he trusts me?" he said his voice straying now, her closeness and smell becoming a distraction.

"I don't think he knows yet and he has to be sure one way or the other. His decisions are evidence-based but he can be ruthless."

"So I shouldn't believe anything he says?" Dominic said, getting a little carried away with the bottom of her shirt.

"You shouldn't 'believe' anything. Either you know something or you don't."

"Maybe I should ask him…"

"What if you don't like the answer?"

"I trust him."

"Dominic, you trust everyone! You trust me for fuck's sake!"

"I never said that…" Dominic said with a smile, knowing she would steal his line.

She pushed him away from her, laughing as she did so, "Why are men such pigs?"

Dominic nodded, wearing a smirk on his face like a badge of honor.

"You don't think I already knew who you were?"

Now it was her turn to wear the smirk and his turn to be surprised. "You did?"

"You lived in Raleigh North Carolina for two years. You did an accelerated degree in computer science with the DF. You were assigned to Special Forces, Third Regiment and you were barely twenty when Ashton put you in the PM's office. You have an on again off again relationship with a girl named Hanna also DF, someone very close to you just passed away and no one is quite sure what you got goin' on with your friend Kevin, also from North Carolina. How am I doing?"

The information could have been gleaned from any low-level, historical and known-associates staff dossier. "So you read my file. No secrets there, chica!"

"Does the 'Sisters of Mercy Orphanage' mean anything to you?"

His smile disappeared and he stared with incredulity. "It's an orphanage on Old Hope Road. Why? Should it mean something?"

"That's where you spent the first eight years of your life."

"I lived at that orphanage?"

She nodded and took his hand in hers. "Which explains why you never talk about your family and your last name."

He felt like pulling away. He felt like shrinking under the sheet that covered him but he stayed rooted.

She drew figure eights on his leg with the finger of one hand and kept his hand in her other.

"What else?"

"It shut down for poor conditions."

"What else?" His desire for raw information overwhelmed him and though unreasonable, he half expected her to reveal the identities of his biological parents.

Olivia shook her head. "I had a long argument with myself over whether I should tell you…"

"Why?"

"I didn't know what you already knew, or what you wanted to know…"

"I've been telling myself I need to find out. I'm kinda on my own now."

"Looking for roots? I get that…"

"I guess…"

She kissed his shoulder and stood up to get dressed. The sun began to set and the drive to Capital would not be short. "Be careful what you wish for…"

She gave him two pieces of information: the SELAND Evidentiary Sequester on the two low level ministers and an address and a messaging tag in Miami. She said SELAND might pull non-essential staff and she would have to leave on one hour's notice. If he ever found himself in Miami, he should look her up because she had grown fond of having him watch her smoke cigarettes at night.

They left the hotel in separate vehicles, she in a taxi he hired and paid for, he in a separate taxi shadowed by his security detail. The next morning, ISEC reported that SELAND pulled non-essential resources in the middle of the night. All he had left was the piece of paper she had given him. He committed her Miami address and messaging tag to memory and then pulled up the SELAND Evidentiary. After reviewing the 10-gigabyte Sequester over the course of the next day he messaged Santo, including a priority urgency code -- that would get the man's attention. It worked. Within two minutes of sending the message, Santo replied inviting him to the upstairs study.

PRESIDENTIAL PALACE – CAPITAL – PRESENT DAY

Inside the study, not the opulent well-manicured wood-paneled study Dominic imagined, Santo sat in a large chair behind a small desk, smoking a pipe. He had his signature bottle of *Hakushu* on the desk. Dominic sat in the chair across from Santo and gave him the SELAND Evidentiary Sequester. Santo traded the *Hakushu* and sat down to pull up the Sequester. At first he seemed flippant, but as data shape outlined story, his attitude shifted to intensity, then anger.

No one questioned Ashton had been blackmailed. The real question was what drove the shift from unwilling participant, to active, enthusiastic conspirator. ISEC admitted the evidence had been easy to come by, as if Ashton had played both sides -- furthering the conspiracy to save his own skin and at the same time, handing the conspiracy to Santo's administration on a platter. The Evidentiary cited phone conversations on a darknet cellular network in which Ashton was a confirmed participant. Trace showed petabytes of protected-class information transferred from Ashton to two camouflaged recipients. The data transferred contained detailed maps of the harbor, blueprints for multiple ships (one of which was chosen for the harbor clean up operation and sank by the conspiracy), as well as outdated engineering drawings of the SELAND towers and network. Also illegally transferred, workaround communication planning for hacktivist/ anarchist flash mob suppression coordination as well as data on civil offense. If the drone tech data had been utilized in some tragic next phase of the conspiracy, the body count could have been astronomical. The evidence was damning, but ironically, Ashton had given the conspiracy outdated versions. For every document illegally transferred, new, updated, revised versions existed. Additionally, ISEC noted that the SELAND Evidentiary would not have been possible if

Ashton had not compromised Dominic's so-called SELAND deck. Having done so, he provided the very evidence that would damn him to the government he worked so diligently to destroy. After two and a half hours Santo closed the Evidentiary. In a moment of weakness, he had made gross errors in judgment when the trouble first started. Ms. Casteñada did have a reason to focus on Ashton's dossier, but still he had to ask, "Where did you get this, Major?"

"Ms. Casteñada …" Dominic replied, deciding not to shade the truth.

Santo leaned back pursed his lips and exhaled loudly. "You must tell me how that came to be," Santo said with a hint of a smile.

"The Bone Room," Dominic said.

"Why would she give it to you, I wonder?"

"'Dunno," Dominic said doing his best to feign ignorance.

"SELAND evacuated their non-essential people last night."

"I read that…"

"You have been cleared of any involvement in this mess, based on a joint ISEC - SELAND 'Q' level investigation."

"Olivia said she couldn't figure out why I was still walking around…"

"It would not have come to that between you and I, but I am relieved the evidence supported my assertion." Santo paused for a moment then nodded slowly in increasing clarity. "You got something going on with Ms. Casteñada?"

Dominic smiled but did not answer.

"I will call elections in three weeks."

"So soon?"

"The sooner the better, I am weary of this place."

"Where will you go?" Dominic asked.

"You mean, where will we go?"

"We?"

"You are coming with us if I have to hold a gun to your head."

"I am?"

"Yes and I will brook no argument! In return you will attend school at the University of Miami and get a degree from an American university. After that, you are your own man. Besides there is someone you know in Miami, no? We leave for Miami in ten days. Family vacation."

"Ten days? You said elections wouldn't be for three weeks!"

"The announcement begins a cycle of violence that will not stop until I exile or I am dead. This is guaranteed, not speculation. It isn't a scenario; we know this. For decades, power flip-flops between the party in power and the opposition. Even so, violence accompanies EVERY election, though the outcome is all but pre-determined. I prefer to exile than die. How about you?"

"I'll have some crazy stories to tell my kids."

"Yes, you will."

"What do you know about an orphanage on Old Hope Road called The Sisters of Mercy Orphanage?"

"Nothing…why?"

"I lived there for eight years."

Santo's mouth dropped and his eyes opened wide. "That is an incredible piece of information Dominic, but there is very little time."

"But it's a start right? A piece of a puzzle?"

"It's the start of a long and difficult journey."

"I need to know...I need to find out..." Dominic's voice broke with emotion mid-sentence, surprising them both. He stood up determined to set course for somewhere, with just this one clue for a compass.

Santo sighed, stood up, poured another two glasses of Hakushu, handed one to Dominic and then sat down again. "Dominic, sit down. I want to tell you a story."

Dominic complied before considering it, more than ready to march out into Hanna's vast and unkind world.

"About twenty-five years ago I had an affair with a dancehall performer, right before I went back to South Africa to help my parents. She was very popular and I was young enough to become obsessed. By the time I returned to the island, times had changed, I forgot the affair and I did not keep in contact. I did not know she had gotten pregnant, that she went full term, or that she gave the child up for adoption. But I did not inquire. At the hospital I read on your chart you had a birthmark. I have the same birthmark, so I asked the hospital for a favor. I asked them to do a DNA comparison."

Dominic shifted his body to the edge of his seat, stood, gut in disarray, torn between a fight or flight response but knowing neither would make a difference. "'Top tell one story..." he said, trying to break a smile as if it were a practical joke. It did not work.

Joseph nodded. "We are kin."

Speechlessness fell on Dominic like a bucket of water. All the memories of the past went reeling past at lightning speed.

"If I had known, had even the slightest inkling, you must believe me, we would not have been strangers. It's improbable but I could not make this up in a million life times."

"What was her name?"

"Your mother's name? Jemma."

Dominic repeated the name out loud, and then twice under his breath. He remained standing in case the flight response proved too powerful, his face hot and his hands and feet cold.

"Dominic, sit down," Santo said, coming out from behind the desk to stand next to Dominic, coaxing him back into his seat, hoping to quell the flight response. He noticed the water welling in Dominic's eyes. Santo thought he understood Dominic's obsession with running to the point of nausea. "I tried to find her but we have not succeeded yet."

"What was she like?"

"She had a big heart like you; a little naive like you. She had hard life."

Having passed the fire of fight/flight and the shock of the conversation, Dominic now had an explanation for Santo's concern, the move from the apartment to the Palace, dinner with the family -- not typical favors the powerful bestowed on those who served them. He knew he found favor but until now did not know why. He certainly never imagined the reason for the favor. What he thought had been luck was actually the pull of blood-kin. He downed the glass of scotch Santo had given him in one gulp. "When did you find out?"

"A few weeks ago…it took me a while to sort it out for myself…"

Dominic sank back in the chair and covered his face in his hands; his body drained of energy. He felt like running but he wanted to stay in this room with a man who claimed to the one person Dominic had yearned for all his life. He wanted to lash out at the walls and windows, hear things crash. He also wanted to hear this man's voice again.

Joseph put his hand on Dominic's shoulder. For the first time in all the time Joseph had known him, Dominic did not withdraw or pull away. Joseph pulled the bottle of Hakushu out of its case and left it on the desk. "I'm leaving this out for you. Take a walk, get some air, this will take a while to sort out I know. Come upstairs tomorrow for brunch and we can talk some more. Promise?"

Dominic nodded once more, face still covered by his hands. He took Joseph's advice. He went outside and walked in the cool night air. The conversation did not spark the crisis he expected. He kept walking, waiting for it. Instead he settled into a relationship he already knew well.

CAPITAL - PRESENT DAY

In a fit of stubbornness or rebellion, he conspired to go to The Bone Room one last time. He left a message with Santo's private secretary. He set up false flags in the ISEC system to indicate he had gone to the Bone Room with a detail. If discovered, they would descend on him at the Bone Room with a fury, but he did not bank on that happening. He expected the credibility of the system flags to go unquestioned. He utilized knowledge he acquired during his time with the President's Office and the familiarity of his face to lull people into letting him do as he pleased. No one paid him any mind.

Before leaving, he took care of one last detail so that he could continue on his way, unimpeded by the past. It required more stealth than he liked to risk. Stealth meant null data values where null was unexpected, a red flag, conspicuous by its presence. His was a task for which triple secret proxies was a minimum requirement. Satisfied he had covered his null-value tracks, he released his code-angel, a stuxnet-42 variant disguised as a lowly searchbot. The searchbot carried an inconspicuous, common demand for status metrics on ISEC Custodial SCADA systems. The data angel needed only the ISEC-searchbot handshake to spread its wings, which it received within milliseconds of releasing the demand. Once inside Custodial SCADA, very little happened. In fact, nothing happened. No alarms sounded. ANTI-INFIL daemons blinked blinked green. The ISEC-SELAND NETCERT on the three petabyte SELAND uplink pipe did not blink. The code-angel waited a full 60 seconds, a lifetime in a world where system responses were measured in nanoseconds. Like the spacefaring rockets of previous generations, the data angel shed its searchbot camouflage, now comfortably ensconced inside Custodial SCADA. For the next three months, it would wait, learning the ins and outs of its new home like a retrovirus. It burrowed past the industrial controls, past multiple layers of security erected to protect processes and records related to people in custody, past disposition documents, behavioral analyses, psych reports and into Medical. From Medical, the data angel made its way to Pharmaceutical, where it buried its head in its wings and buckled down to wait again. It had a random wake code, after which it would execute its primary code and then obliterate itself.

He escaped the perimeter outer video feeds. He relaxed and allowed himself a saunter. Walking alone, no one in front, no one behind, no one to open the car door and no one to usher him into this meeting or conference room, he felt as if he escaped a kind of prison. Tall buildings on the city skyline shimmered in the evening haze. They called to him like drums of the *peristil* many years ago. After walking for forty-five minutes, he realized he had misjudged the distance to the city on foot.

Enveloped by the darkness of the Bone Room, he sat down with a tall glass of ice water and a *Glenmorangie* – something new he discovered. The bartender seemed happy to see him and the girls in the short red leather skirts swarmed him with their usual enthusiasm -- he knew few names and less detail but he enjoyed the attention, being recognized and remembered. Though he had looked forward to being alone, a man approached his table pointing at the empty chair with a hopeful look on his face. Dominic shrugged and nodded, hoping the interloper was not the talkative type. Dominic pegged him for an expat, probably American. The interloper took the empty chair and held up his local beer in appreciation, though the club had a dozen empty chairs and tables. Dominic ignored him, not looking for company or a conversation. He tried his best to appear uninterested but his best was not good enough.

"What are you drinking?" the interloper asked, pulling his chair up closer to the table.

Dominic answered the question in a word: "Single malt." The interloper seemed like an embassy type, tailored slacks, and expensive shirt.

"You work here on the street?" the interloper pressed on.

Dominic decided to try something different. He lied. *"Noosuh! Mi c'yaan take di people-dem yaso..."*

The interloper replied in kind. *"A 'tchroo!"*

Dominic smiled because hearing a foreigner speak the local patois made him smile, no matter how well the foreigner matched the rhythm and tone. "American?"

The interloper laughed out loud. "I should be offended! Canadian, with the embassy."

"Your patois is very good..." Dominic said.

"You are a scholar and a gentleman. I'm Daniel."

"Dominic."

"Barbados?"

"Noosuh! Mi bahn yaso!"

Daniel dipped his chin in apology. "My turn to apologize then."

"No worries..."

"Let me buy you a drink," Daniel offered.

Dominic shook his head. "I'm ok for now."

Daniel was not easily deterred. "I just got here last week and the sun is killing me."

"You'll get used to it..."

"My dad said it served me right."

"Served you right for what?"

"Running off and joining the Foreign Service," Daniel said, laughing at what must have been a private joke.

"What would you be doing if you weren't here?"

Daniel laughed loudly again and raised his glass in salute, "That my friend, is a good question!"

Foreigners were always so easy with that word, 'friend'. So quick to use it, they lessened its meaning with each use, Dominic thought. "I'd be pulling guard duty at a SELAND NOC site, leeward side." He had no sooner replaced his empty snifter on the table than Daniel signaled to the wait staff for another round.

"Ah, SELAND...the closest we'll get to a world government... that's what my dad says!"

"And your dad is?" Dominic asked, wondering about all the 'dad' references.

Daniel laughed again. "He's my dad!" lifting his glass for a toast.

Not wanting to be rude, they toasted Daniel's dad, which set Daniel to laughing again. "So what did you do to get sent here?" Dominic asked, since most new diplomatic corps considered the island a punishment post.

"I applied for a job."

"So what do you think so far?"

"The only upside was the beaches, but I'm in the city."

"The only upside? That bad, eh?" Dominic did not have the energy to be offended.

"That sounded bad. I apologize," Daniel said now self-conscious and embarrassed.

"No worries...it takes getting used to."

"Well this place is an upside. You're an upside. Who do you work for again?"

"I'm not from around here," Dominic said, keeping it simple.

271

"Sounds complicated…" Daniel volunteered, neither asking for more detail, nor expecting any.

"Sometimes…"

"I'm with the consulate…"

"And you hate it already, right?"

"I'm learning *patois*…"

"I noticed…"

"I feel like walking around a little bit…you uh don't feel like walking do you?" Kevin said, standing up as if ready to leave.

"You don't want to just walk around at night, even around here," Dominic said, advice he hoped Kevin would take to heart. Situated outside the Surveillance Regime Control jurisdictional boundary, one took certain risks by doing what might be acceptable elsewhere.

"I know they told me. I figured I'm was better off with a local."

"Get yourself another drink. I don't feel like walking." Talking about the car gave Dominic pause, since walking back to the Palace was no more an option for him than it was for Kevin to walk the streets of Capital at night. He would have to call his own bluff with ISEC.

Daniel remained standing for a few seconds and then sat down again. He seemed distracted and suddenly out of sorts. Drink back in hand; Kevin fell to watching the bartender. Dominic realized the reason Daniel had chosen to sit as his table. "You want another drink?" Dominic needed to buy time. Daniel waived him off, smiling but defeated. Dominic needed to warn him to be cautious. What he liked might get him killed. Dominic sat down again foregoing another drink. He motioned to Kevin, "This isn't Canada."

Daniel made the conversation difficult. "What do you mean?"

"You are who you are and you like what you like…"

Daniel seemed relieved. "I'm out of my element but you looked friendly enough…"

"I can be friendly but I'm not looking for a date."

Daniel smiled. "My dad always said I never listen…"

"You should start. You don't want to end up with a knife in your throat before your first home leave."

Daniel nodded and looked past Dominic, as if someone they knew joined them. Dominic turned and saw a familiar face, not one he could place. The newcomer nodded to Daniel and greeted Dominic the local way. A moment later, he had a name to go with the face – Wilson -- a private contractor who had done some analysis work for ISEC. Odd the man showed up at the Bone Room the same night he ditched his own detail. Wilson harped on him for leaving the grounds without his detail. Wilson wore street clothes, so Dominic knew the man was not on duty. Wilson ignored Daniel and insisted Dominic join him out of earshot in the back of the bar. Dominic waved him off, moments away from pulling rank on Wilson's annoying behavior. Wilson activated his COMLINK and Dominic stepped towards Wilson, who blocked Dominic with his hand. Wilson's hand made contact with Dominic's chest and in his heightened awareness, felt a pinprick. He felt his legs crumble underneath him, and though still conscious, he heard Daniel yelling, before blackness subsumed him.

Dominic heard voices before his eyes opened. He felt the softness of a bed or couch before he recognized the surroundings. He heard a small group of people talking, but no one sounded worried or angry, just average afternoon conversation. The room seemed familiar but his brain refused to focus, to accept any sort of direction. He closed his eyes to focus on himself. His hands and feet were not bound, so whoever hatched this plot did not feel the need to restrain or blindfold him. Studying the light in the room, he knew he had been unconscious for hours rather than minutes. Unsure whether under observation, he maintained the position he found himself in when he became aware. His head hurt but his brain began to emerge from the pharmaceutical cloud. Still he did not know whether he had fallen among enemies or friends.

A familiar voice interrupted his thoughts. "Ah! *Guédé Vi*, you are awake."

Dominic opened his eyes. Baron Semedi stood over him, neither menacing nor angry. The man looked nonchalant and friendly.

Baron Semedi helped Dominic sit up, propped him up with a pillow, and handed him a glass of water. "It was not my intention to kidnap you," he said, "but you have a tendency to run like a cheetah in a tight spot."

Dominic straightened himself in the chair. He recognized the receiving room but what he did not know made it impossible to recommend one strategy over another, so he played compliant, "As you say…"

"I'm glad you are here. Though I wish the circumstances were less dour."

"Dour?"

"Less than ideal or unfortunate."

Dominic felt his usual level of physical control returning -- whatever pharma they used, it had a short residual bioavailability. "Has something changed?"

"Everything is always changing *Guédé Vi*. The question is whether we can keep up."

"You're like a bad dream," Dominic said, uncomfortable not because he feared for his safety but because he did not understand Baron Semedi's motivation.

Baron Semedi chuckled and refilled Dominic's glass with more water. "The water will help flush the pharma from your system."

"Thank you…"

Baron Semedi waved his hand to encompass the room, the house, and the world outside. "The world is your oyster. No one will stop you should you choose to leave."

"Why am I here?"

"We understand Joseph will exile shortly and you will go with him. I wanted to see you before you left," the older man said in a matter of fact, no-nonsense voice.

"You? Wanted to see me?"

"Is that so strange?"

"I find it strange…" Dominic said.

"You do not know the facts and Joseph knows only some of the facts."

Feeling strong enough to sit up of his own accord, Dominic shifted his weight, feeling the fight or flight reaction building inside. He realized Baron Semedi came from a position of knowledge no one imagined he could obtain. "What do you want?"

Baron Semedi shrugged with all the nonchalance in the world and said, "I thought you might like to dance in my peristil before you leave…and meet your mother."

Anger rose in Dominic like a dark, churning wall of water, so strong it forced him to his feet. "You kidnapped me to dance in your peristil? Have you lost your mind? You…" then as Baron Semedi's statement rewound and played again, Dominic stopped mid sentence. "What did you say?"

"You heard me…"

Dominic sat down again. "How…?"

Now it was Baron Semedi's turn to be angry. "You have lived a charmed life, don't you think? You! An orphan with no name in the Office of the President!"

Dominic stood up. "You said I am free to leave. I'm leaving." He fished in his pocket for his COMLINK and realized he did not have it. They must have taken it while he was unconscious. Even that did not stop him. He took three steps toward the door.

"SIT DOWN!" Baron Semedi roared in preternatural tone and volume.

Though prepared for flight, the voice had an arresting effect. Dominic turned to face his interlocutor. He had no argument, nothing he could say to return the advantage to him in the slightest. Facing an emotional dead end he reverted to the diminutive, "What do you want?"

"I want you to listen. Is that so unreasonable?" Baron Semedi asked.

"Why?"

"Before your mother fell for that fool from the city of lies, I loved her. I still love her."

"You know where she is?"

"We will see her tomorrow but first we will dance tonight, yes?" His voice had an entreating quality, as if he felt the need to beg but at the same time not so subtly linking two things together.

"Why tomorrow? She has not seen me for twenty-four years."

"I do not ask you to dance for myself, *Guédé Vi*. It is so you are strong on the morrow."

"Why?" Dominic shifted to the edge of his seat as if something terrible was about to unfold in front of him, as if being ready could stop it.

"She sees but she does not recognize. She hears but she does not understand. She speaks but she is incomprehensible. She is lost, even to herself."

"If you did something to her..." Dominic hissed, fists clenched, barely able to spit the words out.

"Ah...the righteous anger of the abandoned son. I would not hurt her *Guédé Vi*, she brought this on of her own doing. Bad pharma."

Dominic exhaled. "You provoke me!"

"I wanted to tell you your name so that when you leave, you will know who you are."

"How did you know I was leaving?" Dominic asked.

Baron Semedi laughed. "How do I know anything?"

"I have not danced since I was very young."

"You will remember. The *loa* are very close to you."

"They are?"

"You may not remember but I do. By this time tomorrow, you will be back with your father, but before that, you will see your mother and I will tell you your name. That is why I wanted you to come up country."

Baron Semedi brought him a plate of salt fish, fried cassava cake, cold mango and a glass of grapefruit juice. He refilled Dominic's water glass and watched him eat. While he waited, he nursed a beer and relit the cigar he had been smoking all day. "I always wanted children, especially a son, but it was not given to me to have children."

Dominic looked up at Baron Semedi while he ate and nodded but did not say anything.

"Jemma was like fire to me. I loved her like no other woman, but her womb was cursed. Twice I gave her a baby and twice it died in her arms. I never knew the depth of her grief…until she begged me to take you to the orphanage. She never knew the depth of my grief at her request. But I would not have made a good father so I steeled myself and surrendered you to the nuns at the Sisters of Mercy orphanage. It was a terrible place but I promised myself I would be strong and not look back and I did not; not on that day at least."

"What do you mean she was like 'fire'?"

"Driven by the wind; to the east one day, to the south the next; in the space of a few minutes, from ecstatic laughter to tears of desperation. She courted fear and did and said things that made me afraid for myself and for her. Like fire, being near her gave me great comfort but if I got too close, I got burned."

"You said you did not look back. What did you mean?"

"At the time I was wealthy man so I made an anonymous donation to the orphanage for certain upgrades, to provide for the children, the grounds and the staff. As a silent donor, I acquired the ability to ask questions and suggest allocations. I also acquired access to the records of the children, though there was only one I was interested in."

"Me?"

Semedi nodded. "My donations continued for eight years and I was happy to continue. I came to see you sometimes. I did not want to become attached to you. To this day, I have not told her."

"What happened after eight years?"

"After the Armageddon bombing in 2023, reciprocity attacks forced the nuns to shutter the orphanage. In the process of closing out the records, I discovered two of the nuns had embezzled money. This was unacceptable to me. I found somewhere for you to live – Mooma Jacobs -- and filed a report against the orphanage for violations of minimum care regimes for orphans. The investigation proved my allegations. The authorities closed the orphanage. Within days, the orphanage burned to the ground with the chief embezzler inside."

"Did you burn it down?" The thought of the fire as retribution seemed fitting.

"The authorities were unable to prosecute anyone for the fire or the death," Semedi said with a hint of self-satisfaction. "Do you feel well enough to walk? I get tired of sitting inside."

Dominic finished the last piece of fresh mango, emptied his glass of grapefruit juice and nodded. He followed Semedi through the rear of the house and through a small patch of partially landscaped garden. But the garden was not their destination. Baron Semedi continued walking; taking a narrow path that wound around a building Dominic assumed was the *peristil* and out into wild overgrown brush and along a path carved into the brush, making the walk pleasant and easy. Not wide enough for two to walk abreast, Dominic walked behind Semedi until they came to another landscaped clearing, with crude wooden benches surrounded by tall grasses and reeds – a semi-secret oasis. Baron Semedi claimed one of the benches for himself and pointed to the other bench on a diagonal across from him. "I love to be outside," he said as he took his seat.

"This is all yours?" Dominic asked.

"The land is shared between a few families who are responsible for its upkeep. But now it is your turn to tell me something I do not know."

"What do you want to know?" Dominic honestly could not imagine where to start.

"Everything! If Jemma were here, she would be crying and laughing at the same time and she would say 'everything'."

279

"I thought *Guinée* was a real place. I thought if I went there I'd find Mooma Jacobs," Dominic replied, recalling that sadness and how it still lingered.

Baron Semedi nodded. "*Guinée* is here and here," he said, putting his hand on his chest and then on his forehead.

"Hanna left for school in Canada…"

"You are on your own…"

"On my own…yeah…" Dominic said. The wind picked up, rustling the reeds and grasses as if to lift him out of darkening clouds. "Ashton lose his mind…"

"It was not my intention for you to live there, but I was traveling and when I returned it was impossible for me to intervene. I had no leverage."

"Neither did I…"

"Yet in all of this, you are a reasonable man. Where do you think you get that?" Baron Semedi asked, delving deep into the past with his questions.

"*We are reflections of our ancestors, not a chorus but a rhyming verse*, that's what the song says…"

Semedi clapped his hand like a young child. "You do remember! Mercilia told me you had not forgotten but I didn't believe her."

"But I do not know my name."

"I will tell you your name before we part ways, Guédé Vi."

"You?"

"I gave you your name because in her time of great darkness Jemma refused to. I whispered it in your ear before the sisters took you out of my hands. Maybe you will remember it tonight, but if you do not, I will whisper it in your ear before our time is done."

"Is there a time limit?"

"We will be safer once you are back with your father."

"You don't like him."

"I have little use for the man but people need a leader even if they do not wish to be lead."

"You gave him advice."

"I did that on your account, not his."

Dominic stood up because Baron Semedi's words made him uncomfortable. "When Stork died, Ashton broke…"

"She was a strong woman. His children are also broken…"

"Do you think he broke them?" Dominic wondered out loud for the first time. Very little could reliably produce the catastrophe that was Ashton's family now.

"I don't know. Maybe you have some idea…"

Dominic nodded because he did. "Baba Santo says Ashton is flawed."

Baron Semedi smiled. "Already, quoting the father! You do not hold on too long to life's empty scaffolding do you?"

"I don't know what that means…"

"Tell me something else…"

"I cried when Pierre died…"

"No one will hold that against you…"

"People tell stories about you, you know?"

"Most of them are false."

"But some of them are true?"

"What do you want to know?"

"Who are you?"

"I am a man who has made mistakes. I am a man who has had some success, not much different than you."

"Some people say you are *Pwezidan*."

"I am privileged to be *bokor* for those who wish to have me."

"Half the island, they say."

"That is incorrect."

"Do you make the *zombi*?"

"*O bondye!* Where do you get this *vye koze*?"

"People talk…"

They passed the next few minutes digesting lost opportunities for a thousand such conversations that might never have occurred had either made different choices. Baron Semedi sat, pensive and happy. Dominic sat overwhelmed by what he had learned and what it had taken to learn it. The sun began to set, painting the horizon with fire.

Baron Semedi spoke next. "Mercilia told me you remember them well."

"I do," Dominic said, relieved to be talking again. Talking to this strange man felt like medicine that settled the butterflies in his belly.

"You learned to dance when you lived with them. When I saw you dance, that is when I saw Jemma in you. The *loa* were very close to her as well."

"When I went to school up north, I swore I would never forgive Ashton."

"It is good to leave the place of one's birth to see another place, to see the way people live."

"I didn't think so…"

"No, you would not have. You were at the age when boys are most resentful of their fathers."

"How do you know?"

"I remember. I was young once. I suffered all the petty tragedies of childhood just like you and every other child on the earth. Tribulation does not make you special. It is what you make of it that sets you apart."

"The DF, now that was tribulation!"

"It is construed to be so, like plunging steel into fire. It is an established rite of passage but it was not my idea and I meddled in your life no more after you were accepted."

"My Commission?"

"You had an acquaintance in high places. I did not meddle there either. Your success is completely your own."

"You don't find it weird?"

"What should I find weird?"

"That Baba Santo is my father?"

"I have always known, so it has never been weird for me. The world is an odd place. One can be lucky and stricken in the blink of an eye. Stranger things have happened." Baron Semedi folded his hand in his lap, bowed his head and closed his eyes for a brief moment. "I have changed my mind. Instead of dancing in the *peristil* I would like to continue our conversation. Would you indulge me?"

Dominic heard himself replying. He agreed.

When they returned to the house, Baron Semedi offered Dominic the use of the couch to rest, while he disappeared for a few minutes. When he returned, he held a very old and worn book in his hand – a true antique – since mass publication of bound books, hard cover or otherwise, ceased at least a decade ago. He held it out to Dominic. "This is a book from 1969...more than a hundred years old. I bought it on one of my trips north at a bookstore called 'City Lights' in the city of San Francisco. It is by Milo Rigaud."

283

Dominic took the archaic object in his bare hands, afraid he might drop it, that it would shatter. It was titled *Secrets of Voodoo*.

"Here on the island, *vodou* tells who we are and through it, we learn our true names."

Dominic sat down again on the couch with the book, carefully paging through it. The object intrigued him perhaps more so than its subject matter.

"It is my gift to you. It is the only thing I can give you that you can hold in your hands."

"Thank you."

Baron Semedi nodded. "I must rest for a while. We will talk more later, yes?"

That evening, after both napped for longer than planned, Baron Semedi served a meal of fried fish, festival and beer. They ate in silence, staring in turn at the moon and Venus in her shadow. Dominic had forgotten how much silence the country carried – it almost oppressed him. While he slept, a question came to him as a ghost passing in the night, hinting at things he could have remembered himself but did not. With Baron Semedi in such a talkative mood, Dominic asked the question.

"Why do you call me *Guede Vi?*"

The old man laughed. "Is it not a good name? You are a child of the *Guedes!*"

"I am?" Dominic asked in surprise, since this was the first he had heard it.

"Do you not remember?"

"Should I?"

"I thought Pierre would have told you…in good time…"

"If he did, I can't remember."

"Then I will tell you. I remember as if it were yesterday. Do you remember being sick?"

"Breakbone fever…after I got to Pierre's house."

"Yes-I! We were afraid you were being eaten by the *loa*. Your illness lasted much longer than such things normally do and you were not responding to the typical interventions."

"I just remember being itchy…"

"But that was after Pierre brought you to my *peristil* on a stretcher. He hoped to assuage the *loa* eating you."

"And?"

"About half way through the ceremony, you became *cheval* for *Ratalon* and you danced as if your feet were flames driven by a hurricane. Understand, before this you had been in bed for a month, unable to feed yourself. When *Ratalon* finished with you, he threw you against the *Poteau-mitan* and you struck your head hard enough to draw blood."

"And you thought this was a good thing?" Dominic said, finding it hard to accept.

"For twelve hours, we did not know. The fever broke and you told Pierre you were thirsty. That is when the itching began. Ever since that time, seeing you makes me smile. The *Guedes* are pranksters but they can be caustic."

"I don't remember?"

"That is a common occurrence for the *cheval*. While the *loa* is upon him, the human psyche is obliterated so completely that memory does not survive."

"Then what's the point?"

"Spoken like a man from the city of lies! What is *Vodou*, but exploration and introspection of the unknown? If you remember, it is no longer unknown. *Voudou* is not so simple."

Dominic forced himself to repress a smile at the incredulous story coming from the old man, even if he did not disbelieve the chronology of events.

"*Voudou* is finding the essential goodness of your superior self."

"My superior self?" Dominic tried hard not to laugh. The words amused him but his laughter came from also from uncertainty. He wondered whether the old man cast some sort of spell.

"The part of you that sits here peacefully with me and reasons late into the night -- the part of you who loved Pierre; the part of you who sang to Mooma Jacobs at night, the unbroken child inside us all."

"I'll do pretty much anything for fried fish and bammy…"

Baron Semedi laughed again. "Perhaps we are each of us our own *Poteau-mitain*."

"What about the other parts?"

"As I said, the *Guedes* are caustic race and you are a child of *Ratalon*. There is no reconciliation."

They sped away from the white buildings of the sanitorium in Baron Semedi's convoy of black Cadillac Escalades. Dominic and Baron Semedi rode in the middle vehicle and Dominic swore he would not cry as the convoy gained speed on the bumpy gravel road. The older man played the part of the stoic giving Dominic however much space he would take. He did not know how to deal with this kind of grief. The day they had chosen to visit had not been one of Jemma's better days. She had aged so much since Baron Semedi's last visit and had stopped taking care of herself of her own accord. As a measure of how much she had deteriorated, she allowed the staff to cut her hair, now a shade of dirty ash. She mumbled and laughed and groaned and screamed. She stared at both Semedi and Dominic with eyes wide open but gave no indication she recognized the faces in front of her. She had trouble maintaining her balance and drooled when she talked. She needed help to eat and to void. She allowed herself to be bathed once a week. That was the only concession to the world around her. She would not allow them to bathe her more often than every seven days. She also refused medication that might have mitigated the worst symptoms and side effects. Though her condition remained undiagnosed, the doctors concluded her condition was degenerative and would ultimately be fatal.

After about twenty-minutes of driving at a breakneck pace over roads Dominic did not know existed, Baron Semedi took something from his pocket and handed it to Dominic. It was the COMLINK and when Dominic took it in hand, he noticed it was turned on. He queried the old man with wide eyes. "In a few minutes your father's men will swarm our little convoy. We will submit and return you to them. They will be angry. Are you ready?"

"Already?" Dominic asked, realizing he wanted more time.

"You have already been with us too long. Any longer is too dange…ah…do you hear the drone? Now sirens?"

They both looked to the rear and saw drones and vehicles with blue flashing lights in close pursuit. A low flying assault helo swooped dangerously low and close to the lead car, bringing the entire convoy to a screeching halt in a flurry of dirt and gravel. They were immediately surrounded by at least two squadrons of ISEC shock troops with their tell tale mirrored helmets. Baron Semedi cracked open the moon roof and waved a white handkerchief. The assault helo and drones retreated by about one hundred yards. Shock troops reconfigured to cordon off the middle vehicle. Baron Semedi instructed Dominic to open his door slightly, being sure to show both his hands. The troop squadron reconfigured again to concentrate on the open door. Baron

Semedi grabbed Dominic's shirt, pulled him close to him, hissed a name in Dominic's ear and then gently pushed him out the open door of the SUV. The shocktroops enveloped him and carried him to a waiting vehicle. Once safely ensconced in the armored vehicle, the operation sent the success code to their control center and Baron Semedi's convoy was abandoned.

The ISEC response team careened wildly across the island. He had a bloody nose and a dislocated shoulder. They cuffed him like a common prisoner. He repeated the name Baron Semedi had whispered into his ear over and over. The convoy took the same road the garbage truck had taken only months ago. They also lost the attack helo and drones. The convoy did not stop at any of the four checkpoints. It did not slow down until it reached the front of the residence, coming to a screaming stop next to the fountain. His escort heaved him from the car and half-carried, half-dragged him across the driveway and to the bottom of the front portico, where Carly stood with her hand over her mouth. Between exiting the custody vehicle and half way across the driveway, the master sergeant realized the young man in custody held a Cabinet-level post and that treating him like a common criminal might not be the wisest strategy. Midway in their awkward dance, the phalanx stopped, removed the cuffs and allowed Dominic to walk on his own power the last fifty feet to where Carly stood.

Carly hugged him, waving away the response team. She held him at arms length to survey the damage the ISEC team had wrought. ISEC first received instructions from Santo to put Dominic in a holding cell until he returned to the residence, but rescinded the order after a tongue lashing from Carly. "Dominic, what have you done? Are you all right?"

Dominic nodded sheepishly. He never intended to arrive in quite this manner.

"Joseph is beside himself! You have NO idea! Our doctor is just inside."

The doctor took more time than Dominic would have liked. After an icepack for his nose and the man's incredibly strong fingers pinching his sinuses until the bleeding stopped, the doctor poked and prodded at his shoulder, creating more pain than the injury itself. It would need to be wrapped the doctor concluded. After showering and changing clothes, he had to submit to the doctor again so his shoulder could be wrapped. Carly met him in the hallway on the way to Joseph's study.

"Are you sure you're ok?" she said, gently touching his cheek with one finger and then his good shoulder.

"It was a stupid thing to do..."

"I have to agree," she said, though she laughed as she said it.

"I wanted to get out, one last time..."

"We know, Dominic."

"You know?"

"ISEC discovered your plot and put out an alert. A young man from the Canadian Embassy reported something odd at the Bone Room. Why didn't you just ask? ISEC does that sort of thing all the time!"

"Lahwd a massie!"

"Once your COMLINK shut down, it turned into a waiting game. You'd better go wait upstairs. He'll be back any minute."

Dominic nodded, only now realizing how idiotic his whole plan had been and how lucky he was.

The door of the study slammed behind him and the thunderous boom of Santo's voice woke him with a start, unaware he had fallen asleep.

"I believe you two know each other?" Santo said, wearing his pissed off face but polite to a fault.

Dominic turned to meet the sound and realized Santo had brought Daniel, who looked pleased and relieved. "You're all right then," Daniel said, "I wasn't sure what to do. You said not to walk around at night but I saw the policing unit on the corner so I took a chance."

"Thank you. That was very cool of you to do that."

Santo could not resist jumping in. "And you Dominic, were a fool!"

"Yeah...it was dumb, but it made sense at the time..."

Santo rolled his eyes and looked at Daniel. "You have the appreciation of this government at its highest level. You can be assured your ambassador will hear about this."

Daniel nodded. "Thank you, Mr. President."

"If you wait downstairs, Dominic will meet you after we finish talking," Santo said, holding the door to the study open. Daniel understood. A house usher escorted him downstairs.

As soon as the door closed Santo said, "Only pretty dumb? Not completely foolish? Totally crazy?"

"All that..."

"What were you thinking? Were you thinking?"

"I wanted to go somewhere on my own...just me and the world."

"What about our conversations about how dangerous it was?"

"I thought I'd be back before anyone noticed."

"I need to trust you, especially now. I thought you knew that."

"I do."

"You understand I am indifferent to where you go, what you do, or who you see?"

Dominic had never heard such imploring tones, almost begging, and it made him uncomfortable. "Yes."

"We have less than ten days before we leave for Miami. There is only room for error and catastrophe. I don't think you realize how much danger exists in the world."

"No more running."

"Are you sure?" Santo asked, as he poured them both another drink.

"Yessuh."

"You almost killed me with that stunt you know!"

"I'm sorry."

"ISEC reports they recovered you in interesting company."

"Baron Semedi…"

"I don't understand, but something tells me I should."

Dominic shook his head. "He took me to see Jemma."

Dominic's last sentence took all the air out of Santo. "You saw her? You talked to her?"

"I saw her…but it was a nightmare."

"What are you saying?"

"She's in a sanitorium. Bad pharma."

"That's it? All that just to show you a nightmare?"

"He told me my name."

"What's wrong with the one you have?" Santo asked.

"Baba…you know what I'm talking about, my true name, the one they whisper in your ear when you're born, my secret name."

"You follow all that? I'm sorry, I didn't know. I'd heard about it but I didn't know it was important to you."

"Hanna's dad used to lecture her about how I was dangerous because I didn't know my name."

"Really?"

Dominic nodded. "You don't seem angry…"

"Oh I was angry believe me. Carly was upset, my kids were crying…but all's well that ends well. You are not an island any more Dominic. You almost spent your last week on the island with Custodial!" Santo rose and left the room. Dominic could tell he was still angry.

Ten days never passed so quickly as the ten days between his conversation with Santo in the study and when their plane left the ground. Dominic threw his belongings into two black duffel bags and left them where instructed. He did not have much that needed carrying and he had never collected knick-knacks, keepsakes or found objects. After making detailed arrangements to have his media system packaged and shipped, and once the clothes and shoes were in the duffel bags, the decision on what else he would take with him proved more difficult than he imagined it would be. What to do with an odd piece of Hanna's jewelry or an article of her clothing? What to do with a walking stick Pierre found cut for him, or a piece of jewelry from an earlier time? The objects called to him and overwhelmed him. In the blank stare he found an answer: he would take one thing from each person. Hanna's odd piece of jewelry went into the duffel bag but her clothing stayed. The walking stick Pierre carved went into the duffel bag but other keepsakes did not. He took a cedar and pewter "Lion of Judah" Ashton gave him for his birthday years ago. The last keepsake into the duffel bag was a plain white plate and a half-burned candle from Mooma Jacob's funeral and Baron Semedi's book, carefully wrapped in heavy paper to protect it.

Outside the President's Palace, power on the move took shape. Mirror helmeted ISEC shock troops cordoned off the front of the Presidential Palace, surrounding the security apparatus collecting in the circular driveway. Two drones and an un-manned helo circled overhead. Carly sat in the entry way on a huge LV bag while the two Santo kids played tic-tac-toe on a toy made to look like a SELAND deck. She looked nervous and scared. Santo stood in the next room surrounded by ministers and government bureaucrats signing page after page of official documents. Dominic left his duffel bags in the entry and stood next to Carly. She smiled but he could tell she was more nervous that a family vacation would warrant.

"You ok?" he asked, holding his hand out in case she needed that kind of support.

She took his hand briefly in her own. "I'm ok. You? Oh...I almost forgot!" She handed him a small tan envelope.

"*Wah'dis?*"

"Open it!"

Dominic reached in and pulled out a small dark blue booklet. He opened it to discover it was not a booklet at all, but a passport. He took a closer look -- it was a US passport. He checked the front page, surprised to see his picture and even more surprised to see his name: Dominic Santo. Convinced there had been some mistake he handed it back to Carly. "It print up wrong..."

Carly's eyes grew big and she took it from him to inspect it. "What's wrong?"

"Look 'pon mi name..."

"Dominic, it says exactly what it is supposed to say!" She said, her face beaming as she handed it back to him.

"It does?"

"Don't say a word," Carly reached out and took his hand in hers. "We have all the paperwork. You are kin."

Surrounded by a cordon of tactical-black clad ISEC agents, the family walked out of the President's Palace and got into the third of four identical black Audis. The second and fourth Audis held four ISEC agents, each with a high-powered, 15-mm automatic machine-gun. The first Audi would break off as a ruse car. In front and behind the four Audis, three ISEC urban combat vehicles would ride in phalanx formation. The motorcade would be preceded and followed by five ISEC police motorcycles. Overhead four Offensive Drones would provide air cover. The motorcade used neither lights nor sirens but the route was already been blocked, washed and cleared. After sitting in the car for two hours Dominic saw the first of the escorting motorcycles getting underway. The Audi's windows darkened to jet-black and they were off, en route to the airport at the predefined motorcade speed of 75 miles an hour. About a mile from the President's Palace, one of the combat vehicles and the first Audi veered to the left while the bulk of the motorcade maintained course. Looking behind him, Dominic saw a combat vehicle and two escort motorcycles had followed the ruse car. At the airfield, the motorcade gained two more drones as it careened into a hanger where a small jet waited to receive the family. Wasting no time and not pausing for good byes or farewells, Dominic boarded with the family and sat down for the first time in an airplane. Two of the drones accompanied the plane to the edge of the island's airspace. Two hours later, the airplane landed in Miami.

Part Three

"These," he said, "are unpleasant facts; I know it. But then most historical facts are unpleasant."

<u>Brave New World</u>, Aldous Huxley

CHAPTER I

MIAMI - TODAY

<<Tapping The Vein – Complicate It>>

After settling in the family's new penthouse condominium, Dominic spent a couple days feeling his way around town, watching people move, listening to the rhythm and tempo of Miami. He got his drivers license and a bank account. He walked by the boutique shops selling Rolex watches and Hermes bags. He watched the high-end cars parading up and down the streets. Unable to sleep, he ran on the beach at sunrise and did laps in the pool at midnight. It seemed strange – the affluence, the blatant luxury no one recognized as such. No one stopped him on the street to strike up a conversation. People were always in a hurry – trying to get around him, overtake him on the wide sidewalks. Two weeks went by before he realized he walked too slowly for Miami. He did not see much of Santo or Carly but he saw Joseph and Jack, their two young children, and their new nanny, a young Cuban woman named Valeria, quite a bit. It took three weeks for his media system to ship to the condo and another four days for a technician to complete the install and re-align the speaker cubes. He spent hours playing video games with the kids during the hottest part of the day and heard the complaints of young school children as the start of a new school year loomed closer.

He thought about it every day for the first three weeks but he did not message Olivia or find her address on the map. He met the lawyer, the accountant, and the live-in house keeper, none of which were looking for him, but were pleased to meet him anyway. He signed papers for the lawyer and the accountant. Money from his island account would transfer in a couple days, as well as an allowance from Joseph. Until then, he had to make the Bitcoin chip last. If he had complaints about the allowance he should take it up with Mr. Santo, not with the accountant.

Not quite ready to drive on the streets of Miami, he purchased a transit card and studied the transit route maps, building up courage to venture out in search of Olivia. Loath to spend the Bitcoin in hand, the urge to go clothes shopping overwhelmed a fast-fading sense of frugality. He returned to the condo with two articles of clothing and a much-depleted Bitcoin chip, convinced he had been cheated. Embarrassed, he holed up in his room, watching bad soap operas and listening to new music. Despite the novelty, he knew his life, fairy tale that it turned out to be, could not go on forever. Though he could not imagine how it would end or what trouble would find him and make him feel small again. He never had to wait long. Trouble found him easily.

That same evening, after a late dinner with the family, a drink on the patio, some late night media and a restless attempt at sleep, he sat on the floor of his room, his back against the bed, staring out the window – waiting to feel tired. From his vantage point, he saw lighted shrimp boats out near the horizon and night dive tour boats trolling the nearer horizon. The room felt foreign and strange and he could not brag about a decent night's sleep since they arrived. Usually the droll of a media feed induced a kind of weariness, but that night something interfered with his sleep switch. A gentle knock on the door interrupted his frustration at not being able to sleep.

"We need to talk," Santo said, as if he did not want anyone else to hear.

Dominic stepped out of the room into the hallway. Santo wore a grim face and motioned for Dominic to follow him. Santo stopped in front of the workout room, opened the door, ushered Dominic inside and turned on the lights.

Dominic felt nervousness rise, but kept quiet, sitting diminutively on a work out bench.

"Ashton is dead," Santo said, with the pull of death on the living.

Dominic let his chin drop to his chest and let a few moments of silence mark the event. When he looked up his eyes were clear and awake. "How?"

"A medication error."

Again, Dominic dropped his chin to his chest to maintain a lid on the controlled rage he seldom admitted to harboring, and which he knew this moment would spark. So strong was this rage, he thought Santo would see it in his body, arms, and belly. "That's not supposed to happen is it?" he said, keeping his eyes focused on the floor, unwilling to meet Santo's eyes.

"Left to chance, there is a one in a billion chance of contamination."

Dominic looked up at Santo in a squint, as if the lights of the room were too bright. "Ashton was unlucky then?"

"Dominic, there are irregularities in the record."

"Irregularities?" Dominic decided he could face Santo, now that his body fit itself into the situation. He could move about the conversation's pits and valleys with head up, eyes forward. He stood up to match posture with Santo.

"Not random, not a system failure."

"Someone killed him?" Dominic asked, his voice peaking a little higher than he would have liked.

"It appears that way," Santo said, his voice heavy and dripping with all the weight of his years in office.

Dominic lay back on the bench and began bench-pressing the bar on the rack. When he had pushed his arms to failure, he placed the weight back on the rack and stood up, facing Santo fair and square. "I did it," he said with a clear voice, head up, eyes locked on Santo's. Santo took the news much better than Dominic imagined he would. He did not blink or purse his lips or draw in his breath. He did put his hand on Dominic's shoulder and motion for him to sit down.

"You? You'd better tell me…"

"I had to."

"You had to?"

"I've been waiting for ten years."

"You were protecting him just a few months ago."

"I don't like interrogations."

"You've done a thousand interrogations worse that that, Dominic! That's not an answer.

"I lived in his house for three years. For the last year, he came to my room almost every night when he was home."

"You told me there were only two incidents!" Santo yelled.

"He only made two recordings."

"You knew about the recordings?"

"I watched him set up the equipment."

Santo had tears in his eyes now. "You have been holding this inside for ten years?" Now Santo pursed his lips drew in his breath and sat down heavily on the same bench Dominic had been sitting on. "So how did you get from there to here?"

"When he recommended me to your office he thought he was using me, but he didn't know about the monster."

"How did the recordings get out?"

"I toggled the public search stream permissions on the files. I knew Ashton never audited."

"And then?"

"I waited for him to make a mistake."

"Which was?"

"The system deck with the invalid NETCERT…"

"You knew it was a ruse?"

"I knew it was a bad seed. That's when I pointed you to the Sequester in your car after the cleanup operation."

"Who else knows about this…this unpleasantness?"

"No one."

"This could be seen as assisted suicide, not an act of revenge."

"What's the difference?"

"The penalties for assisting suicide in Custodial are much harsher."

"They won't find anything..."

"How can you be so sure?"

"I've had ten years to be sure."

"I cannot imagine living with that…and I would probably have done the same thing…but I cannot ignore this, do you understand?"

Dominic nodded. "So what now?"

"I know a good psychologist here in Miami. He is a friend and more importantly, discreet. I want you to see him."

"Not a lawyer?"

"Only if we have to. This puts me in a difficult position, Dominic. I'm not sure you understand how difficult."

Dominic sat on the bench, exhausted to his core. He nodded, Ashton's 'dog' reference from months ago hanging in the balance.

"I want you to wait a year before you start school. You will live here with us. We'll find you something to do. The

ONLY thing you are required to do is see my friend. Understood?"

Dominic nodded again.

"I need you to talk to me about what's behind your glass eyes." With that, Santo left the work out room.

Back in his bedroom, Dominic lay on his back, feeling the rage he fostered and nursed for ten years dripping like sweat from his body. He focused on breathing and spent a few minutes counting his breaths. Though he expected to feel small, he did not. Though he never expected to feel different, he did. Before sleep overcame him, he whispered a single sentence to himself, bringing an ignoble but definitive end to that sad and shifty character of the very small, Wink.

^gwanweh wink! gwanweh ras-wink!

Dominic woke up the next morning with cabin fever. Uncomfortable in the empty house, he donned an anonymous outfit of basketball shorts, t-shirt and flip flops and started off on his well-mapped trip to the address Olivia gave him weeks ago. He took a driverless transit pod south towards Miami Beach on Harding, over the Julia Tuttle Causeway and then towards downtown on NW 12th St, into Little Havana. It took him a little while on foot once the transit pod ejected him, but he found it – a house on the corner of SW 25th avenue. Neat and tidy with a white steel fence and a gnarled tree near the driveway, it was not what he imagined he would find. From what he remembered, a high-rise condo would have been more her style. As he got closer to the house he heard children talking and playing inside. Someone maintained the front yard in immaculate condition as well as the front of the house.

The whole neighborhood sat in almost a complete silence though it was late on a Saturday morning. Gingerly and diminutively, he lifted the latch on the gate and approached the house. The front door was open to the weather, no bars, and no screen. He raised his eyebrows in amused disbelief as he confirmed two children in the house, a boy and a girl, playing and arguing over a video game. The boy, about 8, looked just like Olivia. The girl…looked just like… the tall man with a thick goatee in the doorway, asking Dominic what he wanted. Not exactly how he planned the reunion, he stammered and asked for Olivia. Then realizing the possible impropriety of his appearance on their doorstep, mentioned he used to be a colleague at SELAND. As the man turned, Dominic saw Olivia coming into the front room and casually waved, as if his visit was a common occurrence. Her eyes grew large, her jaw dropped, she laughed loudly, hugged her husband, saying something to him as she did and ran to the doorway to saddle Dominic with a very long hug. "Don't worry," she whispered in his ear, "I told him you liked men." Of course, despite the long hug and how good it was to see her again, she had some explaining to do.

"Is that your…?" Dominic said incredulously, when he finally managed to separate himself from her.

"Since I was your age, *mijo*."

"Don't call me that."

"Sorry, it's a habit. How are you? I thought you were going to call!"

"I was going to surprise you," Dominic said looking past her and into the house, though the angle of the morning sun made it difficult to see anything.

"Look where that got you!"

"You and that guy have two kids?"

"Yes, Dominic, we are legal," she said sighing, not impatiently, signaling she wanted to 'move on'.

He laughed out loud at himself and his predicament. She played him and played him well. "So, on the island…that was work?"

She raised her eyebrows at his choice of words. "Getting to you was work but I might have gotten carried away."

"Getting to me?" Her story kept getting better and better.

"Look, that's over ok? I'm here, you're here, I don't regret it."

"So you knew from the start, from that night at the Bone Room?"

Olivia nodded.

Dominic whistled to himself quietly, "Lawhd a massy…"

"Does that mean you're over it?" she asked, needling him gently with her hand.

Dominic shrugged. "I'm not complaining. I came by to pick up where we left off…"

Olivia flashed him a slight pout. "I figured you might. That's why I said call first, so I could break it to you slowly."

"How was that gonna' work?"

"I was gonna figure it out when you called."

"What the bouncer's name?" Dominic asked motioning inside the house.

"Are you referring to my legal pair, Dominic?" Olivia said, a little too loudly. "His name is Dudley."

Dominic could not stop himself from laughing. "Dudley?"

"Stop laughing or I'll go in there and tell Dudley everything."

Dominic stopped laughing immediately. "Sorry."

"You should be! Where'd you land anyway?

"Bal Harbor."

"Oooh! Too good for me! Are you staying?"

"Maybe a year…"

"That long?" Olivia seemed surprised.

Dominic nodded. "I have a couple stories to tell you."

"I bet you do! Not now, next week. Dudley's getting nervous. Message me and we'll meet somewhere."

"Ashton's dead," he blurted out, instead of saying good-bye or agreeing.

"I'm sorry to hear that," she said, suddenly cautious, tiptoeing around the subject.

"Don't be. No one else is."

With that he leaned over, left a kiss on her cheek and jogged out of the yard and down the street to the nearest transit pod link. Before taking the transit pod already sitting there waiting for the next passenger, he ran across the street to pick up some street food -- five pulled pork empanadas and a quadruple café Cubano. He'd have to pull a few tricks to get the food into the transit pod but having not eaten breakfast, he felt hollow and empty inside. Though hard-pressed to give it a name, he felt better for talking to Santo the night before, although for most of his life he swore he would never talk about it with a single soul. He let four transit pods go by before he found one without the new food sensors. He sat back in the pod devouring his empanadas while the pod took him noiselessly back to Bal Harbor and the office of a Dr. Kim, a small and unassuming office sandwiched in between a Prada shop and white table-cloth Spanish café inside the Bal Harbor Shops on Collins Avenue.

He promised Santo he would stop by Dr. Kim's office, introduce himself and get on the doctor's calendar. When he found Dr. Kim's office, his body was just beginning to 'buzz' from the café Cubano. Dr. Kim stood in the doorway to his office, peering out over the crowd of people mulling around the shopping center. Dr. Kim seemed to recognize Dominic as he approached.

"You must be Joseph's son," Dr. Kim said, extending his hand.

Dominic shook the man's hand, "I'm Dominic," he said. Dr. Kim stood six or seven inches shorter than Dominic, with carefully groomed grey hair, tan slacks with brown loafers and a carefully pressed burgundy shirt over a searing white undershirt. He wore a small gold band on his left index finger and an intricate jade bracelet on his right wrist. He had a soft voice with an Asian accent.

"Come inside and we can talk for a minute. Joseph said you might stop by today." They entered a small but immaculate office with mahogany tabletops and counters, slate floors, black leather modern furniture, an antique grandfather clock and an old-model electronic scribe. "Sit down Dominic. I just need to get to my calendar. Do you want something to drink, some water perhaps?"

"Thank you, I'm ok."

"Joseph told me you've been through a lot and you wanted to talk to someone. Do I have that right?"

"He asked me to talk to you. I said I would."

"Excellent. How about we start two days from now after lunch, about 1.30?"

"OK." Dominic stood up to leave.

"Anything in particular you want to talk about?"

"No."

"Fifty minutes can seem like fifty years with nothing to talk about."

MIAMI – ONE WEEK LATER

Two days later, Dominic sat in the black leather recliner Dr. Kim offered him and Dr. Kim sat across from him in a large, high-backed chair that made him look small. Dr. Kim flipped a switch on the media scribe eliminating the need to take notes. The office lighting switching to low-key, not dark, but muted. Dr. Kim had the look of a patient man but Santo told Dominic not to underestimate him, that he had his own stories to tell. Dr. Kim had poured them both glasses of water and set them on the small table between them.

TRANSCRIPT EXCERPT
SESSION 1
RECORDING 1
(K) DOCTOR: KIM
(D) CLIENT: SANTO, D

(K): "Thank you for arriving on time Dominic. We're going to be spending a little bit of time together so trust and respect are important. Do you agree?"

(D): "Yessuh."

(K): "You may call me Dr. Kim or just Kim. May I call you Dominic?"

(D): "Yessuh."

(K): "Good. See that wasn't so hard was it?"

(D): "Nossuh."

(K): "Sometimes the person in that chair has a problem to solve, so they know, within rounding error, why they are here. They may be the lucky ones. Others aren't so sure. They have to explore, to stare into the abyss. Which do you think you are?"

(D): "I am not lucky,"

(K): "If you were to guess what would you say Joseph's reason was for asking you to talk to me?"

(D): "He is afraid."

(K): "Afraid? Joseph is not easily frightened."

(D): "He wanted a son but he got a monster."

(K): "Monster? Who is a monster?"

(D): "I had one inside me."

(K): "You had one? No more?"

(D): "It died when another man died."

(K): "Which man?"

(D): "The man who made the monster inside me."

(K): "Which man is that?"

(D): "His name was Ashton."

(K): "How did Ashton die?"

(D): "He died from contaminated insulin."

(K): "I see. He made the monster?"

(D): "Yes."

(K): "Let's stop for a minute. Sometimes we have to give the body time to catch up with our words."

(D): "Your office is quiet."

(K): "People need quiet to do the work they must do when they come here."

(D): "It's too quiet here. Everywhere is quiet."

(K): "We live inside our houses and heads to a greater extent than other places. It makes us hard to read and hard to reach. How did he make a monster inside you?"

(D): "The way a man makes a baby in a woman."

(K): "And this started when?"

(D): "I was almost fourteen."

(K): "Tender years…"

(D): "Unpleasant years…"

(K): "What did you think when he died?"

(D): "I already knew."

(K): "You already knew?"

(D): "I killed him."

(K): "You killed Ashton?"

(D): "Yes."

(K): "I did not expect this level of honesty so soon. Do you think of hurting other people?"

(D): "No."

(K): "Yourself?"

(D): "No."

(K): "Ashton was revenge?"

(D): "I didn't call it that. Is 'eye for an eye' revenge?"

(K): "You're talking about reciprocity…"

(D): "Yeah, that's the word."

(K): "'Eye for an eye' is the definition of revenge. Reciprocity is not usually an end game. Ashton is dead. You are here."

(D): "I died 161 times. Ashton died once. It's not 'eye for an eye'."

(K): "I know Ashton hurt. Let's set the revenge conversation aside for now. We'll come back to it later.

(D): "You asked about revenge, not me…"

(K): "OK. Why do you think Joseph is afraid?"

(D): "He only knows technology, the chain of command, and favors and none a dem fix."

(K): "Do you need to be fixed?"

(D): "*People-dem cya'an fix! Sum bahnn lucky, sum broke, sum too soon, sum too late.*"

(K): "People cannot help themselves then?"

(D): "Maybe the lucky ones…"

(K): "You don't consider yourself lucky?"

(D): "*From mi bahnn mi very unlucky.*"

(K): "You've switched to your local patois…"

(D): "Sorry…"

(K): "I could say you are lucky. I might even say that you helped yourself."

(D): "Yuh nuh know me."

(K): "Weren't you afraid I might turn you in?"

(D): "Baba Santo said you were discreet."

(K): "You trust Baba Santo then? Does he know you?"

(D): "I trust him but he doesn't know me yet."

(K): "Does he trust you?"

(D): "Not any more."

(K): "Do you ever think of hurting yourself?"

(D): "Why would I do that?"

(K): "I don't know I'm asking if those thoughts cross your mind."

(D): "You asked me that earlier."

(K): "Do you think of hurting or killing other people?"

(D): "No. Why do you keep asking me that?"

(K): "We've covered a lot of ground today, much more than some people cover in a lifetime. Sometimes answers change."

(D): "What happens if my answer changes?"

(K): "There are rules I must follow."

(D): "What kind of rules?"

(K): "By law I am bound to report any person who may be a danger to themselves or others."

(D): "Will you report me?"

(K): "I think you are hurt more than you are dangerous, but an aspect of your voice and your eyes worries me."

(D): "I have glass eyes…"

(K): "You didn't have glass eyes a couple of days ago."

(D): "Will you report me?"

(K): "What would you do if I said yes?"

(D): "Call Santo."

(K): "Would he help you?"

(D): "Maybe..."

(K): "Has anyone else hurt you the way Ashton did?"

(D): "No."

(K): "Are you sexually active?"

(D): "Yes."

(K): "Gender preference?"

(D): "Women."

(K): "Exclusively?"

(D): "No."

(K): "Our time is not up but I think we should stop. I would like you to stay until our time expires. Will you do that?"

(D): "I'm getting hungry…"

(K): "Our time expires at 10 minutes to the hour."

(D): "No more talking?"

(K): "If you wish to talk I will listen."

(D): "Do you like Miami?"

(K): "It is not Japan."

(D): "You're from Japan?"

(K): "Yes."

(D): "Why did you come to Miami?"

(K): "Because it is not Japan."

(D): "Something happened in Japan?"

(K): "The tsunami of 2011 and the Fukushima nuclear disaster."

(D): "Is that why you are sad?"

(K): "I lost my parents, my wife, three small children and my home to the wave."

(D): "That's a lot to lose…"

(K): "Yes. Let's make an appointment for next week."

(D): "OK."

When Dominic emerged from Dr. Kim's office, Santo surprised him on the pedestrian mall. They got into Santo's big, new, white Bentley and Santo said they were going to get burgers. Santo smiled as they pulled out of the parking lot and when he put the top down Dominic smiled as well. At the burger shop they ordered and found a table in the back of restaurant where it seemed quieter, though it was still loud for a small place. Dominic ordered the biggest burger on the menu and a chocolate milkshake. Santo ordered sweet potato fries. For the first few minutes, Santo watched Dominic eat as if he had never eaten in his life. It was an amazing sight to see so much food disappear so quickly. Before Santo thought to reach for the BBQ sauce for his fries, half the milkshake was gone along with three quarters of the burger.

"How do you like Dr. Kim?" Santo asked finally.

"He's OK…"

"Good. What did you talk about?"

"I told him what I told you."

"What did Dr. Kim say?"

"He said I had glass eyes. He kept asking if I thought about hurting myself or other people."

"What did you say?"

Dominic stopped eating, put his hamburger down and looked hard at Santo. "Can we talk about something else?"

"Sorry. Of course," Santo said as a wait staff dropped off another drink for Santo.

"Hanna flies in a couple weeks. Should I get a hotel room?" Dominic had messaged her from the transit pod on the way to Dr. Kim's office and she replied immediately. She was ecstatic.

"What's wrong with your room?"

"Nothing! But…"

"There is no need to ask, but you must introduce us!"

MIAMI – SIX WEEKS LATER

TRANSCRIPT EXCERPT
SESSION 6
RECORDING 6
(K) DOCTOR: KIM
(D) CLIENT: SANTO, D

(K): "So, how was the week just past?"

(D): -------

(K): "I cannot understand when you shrug your shoulders."

(D): -------

(K): "I see, I expected as much. There is almost physical pain, yes?"

(D): "Yessuh."

(K): "Thank you, I know that was difficult. Am I correct to assume you did not have a good week since I saw you last?"

(D): "Yessuh."

(K): "What happened?"

(D): "I hid in my room."

(K): "Did you learn anything in your seclusion?"

(D): -----

(K): "I understand why you prefer silence but it is important to keep moving forward. Do you lift weights?"

(D): "Yessuh."

(K): "How do you build muscle?"

(D): "Push to fail…"

(K): "And when the muscle fails?"

(D): "Recover…and go to failure again."

(K): "That is what we are doing here, Dominic. We push to failure and start again."

(D): "Silence is failure?"

(K): "Not always, but in the way you are using it, yes."

(D): "I stayed in my room. I felt dirty inside...where the monster was..."

(K): "Yet, you are here now. How did that happen?"

(D): "Joseph's kid wanted to play video games."

(K): "Did you?"

(D): "Yeah..."

(K): "It's good to see you smile, it's good to hear your voice."

(D): "That's what Joseph said at dinner last night."

(K): "Joseph still puzzles you, doesn't he?"

(D): "Sometimes..."

(K): "Did Ashton puzzle you?"

(D): "No..."

(K): "Ashton was a known quantity?"

(D): "I knew who he was...what he wanted..."

(K): "And your puzzle with Joseph is..."

(D): "I don't know what he wants..."

(K): "And if he wants nothing?"

(D): "Everybody wants something..."

(K): "If I want something from you, I ask you. If Joseph wants something, he will ask. I ask you for conversation. What has Joseph asked of you?"

(D): "Nothing..."

(K): "That bothers you..."

(D): "It doesn't bother me, but I don't know what he wants."

(K): "Maybe nothing."

(D): "Maybe…"

(K): "The 'monster', has it returned?"

(D): "No…"

(K): "I suspect we will need to backtrack over unpleasant ground. Your words from a week ago came ahead of their time and your body, emotions and your mind struggle to catch up."

(D): "You mean feeling seasick when I'm standing on concrete?"

(K): "It might feel like that, or the need to hide, to be invisible, to wall yourself off in the real world."

(D): "I didn't feel like that before…"

(K): "We are not just talking here. We use words but this is excavation. You are an archeologist finding meaning in the experience of life. Excavation is work."

(D): "You didn't tell me?"

(K): "It's better you find out for yourself."

(D): "I thought you knew everything…"

(K): "I only know what I know and you know what you know."

(D): "So now what?"

(K): "I'd like to go back to my earlier question, about last week and whether it was like a moth inside its cocoon."

(D): "I'm not a caterpillar."

(K): "What happens between the time the caterpillar spins its cocoon and when the moth comes?"

(D): "I'm not a caterpillar!"

(K): "I will tell you. The caterpillar becomes what it always was, not small and bound to the ground like a serpent, but a creature of the air and the wind."

(D): "So if I stay in my room long enough, I'll turn into a moth?"

(K): "The caterpillar does not 'turn' into something it is not. It is and was always both things. You cannot have one without the other."

(D): "What are you talking about?"

(K): "I'm talking about becoming who you want to be, regardless of who you think you are or have been in the past."

(D): "I'm not like you, Dr. Kim. I don't see lessons everywhere. I'm not a caterpillar or a moth. The stupid things people do don't have that much power."

(K): "What you do, say and most importantly think, have incredible power – for you."

(D): "They do?"

(K): "If you let them…"

MIAMI – TWO MONTHS LATER

Joseph and Dominic created their own evening ritual, involving patio deck chairs facing the western sky, a fair amount of silence, a glass or two of scotch and snatches of conversation between stargazing. Though neither would admit it, a bit of catnapping. Sometimes, Joseph enjoyed a cigar and Dominic complained about the smoke. Sometimes, the kids joined their father, crowding the deck chair. Although the last couple of times, Jack opted for Dominic's chair. It was their time. The kids would always get called inside at some point, leaving Joseph and Dominic alone again. Sometimes the transition triggered conversation and other times, silence prevailed.

"I was worried about you last week." Joseph said.

"Sorry…"

"I almost knocked Wednesday night."

"Why didn't you?"

"The lights were off, I didn't know if you were sleeping."

"I was just staring out the window…I felt like hiding…"

"When Jack was small, he loved to play hide and seek but he was too scared to hide on his own so he always wanted to be the seeker.

"He's the one who walked into my room and told me I smelled. He had some new video game he wanted to play."

"So next time, I know to send Jack."

"Joseph?"

"Dominic?"

"Why did you leave South Africa?"

"I don't know that I left South Africa as much as I simply never went back."

"You and Dr. Kim do the same damn thing. Who cares whether you left or you never went back? You're not there now."

"What I mean is that when I departed South Africa for the first time, I had every intention of returning. It just never happened."

"You left your parents in South Africa…"

"I did."

"Why?"

"Because they were constant and I was weary of constants."

"I could sit here forever…"

"I know the feeling, son. I know the feeling."

"Why did you come here, to Miami, instead of going back to South Africa."

"You are full of questions tonight…"

Dominic pulled himself up in the deck chair to look at Joseph directly. Something had changed. An imperceptible nervousness enveloped their conversation like a cloud of gnats one does not see until one is breathing gnats. "I have alot of catching up to do, no?" Joseph seemed to do battle with himself, his discomfort with the conflict showing in the set of his shoulders and creases of his frown.

Joseph sighed loudly and took a long puff on his cigar.

The change in mood set Dominic's teeth on edge. He realized how comfortable he had become with Joseph, with the family.

Joseph also pulled himself up in the chair to face Dominic. "I don't know why I thought you wouldn't ask, but you have, and I am going to tell you."

"*Wah yuh a chat 'bout, mon?*"

Joseph leaned forward and placed his lit cigar on the floor at his feet. "You trust too easily, you know, *bredda*. It forces people to earn the trust you put in them."

Dominic whistled softly, brushing the wafting cigar smoke away from his face. He walked to the edge of the balcony and looked down at the nighttime traffic below. This was not the conversation he expected.

"I did not mean that as harshly as it sounded. I'm sorry. Please come and sit down."

Dominic went back to his deck chair and sat down, facing Joseph.

"Are you familiar with UN2 and the International Court of Justice?"

Dominic nodded.

"So you know that two countries are not signatory to either."

Dominic nodded again, but still he did not understand.

"There were rumors that actions of our government might be referred to the ICJ."

"So you came to Miami…"

"As a coward and in fear…"

"The US does not extradite to the ICJ."

"It does not."

"Just rumors?"

"Let us call them 'confirmed rumors'."

"That's why you called elections so soon?"

"It was a factor, but not the only reason…"

"But somebody had to make the referral…" Dominic stood up again, unsure about the feelings in his gut and in his head. Standard practice would have been to dissect the situation in search of something he could blame himself for. The cigar smoke made him lightheaded and the whisky went to his head when he stood up. When he sat down again, Joseph stood up and switched chairs, sitting down next to Dominic. He put his hand on Dominic's shoulder and sighed loudly.

"You made me very happy when you chose to join us here. Nothing has changed. Do you understand me?"

Dominic nodded. For the second time in his life, another's hand on his shoulder made him feel strong and he did not pull away.

TRANSCRIPT EXCERPT
SESSION 14
RECORDING 14
(K) DOCTOR: KIM
(D) CLIENT: SANTO, D

(K): "So how was the week just past?"

(D): "OK. Hanna arrives tomorrow."

(K): "Who is Hanna?"

(D): "My best friend, my girlfriend...sometimes..."

(K): "Sometimes?"

(D): "Sometimes."

(K): "As a member of the President's staff you must have been exposed to things that you did not approve of, that made you uncomfortable."

(D): "I didn't like interrogations."

(K): "Why?"

(D): "It wasn't a fair fight."

(K): "How did you deal with that?"

(D): "When Ashton was under the gun, I told Baba Santo even the Americans rejected special techniques. He didn't like that."

(K): "You were uncomfortable with methods??"

(D): "There's other ways."

(K): "Other ways?

(D): "Other ways to get what you want."

(K): "Did you get what you wanted?"

(D): "I got what Santo wanted…"

(K): "How?"

(D): "I bartered assistance for Ashton's children for information. He called me a devil."

(K): "Will they get the assistance?"

(D): "I don't know…"

(K): "Did you follow through?"

(D): "I left instructions about Straightedge. The other two I don't care about, they were too much like Ashton."

(K): "Do you feel bad about that? Not following through?"

(D): "I hope Straightedge gets a break…but who knows what will happen."

(K): "Do you think that Ashton made a real monster inside you? The kind that spits fire and lives in a dark cave?"

(D): "What?"

(K): "You said that Ashton made a monster inside you. Is it a real monster inside you?"

(D): "It felt real…like it wanted to get out and do damage, but if you cut me open you wouldn't find it."

(K): "Why?"

(D): "I just called it a monster…"

(K): "Some people don't make that distinction. I'm happy you do."

(D): "You're trying to figure out if I'm crazy."

(K): "We have a 50% chance of being right."

(D): "You're crazy."

(K): "Why do you say that?"

(D): "I'm sitting here with you."

(K): "So you disagree with my assertion?"

(D): "Just because I can be, doesn't mean I am."

(K): "If it can be imagined it can be done."

(D): "So I should imagine that I'm right?"

(K): "Perhaps its easier to start with the premise that you are 'not wrong'."

(D): "You're saying killing Ashton was 'not wrong'"

(K): "Murder has been proscribed in almost every civilization society and culture since the dawn of the human race yet humans are without exception the most murderous species on the planet."

(D): "You make it hard to get to 'not wrong'."

(K): "It was not my intent to make it easy or hard. I'm not talking about specific actions that can also be 'right' or 'wrong'. I'm talking about being on the side of right, not broken or damned, even if that person sometimes does things that are 'wrong'."

(D): "You want me to pretend the world is round?"

(K): "We both know the world it isn't"

(D): "The world is a reciprocating saw."

(K): "Do you know why Joseph asked you to come see me?"

(D): "I told him about the monster…"

(K): "My guess is that he would have asked you to see me whether or not you showed him the monster."

(D): "Why?"

(K): "He feels guilty."

(D): "*A fi 'im problem…*"

(K): "Yes it is. But he has accepted that guilt. He mitigates its effects without walling it off somewhere inside him where no one can see it."

(D): "You think I put the monster in a box so no one could see it?"

(K): "I don't know, but that is why we are here. You tell me."

(D): "So I can answer the question and be right 50% of the time?"

(K): "Yes! Exactly."

(D): "Gimme' a break…"

(K): "If the creation instinct created the universe using words, I think we lesser gods can create and re-create ourselves with words as well."

MIAMI - TEN MONTHS LATER

Hanna arrived for her sixth visit in a whirlwind of smiles, laughter, hugs, and too much luggage. Joseph let Dominic drive the Bentley to the shuttleport to pick her up – a reward for Dominic's progress with Dr. Kim. Nervous about seeing Hanna again, he bit his lip while he drove.

Joseph noticed and chuckled to himself. "You're not nervous about seeing this girl again, are you?"

"Nossuh!"

"You're nervous about something! Maybe I should drive," Joseph pushed back a little, still highly amused.

"Why? Did I do something wrong?"

Joseph burst into loud rolling laughter, slapping his knee for effect.

"'Top mek free wit'mi yuhnno, Joseph!"

Joseph could not stop laughing partly out of satisfaction Dominic had started calling him 'Joseph' instead of 'Baba'; partly because he had become endeared to Dominic's particular brand of gullibility. *"B'watch ya! Uno nuh mek di car run off road!"*

Dominic stopped biting his lip and resettled himself in the driver's seat. The car felt too big, but he never declined a chance to drive it.

"Taking her anywhere special?"

"The bedroom," Dominic said, biting his lip again.

"Yuh too bright!"

"Dunno where to go. All I know is Bal Harbor and Little Havana."

"Little Havana? What were you doing in Little Havana?"

"I went to see Olivia."

"Oh you did, did you? A little booty call before the girlfriend flies in?"

Dominic smiled but bit his lip again. "She's legal with some guy named Dudley. She has two kids."

"Dudley?" Joseph started laughing again.

Dominic shrugged. "She said what happened on the island was work."

"What do you think about that?"

"I'm not complaining."

Dominic saw Hanna's telltale curly reddish hair before anyone else as she exited the jet way. He saw her before she saw him and watched her walk, head down, inwardly focused, casually dressed, calm, cool, collected and more beautiful than he remembered. In jeans and a turtleneck she drew him to her like a magnet. She did not see him coming and when she did it was too late. Their bodies merged in the middle of the departure gate. People smiled and maneuvered around them. Joseph stood back watching; smiling and content.

TRANSCRIPT EXCERPT
SESSION 30
RECORDING 30
(K) DOCTOR: KIM
(D) CLIENT: SANTO, D

(K): "So how was the week just past?"

(D): "I miss Hanna."

(K): "Good. Did you tell her?"

(D): "Yeah, we talked a lot…"

(K): "That's all?"

(D): "Yeah…I mean no, we had a lot of sex, I mean a lot, but we never stopped talking, all night sometimes."

(K): "I am happy to hear that."

(D): "You're happy I got laid or you're happy that we talked a lot?"

(K): "Both, Dominic."

(D): "I'm happy I got laid, the talking just happened."

(K): "Of course you are. But we aren't in the one word answer mode anymore. You're letting yourself show through."

(D): "Are you going to tell Joseph?"

(K): "I owe him my thoughts every three months, only in the most general of terms."

(D): "Sometimes I don't understand what you're saying but I just nod anyway."

(K): "Would you agree that this time we spend together would be harder if you did not trust me?"

(D): "I guess…"

(K): "Why did you trust me Dominic?"

(D): "Joseph said you were discreet."

(K): "On that basis, you walked into my office and rolled out the magic carpet of your life in the very first session."

(D): "You told me to think of something to talk about!"

(K): "Did you have a reason to trust me?"

(D): "Only what Joseph said…"

(K): "Dominic! Don't go dark on me – no glass eyes in here, sir! Keep your head up! Keep your head in the game. I know this is hard work. Did you have a reason to trust me?"

(D): "I trusted Joseph."

(K): "Good! You trusted what Joseph."

(D): "Olivia told me I should be more paranoid. But I'm not…less trusting…"

(K): "How does being trusting get you through the day? What problem are you solving by walking blindly into situations without asking questions?"

(D): "You're asking me?"

(K): "There is no one else."

(D): "I don't know…"

(K): "We are going to stop here for today. I hope you will think about my question until next time and we can pick up where we left off."

(D): "Dr. Kim?"

(K): "Yes?"

(D): "Last week I had a dream. I was at Ashton's funeral, crying like a little kid…"

(K): "Now the monster inside is gone human feelings fill the void like rushing water filling an empty cave."

(D): "I didn't kill a monster…I killed a man…"

(K): "Many a hero's myth involves the slaying of the dragon, a mythic existential monster."

(D): "I'm not a hero."

(K): "You do have a man's life on your hands. We cannot forget that."

(D): "I won't forget…"

(K): "Good. In the end we will have to deal with that but there is much work to do before hand."

(D): "I'm not a caterpillar or a moth or a hero."

(K): "We are all heroes in the myth of our lives. We wake up each day, kill the myth and eat it. At night, the myth is reborn, to be killed and eaten the next day. If the myth you have written makes you a 'trusting' hero then you must 'trust'… but not at your own expense."

MIAMI - ONE AND A HALF YEARS LATER

Joseph dropped him off outside the glass-enclosed skyscraper that housed the global SELAND headquarters. At eighty-eight floors, it remained the tallest building in Miami's new business district, as well as the object of much hatred and not a few protests. He felt strange to be dressed in a suit again, nervous as he made his way through the many and copious security layers that evolved between the outside world and SELAND's sensitive underbelly. The ingress security contingent consisted of bald men in their fifties, former linebackers or perhaps even rugby players, with permanent frowns and the telltale earpiece running from their ear and behind stiff white collars, humorless but not unfriendly. Dominic passed through three layers of sensing technology, an iris scan and a voice scan. All this for a job interview! Rumor had it egress security was just as intense. He waited patiently in a non-descript, forgettable waiting room. He pressed all the buttons on the drink dispenser but it seemed to be inoperable. He read the brochures on the table, showing smiling healthy people with technology in hand to solve the problems of the world with less than ideal solutions. That was the SELAND motto: 'Don't let the perfect be the enemy of the good'. Joseph and Olivia had both submitted recommendations on his behalf for a new geospatial analyst position. They both thought he was a shoe-in. Although Dominic did not think the first COMLINK conversations had gone well, he had been invited to a twelve- minute face-to-face interview.

TRANSCRIPT EXCERPT
SESSION 56
RECORDING 56
(K) DOCTOR: KIM
(D) CLIENT: SANTO, D

(K): "So how was the week just past?"

(D): "I'm working like a dog…"

(K): "Do you enjoy the work?"

(D): "I'm still learning. There's so much to learn."

(K): "Last time you mentioned you might have some news…"

(D): "She finished law school last month and took the licensing exam…in Florida."

(K): "That sounds auspicious. Wasn't she in Montreal?"

(D): "She was. She called me two nights ago to tell me she got hired on with Shutts and Bowen."

(K): "I feel like there is more news coming…"

(D): "We found this condo on the waterfront where we can both walk to work…Joseph's giving us the down payment."

(K): "Congratulations Dominic! I'm very proud of you."

(D): "I'm kinda scared…"

(K): "You should be!"

(D): "Hanna and Carly are out buying furniture. After I'm done here, we're getting a 55-gallon tank for Japanese Snapping Shrimp and Ghost Eels."

(K): "Admirably domestic Dominic. What about your manager?"

(D): "She still looks at me like I'm a pre-schooler. I'm always bugging her with questions."

(K): "Who raised the subject of the condo first?"

(D): "Me."

(K): "Interesting. What was her response?"

(D): "She said 'I thought you'd never ask…'"

(K): "And that was it? The deal was done?"

(D): "No. There were a few things I had to tell her…"

(K): "How did that work out?"

(D): "She cried…she made me cry…"

(K): "What did you tell her?"

(D): "I told her everything, even my name."

(K): "Your name?"

(D): "On the island, your parents give you a birth name you're supposed to keep secret. It's not the one people use to get your attention. They say if you tell a girl your true name it means you want a life together."

(K): "Is that why you told her your name?"

(D): "I told her my name because her father always warned her away from me because I didn't know my name."

(K): "So now she can tell him your name?"

(D): "She won't do that and he wouldn't let her. But he'll be a little happier I know what it is. Maybe he'll ease up on the whole 'cohabitation' thing he's on right now."

He met Olivia on a Wednesday, at a bar in the financial district, downtown Miami. She had none of the pull he remembered from the Bone Room. She sat down in a frazzled state, ordered a glass of wine, completed a text message and lit a cigarette before she looked at him and smiled in greeting. He noticed things now he had not noticed before. Little things. She looked older, still attractive, still stylish, but something was lost. Maybe it was because he had seen her kids, seen Dudley, seen the house with the game controllers on the living room floor.

She took a sip of her wine. "Stop staring at me, mijo."

"Don't call me mijo."

"Sorry."

"I got the job at SELAND."

"I noticed. Congratulations! I knew you would get it. I'm so happy I'm out."

"How's the fam?"

"Nice. They're fine. You and Dudley should grab a beer sometime."

"I don't think so…"

"I was kidding."

"Oh."

"You were going to tell me all the good gossip…"

"Can't. I'll lose my clearance. Why'd you quit?"

"Priorities. My kids almost forgot what I looked like."

"What about Dudley?"

"If you were nine, would you rather see Dudley's face or mine when you woke up in the morning?"

"I'm not nine."

"It was a rhetorical question."

"What's that?"

"A question you don't have to answer."

"Then why'd you ask it?"

"Ay Dios Mio! You sound like my kids!"

"I'm not a kid."

"I know this!"

"This is the last time, isn't it? We can't talk shop. What are we gonna' talk about?"

"You're losing your accent already. That's sad."

"You're changing the subject."

"You're like a pit bull. If you want to do this again, you gotta' lighten up."

"I'm not sleeping…"

"I can tell. You'll feel better in a couple weeks."

Dominic picked at the sandwich he ordered for lunch. He had been hungry when he left the SELAND building, but his appetite cratered between the cross walk and Olivia's last sentence. "I told you Ashton's dead?"

"You did."

"I can't tell you anything else though."

"I don't want to know."

"You're different."

"I hope so."

"I think I'm gonna' go back to my building." Meeting Olivia seemed like a good idea at the time, but like his last trip to the Bone Room, that only proved that he had not been thinking -- at the time.

"Is this good bye?"

"Yeah, I think so."

"You don't sound too sure of yourself."

"I'm not…"

"Take care of yourself, mijo. Try and stay out of trouble."

Dominic stood up. "Don't call me mijo," he said, and left the bar to jog back to his office. Running felt good and as he ran, he changed his mind. Meeting Olivia had been a good idea, but he would not do it again.

MIAMI – TWO YEARS LATER

There was much to think about during the shuttle to North Carolina. Kevin had finally sent out his marriage invitations and Dominic could hardly refuse. They had messaged each other numerous times, maintaining a long message thread on how their friendship had mutated over the years. Kevin seemed different, less uncomfortable, more grounded, not as explosive or angry. Hanna never met Kevin and Dominic doubted she ever would even if Kevin belonged to a world Dominic could not just leave behind. He missed the less stylized, spontaneous, fiery camaraderie he remembered from their younger days. He was not nervous this time, but his private myth, which Dr. Kim said was under construction, seemed always on the verge of collapse, and that was nerve-wracking. Not needing to wait for his bags, they exited the shuttle port's roundabout causeway in record time. Dominic showed Kevin pictures of Hanna. Kevin reciprocated with pictures of Rafi'a, his new bride-to-be -- a beautiful but very young woman from New Sumer – the latest least-worst solution to emerge from the reformed UN2, as it was called.

"You seem different," Kevin said as they returned their pictures to their treasured hiding spots.

"You too…"

"The new GNRMs are almost better than sex."

"GNRMs?"

"Genomic neurotransmitter response modifiers."

"Psych-grade pharma?"

"It did the trick for me…"

"Are you ready for this?" Dominic asked since they would be in the transit pod for more than ninety minutes.

"Hell no!" Kevin replied looking out the window. "I'm doing it for my mom. Her cancer came out of remission a month ago."

"I'm sorry Kevin."

"Dad's in rehab and he's being an asshole so they won't release him for the wedding so it's just Moms and you for family!"

Dominic felt the past creeping into the transit pod. "I'm glad I could make it up."

"I got you a hotel room."

"OK."

"Mom's home now. I didn't want you to have to deal with all that sickness. I dropped out of school to take care of her."

"Does she have a good doctor?"

"There are better, but she wants to stay close to home."

"I understand that…"

"I don't…"

"How is Rafi'a?"

"Like a rock star. She's my mom's nurse."

"Lawhd a massy! You always did have a talent for getting yourself wrapped around a lamppost."

"I got mixed up with you!"

"You still doing those pencil sketches?"

"Nah…I burned all that shit a few years ago. I remember every single one of them used to mean something. When I went back to look at them I couldn't make heads or tails out of any of 'em. It's like I was drawing shadows over shadows over shadows until you couldn't see the white space anymore."

"I could never make out any of it."

"You asshole! You used to stand there and listen to me talk about those fukken drawings and the whole time you thought I was crazy?"

"I didn't think you were crazy but I didn't have a clue what you were talking about…"

"I don't even remember what they were supposed to be…"

"Neither do I…"

"I thought you were pretty cool listening to me all that time, now I know you're an asshole, just like everyone else." Kevin laughed as he punched Dominic's arm with his fist.

"Where are you going for your honeymoon?"

"New Sumer. She hasn't seen her brother since the partition."

"Be careful…"

"She showed me pictures of how they travel. They drive around in an armed convoy. It's crazy! I can't wait."

"Admit it, you're an adrenalin junkie!"

"Everybody's a junkie for something. I need something to tell me I'm alive. It's like I'm asleep over here."

The transit pod stopped finally in front of a suburban, two-story garden hotel and much like Dominic had done when Kevin had visited, Kevin stayed in the transit pod with plans to pick Dominic up later to have dinner. Since Kevin would be getting married in less than twenty-four hours he was not allowed to see Rafi'a so it was just the two of them for the bachelor party. Later after dinner they sat at the bar nursing double shots of 21-year Lagavulin, Kevin mentioned the survivors of the zombie plague in the old horror movie, *28 Days Later*, drank Lagavulin. "We're all survivors of a zombie plague."

"For guy on psych-grade pharma who's about to get married, you're pretty fukken depressing," Dominic said holding the dark aromatic liquor up to the light.

"Hold on! When did you start drinking?"

"About a year ago."

"Some heavy shit went down, eh?"

"You could say that…"

"You gonna' tell me about it?"

"Can't. I'll lose my clearance."

"Bullshit!"

"Really! I told you I got on with SELAND. I'm with their GIS unit."

"JesusHChristInAChickenBasket! My best and only friend signs up with those grey hat bastards! Why not OpenSource? Why not fukken AnonLulz, for fucks sake! Jheez! You are a mess!"

"There's more money with SELAND."

"So join a fukken' commune or something!" Kevin was smiling but Dominic knew he was half serious.

"They don't have Lagavulin…"

Kevin raised his glass in a silent toast. "I don't trust myself. That's the real reason I got you a hotel room. There. I said it with my outside voice," Kevin said, staring into his empty glass.

Dominic nodded. "I'm fine here but if you don't pick me up in the morning, I'll miss your wedding."

Kevin looked up and smiled. "I guess you're not such an asshole after all." He stood up. "Be outside at 10 am. Those transit-bitches don't like to wait."

Since taking the position at SELAND Dominic spent an inordinate amount of time in the GIS lab on the 16th floor. They made it easy to stick around – a food court that was always open and heavily subsidized, ping-pong tables, pool tables, a gymnasium with basketball courts, three rooms of workout equipment and an indoor swimming pool. Beverage dispensers liberally sprinkled throughout the building seemed to be constantly dispensing caffeinated drinks, and if coffee did not make the grade, there were always the refrigerators stocked with energy drinks and water. Sometimes time got away and he crashed in one of the small cot rooms. His workspace became a miniature library, piled high with single copy prints that never left the room. In the age of SELAND, the closest the world ever came to paperless workflow, the documents which governments considered most valuable were single copy prints. On top of the pile, a document enclosed in a tan envelope, from the government of the country of his birth, almost got lost in the shuffle. The judicial summons the envelope contained demanded he stand for charges in the death of one, Ashton Smith, a known political enemy of the former President Joseph Santo. He had been expecting something of the sort ever since they left the island and now that it had come, he felt relieved. Joseph and Carly would neither appreciate nor approve the decision he had come to since the letter arrived. It was his good luck they agreed to have dinner together that night.

Dinner was elegant as always – grilled shark steaks with a green olive, dill and orange rind salsa, wild rice and asparagus. The kids were upstairs and Hanna was traveling on business so it was just the three of them at the table, ideal for the conversation Dominic intended on having, as much it would pain him to do it. Nervous and uptight, he let the dinner progress through its inevitable stages, eschewing the aperitif and the wine. Desert consisted of a massive cheese plate, pistachios from Iran and a clover honey. Joseph and

Carly drank Madeira, which he had not developed a taste for. Finally as they all picked at the last of the cheese plate, the pistachios having been devoured first, Dominic could stand it no longer. He fished the envelope from his back pocket and put it silently on the table.

Nobody moved. Perhaps no one recognized its importance. Then, in a second, the atmosphere blinked from quiet and satiated to nervous and scared. Joseph snatched the envelope from the table and tore into it, almost ripping the letter inside. His face reddened as he read it, the veins in his temple suddenly visible. "Where did you get this?"

"It came to my office at SELAND today. They sent it by SELAND messaging and hardcopy." Just to have gotten this far allowed Dominic to breathe again, but he held his breath and bit his lip.

Joseph handed it to Carly, who read it and gasped. She was uninformed where affairs of state were concerned.

"I need your help," Dominic said, the first time he made that admission to anyone.

"What do you want to do?" Carly asked.

"I'm not sure…" If Dominic thought the letter disturbed Joseph, what he saw a minute ago was nothing compared to what followed.

Joseph jumped to his feet, threw the letter on the table, and slammed the wall behind them with his fist. Surprisingly, it did not crack, dent or collapse. "You're not sure? *Yuh mind gone, captain*? You catch a deathwish?" he yelled, the volume of his voice causing the glassware on the table to shiver.

Dominic did not stand or look up in reaction. "Nossuh."

"Mi seh! Yuh mind gone! Yuh cyaa'n traipse dun deh yuh know!"

"Dominic, what you are saying?" Carly asked, carefully folding the letter and replacing it in its envelope.

"Mi nuh a' wahdo d'bredda ya! Nuh boddah reason wit'im, Carly. Him mind gone but it mek up."

"Joseph, don't be like that," Carly said, nodding apologetically at Dominic, moving to stand behind her husband, her hand on his shoulder. That seemed to do the trick because when Joseph turned around, he had lost his earlier bluster.

"This path you're on is a dangerous one. Are you prepared to accept the consequences?"

"I don't know what the consequences are."

"That's the problem – no one knows. They are not interested in extenuating circumstances. This is political – they do not care who gets crushed in such a process."

"Joseph, Dr. Kim was your idea. You started this."

"What are you talking about, Dominic?" Carly asked, setting her wine glass down in the realization she had missed something critical.

"There may be merit to the charges," Joseph said quickly and quietly as if defeated, deflated. "Go ahead Dominic, tell your most adoring fan the ugly truth."

He never envisioned telling anyone his innermost secrets. For a few days after his conversation with Joseph, he wondered how even that had happened. He wondered how and where the levy had broken; how the wave of history flooded a relationship just forged. Thus, Joseph's suggestion that he include Carly in that flood of emotional darkness seemed foreign, as if Joseph made the request in a foreign language. He stared at the envelope for a few moments, castigating himself for raising the subject at dinner…though it seemed like a good idea at the time. Unable to frame his words, he let the flood take its course. "I contaminated Ashton's insulin and he died."

Carly gasped and covered her mouth with a well-manicured hand. "Surely it was a mistake. It was unintentional, right?"

"It was not a mistake."

"Because of what he did to Joseph's government?"

"No."

"But why?"

"He has personal reasons," Joseph added, staring directly at Dominic, as if Carly was not in the room, "the most personal reasons a person can have."

"You can't go back there. It's too dangerous."

"I killed a man. What do I do?" Dominic asked, getting to the dark heart of it in a roundabout way.

"I do not know what you do, but it is NOT THIS!" Joseph yelled, striking the dining table with his fist.

Dominic kept his seat and his head down. Having the letter in front of him gave him something to focus on, to avoid the body language that signaled confrontation, to make things worse than they already were. "That's why I said I need your help."

That got Joseph's attention and Dominic saw him pivot from the train wreck mood he had allowed himself, something different, one more accommodating, with less volume. "You did say that, didn't you...I almost missed it..." Joseph said, taking his seat again and putting his hand on top of Carly's, gingerly picking up the letter once more.

"I need to do something with this."

"You sound like Dr. Kim," Joseph said, his face hidden behind the letter he decided to re-read.

"Dr. Kim was your idea..."

"The problem with Dr. Kim is he doesn't stop at good enough. He has to take things to their absolute logical end." Joseph put the letter down and took a long look at the young man in front of him, knowing whatever brought him to this point; Joseph had little to do with it. Despite the odds, he could not help admiring how the world worked. "Forgive me for yelling earlier and my harsh words. I did not mean what I said."

Dominic nodded, choosing that moment to look up. "I don't know what to do with this," he said motioning to the letter. It was difficult to keep the water welling in his eyes.

"We will find a way. I know people who will talk to me."

TRANSCRIPT EXCERPT
SESSION 99
RECORDING 99
(K) DOCTOR: KIM
(D) CLIENT: SANTO, D

(K): "So how was the week just passed?"

(D): "One of my Ghost Eels died…so that sucked. I did what you suggested about the fights Hanna and I were getting into, and it worked, damn you!"

(K): "We are coming to the end of our conversation. There are only two sessions remaining on your commitment."

(D): "Two?"

(K): "Yes."

(D): "So what now?"

(K): "When Joseph first contacted me, I was reticent. He gave me the backstory and it crushed me. He asked if I could help you re-write your story into one of your own making."

(D): "We did that, didn't we?"

342

(K): "You did."

(D): "Don't write yourself out."

(K): "How is your son?"

(D): "He's great! He keeps us up at night. We drink A LOT of coffee!"

(K): "And Hanna, how is she?"

(D): "She gets tired and sometimes she ignores the baby but her doctor said that will pass."

(K): "Have you decided what you will do about the Ashton Inquest?"

(D): "The government filed charges and we answered *in absentia*. The charges will stick but the sentence will be commuted."

(K): "Can you return to the island?"

(D): "I'm an immigrant."

(K): "Is that something you can live with?"

(D): "I was lucky…they could have insisted on extradition."

(K): "But now it is done, finished."

(D): "I still think about him though…even more after my allocution…"

(K): "You don't grieve over the past, do you?"

(D): "A few days ago, I started thinking about it and I thought I was gonna bawl…"

(K): "What did you do?"

(D): "I went to the pool and did laps until I was so tired I could barely get out of the pool."

(K): "One day, you must tell me about your Vodun experience. Is it something you think about often?"

(D): "No. The drums move my feet."

(K): "What happens when you dance?"

(D): "I don't know…"

(K): "If you had the chance to dance again, would you?"

(D): "It's not the dancing that stays with you, it's the fire…"

(K): "You have a word on your island that means unity or solidarity, though it is mostly associated with rebellion and destruction…"

(D): "FIYA!"

(K): "So this fire inside, can you still feel it?"

(D): "I don't spend a lot of time looking for it…"

(K): "Maybe you should…"

Epilogue

*Those who cast out devils should be careful
lest they cast out the last good thing in them.*

Friedrich Nietzsche

If the million and their children cannot be forgiven for one thing, it is that they have surrendered their sense of history in exchange for paper money. Such accusations are never thrust upon them. Their rage is great.

The million have children and grandchildren and great grand children to spend in the most gruesome horrible ways. Honor, innocence and life itself is bought, sold and murdered by children with soft voices who do not remember that where they stab swing slash a river used to run.

Faces overflow with laughter, constricted in anger, resigned with sadness, brightly lit with hope, singed as if in a fire, with fear. These are memories etched in stone. Memory is like an ocean, a mother, a doctor bird, or the thick market woman who wants to sell me her ginger.

People run through me like a river, like blood.

What can I tell you fourteen years later that you do not already know?

I do not know what happened to Worm and Scorn and doubt I ever will. I did not say goodbye to Melia or Miss Missy and since they were off-grid, it is unlikely I will be able to explain myself. I heard that Mercilia died eleven months after Pierre. Jemma, the woman who bore me, died in her sleep, four years after we left the island, just days before my graduation from the University of Miami. Guede Baron Semedi died violently under suspicious circumstances. Joseph was right. More than two thousand election related deaths occurred on the island after we left. Straightedge was moved to a new, clean, contemporary national facility. I heard he is doing well on medication and has transitioned to a halfway house. Olivia and I reconnected after Hanna died and we are close friends now. My son calls her "Auntie". She still calls me 'mijo'.

I lost Hanna and Dr. Kim to the Yemeni Flu Pandemic of 2106 and have been in a foul mood ever since, as has much of the world. Social scientists proclaim that with only four degrees of separation between any two people on the planet, everyone lost someone in the 2106. I saw Kevin a couple of times after Hanna died, but the friendship I remembered proved difficult to sustain. His moods returned, Rafi'a behaved obstinately and his dogs urinated on my shoes. Kevin and Rafi'a talked about immigrating to New Sumer, to buy into the latest form of communal living – a commune with equity. New Sumer hit upon equity communes as a way to lure people to the newly established territories and fill the vast open spaces with which it had been saddled. Like a marshland needed reeds and grasses to hold the mulch in place, New Sumer needed settlements to give it legitimacy, to prove that people lived there out of choice not as political refugees or asylum-seekers.

Elements of SELAND have been judged too intrusive and destructive of basic individual rights. Governments across the globe are reconsidering the autonomous technology treaties as too expensive without accompanying upside; meanwhile technology control regimes and treaties are being strengthened. This should not imply that fundamental issues are finding resolution or that there is new, ideal thinking afoot – there is not. It may be that the chaotic years have passed and a dismantling of chaos-induced scaffolding has begun. Such things are not for me to say. For one can only talk about these things when they are far enough into the past to discuss them dispassionately, or perhaps to mythologize them. I don't know how much longer SELAND will keep me, but I look forward to an assistant professorship at the University of Miami.

My son Jules is my life, my reason for living. Like me, he has been in a foul mood since his mother died (or because he has reached that age of foul moods) but he's in love with his grandfather Joseph. If his messaging metrics prove anything, there's a girl somewhere in the wings of his life. He has a female Pug he named 'Daisy,' which has become his pride and joy. Though only fourteen, he is nearly as tall as me with the lanky build of the basketball player he dreams of being. Though his emotions are still too large for his body, it makes me smile to see this heap of a child, all bones and angles, lying on the floor with his little dog sitting on his chest. The dog lies with its head flat on his chest, its nose touching Jules' chin. I don't know what they do in that pose but they will stay like that for hours. Jules says they are talking. Some days, he wakes up with Hanna's pragmatism with an answer for everything. Other days he wakes up with my stoicism and I cannot get a word out of him. He has four good friends who are trying to start a death metal band. I told him I'd rent him a studio in San Francisco when they finally got their gear together. Two days later, he figured out that San Francisco was not a neighborhood in Miami; that it was on the opposite coast and he did not talk to me for an hour. Sometimes I love him to death.

Sometimes I don't know what to do with him or his damn dog. Everything is as normal as anything can be.

Some people are dangerous because of what they do to themselves and to others. Others are dangerous because of what they do not do. Some are dangerous because of what happens to them regardless of what they do or do not do. Others are born under a dark star, or have ancestors who committed heinous crimes. Others are possessed by the wrong *loa*. This is what Hanna's father said about me for most of her life. Even after Jules was born and we filed papers for a civil union and Hanna told him I had learned my birth name, he still maintained I was dangerous because I had lived so long without it.

People take what they want from the unattached and I was an un-tethered but stranded fixture on Old Hope Road my entire life, though for much of that life I remained oblivious. Incredibly, I did not lose what I did not have - my name. Before Joseph, Dr. Kim, Hanna and Jeremy, I loved one person -- old blind Pierre. He brought me to the edge of the *houngan*, letting the rhythm of *Rado* and *Pethro* move my feet into and around the *peristil*. He took me to see *bokors* of the right hand and the left, so that I might look past the stars and 'become god'. I learned the world stepped back in fear of the fire I found inside and I felt safe as if in a cocoon, untouchable and far away. Of course I did not live in a cocoon nor was I untouchable or far away.

It is likely that what one seeks from an epilogue is not the tying off of loose ends, the ambiguous and ambivalent statements about justice done or the irony of terrible deeds unpunished – but a wrapping up of the emotional demi-urge, a participation-mystique if you will. I am not sure this epilogue is that. I wonder why we find it so easy to see our selves, and the world, as fundamentally flawed; to call ourselves broken, found in wanting – as if some transcendental scoreboard is irrevocably and permanently set to our disadvantage. In my unguarded moments, I question such baseless assumptions. Can we not restate our assumptions on our terms? Can we not claim for ourselves the 'essential human' or the 'superior self'? For a wise man once told me, 'you are who you are and you are the only person you can be absolutely right about'.

<<Pearl Jam – Who You Are>>

CPSIA information can be obtained at www.ICGtesting.com
Printed in the USA
BVOW041029140512

290161BV00001B/216/P